DEEP HOSTAGE

MIKE SEARES

BOOKS

By Mike Seares

John McCready Thrillers

Deep Steal
Deep Impact
Deep Hostage
Deep Control

Vinci Books

vinci-books.com

Published by Vinci Books Ltd in 2025

1

Copyright © Mike Seares 2020

The author has asserted their moral right to be identified as the author of this work in accordance with the Copyright, Designs and Patents Act 1988. This work is a work of fiction. Names, characters, places and incidents are the product of the author's imagination or are used fictitiously. Any resemblance to actual persons, living or dead, places and incidents is entirely coincidental.

All rights reserved. No part of this publication may be copied, reproduced, distributed, stored in any retrieval system, or transmitted in any form or by any means, including photocopying, recording, or other electronic or mechanical methods, nor used as a source for any form of machine learning including AI datasets, without the prior written permission of the publisher.

The publisher and the author have made every effort to obtain permissions for any third party material used in this book and to comply with copyright law. Any queries in this respect should be brought to the attention of the publisher and any omissions will be corrected in future editions.

A CIP catalogue record for this book is available from the British Library.

Paperback ISBN: 9781036704001

Printed and bound in Great Britain by Clays Ltd, Elcograf S.p.A.

Chapter One

Eight months ago

With the mercury hitting a hundred and ten degrees Fahrenheit, and humidity at ninety-eight percent, the Paco district of Manila at midday was not a place for the overweight.

But despite the all-encompassing heat, the conditions were not on the mind of Manny Pincher as he eased himself out of the burdened rickshaw. Weighing over four hundred pounds in his boxers, his huge bulk made the average sumo wrestler look anorexic, but his mind was elsewhere as he subconsciously mopped his glistening brow with an already dripping handkerchief.

Mr. Chin, the rickshaw driver, heaved a sigh of relief, wiping away an equal amount of sweat as he watched the kaftan-adorned Pincher lumber across the road.

Chin was in his sixties, thin as a rake, and used to students and tourists, even backpackers with huge rucksacks, but the American was something else. He had paid well—too well really for the short ride from the Sheraton Manila Bay hotel. The tip had been a week's wages. Even so, it hadn't been worth it.

He arched his back in pain, trying to ease the strain from the half-mile run, and then glanced over as Pincher miraculously made it to the far side of the road without a single collision with any of the numerous bicycles and rickshaws that swerved and veered around the moveable chicane, their little bells tinkling in protest.

Mr. Chin watched as Pincher headed for a side street. He hoped he'd never see the man again. There was something about him that wasn't quite right, and it had nothing to do with his weight.

As Pincher reached the far side of the road he glanced at the rickety array of abandoned, half-built houses that lay in an uneven row down the street ahead. A couple of them had bamboo scaffolding supporting the outside walls. Seemingly the builders had clearly been on half pay when they had constructed them. They were built from wood, and none of the upper floors were aligned with any of the others.

He pulled a piece of paper from his pocket and checked an address.

Number six.

The details on the paper matched the number on a wooden post leaning against the wall of the third house along on the right-hand side.

He walked toward it, his garish yellow flip-flops sliding across the dirt of the road, sending up a trail of dust in his wake.

He shoved the paper back into his pocket and pulled out a Snickers bar. He tore off the top of the wrapper, dropping it on the ground, and took a bite of the chocolate.

As he did so, a mangy mongrel emerged from under a wooden deck at the front of one of the houses. It walked over to the wrapper and sniffed it. Pincher glanced down at the pitiful beast. Most of its fur was scabby. One of its ears had been half bitten off, and it had a slight limp in its front left paw.

Pincher held the chocolate down so the dog could smell it. The dog approached slowly, cautiously. It had almost reached the bar when Pincher pulled it away and kicked the mutt in the ribs. It yelped in pain, hobbling over to cower behind an overflowing trash can next to the closest building.

Pincher laughed, stuffed the remains of the bar into his mouth, and threw the rest of the wrapper onto the ground. He then walked over to number six and pushed open the door.

It creaked and groaned on its hinges.

It was dark inside.

The door hadn't been locked. He could tell by the state of the place that it had been used by anyone who had chosen to gain entrance. There was a strong smell of urine and rotting waste. He wrinkled his nose at the stench. Why couldn't his clients choose a civilized location for once? But they were paying the big bucks, and his was not to reason why.

He had been told he had to proceed upstairs. He took one look at the narrow, uneven set of wooden steps and wondered if he'd survive the exertion.

Five minutes later he emerged at the top, wheezing hard.

He found himself in a large room.

The whole level of the house was open. There were no internal walls, and there was only one window at the far end, which was covered with a bamboo blind.

The sole illumination came through the uneven joins in the walls that let narrow shafts of light stab across the room. But for what Pincher needed to do, he didn't need a whole lot of light.

In the center was a table and chair, and, as he had known there would be, on the table was an open laptop, its screen emitting a bright glow, like a beacon drawing him forward. There was a USB stick protruding from the side. The laptop was sitting on a raised box about two inches high. It had the same dimensions as the computer.

The only other object in the room was a small high-impact case, about six inches square, sitting on a narrow shelf beneath the window.

Pincher crossed over to the table and sat down on a chair he was sure wouldn't survive his visit. He glanced at the laptop.

The screen was blank except for two document icons in the lower right-hand corner.

As he sat down, a messaging app opened.

He immediately glanced around the room. In one of the far corners, in the shadows, he could just make out a small blinking red light. He couldn't see the camera he knew it would be attached to, but they were watching, of that he could be sure.

He turned his attention back to the screen.

A message had appeared telling him to open the first document on the desktop.

He did so.

Contained within it was a description of information his

client wanted him to access. Once the files were downloaded they were to be put on the USB stick plugged into the computer.

Pincher read through the instructions again.

He smiled.

This would be easy.

Normally there was something that might challenge him, but for one of the premier hackers on the planet, retrieving the security protocols, original blueprints, and details of the senior personnel of a building was child's play —but hey, it was their money.

He rolled his shoulders and started to work.

His fingers flew over the keys. As they did, screens opened within screens, accessing controls and corners of the web few knew existed. It took him all of ten minutes to retrieve the files that had been requested and transfer them to the USB stick.

He had no idea what they were. It was none of his business. He never wanted to involve himself in his client's requests; that could get him into a whole lot of trouble. But he had briefly caught a glimpse of the schematics he had downloaded. As the plans had streamed onto the screen he'd noticed high-tech elevators, secure, pressurized rooms, even a tunnel carved out of rock. It looked impressive.

Once the files were securely on the USB stick, he clicked on a COMPLETE button within the messaging app. A return message confirmed his $100,000 fee was ready to transfer.

He sat back, a smile on his face.

But there was the second document on the desktop.

He clicked on it.

The file also contained instructions. As he read through,

an even broader smile spread across his face, particularly when he saw his fee.

This was more like it.

A challenge…

…with a price to match.

He interlinked his fingers, stretching his palms outward, like a conductor about to control an orchestra, which, in essence, was what he was about to do.

He concentrated on the screen, thought for a moment, and then let his fingers play across the keys. He would have to go far deeper into the web to find the tools to hack into the Pentagon.

As he worked, he felt a thrill spread through his body that was better than sex.

While Manny Pincher was not adept in the physical world, he was a supreme athlete in the digital one. There may well be people who could run faster, jump higher, swim further than him, but there were few who had the dexterity, ability or talent to go where he was going now.

It took longer this time.

Twenty minutes.

But when he had finished, he had the complete schedule for the US Navy's covert vessels research and development program.

He transferred the documents onto the USB stick and clicked COMPLETE.

A return message confirmed his fee had grown by $500,000 to a total of $600,000 and was now ready to transfer.

But then another message beeped.

It instructed him to take the USB stick and put it in the case by the window.

That was strange.

What could be the purpose of that?

But again, his was not to reason why.

Anyway, his head was filled with the thoughts of what he was going to spend the money on. There was a red, second hand Ferrari Testarossa at the dealership in Mandaluyong that had his name on it.

He ejected the stick, pulled it from the side of the computer, and shambled over to the window. He opened the highly protective case, placed the USB stick inside, and closed the top securely.

When he returned to the computer, there was a message instructing him to place his eye close to the laptop camera to confirm the transfer of funds.

He sat down and moved forward to look into the tiny lens at the top of the screen.

As soon as his corneal pattern had been confirmed, there was a beep.

It was the last thing Manny Pincher ever heard.

The explosives in the box beneath the laptop detonated, blowing off half the American's head, totally destroying the laptop.

The blast wasn't enough to damage the room. In fact, more damage was done by Pincher sliding off the chair and crashing to the floor, splintering a number of the floorboards.

He would never see the young girl, who, ten minutes later, ran into the room, picked up the case by the window, retrieved the camera from the corner, and ran out again without a glance at the massive hulk lying on the floor.

It also meant he would never hear the faltering patter of tiny feet as the mangy dog hobbled up the steps and into the room.

If Pincher had been alive he would no doubt have felt a

warm sensation in his left foot, one that would have turned into a sharp pain, as the starving mongrel, first started to lick his foot, and then chewed and gnawed ravenously through the bones in his toes.

Chapter Two

Six months ago

The tiny bubble started its desperate bid for freedom from around a hundred feet underwater. Along with countless other small silver spheres, it headed up toward the pale moonlight that was imperceptibly breaking through the surface somewhere above.

When it reached a depth of thirty-three feet the water pressure had reduced by half, allowing the bubble to expand to twice its size. It had now become dome-shaped, resembling a quivering spaceship as it hurtled ever upward. With its increase in size came an increase in buoyancy and therefore speed.

When it finally broke the surface, it was traveling far faster than the fifty feet per minute at its birth, and it had again doubled in size, this time between thirty-three feet and the surface—a perfect demonstration of the physics of Boyle's law.

With a small pop, it expelled its gas into the atmosphere

in a joyous gasp, now free from the constraints and tethers of the inky black depths below.

The makeup of the gas was eighty percent nitrogen, sixteen percent oxygen and four percent carbon dioxide. The exact composition of exhaled human breath.

The surface began to froth with the now constant release of gas from the regular stream of bubbles rising from the depths. Between the shimmering silver balls on their upward charge, a flickering, dancing light could be seen, growing brighter by the second. It was an erratic, haphazard light that seemed to represent a panic all of its own. Within seconds it was flashing across the surface, heralding the arrival of something greater. As if in support of the imminent event, the bubbles joined as one in a frothing mass of incandescent light sparkling in the water.

Suddenly, the neoprene-clad hand of a fully equipped scuba diver broke through the surface. Droplets of water cascaded in all directions, backlit by the moon like some sort of surreal special effect.

As the diver rose up, the momentum of the high-speed ascent sent his upper body three feet out of the water.

With a gasp, Ilya Kozak ripped the Oceanic Omega demand-valve from his mouth, sucking in the life-giving air. As his body settled back, he jabbed the direct-feed control on his buoyancy compensator, injecting air to provide lift and keep him on the surface without struggling. Pushing the dive mask to his forehead, he looked around desperately in all directions. Even in the moonlight, his young East European features were evident, almost beautiful, despite the harrowed, anguished expression he currently wore. All around, the sea was an oily calm, the moonlight sending an uninterrupted ribbon of glistening silver to the horizon.

He stared in all directions, flashing the dive-light

across the surface as if looking for someone, but he was alone. As he turned, he spotted land in the distance. Trying to focus, he made out a harbor at the base of a cluster of lights. It looked like there were buildings, and movement—yes, a vehicle's headlights, people walking around, and the muffled hum of a generator drifting on the night air. He finned madly out of the water, waving his arms and yelling at the top of his voice, but no one heard him.

The sound of the generator hid his plight.

He shouted again, but to no avail. In desperation, he took another look round, then struck out for the harbor. It was a harried, frantic, overarm stroke, his fins beating the water in an undisciplined effort to propel him toward safety.

At a depth of a hundred and eighty feet, it was pitch-black on the vertical rock wall, but it didn't stop the speckled leopard shark from hunting for food. It cruised lazily along the drop-off, its six-foot-long muscular body weaving stealthily through the water.

It was rounding a corner when its senses suddenly became alert.

Something was coming.

Something unusual.

Slowly, from around the vertical drop-off came a glow of light, increasing in intensity with every passing second. Along with the glow came a distant drone that became louder, eliminating the presence as some form of bioluminescent sea creature.

Suddenly, shafts of light, like spotlights on a foggy night, split through the murky water, highlighting the wall in stark relief. The shark, wary of the unknown, and of what was coming, made a decision. With a violent twist of its body and a flick of its tail, it disappeared into the depths.

Then, with the whine of twin water-jets that could drive her through the water at over fifty knots, the man-made invader rounded the point. It had a profile resembling that of a highly evolved sea creature rather than a technological invention. *Deep Intruder* was the US Navy's most sophisticated and advanced military special forces submersible. A formidable weapon. An underwater Apache.

The sub cleared the rocky point, tracking slowly along the wall.

There was no conning tower, merely a flush-fitting hatch, which resulted in a smooth profile resembling the eager poise of a dolphin, whose motions, shape and skin texture had been studied over thousands of hours to produce the perfect through-water body covering. This smart-skin surface was in a constant state of flux, as real-time micro changes to its surface adjusted to the water conditions to minimize drag.

The front of the sub was a transparent dome, merging smoothly with the main hull, enhancing the cetacean-like appearance and providing the operator with a full one-eighty-degree visibility, both vertically and horizontally. The dome's design had been optically corrected to produce zero distortion, a feat comparable to the preparation of the mirror for the Hubble Space Telescope, though this time, they got it right first time. On the underside of the sub was a lockout hatch to allow entry and exit for divers.

At around thirty feet in length, *Deep Intruder* wasn't large, but her size and shape gave her stealth capabilities necessary for her role as a SEAL Delivery Vehicle. She also had full independent lockout capabilities for all on board. Her ceramic carbon fiber construction provided strength and integrity, and the double internal compartment design allowed a mix of one-atmosphere and ambient pressure-related missions to be completed. She carried a secure communication system, visible as an array of antennas on the top of the sub, which was capable of operating anywhere in the world. To provide protection, and attack capability, there were multiple weapons systems slung on small drop-down wings that emerged from the smooth hull when required.

Inside the sub, Captain Frank Cardiff pulled back gently on the joystick and rocked it to the right, trimming *Deep Intruder* onto a level track to head straight out into midwater, away from the drop-off, at a depth of a hundred and seventy-five feet.

Mid-fifties, and with over twenty years' experience in submersibles, Cardiff represented the epitome of relaxed calm in a workplace that was a high-tech bubble operating in one of the most inhospitable environments on or off the planet. He scratched at the stubble on his chin and checked the depth readings and trim controls.

"Looks like she's running A-okay for now. Anything on sonar?" The question was directed at Mateo Ramirez, who was seated just behind Cardiff in the cramped interior. Ramirez was an enthusiastic twenty-something technical geek with short dark hair and an angular face, one that currently wore a look of extreme concentration. He was usually lost in the technical aspects of anything he was doing, and the danger and frightening reality of the depths the sub operated at never strayed into his mind. He was there to oversee the technical performance of the test dives, and that was what he would do.

"What do you expect?" he replied. "This is the final trial before she hits the beaches. We ain't gonna have no problems... Oh yeah, and sonar's clear from the wall. We're ready for whatever they can throw at us."

Cardiff smiled. He liked the enthusiasm of the youngster but didn't necessarily share his confidence in technology. Not that there was anything wrong with the sub. He just knew from experience that you had to expect the unexpected.

"Okay, here we go," said Cardiff calmly.

He flicked a switch that lowered the weapons pods into position on the outside of the hull. He then eased forward on the throttle control. The sub accelerated slightly, moving further away from the wall and out into the murky depths of the Pacific.

Ilya Kozak was exhausted.

He had been finning for over twenty minutes, but the current had been against him. He could feel his energy disappearing. He had to reach the small harbor he had seen when he surfaced.

It wasn't only his life that was at stake.

The water had developed a slight chop. As he swam, he gagged and spluttered, desperately trying to draw in the air his body needed, the supply long since exhausted from the cylinder.

He had to stop.

Just for a minute.

He trod water for a while, getting his breath back, preparing for the final push.

When he was ready, he set off to cover the hundred yards that would take him to the stone harbor wall.

He could make out some steps. They seemed a million miles away. If he could just reach them.

Ten minutes later he made it. There was no sign of anyone above, but all he needed to do was climb out of the water, rest, and then he could find some help.

But time was of the essence.

He hauled himself out onto the first of the steps. The water sloshed around his body. Green algae clung to the stone, making movement difficult and slippery. He managed to throw off his gear and half walk, half crawl to the top of the harbor.

When he finally made it, he was so exhausted he rolled onto his back for a moment and closed his eyes, breathing heavily, thankful he had reached safety.

But a second later he froze.

There was the sound of running feet and then a series of aggressive metallic clicks. Slowly he opened his eyes, and his heart almost leapt into his throat.

He was staring into the muzzles of four M16 assault rifles. The eyes of the men behind the sights left no room for interpretation.

One of them leaned forward, the muzzle of the gun inches from Kozak's face.

"Don't even move, pal!" said the gruff American voice.

"Please… My friend. You have to find my friend," said Kozak, desperately.

Deep Intruder was currently undergoing final weapons trials from a small, low-profile naval base located on the ocean side of the Point Loma peninsula to the west of San Diego. It was just south of the Wastewater Treatment Plant, and on a warm, sunny day, with the wind in the wrong direction, the works made their presence felt in the most unpleasant way imaginable, but in the military, you always had obstacles to overcome.

The base consisted of a number of buildings, which housed medical, recompression and training facilities, two large test tanks, accommodation blocks, offices, car parking spaces, and a control room and small harbor.

As well as the base for the sub, the facility was home to the US Navy's special forces underwater warfare unit, a division of the famous SEAL teams that trained at the main naval base at Coronado on North Island, on the other side of the peninsula. In fact, some even referred to it as 'Coronado lite.'

Few people knew of its existence, let alone the work that went on there.

The air force had taken all the glory with their infamous Area 51. Somehow though, 'Underwater Flying Objects' didn't quite cut it with the public at large. But the high-tech vehicles that were developed, and the research carried out at the facility, were every bit as exotic and sophisticated as their airborne cousins in the desert. In fact, the navy were quite happy for the public to believe in lights in the sky over Dreamland, even though they were merely advanced flying machines with revolutionary propulsion systems and stealth capabilities. It took the pressure off the Coronado drop-offs, which had many secrets of their own to hide from prying eyes.

The operations room for *Deep Intruder* was located in a building overlooking the harbor. Physically, it was like a covert airport control tower with blacked-out, one-way windows. But that was where the similarity ended. Inside, the space was arranged over a two-tiered level, lit in the dull glow of subdued lighting. There was an air of quiet calm and determination, unlike the hectic, frenetic world of pushing tin at airports around the world.

The lower level, next to the all-encompassing windows that looked out onto the harbor, contained the operators, who monitored displays showing video feeds from the sub. Above the windows, a graphical display showed the sub's location in relation to the coastline and the underwater firing range that was located just offshore.

The technicians had at their disposal a formidable array of equipment they could utilize to test and challenge the numerous complex systems on the sub—some of them more real than the occupants might have liked—but that was the nature of the game.

The test controller, Steve Carnegie, checked the screens to make sure everything was in position for the exercise that was about to start. He then swiveled in his chair to talk to the man who was stood directly behind him. He paused to take a breath before speaking. You wanted to be very clear in what you said when you spoke to Commander David Bryce.

Bryce was a tall, hard-bitten naval officer, who was head of the US Navy's underwater warfare operations. He took no prisoners and didn't suffer fools gladly.

"Sir," started Carnegie. He then pointed at the large screen in front of him. "This is *Deep Intruder*'s current position. The green lines mark the zone boundary, the small red dots, the drones. We have full control at all times, but they can be set for AI, forming their own attack scenarios."

Bryce looked at the screen. He was briefly distracted by activity on the harbor wall he could see through the windows, but then his attention flicked back to the display.

"How many drones will be in the trial?" he asked.

"Four, sir. There'll be an initial attack by two, with one

surveillance drone, and a third that will act as a decoy. It should give a good workout for the tracking and defensive systems of the sub."

Bryce nodded. He was about to ask a further question when a young rating ran up and spoke to Carnegie. Bryce couldn't hear what was said, but Carnegie's expression turned to one of irritation, but also concern. The rating turned, nodded at Bryce, and then left.

"Anything I should know about?" asked Bryce.

Carnegie reached for the comms mike that would allow him to talk to *Deep Intruder*. He glanced up at his superior officer. "We're going to have to abort the trial, sir." Bryce raised his eyebrows. "Some sports diver's gone and got himself in the test area. He just climbed out onto the harbor. Seems his buddy's missing on the drop-off. It's a thousand feet plus down there. If that's where he is, there's not much hope. But we need to check it out. See if we can help."

Bryce gritted his teeth but nodded slowly.

Civilians!

Carnegie flicked the comms mike. "*Deep Intruder*, this is control. Frank, we have a problem."

Chapter Three

Ilya Kozak sat on a white treatment couch in a clinically clean medical examination room. It wasn't so much a couch, more a recliner with a padded cover that could be raised electrically to different angles depending on the condition of the patient. He had been given a bland gray jumpsuit to wear, which was slightly too large and certainly wouldn't win any fashion awards.

Once the situation on the harbor had calmed down, and the leader of the armed unit had realized Ilya wasn't a threat, messages had been sent and he'd been escorted in a Humvee to the medical facility a few hundred yards from the harbor. He had then been taken into the building and to an examination room, which was where he was now currently sitting.

An armed guard stood watch by the door.

Ilya looked at the room around him. It was quite large and was clearly used for more than just treatment and diagnosis. In fact, it was more like a research lab. Along one wall was a wide laminate worktop that had scientific equipment, microscopes and other paraphernalia laid out across its length. There were also a number of computers with widescreen displays showing information and graphs he couldn't understand. Suspended high on one wall, facing down toward the room, was a TV. The room had no windows, and he knew from the journey in that he was below ground level. In one corner he could see that his diving equipment had been brought over. It had been packed into a large holdall.

He was about to stand and stretch his legs when he heard clipped footsteps from outside the door. A moment later, a young, blonde-haired woman walked into the room. She nodded at the guard, and then her gaze came to rest on Ilya. She briefly looked him up and down, and then smiled and walked over. She was around thirty years old, with a fresh, outgoing face, bright and intelligent, but she moved as though she was in a hurry—that there were things that had to be done. She carried a clipboard in one hand, a pen in the other.

"Hello, I'm Doctor Fletcher," she said breezily.

From the name tag on the left breast pocket of her lab coat, Ilya could see that her first name was Connie.

"Hello," he said quietly, but then, with more fervor, "My friend… you have to find my friend."

"All in good time," said Connie. "Now, I understand your name is Ilya Kozak. Is that correct?"

"Yes."

"And you were diving on the drop-off?"

"Yes, that's right. About eighty feet. We were caught in a current. My friend just started sinking. He was there one minute, gone the next."

"Was he still breathing when you saw him last?"

"Yes, I am sure. His bubbles."

"You know you were in a restricted area? All around here is a military zone. You could both have been in danger, and not just from the depth and current."

"I am sorry. I did not know that," he said meekly.

Connie looked at him, as though gauging his answer. "I'm sure my colleagues will do all they can to find your friend. They have some pretty sophisticated kit. One of their submersibles is conducting a trial in the area. If anyone can find him, they can. For now, we just need to do some tests to make sure you're okay. We have recompression facilities on-site, so if you need treatment, we can look after you." She glanced over at the guard by the door. "Thanks, Alec. That'll be all."

The guard nodded and left the room. Connie turned back to Ilya.

"Now, I just have to ask you some questions and take a blood sample."

He looked up at her apprehensively. "Will it hurt?"

Deep Intruder's lights blazed across the rock wall.

After receiving the message from the control room about the lost diver, Cardiff had turned the sub around a full one-eighty degrees and headed back toward the drop-off. He and Ramirez were now focused. They were both divers, so any help they could give to a fellow aquanaut was forefront in their minds, even if he had been in a restricted zone.

Ramirez was hunched over a sonar display that could look far beyond the reach of the lights. It was combined with an overlay from thermal imaging cameras that could pick out temperature changes in the environment ahead. If there was anyone alive out there they'd be able to pick them out within a several-hundred-yard radius. For now, all he could see was the wall with specks of heat where small life forms ducked and dived through the darkness ahead.

They had been traveling silently for around five minutes when Ramirez looked more intently at the display. In the middle of the graphical outline of the wall, a small red area started to grow. He checked the depth reading—two hundred feet—and then looked back at the screen. The colored patch was definitely getting larger.

"Could be something ahead," he said calmly. "About a hundred yards."

Cardiff slowed the forward motion of the sub and peered out of the dome. All he could see was the sheer wall to the right and the blackness of the ocean beyond the reach of the lights.

"Fifty yards." Ramirez stated from the rear.

Ahead, Cardiff could now see a glint in the dark. Something was reflecting back at him in the beams of light. At the same time there appeared to be a distortion in the rock. It seemed to roll out and flatten, forming a narrow ledge on the otherwise sheer wall.

"Could have something here," said Cardiff.

As they moved slowly forward, the outline of a diver could be seen lying on the small ledge.

"Okay, looks like we've found our man," said Cardiff matter-of-factly. He squeezed the comms trigger on the control stalk. "Control, this is *Deep Intruder*. We've found a body."

Immediately there was a crackly reply over the speakers.

"Okay, Frank. Any movement?" said Carnegie.

"Not as yet. And no bubbles. Looks like he ran out of air. I'm afraid it's a recovery mission now. I'll keep you updated."

"Sorry to hear that. Let us know when you need surface pickup. Control out."

"Roger that. Cardiff out."

In the control room, Carnegie turned to Bryce, who was standing impatiently behind him.

"No hope?" asked Bryce.

"He's at just over two hundred feet. As you know, air at that depth is pretty narcotic. Probably what put him to sleep. O-two poisoning would do the rest. If there's any left, of course." He was about to continue, when there was a beeping noise from the panel in front of him. He turned back to the display, and a confused expression crossed his face. A red dot was moving toward the main pulsing yellow marker that indicated the position of *Deep Intruder* on the drop-off. "That's strange."

"What is it?" asked Bryce.

"There shouldn't be any drones out there. AI's inactive." He flipped a couple of switches. Four other dots suddenly appeared on the display, well away from the still-moving red dot. "They're all accounted for." He paused. "There's something else down there and it's not one of ours."

Cardiff gripped the manipulator controls and brought the two remotely controlled arms down and level, ready to scoop up the body. They were just sliding under the diver when Ramirez leaned forward. "Hey, he's wearing a rebreather. There wouldn't be any bubbles."

Cardiff paused. "So why were we told his friend had seen bubbles before he lost sight of him?" They both looked at each other, puzzled. When they turned back to look forward, they knew the reason why.

Without warning, the 'body' reared up and turned to face the sub.

The figure looking in at them was dressed in a black drysuit. He was wearing a compact full face mask with the distinctive twin hoses that swept round the back to connect to a rebreather. There was a small cylinder mounted horizontally across his waist. Cardiff was stunned at the development. He was about to rejoice at the fact they'd found the man alive, when the figure did something extremely unexpected and extremely concerning.

He leaned forward to place one hand flat against the dome of the sub. He then raised his other hand. In it was a drill-like device connected to a short hose, which, in turn, was connected to the cylinder across his waist. The hand moved forward until they could see the pointed end of the drill make contact with the center of the dome in front of them. The dome that was keeping out over six atmospheres of water pressure.

The man's eyes looked directly at them.

"Good evening, gentlemen." The voice echoed out of the comms speaker. It was laced with a heavy, what sounded like, Russian accent. As they stared at the man, his eyes never wavered. Cardiff and Ramirez were rooted to their seats.

"What the hell?" exclaimed Cardiff. He pulled the comms trigger and spoke quickly. "Control, we have a situation here. Control…!"

Unseen by those inside, another diver, similarly clad in black and using a rebreather, landed on top of the sub. He immediately attacked the array of sophisticated antennas at the front, destroying them.

A crackly voice came over the speaker.

"Control, go ahead Frank, what's the—" And then it cut out.

Cardiff persisted. "Control. Do you read? Over… Control. Do you read? Over?"

Nothing.

"Jesus! What the hell's going on?" Cardiff returned to stare at the man holding the drill to the dome. Suddenly his voice came over the speaker again.

"They can't hear you. My friend has seen to that. Do as I say and you may live. Refuse and…" He gripped the trigger on the drill. Immediately there was a flurry of bubbles from the air-driven tool. A high-pitched whine filled the sub. The dome itself vibrated as the drill started to burrow into its surface. A second later it stopped. "…You can guess what will happen." The diver paused. "Open the hatch!"

"No way!" said Cardiff.

Without warning, the drill started again. It wouldn't be long before it penetrated enough of the material to cause a catastrophic failure, from which there would be only one outcome. A second later a small jagged line splintered out from the point of impact.

Cardiff realized it was all over.

"Jesus! Okay… Okay," he said. "You've made your point." He stared out of the dome with venom. "You win. Just give me a minute. I have to equalize the pressure."

Once Cardiff had equalized the internal pressure to that of the water outside, he turned to Ramirez and spoke quietly. "Open the hatch." Ramirez stared back. There was fear in his eyes.

He moved slowly to the rear of the sub and began turning the large metal wheel on the lockout hatch in the floor. When it was undone he glanced at Cardiff, who nodded. He pulled the hatch open. Immediately a black-clad figure climbed in. Before he even looked around, he pulled a small gun from a pocket on his drysuit and shot Ramirez dead. The sound in the confined space was deafening.

"Noooo!" cried Cardiff, but the man had turned the weapon on him. Once Cardiff was confined in the cockpit, the man at the front of the sub removed the drill from the dome.

A minute later he was sitting inside, with the hatch closed, but not before Ramirez's body had been unceremoniously shoved into the depths. The man removed his gear, pulled down his drysuit hood and stared menacingly at Cardiff.

Frank Cardiff was a veteran of numerous American military operations. He didn't scare easily. He had been trained to function and survive in life-threatening situations. This definitely counted as one of them. After the initial shock, his training and instincts kicked in. They allowed him to calmly observe the new arrivals, while at the same time calculating options and odds. None of which, right now, looked particularly in his favor.

The man, who was clearly the leader, continued to stare at him. He was in his late thirties. He had a hard, weather-beaten face. It was a face that had seen much trauma in its time. One that had endured and triumphed. One that carried no empathy or feeling, just determination and drive. When Cardiff looked into those eyes, he felt fear. He could expect no mercy. No negotiation. This was a man who was here to win at all costs.

Cardiff spoke evenly. "Who the hell are you? What do you want?"

The man looked away, thinking for a second, then stared directly at Cardiff. "My name is Andriy Kozak. You might say my friends and I are tourists, visiting your land of opportunity." He glanced around the sub before returning his gaze to Cardiff.

"What, you think you can just steal this thing?" said Cardiff.

Andriy simply smiled and nodded at the other diver. The man pulled open the hatch. Andriy looked at Cardiff and nodded at the hatch. A thin smile traced across his lips.

This was something Cardiff had not expected. His mind was spinning. Options. Angles.

There were none.

"You're kidding, right?"

Chapter Four

Ilya Kozak's blood sample had been taken and it hadn't hurt one bit. He had been through worse in his life—much worse. The test, though, had given him the pleasure of having the attractive doctor hold his arm in her hand. Her touch had been delicate, but assured. Her hands were soft and her proximity had meant he had caught a waft of her perfume, which was also delicate but at the same time sophisticated. He had enjoyed the moment while it had lasted, but now she had taken the sample and said she'd be back in a few minutes.

He checked his watch.

He was on a schedule. Time was ticking away.

He hopped down off the couch and ran over to his gear in the large holdall. He wouldn't be needing most of it, but the holdall would come in handy.

He unzipped the bag and removed the equipment. He found a dive slate under his fins in the bottom of the bag. It was housed in a small plastic frame. He opened up the cover. From beneath the slate he pulled out a sheet of waterproof paper. On it was a schematic. He glanced at it quickly, found his current location on the map, and then oriented it in the direction he was facing.

There was a storeroom he was desperate to find.

Once he was sure he had the route locked in his memory, he stuffed the map in his pocket. He then retrieved a dive knife and a small torch from among his equipment. He slid them into one of the large pockets on the front of the jumpsuit. Next, he picked up the now empty holdall and moved quietly to the door. He peered cautiously around the corner into the corridor beyond.

The passageway extended in both directions for about thirty feet. At each end another passage crossed as a T-shape. An orderly passed the end of the right-hand passage, which was where he needed to go. The passage was well lit. He ran quickly to the end, keeping close to the wall. The map in his head told him he had to turn right. His destination would be the third door on the left. He risked a glance around the corner. The orderly was disappearing further down the corridor. Ilya moved quietly into the new passage and ran to the third door. He checked the nameplate—RESEARCH STOREROOM.

He opened the door and moved inside.

The lights were off. He pulled out the torch, shielding the beam. He swung it around the room. It was of medium size, with tall storage shelves arranged in rows. He quickly shone the beam along the shelves until he found a large box on a bottom shelf. He read the label—HEMOFILTERS: SECOND TRIAL. He pulled the box off the shelf and opened up the top. Inside were stacked rows of small semi-transparent plastic cases, each about a foot long by four inches wide. He could see they contained what looked like wearable instruments of some kind.

It was what he was looking for.

After a quick glance toward the door, he opened the empty holdall and transferred the plastic boxes into the bag. He then returned the large cardboard box to the bottom shelf, zipped up the holdall and moved back to the door. He turned off the torch and listened. When he was sure there was no one coming, he carefully opened the door and turned left. This, he knew, would take him to some stairs that led up to a door that would take him outside close to the perimeter of the base.

He had just rounded the end of the corridor, when behind him he heard the clipped footsteps of Doctor Fletcher returning to the lab.

He ran as fast as he could for the door that led outside.

Captain Frank Cardiff stared at the open hatch and the small round pool of dark cold water in the middle. He had done all the sums. Calculated all the odds.

There was only one option.

Once he was outside the sub, he had a couple of hundred feet between him and certain death. It wasn't impossible, but it was also not easy. He had frontline special forces training, but those were skills way past their sell-by date. You remembered, but you became rusty. Back in the day, he might have thought it more of a breeze—a challenge—but right now, sitting, staring at that circle of water, a small finger of fear crept up his neck. And despite what he told himself, despite the confidence he willed into his brain, realistically he gave himself a chance of no more than one in ten.

"I'm waiting," came the emotionless statement from Kozak.

Cardiff moved over to the hatch and climbed into the water. He didn't want to give the watching men any satisfaction, so he gritted his teeth at the cold that enveloped his body. He looked up at Kozak.

"They'll hunt you down. You won't get away with this."

Kozak looked at him for a moment. "Would you die for your country?"

"If it came to it," replied Cardiff, "yes."

Kozak smiled, nodding slightly, then gave a single nod to the man at the hatch. The man forced the top down as Cardiff hurriedly filled his lungs with the last breath he might ever take.

Once the hatch was closed, Kozak moved to the front and took control of *Deep Intruder*.

Outside, he could see the sub's previous pilot desperately striking out for the surface. He had to admire the man, but he knew he would never make it.

Kozak grabbed the controls and turned the sub to follow Cardiff's progress. He watched him in fascination, the lights illuminating his body against the black water beyond. And then, as if he had grown tired of the sport, he flipped down the weapon controls. Outside, the two armed wings folded down into an aggressive attack profile. The short arms bristled with torpedoes and armaments of various sizes.

Kozak looked over the options. He had learned the manual by heart, the one that had come from the now dead American hacker. He selected a small torpedo, brought up a crosshair targeting display, and lined up on the figure that was swimming up and away from the sub.

Before he ended the man's life, he saluted a fellow soldier. And then, thinking back to Cardiff's statement that he would die for his country, he looked out into the gloom, pressed the launch button, and watched the torpedo streak for its target.

"So would I," he said, sitting back in the pilot's seat as Frank Cardiff was blown apart in an explosion of bubbles right in front of him.

A moment later, his murderous act was forgotten. He quickly checked the sub's status and then pushed the joystick forward, at the same time pulling back on the controls that would take them up.

Ten minutes later the stealthy black craft broke through the water into a light chop that covered the ocean as far as the eye could see. Everywhere was pitch-black. They were now some distance from the naval base, further along the coast. Kozak checked that the auto-pressurization system had balanced the pressure as the sub had ascended. He crossed into the rear and pulled open the top hatch, climbing out and breathing in the fresh, clean air. He looked toward shore. It was around half a mile away. He pulled a walkie-talkie from his pocket and checked his watch.

Five minutes to spare.

Doctor Connie Fletcher was looking forward to going home and grabbing some much-needed sleep. It was going to be a busy day tomorrow. The call to come and check over a sports diver who had got himself into the test zone hadn't been welcome, but when she'd heard another diver was missing and that he could be injured himself, she had driven in without question.

She was now even more happy, as the man's results had come back negative for any form of bubble issue that would indicate he was at risk from the bends. That was something she wouldn't wish on anyone, as it could result in skin rashes, severe pains in the joints, even neurological issues that could leave you paralyzed for life.

All she had to do now was give him the good news, get him to sign a couple of forms, and then he could go and wait in the small canteen until they had word of his friend. She would then be free and clear—he was someone else's responsibility.

She was just checking through the list of questions on the form he had to sign and was looking down as she entered the lab. When she glanced up, she stopped dead and frowned.

It was empty.

What was more puzzling was that the man's dive gear was all over the floor and the bag was gone. She wished now she'd asked the guard to stay. It wasn't good to have the public running around loose on the base. She mentally and physically kicked herself.

Where the hell could he have gone?

Ilya Kozak hauled himself over the perimeter fence and ducked down into a line of small bushes. He glanced back to check he hadn't been followed, then, crouching low, he ran up the slope until he reached a small path he knew would be there. Five minutes later he had found the Kawasaki KX450 motocross bike he had hidden under some loose scrub two days earlier. He dragged it out from its concealment and glanced around again before jumping on. He pulled out a walkie-talkie and checked his watch.

One minute to go.

Fifty seconds later the speaker crackled.

"This is Andriy. We have control."

Ilya pressed the TRANSMIT button. "I hear you, Andriy. I have the package."

The reply was immediate. "Well done, my brother. We are on our way."

And with that, Ilya pocketed the walkie-talkie, kick-started the bike, and skidded off into the night with a spray of gravel.

Chapter Five

The following morning, Lieutenant Mitch Harley walked along a corridor in the main block at the naval base and turned to face an imposing wooden door at the end of the passageway.

The last door.

The door beyond which the buck stopped for many a covert mission he'd been sent on. The nameplate read **COMMANDER DAVID BRYCE**. It was a door through which, if you passed, you needed to be on top of your game, and one behind which anything could happen.

Harley took a deep breath and knocked firmly on the thick oak panel.

"Come in."

He pushed the door open and walked into the familiar office. The room was small, with books and files on shelves on the walls, but there was a view across the harbor to the open ocean beyond, making the space feel expansive rather than oppressive. That feeling would come later depending on the reason for your presence. Harley walked in and stood stiffly in front of the desk.

Bryce was seated, writing something on a form. He looked tired, but alert, despite having been up all night. He put the pen down and glanced at Harley.

"Sit down, Lieutenant."

"Thank you, sir."

Bryce looked at him thoughtfully for a few seconds. "Bad incident last night, Mitch."

"Yes, sir, it was. Do we have any news on Frank and Mateo?"

"Mateo's body was found washed up about a mile along the coast. A number of body parts were also found. We're confirming they're Frank's, but there's little doubt."

Harley gritted his teeth, his anger growing.

Bryce continued. "And there's no sign of *Deep Intruder*. She's vanished."

"Seems it was well planned."

Bryce nodded gravely. "I don't need to tell you the implications of this. Aside from the tragedy of the deaths… murders… of our men, *Deep Intruder* must be found. Not only is the loss embarrassing… in the wrong hands, there's no knowing what use she could be put to. The consequences don't bear thinking about."

"Do we have any leads?"

"Not right now. There's been no chatter that an operation like this was in the works. It came out of nowhere. All our resources are being coordinated to find these bastards."

Harley was silent.

"I want you and your men to be on a half-hour readiness to deploy when we have a target. Is that understood?"

"Yes, sir."

"What are your movements today?"

"I'm scheduled to meet with Doctor Fletcher after this for medical trials and then I'm training in the large tank this afternoon. I'll be on base all day."

"Good, stay close. This is going to be a tricky one. But when you get the order to go, you go in hard and fast and take no prisoners."

"That won't be a problem, sir."

Harley was the epitome of a US Navy SEAL. Tall, broad, super fit, but with an easy-going air about him that belayed the violence that could be unleashed from within.

He had been in the service for six years. A background in the marines had led him to Coronado. He had an aptitude for underwater work and had focused on that skillset above all others. Put him in the water against any other adversary and you would be a foolish man to bet against him.

He walked out of Bryce's office and made his way into the sunshine of what looked like was going to be another hot day. There was barely a cloud in the sky. The sea was millpond flat. A beautiful day. If it hadn't been for the events of the previous night he would be walking with a spring in his step. But the events had occurred and he knew before long he would be called into service by his country to right a wrong that, this time, was far too close to home.

As he walked through the base he was greeted with friendly salutes from junior ranks, but the protocol was conducted in a relaxed style, as was prevalent among many of the world's special forces.

He reached the larger of the two water tanks. It was two hundred feet long, fifty feet wide, and twenty feet deep. It was where they spent a large amount of time honing tactics and testing equipment before taking them to the open water that was only a couple of hundred yards away.

Currently, two of his men were conducting live fire exercises with torpedo launchers from diver propulsion vehicles (DPVs). One side of the tank had a viewing panel of glass that extended for thirty feet close to the target zone. Harley peered through. As it was a training pool, they needed to analyze the capability of the weapons as well as the operatives, so the water was crystal clear. All testing and training was recorded on cameras that covered the length and breadth of the tank so analysis could take place later to refine performance and outcome. Similar protocols were in place at NASA. Both organizations worked with impossibly fine margins where a slight divergence could spell disaster.

As Harley peered through the glass he saw a moving target appear to his left. It zigzagged across the width of the tank. It was an autonomous drone, programmed to take evasive action against any threat its sensors picked up.

Then, from the right, he could see two shapes approaching at speed. They were moving fast, one ahead of the other. As he watched, they took the form of divers holding onto sleek DPVs. The lead diver approached the drone from the side. The drone spun, engaging the target. Lights lit up across the top, but before it could fire, Harley heard a whooshing sound. He glanced behind the drone. The second diver had unleashed a small torpedo from his DPV on the far side. A classic pincer movement. The weapon sped fast and true for its target, seemingly anticipating every evasive action the drone took. In fact, there was no anticipation involved, the reactions of the drone and the torpedo were working far faster than the human brain could follow. The torpedo was merely reacting to the actions of the drone. A second later there was a small explosion.

The drone disappeared in a mass of bubbles. One of the divers did a victory pass behind the window, barrel-rolling his DPV as he went. Harley smiled and gave him the thumbs up. He then turned and walked toward the long squat building beyond the side of the tank.

When he walked into the lab, Doctor Connie Fletcher was peering down a microscope at a petri dish. The TV up near the ceiling was showing CNN. The sound was muted. He leaned against the door for a few seconds. Briefly, the anger he had felt earlier dissipated as he watched her work. Nothing had happened between them, but there was a chemistry he was sure could be turned into biology if he just had the guts to ask. Put him in life and death situations around the world—no problem. But women, they were a whole different threat assessment.

As if sensing his presence, Connie looked up. She seemed to be fighting to try to hide the smile that almost spread across her lips. She was playing the game as well. She leaned back in the chair and swiveled to face him.

"Hello, Lieutenant."

"Hello, doctor."

She gave him a look. "At least you're on time for once."

"How could I miss my favorite appointment of the week."

Her face then became serious, and what little of the smile had been there, faded. "Okay, go and sit on the recliner and lean back."

Harley walked across to the recliner and sat on the side. He looked at her. "Hey, you okay?"

She turned to face him. He could see the sadness in her eyes. "One of them was here, Mitch. I was looking after him."

"There was no way you could have known. "

"Maybe I should have asked more questions. Left Alec on guard while I was away…"

"Connie… Connie… Look at me."

She looked at him.

"It's alright. It wasn't your fault. He had us all fooled."

"But Frank… and Mateo."

Harley's face hardened. "I know, and make no mistake, we'll find those who did this."

She took a deep breath and composed herself. "Okay, you ready?"

"As I'll ever be."

"I'll be back in a minute."

She left the room, leaving Harley thinking about what he would do to those who had killed his friends. He was working on the fourth scenario when Connie rushed back into the room.

"They're gone!"

"What?"

"The second batch of test samples. All gone. That guy who was here. He must have taken them."

"I'll let Bryce know. He's not going to be happy."

Harley had a five-minute conversation, which seemed to be all one-sided once his reason for calling had been established. He put the receiver down.

Connie looked at him apprehensively.

"Not happy, but that was to be expected." He glanced at her. "Don't worry, no one's blaming you."

She didn't answer. Instead, she indicated for him to lie back on the recliner. She walked over to the side table and snapped open a small plastic case measuring about a foot by four inches. Harley could see a printed label on the top that said HEMOFILTERS: THIRD TEST BATCH.

She pulled out a device about three inches long by two

inches wide that was attached to a wrist strap. Underneath were two short, thin plastic tubes with stoppers in the ends of them. She took out a small vacuum-packed pack about an inch square. She ripped the top off and removed two thin needles. Each had a small plastic connector on the end. She then deftly pulled the stoppers from the tubes on the device and attached the needles to each of them. She then crossed over to Harley.

"Okay, you know the drill. Roll up your sleeve."

He could see a tension in her movements and glanced at the device with the two needles now protruding beneath.

"You sure you're okay to do this?"

"I'm fine," she said firmly.

He glanced at her, and then, not taking his eyes from her, rolled up his sleeve. When she saw his arm, she frowned slightly. "I hope you never get busted by the cops, they're going to think you mainline every day."

Harley glanced down at the underside of his arm and realized the puncture holes and distorted veins didn't look good.

"Don't worry, doc, I'll just tell them you're my dealer."

She raised her eyebrows, then sharply pushed the device down on his arm. The needles penetrated his skin and veins.

"Owwww! Shit! What was that for?"

"For sometimes being almost adorable, Lieutenant. And don't be such a wuss!"

He looked at her warily.

Connie was then all concentration. She attached one end of a small cable to the side of the device. The other end was plugged into a computer. She clicked some keys. A window opened on the screen. At the top was a heart rate monitor showing Harley's heart rate. Below was a graphical interface that had an X and Y axis. Currently there were no readings on the graph.

Connie reached over to a small metal tray next to the computer. On it was a syringe containing a clear liquid. She picked it up and turned to him.

Harley smiled. "Go on, Doctor Death, do your worst!"

"Do not tempt me."

She moved forward and carefully injected the liquid into Harley's arm. "Okay, now just relax. Lean back, close your eyes and think of something pleasurable."

"But they'd have to be open, looking at you."

She rolled her eyes.

"Focus, Lieutenant." But there was the hint of a smile.

"Are we making progress?"

"I think so," she replied. "The hemofilter is removing ninety-five percent of bubbles in the critical size range. We need it to achieve ninety-nine. If we can get to that level we should be able to pretty much eliminate decompression issues from deep diving operations. Take out the bubbles that can block the lungs and arteries, we solve the bends. Just a lot of trial and testing before we get there."

"And in the meantime I'm your personal pin cushion."

She grinned at him. "Finally, we've found a use for you."

Harley gave her a look. As he leaned back in the chair his gaze flowed past her to the TV in the background. "Hey, turn it up."

Connie glanced at the screen and then grabbed the remote.

A female presenter was speaking into camera in a studio. Behind her was a photograph of the naval base. She was talking about an incident that had resulted in a lockdown on the surrounding roads. She then transferred over to a reporter on location who was standing at the side of the

I-5 with gridlock in both directions. Single-file traffic both ways. Next to him was a motorcycle cop from the California Highway Patrol. He looked like he'd just walked off the set of *CHiPS*. The reporter turned to him.

"Okay, so what can you tell us about the congestion motorists are experiencing at this time?"

The cop turned to look earnestly at the reporter. He still wore his helmet and kept his Ray-Bans in place against the glare of the sun.

"Well, all I can tell you," he said in a slow Texan drawl, "there was some sort of disturbance over at one of the facilities at the naval base. All roads in the surrounding area are being screened for potential suspects."

"Do you know how long travelers will be affected?"

"No, sir. We're here as long as we're told to be here. But I wouldn't expect it to ease for much of the day."

"Thank you for your time, officer."

"No problem." The reporter turned to camera. The cop turned back to the road where a glacier-white Audi RS TT Roadster was inching along in the queue.

"So there we have it," continued the reporter." Looks like a place to avoid for the rest of the day. Now, back to the studio."

Connie turned the volume down. Harley glanced at the screen.

"Won't do much good. They'll be long gone by now. These guys are pros."

"Don't I know it," said Connie.

On the I-5, the motorcycle cop stretched his back and watched as the reporter and his cameraman packed up their gear and loaded it into the back of a small SUV with 'San

Diego News Channel' written across the side. He turned back to the never-ending flow of traffic inching forward in line and sighed.

It was going to be a long day.

As he glanced along the queue, he noticed a woman in a white Audi RS TT Roadster. There was something about her. She sported a pair of stylish sunglasses. Her hair was drawn back into a ponytail and she wore a smart black business suit. She was tapping her fingers on the steering wheel and was stretched back in her seat, her head leaning against the headrest, absorbing the full rays from the sun.

The Audi inched closer.

As it approached, he could hear the gravely strains of Rod Stewart emanating from the speakers. He winced. She had almost been perfect.

As the car drew alongside, he walked over. The woman looked up and gave him a broad smile. Six foot four of muscled California Highway Patrolman went weak at the knees.

"Hi, officer. Any idea what all this is about?"

"Sorry, ma'am. Something to do with an incident at the naval station. All I know. Looks like you'll be here for a while."

The woman frowned.

"That's a pain. I have a job interview over at Imperial Beach at eleven."

The cop checked his watch. "You might make it, but it'll be touch and go."

"Ah, well," said the woman. "At least I have my music to keep me company." She smiled that smile again.

"Not sure you can call that music, ma'am," the cop said with a straight face.

She looked up at him indignantly. Then she lifted her

shades, revealing a pair of stunning green eyes. The cop swallowed.

She smiled mischievously, putting on an innocent voice. "Not exactly against the law, though, is it, officer?"

"Not right now, ma'am, but I'm sure it will be one day."

She grinned. "Philistine."

"No, ma'am, I'm from Texas."

The queue started to advance.

"Move along now. You have a nice day."

"Ciao, officer. You too."

The Audi moved off slowly. The cop watched it go and then let out a sigh. Somewhere out there, there was one lucky guy—and then he mentally corrected himself—or girl.

He hoped it was a girl.

Chapter Six

Today

He could hear it before he could see it.

The noise started out as a distant drone that grew in intensity. There was a crackle from a walkie-talkie attached across his chest.

"Incoming. Should be with you any second."

John McCready lifted the pair of Oakley sunglasses onto his forehead, momentarily revealing his piercing blue eyes before covering them again with a pair of Zeiss binoculars. He pointed them down the majestic length of Loch Lomond in Western Scotland to try and pinpoint the small target that would be approaching at several hundred miles per hour. He adjusted left, right, and then saw it. It was small but was growing larger by the second. He held onto the glasses with one hand, keeping the target in sight, then lifted the walkie-talkie and pressed TALK.

"Roger, Craig. She's in sight now. Should be with you in about twenty seconds."

"Copy that."

McCready watched the object coming closer. He could now make out more of its shape. It was about fifteen feet long and had the profile of a fat cruise missile, but waging war was far from its purpose. Two stubby winglets sprouted from each side, and on the top, at the rear, were two angled tail fins. Along the sides, at the front, two large forward-pointing moldings that looked like thick spears gave it an aggressive feel.

It was almost upon McCready. He no longer needed the binoculars. He lowered them just in time to see a streak of white flash past him. As it flew by, he could make out the light blue lettering on the side spelling out SKYLINE.

And then, with a roar, it was past.

Immediately, it started an upward turn into a near vertical climb. McCready watched as it rose higher and higher and then rolled over to arc straight down and head for the loch below. He turned his gaze to the water at the base of the two-thousand-foot mountain he was currently perched halfway up.

The loch was nearly a mile wide at this point. In the middle he could make out a large area marked out with a circle of brightly colored red buoys. It was about two hundred yards in diameter. On the right-hand side, a fast RIB with twin 200hp engines mounted on the back was moored up. There were two people sitting on its thick buoyancy tubes. On the shore immediately below him was a slipway and a car park. He could make out a number of 4x4s and a flatbed truck parked up.

McCready watched the descent of the craft toward the water. He was waiting for something specific to happen, which should be about… NOW.

It happened, but not in the way that it should.

The two long moldings on either side of Skyline should have fired small retro rockets precisely calculated to slow the craft and bring it to an almost dead stop just feet above the surface—the idea, to cushion the impact and protect any cargo inside. Instead, what happened was that one of them fired but not the other. This spun the craft into the water with a mighty 'THWACK' and there was an explosion of spray. The craft cartwheeled across the surface, narrowly missing the RIB, causing the occupants to duck as it flew overhead.

McCready watched in shock as waves from the impact rippled out across the otherwise smooth surface of the loch. After a couple of seconds the craft slowly slipped below the water. He continued to watch. Ten seconds later there was an eruption of bubbles. This was followed by the appearance of the craft, now cocooned in bright orange flotation bags—at least the emergency buoyancy system had worked.

He picked up the walkie-talkie.

"Well that didn't go quite to plan."

"No shit! You better come down."

"On my way."

Twenty minutes, later McCready waited for a lorry to pass by on the main road at the bottom of the mountain. He then crossed the road to the car park beyond and made his way over to the group of vehicles parked by the water.

As he reached them, the RIB was just approaching the slipway with the long white craft in tow behind. There was a large dent on one side of the nose cone. It was looking pretty sorry for itself with the array of flotation bags strapped to the sides. He walked over to Craig Richards, whom he had been speaking to over the radio.

Richards was McCready's business partner and his closest friend. He was in his mid-fifties, somewhat gruff in his outlook on life, but a staunch ally, and someone McCready trusted with his life. They'd been through many adventures together, but this latest enterprise was one of the most exciting and challenging yet, as they aimed to take their company, Ocean Oil Exploration, in a whole new direction.

Richards glanced at him, shaking his head.

"I thought we'd cured this. That's the third time the retros have failed on that side."

McCready walked with him as the RIB pulled into the slipway.

"Could be something in the software just not triggering the charge."

"Maybe. Maybe not."

McCready watched as Richards chatted to the boat driver and others on the team. They prepared to lift the craft out of the water and onto the flatbed truck using a small crane on the back. There would need to be a detailed investigation when they returned to base in Aberdeen.

The Skyline system had been in development for a number of years, but it was only now receiving its real-world testing. It had been problematic from the start. They had thought, though, that they'd resolved this particular issue.

It was designed to be a fast aerial delivery system, getting medical and critical supplies to where they were most needed in times of crisis or disaster. It had a parachute system to allow it to land safely on land, but there was the rocket system for water landings, where there often had to be pinpoint accuracy—the recipients might not always be able to move far across the water to reach it. Powered by small jet thrusters and controlled by military precision GPS, it could, in theory, splashdown within a twenty-foot radius anywhere on the planet. On land it was launched from a mobile shore-based launcher, but it could also be air launched from a pylon slung beneath the wing of an aircraft. All sexy stuff. While today's test had been from the back of a truck located twenty miles to the north, the aerial launch trials were due to start soon using a recently acquired second-hand Boeing 737 that had been fitted out for the drop tests. All they needed before the trials could begin was the hiring of a suitable pilot who was willing to do the things they needed to do, often above and beyond the call of duty. This was something they'd be hopefully sorting out in the next few days.

"Okay, guys, get her back to base. We'll go over the debrief when we get there." Richards watched as the flatbed drove across the car park, the damaged Skyline secured under a large gray tarpaulin. He walked back over to McCready who was checking a message on his phone.

McCready looked up as he approached. "Sarah can make it tomorrow night. You still on?"

Richards snorted. "You kidding? Free booze at the McCready house. Yep, I'll be there."

"Hey, it's your turn to bring the booze."

"Yeah, right."

"So, what time at Queensferry in the morning? And you're sure this pilot is who we need?"

"The race starts at ten, so meet up nine thirty. They're laying on bacon and sausage rolls at the Three Bridges pub, so you can stock up for the day." McCready smiled. "As for Charlie... pilots don't come any better. Wait till you guys meet. I'm sure you'll agree."

McCready looked skeptical.

"Have I ever let you down?"

McCready was about to reply, but then he remembered that the last two recommendations his friend had made had proved to be solid gold. The first was Eugene Porter, an explosives expert, who'd be joining them in Queensferry for the Red Bull air race; the second, Mac Logan, was an expert technical diver and sub driver. Both had been invaluable on an operation at the end of the previous year.

"Okay, I reserve the right to reserve judgment."

Richards smiled. He glanced at McCready's phone. The background picture was of a woman in a wetsuit with a wide smile and dancing green eyes. She stared cheekily at the camera and looked full of life. He gave McCready a quizzical expression.

"You sure that's wise to still have that on there?"

McCready glanced at the phone, and the picture of Clare, before quickly putting it away. He put his hands in his pockets and looked straight at Richards.

"Don't you think it's time to let go?" said Richards gently.

McCready looked out across the calm water, the afternoon sun warming his face.

"I'm fine, really. I've moved on."

"You sure?"

"Okay, it was a shock, I admit. I wish she could have called or something. Reading a message saying she was seeing an old friend who had become *more* than an old friend kind of hurt, and that she's now working with him in LA is not exactly great."

"Yeah, but John, think about it. She found you in bed with another woman—no, an eighteen-year-old girl—and I know you've explained the circumstances and that nothing happened, and I believe you, but you have to admit, the optics aren't exactly great!"

McCready glanced at him, knowing he was right. "I suppose. I just wished she'd given me a chance to explain."

Richards put a hand on McCready's shoulder.

"Okay, I'll bring the booze tomorrow night. My treat. Drown all your sorrows."

McCready smiled. "See you at the Three Bridges, nine thirty."

Richards waved, and with that McCready climbed into his Corris Gray Range Rover Sport and gunned the engine. He lowered the window, and as he turned round, about to drive off, Richards shouted at him, "At least you've got your bloody taillight fixed!"

He grinned and drove smoothly out onto the main road and headed west.

McCready had finally managed to get his rear light fixed after it had been broken during an incident with two employees of his former boss who had made huge efforts to run him off the road.

As the memories came flooding back, his face turned serious. It was only about a mile further along the loch, among a dense patch of trees, that a good friend and colleague, Steve Donovan, had been killed in the same incident.

Other memories also filled his mind.

Much had happened in the previous six months, since an operation in the Western Pacific that had nearly killed himself and Craig. He still bore the scrapes and scars, which included a bullet and knife wound, and, some might say, a broken heart. One thing that had come out of it, though, was a somewhat complicated relationship with a certain Mr. Martin Steel. The man worked for the British government in a security capacity, one that was actually able to get things done—no questions asked. One of the questions McCready had asked, was, how do you transfer $100 million dollars worth of gold into usable currency. The gold had been acquired during a period of time that had changed McCready's life. It had been to right an injustice, and while technically he had bent the law further than Uri Gellar could bend spoons to achieve this, it was the kind of bending Martin Steel could understand. They had at one point come to an arrangement that McCready would keep the gold, but that still left the problem of transferring it into a usable form, so after much deliberation McCready had gone back to Steel, asking for his help, saying that half the gold could be returned to be used by Steel and the government as he so wished. Steel had appeared surprised at the offer, but after careful consideration had accepted. It had cemented their fractious relationship and, McCready hoped, put it on a more stable and trustworthy footing.

Two weeks later, the gold had been delivered to Steel. A month after that, the balance of Ocean Oil Exploration's business account had changed somewhat... most definitely for the better. In fact, Craig had received a phone call from a very excited and enthusiastic bank manager.

This new liquidity meant that McCready had been able to share out a large proportion of the money to those who had participated in the original operation. However, after a meeting, where everyone had been allowed to have their say, it was generally agreed that each individual would take a reasonable figure for general living and to buy a few luxuries, but that the majority should stay within the company to explore new directions. The group had included Porter,

Logan, Craig and himself. But there were two others who were an issue. Sarah, who would be coming over to the house the following evening, was the wife of McCready's late brother, Sean. His death as a result of actions of his former boss, Malcolm Mercer, was what had triggered everything in the first place, resulting in Mercer being relieved of the gold. They had all agreed that a portion of the money should be used to set Sarah and her baby girl, Shauna, up for life. She had wept openly when she saw the check they presented her with. It would never bring Sean back, but it meant she could now move on with her and her daughter's life without any financial worries.

The other individual McCready wanted to share some of the cash with was Clare. It was how they had met. He had coerced her into becoming involved, against her better judgment, and for that he would always feel responsible. But if he hadn't, they would never have met, though now he was wondering if it had been worth it. But the thought was only for a second—of course it had been worth it. He didn't think he would ever meet anyone else like her. She had gone along with him because she had believed in him. As a result, she had lost her job. In fact, when McCready thought about everything that had happened between them, he could easily see why she would opt for a safer, more stable, life, which had been the words she had used. As a result, he had never contacted her, but he would watch from afar, and if she was ever in trouble, or needed money, he would be there to help.

The balance of the funds had then gone into a rethink of the direction the company McCready and Richards had founded ten years earlier. It had originally been set up to handle the thriving oil industry in the North Sea, while at the same time involving itself in the design and research of underwater technology and equipment. With the oil industry rapidly declining, and with the recent injection of cash, it had been decided to close down that side of the business and concentrate on technology design and development. With this in mind, the company had been rebranded as Ocean Tech. In line with this there had been many changes at the HQ, which was based in Aberdeen.

Despite the issues in his personal life, McCready thought a chapter had been turned, and he smiled ruefully to himself as he stared out at the beauty of Scotland passing by beyond the Range Rover's windows.

He could now look forward to fresh new challenges in the years ahead and put the past behind him.

Chapter Seven

The smog hanging over Los Angeles was particularly bad. It lay in a dense layer over the main part of the city, shrouding it in a muddy, cloudy mist. But at a height of fifteen hundred feet, the smart red and white Airbus ACH160 executive helicopter was well above the pollution. It had just taken off from the private terminal at LAX and was still climbing for the short trip across the city.

Sitting in one of the four comfortable leather seats in the rear cabin, Clare Kowalski stared out at the view. She was dressed in a smart blue business suit with a white shirt beneath. Her hair had been cut shorter than usual to fall just below her collar.

New life—new look.

Sometimes she loved the city. Sometimes she hated it. Today the view was not so great, but her mind was so preoccupied she barely noticed it. Sitting next to her was Randal Watson, adviser to the president, and part of the advance team for the forthcoming arrival of the leader of the free world to the building where she was now working.

Watson was in his mid-thirties, slightly balding, with a lean, wiry physique. But he was sharp as a tack and Clare thought they could work well together. He was currently buried in a scheduling timesheet that was displayed on the screen of a compact laptop.

A lot had happened in the last five months since she'd accepted the job of assistant manager at the Omega Complex. To the outside world, the facility was merely a conference center, but underneath, it represented a building with the most secure capability of virtually any on the planet. She had stared in amazement when she had first been given the tour. It was for the challenge of helping to run this groundbreaking complex, as well as knowing the importance of the meetings of world shakers and movers it would host, that Clare had accepted the position.

Another major factor that had been part of the decision had been personal. When Brad Walker, the manager of the complex, and an old flame from college, had come back into her life and had been the one to offer her the position, she felt the planets had aligned. She had just been through a difficult period in her professional and personal life and this represented a whole new chapter. It had been difficult with regards to the guy she had given up for Brad, but she thought it had been for the best, and now, five months on, she was glad she'd made the decision. They worked hard together and they played hard together. Right now, she was more than happy.

She glanced at Watson. He was still staring at the laptop. She looked out of the large rectangular window as the patchwork of streets and buildings sped by below. If only you could always get around LA like this.

They were just approaching the main part of the city. Below, she could make out the concrete spillway that made up the Los Angeles River, now almost bereft of water after the hot summer. It always reminded her of one of her favorite films, *Grease*, where at the end of the film John Travolta's character, Danny Zuko, has a race in a 1950s convertible along the slopes and bed of the dried-up waterway.

Up ahead she could see the Hollywood Hills, where her house was located. In fact, as she stared down, she could just make it out at the top of Laurel Canyon.

The helicopter curved round in a smooth turn, running parallel to the hills for a while. It was lining up to come in to land. Below, they passed over the new Griffith Park reservoir that had only recently been completed. It had been a huge help in rectifying LA's water supply problem—something that had plagued the city for years. Its four-billion-gallon capacity had been a big boost to the city, particularly after the water quality issues there had been at the Stone Canyon Reservoir.

As they sped over the ruffled surface of the water, and then the high dam wall, Clare saw the Omega Complex come into view.

She turned to Watson.

"We're almost here, Randal. You might want to take a look."

Watson looked up from the screen and glanced out of the window. He was about to return focus to his work, when he saw the complex and had to stop and stare.

It was located at the east end of the range of hills and had taken over part of Griffith Park. This had caused a stir at the time as even some of the holes of the golf course had had to be relocated. It was about half a mile from, and slightly below, the reservoir. The main building was two hundred feet high. From above, it was designed in the shape of an omega symbol. The sides were made up of wide, curved glass panels that reflected the morning Californian sunshine.

The center of the building was hollow, forming a two-hundred-foot-tall atrium. Offices and accommodation facilities were arranged around the central core. The roof was made up of a dome of glass squares, which cast moving shadows below as the sun moved across the sky during the day, creating an ever-changing environment within.

The helipad was located on the right-hand side of the roof. On the left were a number of sophisticated antennas and communications dishes. They were some of the most advanced in the world, and played an integral part in the security of the complex.

Watson was still watching as the Airbus swung round in a wide arc and came in to hover above the large red 'H' in the middle of the white rectangular pad.

A second later they touched down. The pilot killed the engine and the rotors slowly came to a stop. Once they were stationary, a woman dressed in a smart red and gray uniform ran up and opened the door on Clare's side. Clare climbed out, and after closing his laptop and putting it in a briefcase, Watson followed her onto the pad.

They stood briefly before being escorted by the woman to the entrance of the helipad lobby at the side. Once inside, Clare thanked her and turned to Watson. They were in a small reception area with large windows and wide comfy couches.

"Enjoy that, Randal?"

Watson looked impressed. "Very nice, Clare. I hope the rest of the place lives up to the good things I've heard."

"I'm sure it will. If you could just give me a couple of minutes and then we can start the tour."

Watson put his briefcase down and looked around the room. The walls had large-scale prints of the complex taken at different times of day and night. He strolled over to look at them.

Clare walked out of the room and along a wide open-plan landing. It led through to the center of the massive atrium. She was always in awe when she was in this space. The atrium itself was a hundred feet across. All the functionality was located around the edge. It consisted of twenty floors of offices, meeting rooms and accommodation. The main conference rooms were on the lower levels. The accommodation was in the middle. The offices were on the upper levels. However, the really impressive part of the complex, and what made it unique, was located below ground level.

For now, she walked around the atrium, past two doors on her left, until she came to the manager's office. She could hear a voice from behind the door talking on a phone. She opened the door and walked in.

And smiled.

There, standing by the window, was the man she had changed her life for—Brad Walker. He was looking exactly as he had when she had seen him for the first time in years, as he had stood in the office at West Coast Recruitment in San Diego six months earlier—tall, broad shouldered, and with a slightly arrogant silhouette that she knew was only a front and one that she could break down in moments.

He finished up his call and turned to see who had entered. As soon as he saw Clare, he smiled.

"I haven't got long," she said. I have to give Randal Watson the tour. Last-minute checks before the president arrives."

"And the rest of them," said Walker.

"Yeah, and the rest of them."

The forthcoming event was to take place over the following five days. It was a summit between the Russian and American leaders to try and address climate change issues, as well as thrash out arms control limitations. This was in the wake of the American president's predecessor, who had torn up agreements left, right and center, and which now had to be stitched back together. But given the president's desire to play hardball with an equally hard man from Moscow, it wasn't going to be easy.

Thankfully, that wasn't Clare's problem. All she had to do was keep the coffee flowing and make sure everything ran smoothly, including security. Given the capability of the facility, though, that was the least of her worries. There had been no information from any of the intelligence agencies as to any potential threats, so it was likely the summit could be treated as a glorified shakedown and trial run of the systems and protocols of the newly completed complex.

"Come here," said Walker with a grin.

Clare glanced around. "I can't. Randal's waiting in the lobby. I said I'd only be a couple of minutes."

"Amazing what you can do in a couple of minutes," said Walker as he started to cross over to her. She stood still, letting him come. She watched him. When he reached her, he bent forward and gave her a long, warm kiss. As he drew away she wanted to prolong it and draped a hand around his neck preventing him from moving. He didn't object. When they did break apart she looked at him with an inscrutable expression. "I suppose that could be classed as sexual harassment in the workplace."

Walker looked at her for a second. "Then what the hell would you call what you did last night?"

"My resignation will be on your desk in the morning," said Clare with a guilty grin.

"Go to work! I'm not paying you to hang around molesting me all day. That's a whole different job description," said Walker.

Clare turned for the door, pulling a face as she went, but she was smiling as she walked back to the lobby.

Yeah, she was happy.

Five minutes later she'd briefed Watson on what they were going to see. He'd picked up his briefcase and they'd walked out onto the walkway that encircled the top of the atrium. They walked over to the edge. There was a glass barrier, four feet high, all the way around. Where they were, the barrier looked like it could slide to one side.

When he glanced over the edge, Watson whistled quietly. "Wow, that's impressive."

"You ain't seen the half of it," said Clare.

She tapped her Apple Watch.

"We're going to use the lift-track system, which makes it easy to get around the complex. It serves all the levels, as well as the cocoon, which I'll show you after the security center. You call a capsule by an app, as on my watch, or else you'll be provided with an electronic band for your stay. The system knows where you are and sends a capsule to your position. The entry points are every thirty degrees around each level."

Watson watched as a large glass capsule rose up on a vertical track further around the atrium. Once it arrived at their level it moved horizontally around the side until it reached them.

Clare continued. "Once you're inside, you use voice-recognition to state your destination. All those with clearance have their voices recorded when they enter the building and pass through security."

As she finished, the capsule arrived. The two curved glass doors slid smoothly aside, along with the section of glass barrier. She let Watson walk in first and then followed. The doors closed automatically behind.

"Level One," said Clare.

"Destination Level One confirmed. Please hold on," said the computerized female voice.

The capsule moved horizontally around the atrium, and then, when it reached the vertical track, started to descend.

Watson continued to stare around at the impressive structure surrounding him. He could see other capsules moving around the levels and ascending and descending.

Clare continued. "The main construction of the building is with super-strengthened steel surrounded by high-impact concrete. The windows are pressure-proofed and designed to survive moderate explosions. They'll easily withstand bullet hits… also, RPGs and other small portable missile systems."

They were now two-thirds of the way down.

"I'm impressed, Clare. It's an amazing place."

The capsule glided to a smooth stop at the bottom. As the doors slid open, a couple of businessmen waited to enter. They nodded at Clare as she walked out with Watson.

They were now standing on the floor of the atrium, and if possible, it looked even more spectacular from down there. Most of the area was taken up with stone engravings depicting the nations of the world. In the center was a large statue of hundreds of people holding up a symbolic rendering of the planet high above them—a bit like the soccer World Cup trophy on steroids.

After Watson had spent a couple of moments taking it

all in, Clare led him over to the side of the atrium. They passed through a double set of pneumatically sealed doors, which acted as an airlock, and led to the security center.

Once inside, they were standing on a slightly raised section that ran the full length of the space. It looked out over an area that resembled a military ops control room. Steps led down to the lower section. Long workbenches lined three sides. Spread across these were a series of computer workstations with large widescreen displays. Above them, CCTV displays showed views from cameras throughout the complex. There were four controllers sitting on wheeled office chairs to aid movement. They were currently going through a procedural checklist in preparation for the presidential visit. One of them looked up. Clare waved.

Harry Patterson was a bear of a man. He was the senior security controller and, as he walked over to Clare, he had a smile on his face.

"Hi, Clare. How's it going?"

"I was about to ask you the same thing... Harry, this is Randal Watson. He's with the president's team. Just giving him the tour."

Randal and Patterson shook hands.

"Nice to meet you Mr. Watson. We aim to keep you all safe and sound for the duration."

Watson was looking around at the screens. "That's good to know. You certainly seem to have the kit."

"That we do," said Patterson. "Could I just borrow this little lady for a couple of minutes? Won't be long."

"Of course," said Watson.

Patterson led Clare down onto the floor and over to one of the computer screens. Some of the technicians looked up and smiled as she passed.

"Everything okay?" asked Clare.

Patterson indicated a screen that showed a series of figures and data relating to a recent test.

"So far. We've run a general simulation, and then specific chemical, biological, even nuclear attack scenarios. All except the last one, we're well within predicted results. Your guests are going to be well taken care of."

"Great. How's the tunnel issue?"

Patterson clicked a mouse. He moved it to bring up a schematic of a tunnel. At one end was the Omega Complex, at the other, an opening in the Griffith Park reservoir dam buildings. It was an escape tunnel to be used as a last resort if the complex ever came under attack and there was no way out. Patterson manipulated the mouse, which moved the 3D graphic around. He zoomed in to a point in the tunnel about halfway along. "Around here there's still a slight leakage for about twenty feet, but well within tolerances."

He then clicked the area on the tunnel graphic. A CCTV image came up. It showed two workmen and a pickup truck working close to the wall on one side.

"Okay, I'll go check on Hank and Josh later. For now, I have to finish Randal's tour," said Clare.

"Okay, be safe, little lady."

"Always am, Harry. See ya."

And with that, she turned and walked over to Watson.

"Okay, let's show you the rest of it."

Chapter Eight

Bacon rolls smelled far too good.

At least that was John McCready's assessment as Richards handed him one. It was piping hot and a dribble of tomato sauce leaked out of the side. He wiped it up before it escaped and landed on his denim shirt. He licked his fingers and took a bite.

The taste was as good as the smell.

McCready, Richards and Eugene Porter were standing in a car park outside the Three Bridges pub. It was located at the side of a marina in the small town of Queensferry, about eight miles to the west of Edinburgh. The town looked out over the Firth of Forth and was smack bang in the middle of the three bridges that spanned the wide expanse of water.

For many years there had only been two, The Forth Road Bridge, which, as its name suggested, carried road traffic across the water, and, to seaward, the iconic Forth Bridge, or rail bridge, which had opened in 1890 and was regarded as an engineering masterpiece. The structure had also descended into folklore as a way of describing a never-ending job, in so much as a job was like 'painting the Forth Bridge.' These two bridges had been joined by a second road bridge in 2017, called the Queensferry Crossing, built to help deal with the increase in traffic and situated just up river from the existing road bridge.

The car park was full, and there was a buzz of excitement and anticipation from the two-thousand-strong crowd of spectators that lined the waterfront and gathered in groups further along the shore. There was a great family vibe, as parents and kids laughed and shouted. Ice cream sellers were doing a brisk trade. Everyone was happy enjoying the bright morning sunshine.

A moment later, a fast single-seat aircraft shot over the heads of the crowd with a roar. It was red, with a white stripe down its side, and was the first of a series of overflights by the competitors in the day's Red Bull Air Race.

Red Bull had, over many years, become synonymous with adventure sports and daring events. There was no better example of this than the air race. It consisted of a series of rounds taking place across the world. Pilots had to navigate a course, negotiating various obstacles and completing a number of tricky maneuvers.

The course was outlined by massive red and white air-filled pylons, eighty feet high. These included: a start and finish gate; three to four, two-pylon gates; a chicane made up of three individual pylons; and a vertical turning maneuver. The one that completed it in the quickest time, with the smallest number of penalties, was the winner. All this in a single-seat piston aircraft flying at speeds of over two hundred miles per hour, pulling up to twelve G, often mere feet off the deck. There had been numerous instances where pilots had hit the inflatable cones with little damage, but also a number where it had resulted in serious accidents. It was an adrenaline junkie's nirvana.

It was a beautiful day for the event, which was taking place in the early autumn sunshine of what had been a hot summer in Scotland. Everyone was wearing T-shirts. Most had baseball caps to shield their eyes against the sun as they looked to the skies. McCready glanced down at Porter's shirt. It was black, with **BIG BANG THEORY** scrawled across it in large white letters.

"Subtle."

Porter glanced down. "Like to keep things simple, guv."

McCready smiled.

But their attention was quickly drawn back to the skies above as an announcer introduced the pilots over a tannoy. As each name blared out, a small plane shot over the crowd, completed a barrel roll, and soared out over the water of the Forth. There were eight in all. Each roll was greeted by whoops from the crowd.

The course itself was laid out in a series of snaking gates that ran beneath the bridges. But before the main race got underway the pilots put on a spectacular display, following nose to tail and looping over and under the bridges one after the other. The display ended with trailing multicolored smoke trails from behind the planes.

"Okay, so which is our guy?" asked Porter.

McCready and Richards exchanged glances. "The blue and yellow one with white wings. Charlie Menzies," said Richards.

Porter looked up at the sky, shielding his eyes from the glare. He found the plane coming off the top of a loop above the Forth Bridge.

Over the next two hours the crowd were treated to an amazing display of flying skill. By the end, it came down to two planes that could win. The first, a black aircraft with graphic flames across the fuselage, was going for the record. It weaved dramatically in and out of the cones, clipping the last one and earning a penalty. It was then down to the final run. Charlie Menzies needed to beat a previous best by two seconds to take the win.

All eyes were on the small MSX-R aircraft as it lined up for the run.

A horn sounded and the plane looped round to speed through the starting gate.

The clock started.

It shot through the first gate and turned quickly to the left under the Queensferry Crossing. A shimmy to the right and it was through the second. There was a wide bank round and then it twisted left, right, left, powering on the G-forces through the chicane. It clipped the outside pylon at the exit, the thin material blowing free in the wind as it was severed by the wingtip of the speeding plane.

Penalty points.

The clock read a second under the previous best time. There was now a long run under the Forth Road Bridge, a sweeping right and another gate, followed by a dash beneath the rail bridge and then a gate followed by a high looped turn and back down to rerun the course in reverse. The plane was now a second up.

There was a buzz from the crowd.

But suddenly someone shouted.

"Look, there!"

A finger pointed up into the sky between the two road bridges. There was a gasp as people looked up. High above, an orange and white hang glider was banking round to track in between the bridges, seemingly oblivious to the action taking place below.

The announcer shouted a warning over the tannoy, but the hang glider remained on course to run straight into the path of the speeding MSX-R.

The small plane powered on, now seconds from the finish gate and certain victory.

Two-point-five seconds up.

But then, ahead, it must have seen the hang glider in its path, as it made a violent turn to the left to avoid a certain collision. It was now heading straight for the crowd and losing height. The engine pitch increased as the pilot fought the airframe.

There was a cough and splutter.

The engine was going to die.

A catastrophe seemed inevitable.

But the pilot managed to wrench the controls back, flipping the aircraft vertically on a dime, stopping any forward momentum before the engine finally gave out. There was a deafening silence from the lack of engine noise that had been there a second before. It looked like there was no hope for the pilot, as the plane, now an uncontrolled mass of flying scrap, headed for the water.

But then something miraculous happened. The small canopy slammed open. A figure emerged, pushing away from the upside-down cockpit. Pilot and aircraft dropped like stones for the water a hundred feet below.

The stunned crowd could only watch.

Two thousand people held their breath.

There was a massive splash as the plane hit the water.

...and then silence as the aircraft bobbed gently on the surface.

No sign of the pilot.

The silence was split by the growl of a rescue boat as it sped out from the marina. Concerned mutterings started in the crowd. They grew until everyone was chattering, desperate to learn the fate of the pilot.

Porter continued to stare out over the water. "Looks like he's a goner. Bloody amazing flying, though. He saved the crowd."

McCready and Richards continued to stare, saying nothing. They were equally concerned.

The boat circled round behind the plane, out of view. There were a tense few minutes, but suddenly there was a roar from one side of the mass of onlookers. The RIB appeared from behind the wreckage. There was now an additional person sitting in the boat, and this one was wearing a helmet. The crowd cheered.

McCready and Richards glanced at each other with relief. Along with Porter, they headed for the jetty.

A couple of minutes later they were standing watching the boat come closer to shore.

As they watched, the pilot seemed to be chatting happily to the boat crew. When the boat moored up, Richards stepped forward and helped the pilot up.

"Great flying, Charlie, but you screwed up that last bit!" he said cheerily. McCready and Porter watched on.

The pilot reached up to remove the helmet. As it was pulled free, a mass of long water-drenched red hair flowed down around her neck. She glared at Richards.

"G'day, Craig. Like to see you do better!"

Porter was staring in shock. "Strewth, guv. There's a bloody sheila flying the plane!"

Richards, McCready and Charlie all turned to Porter.

"Eugene, meet Charlie Menzies. Best goddamned pilot I know. Used to fly F-16s and choppers for the Australian Air Force until she got bored," said Richards. "And then took up wingsuit flying to put some excitement back in her life!"

Porter just stood there in shock, mesmerized by the heavenly creature in front of him. Charlie stuck out her hand. "Good to meet you, Eugene. Look a little tongue-tied, there, mate."

Porter held out his hand and shook hers, but he was in a trance, unable to speak. He just glanced between McCready, Richards and Charlie.

An hour later, after Charlie had been checked over by the medics and had showered and changed out of her flight suit, she wandered back over to join the group, who were enjoying a beer in a garden at the rear of the pub. They bought her one—Foster's—and then she turned to Richards.

"So, Uncle Craig, hear you might have a job for me?"

Porter looked at Richards.

"Uncle Craig?" said Porter.

"Distant relations. Dark side of the family," said Richards, as if in explanation.

Charlie raised her eyebrows, but her eyes were smiling. "I'll tell Mum you said that!"

They all laughed, and then Richards recapped the new direction the company was taking and their need for a pilot for the 737 test bed, as well as other possible opportunities. They got involved in some interesting projects now and then, and while McCready had flown before, he was no expert. Having an experienced pilot on the team could prove to be useful.

After listening carefully, Charlie looked across at the three men and took a swig of beer. A wide grin spread across her face.

"Well, nothing much else on right now, so may as well give it a go."

They all hugged, but Porter was particularly reluctant. Charlie laughed and pulled him close. "Can't forget you, you chubby little chappie, can we?"

Porter didn't know which way to look.

Once the beers were finished, McCready checked his watch.

"Okay, I gotta go. Charlie, lovely to meet you. I'm sure we'll catch up in a few days. Eugene, always a pleasure, and for once everything's still in one piece. Okay, the plane isn't —but not your fault this time. Craig, see you about seven at the house? Sarah will be there around six… so whenever, and don't forget the beer!"

"Just a few things to check in on back at base, but I'm sure they can manage without me for one night. Should be able to make seven."

And with that, McCready walked over to the Range Rover. As he climbed in he took a final glance at Charlie. She was certainly going to be an interesting addition to the team. But it would take him some time to get over the expression on Porter's face when she'd pulled off her helmet.

Chapter Nine

The west coast of Scotland was a beautiful part of the world. It was why John McCready had decided to build his home there. It was wild and untamed. Just the way he liked it.

The house was a labor of love he had toiled over for six years, slowly adding to, and improving, as time had gone by. But it was now complete. He had finally finished a games/hobby room that had had an issue with the construction material of one of its walls. The property provided him with the home he had always wanted. Sturdy, stylish, yet functional. It was cozy inside and was built on a sloping hill at the side of a wide, curving bay. Its location at the end of a half-mile dirt track also meant it was off the beaten path, and it gave him the solitude he found he was drawn to more and more as the years went by.

Having returned from the air race, he had taken his Suzuki trial bike out for a ride over the surrounding hills and scrubland.

He now sat on the bike, high up on one of the cliffs at

the end of the bay. As he looked across at the view, he saw what was left of an old derelict house that had once been used by a biker gang. McCready and the gang had had a difference of opinion that had resulted in the destruction of the house and the gang never returning to the area.

The sea was as it had been for much of the summer, mill pond flat. That was one of the things he loved about the place. It was seasonal. You could have calm water reminiscent of more tropical climes, and you could have raging storms that flew across the horizon as though the wrath of the gods was on display for all to see. All of this he could watch from behind the thirty-foot glass frontage of his living room.

He took another look across the water and then gunned the engine. He rode across the scrubland at the side of the beach and then down onto the sand that extended the full width of the bay.

As he sped across the sand, his tires left a distinctive pattern in his wake. He moved closer to the water lapping at the shore, speeding up, relishing the spray that flicked up into his face leaving a salty taste in his mouth.

He continued until he reached the end of the beach. Once there, he parked the bike and climbed up onto the rocks that bordered the bay. He had gone about twenty feet when he spotted something in the water. It had just dipped below the surface. A few seconds later the smooth head of an otter popped up and looked around. McCready recognized her immediately, a bond that was reciprocated, as when she saw him, she swam over.

Mira had had two pups, which she had brought up alone after the death of her mate. McCready had been incensed when one of them had been killed by the gang from the old house. A fact, more than any other, contributing to why the gang was no longer there. Mira had continued to bring up her second pup, but recently McCready had noticed he had gone off on his own. He had seen him foraging for food separately, away from his mum. That was good. The circle of life was continuing its never-ending cycle.

What he hadn't known was that Mira now had a new mate. He realized this when, a couple of minutes later, a large male otter sped through the water and climbed onto the rocks six feet away. He was initially wary, but when he saw Mira interacting with McCready, he came over, and within a couple of minutes all three were close together on the rocks. McCready had to smile. He was happy for her. And then something struck him, something that all of Craig's advice could not have achieved. Animals and humans were not so different after all.

Mira had moved on.

Maybe it was time for him to move on too.

He stood up.

After a couple of minutes, the otters lost interest and ran off to frolic together in the long kelp fronds that bordered the rocks just below the surface. McCready watched them briefly. He then pulled out his phone. He looked at the picture behind the icons. He opened WALLPAPER SETTINGS, hesitated for a couple of seconds, and then hit DELETE.

Yes, it was time to move on.

He jumped back on the Suzuki and headed up to the house.

Half an hour later he'd hosed down the bike, leaving it to dry in the afternoon sun on the flagstones at the rear. He then showered, changed into an open-necked white linen shirt and tan slacks, and put on Nina Simone on the hi-fi.

The music wafted through the house from multiple speakers.

Twenty minutes later the doorbell rang. He smiled, walked over to the front of the house and opened the door.

Sarah McCready looked radiant.

She was dressed in a light blue dress with four large buttons down the front. She smelled of flowers. She put down the baby carrier, which held a sleeping Shauna. The baby was almost too big for it, but she felt it would give her somewhere safe and secure to sleep while she was at McCready's.

She reached up to hug McCready. He kissed her on the cheek and they held the hug. There was nothing but love and respect between them, and McCready was so happy to see some of the spirit he had known she had return, and for her to flash that wonderful, disarming smile again for all the world to see. He was sure she would never get over Sean's death, but equally, day by day, she was beginning to deal with the loss and allow a small piece of happiness to creep back into her life.

When they broke the embrace, McCready turned his attention to the cot.

"And how's my favorite niece?" he said.

"Careful. She's sleeping. And she's your *only* niece."

"Still my favorite," grinned McCready. He reached into the cot and drew back the light blanket that covered the sleeping baby. He marveled at her small, perfect features and stroked her soft cheek. A far away expression crossed his face. Was *this* what he really craved? A family, stability. Not racing round the world, risking his life trying to right wrongs and do the right thing?

Sarah looked at him thoughtfully, but then he snapped

out of it. He stood quickly, picking up the cot by the large carry handles on top.

"Okay, let's get you inside," he said to Shauna, and then to Sarah, "You like a drink?"

Sarah looked indecisive as she followed him in. "Just lemonade, thanks. Got to drive this little one home later."

McCready smiled, put his arm around her shoulder and closed the door behind them.

Half an hour later Craig Richards rang the bell. No baby carrier—a crate of beer. McCready let him in. They walked through the split-level house and out onto the deck at the first-floor level that looked across the bay. There was a table and three chairs set up. The sun was going down and there was barely a breath of wind. Richards and Sarah hugged. He then made a fuss over Shauna, who was still sleeping but gurgled cutely as he tickled her chin.

The three friends relaxed over dinner, recounting tales from the past. Sean came up in the conversation, and McCready watched as Sarah coped bravely with the memories. It felt good to be among friends. No more adventures for him for a while, he thought.

This life was good.

It could be good.

After polishing off a plateful of lemon cheesecake topped with cream, Sarah checked her watch. It was nine and the warmth of the day was receding.

"I have to go, guys. Thanks so much, John. It was lovely." They all hugged. McCready saw her to her car and watched as she drove away. Probably his two favorite girls in the whole world right now.

When she had gone, he walked into the small oak-topped bar next to the dining area, picked up a bottle of whisky and a couple of glasses, and went back out onto the deck. He dropped a glass in front of Richards, unscrewed the top and poured them both a shot.

"She's looking good," said Richards.

"Yeah, I think she's doing great. I can't always tell, and it's going to take time, but I think she's over the worst."

There was silence for a moment.

"And you?"

McCready was staring out to sea.

"Yep, I'm good. Life goes on." He paused and then turned to Richards. "I don't know, Craig. Sometimes I think I want to stop. Settle down. But I tried that. It didn't work. Maybe it's not for me."

"Maybe," said Richards "But, and I know it's a cliché, maybe you just haven't met the right one."

McCready gave him a look. "I thought I had."

Richards proceeded carefully. "Okay, but when options are off the table, you have to look elsewhere."

"You're one to speak. I mean, you've been through enough relationships."

Richards thought for a second, and then smiled. "Yeah, guess you're right. Who am I to give advice? But it does kind of make my point... You have to start with that feeling. You know, the one where you're hit by lightning and can think of nothing else. Then just see where it goes from there."

"And that's happened to you?"

Richards grinned and reached into his pocket to pull out his phone. He took another gulp of whisky and then scrolled through his photos. He stopped when he found what he was looking for. He took a long look at the picture and then passed the phone to McCready.

McCready took the phone and stared at the photograph. It was of a very beautiful woman. She had long brown hair that reached the whole way down her back. She was wearing some sort of dancer's costume and her face was strong, Slavic, with high cheekbones. Her expression was almost one of defiance, as though she wanted to take on the world. But her eyes were deep and brown and exhibited a softness that McCready felt sure would make her a warm and exotic person to know.

He passed the phone back to Richards. "Who the hell is that?"

"That, my boy," said Richards with a bit of a slur, "is Kristina."

"How do you know her?"

"Well, we were in touch for over a year, but then it all sort of fizzled out."

McCready was starting to become suspicious. "So how often did you see her?"

At this, Richards looked slightly sheepish. "Well, we didn't actually meet. She was this exotic dancer from Nikolaev."

McCready saw the light. "You mean you met her on one of those Russian dating sites!"

"Er, well, maybe. Yes. But she wrote to me for months."

"At what cost?"

"Well…"

"Come on, Craig. You fell for that? The person writing to you was probably some over the hill Russian shot-putter that smoked twenty a day and drank like a fish!"

"But she is gorgeous."

"Yeah, she's bloody stunning. But it doesn't change the facts."

"Anyway," said Richards, taking another drink, "*that* was love at first sight. I would have crossed oceans for her."

McCready shook his head, smiling.

"So, was Clare that for you?" asked Richards. "Someone you would drop everything for, unconditionally, no questions asked?"

McCready hesitated for a second, then his expression turned distant. He looked out toward the horizon. The stars were starting to come out.

"Maybe." He paused. "There was someone else, though. But that was a long time ago."

Chapter Ten

Twenty-five years ago

John McCready looked at the map in the waterproof cover and then tried to orient it with the topography he saw ahead of him. It shouldn't have been too difficult. Mountains ahead—sea behind. When he was happy, he checked the name of the village he was heading for. He had been told there was an amazing river close by whose waters ran red with iron oxide washed from the sandstone, and that if he was exploring this part of Peru, he shouldn't miss it.

He then set out at a brisk pace.

His backpack weighed about eighty pounds. He had enough provisions to last him a couple of weeks, as well as a tent, cooking utensils and waterproofs—it rained a lot in Peru. What lay ahead was his first great adventure since leaving school a month earlier. He had spun the globe and promised himself wherever his finger landed he would buy a one-way ticket and see what happened.

Since the death of his parents, three years apart, and his father only six months before, he'd been lost in a world of despair. No direction to his life. His teachers had said he had the aptitude to do pretty much whatever he liked. He could have gone to university. But he had faltered. His grades had deteriorated, and from a qualification point of view, university was suddenly not an option.

He had eventually pulled himself together and decided that the best thing would be to head out on his own to experience some of the world. Leave his old life behind for a while.

Change of scenery—change of outlook.

His parents had always been adventurers. They had loved the big wide world, the environment and the animals in it. In fact, it was his mother's dedication to protecting the wildlife of the planet that had led to her death when he was fifteen. She had been working on a Sea Shepherd environmental ship when she, and a number of colleagues, had been run down in a fast RIB by a Japanese whaler and killed. It was something he would never forget—and never forgive. But the desire for wanderlust was enshrined in his soul and his DNA. So now he was heading off to find adventure of his own, and, if he had thought about it long enough, maybe to find himself as well.

He soon realized he loved being on his own. Camping out at night under the stars, hearing the call of the wild, the sound of the planet going about its day. In a strange way it brought him closer to what life was about. Closer to who he thought he was as a person.

On the third day of the second week, he was feeling tired but exhilarated. He had found the river, and it had been a truly startling sight. It was as though the land was bleeding, as blood-red water flowed through pristine green valleys. It was an image he would never forget.

But now, as he headed higher into the Andes, he found himself approaching a small village. He was breathing more heavily from the altitude and was walking on what was little more than a dirt track that meandered through a straggly collection of huts and small buildings. There must have been a school nearby, as a stream of kids, aged from about eight to eighteen, were making their way down the street. Some were walking studiously, their small satchels on the backs of clean uniforms, while others were horsing around, kicking and jumping at each other.

McCready noticed a young boy, no more than eight, at the back of the line. He was quite small and held back slightly, his head bowed. He had a somewhat vacant look about him, as though his mind was elsewhere. He glanced up occasionally, and it looked as though he was hoping to avoid eye contact with the other kids. Suddenly, one of the older boys spotted him. He called his friends over. They headed toward the boy. When the boy noticed them, a flick of fear crossed his face. He tried to run, but the older boys were faster. They easily caught up, surrounding him. They taunted him, pulling at his satchel. Finally, the straps gave way. They ripped it from him, tipping the contents onto the ground. Papers, pens and a couple of small toys spilled out onto the mud. They were trodden into the dirt.

McCready moved toward the group.

"Fernando!"

The cry came from the side of the street. McCready looked up to see a girl running toward the boy, who was now on the ground crying. She couldn't have been older than sixteen. She was wearing a pale pink dress with flowers on it, and she was the most beautiful thing McCready had ever seen. She had a small oval face with large brown eyes, which were now filled with hurt and anger. Her hair was jet black and swept back, flowing over her head to fall in thick waves halfway down her back. There was a real fire in her expression as she ran forward. When she reached the boy she crouched down, flinging her arms around him in a protective embrace. She looked up at the group, fury in her eyes. She shouted at them. She knew no fear. McCready couldn't understand her words, but one of the boys pushed her over.

She fell down with a cry.

McCready took a deep breath, lowered his backpack, and then walked purposefully toward the group. Before they knew what had happened, he'd pulled the nearest boy away from her and stood in front of them.

"Back off! Now!"

They stared at him, not understanding, but then the tallest one advanced and threw a punch. McCready ducked and replied with a fist straight into the solar plexus. The boy groaned and slumped to the ground. McCready turned to the girl, who was watching him in stunned amazement.

"Go! Go!"

In case she hadn't got the message, he shooed her away with his arm. She quickly bundled up the small boy and fled to the side of the road. There, she spoke to him quickly, indicating for him to run away down the street, before looking back at McCready.

When McCready turned back to the group, there were now five. Another, older one, had joined them.

The odds were decreasing. Not good.

But then he thought of the kid—he didn't like bullies. He thought of the girl—he thought he was in love. And he thought of his mother and the fact that far greater bullies had ended her life for doing the right thing. Here, now, whatever happened, he knew he was doing the right thing.

That was all that mattered.

He let them come at him. He lashed out with a fury he didn't know he had. He saw two of them fall, before a third, coming at him from the side, hammered a fist into his head. The next thing he knew he was on the ground.

There was the glint of a blade.

A second later he felt a sharp pain. There was a warm sensation in his side. He looked down to see blood oozing onto his shirt. The area was growing larger and larger, now spilling out onto the dirt of the road, staining it red. He heard a shout, and suddenly the boys ran away.

The street was deserted for a moment.

He started to feel dizzy. He couldn't stop it. Everything was becoming fuzzy. It was getting darker and darker. The last thing he remembered, before completely succumbing, was a pair of the most beautiful dark brown eyes staring down at him with worry and concern.

And he knew, there and then, that if they were the last thing he ever saw, it would have been worth it.

When McCready awoke, it was dark. There was the sound of insects in the night. As he slowly regained consciousness his side started to hurt. And then it started to really hurt. He reached down and felt a thick bandage. And then the pain was so great he had to cry out. A moment later, as he tried to fight the agony, he felt a cool cloth dabbing his forehead.

"Shhhh. It okay," said a voice in faltering English. The voice was soft and calm, and somehow, despite the pain, he found he was losing himself to the sound.

Again, he heard it. "Shhhh. It okay. You safe."

Again, the soothing dabbing of the forehead. He managed to open his eyes, and there, a foot above him, were those deep brown eyes he had seen out on the road. They looked concerned, but they also looked calm, and McCready felt a wave of warmth like he had never known wash over him. For some reason he felt completely and utterly safe.

She spoke again, softly. Soothing. "You save my baby brother. Thank you." She paused as she concentrated on wiping the sweat from McCready's brow. He felt he was burning up. Like he had a fever.

"What is name?" she asked, again in that dreamy, calming voice that so relaxed him.

"John... John McCready," he managed, but even that was said through clenched teeth.

"John..." She smiled. "My name, Carlita."

For some reason, when she said his name it sent a bolt of electricity through him that he could feel even above the pain.

"Carlita!"

The shout came from beyond a door.

They were in a small room. The walls were a haphazard collection of upright planks that fitted none too well. The roof was made of corrugated iron.

"Okay, Mamma," Carlita answered.

She looked down at McCready with such tenderness and care that he thought he never wanted to move from that spot for the rest of his life.

She watched him for a moment, and then leaned down and kissed him gently on the forehead.

"Sleep, John." And with that she was gone.

McCready lay back, and as he drifted in and out of consciousness, he felt he had died and gone to heaven.

For the next month, McCready stayed with Carlita and her family in the small village. Why did he have to go and see the world when his whole world was right here with this amazing girl who had come into his life? He helped out with repairing things that needed fixing. He helped her father with the small area of land where he kept several cows and a mixture of goats and chickens. The rest of the world could go to hell as far as he was concerned.

Life was perfect.

Fernando thought of him as some sort of superhero. It turned out that he was autistic, which was why Carlita had been so protective of him. She had told McCready she would do anything to keep him safe, whatever the cost. His autism displayed itself in sometimes subtle, and sometimes not so subtle, ways. While he would often be distant and seemingly not paying attention to a conversation, he could suddenly spout some incredibly insightful and intelligent discourse on the subject under discussion, before slumping back into a seemingly quiet and serious state. For an eight-year-old, he also had an amazing ability to understand highly conceptual theories, which he must have read on the internet or seen on TV, and from which he would make lengthy and believable assessments and predictions, but which no one could verify as the ideas were way over their heads.

In complete contrast, he also had a mischievous side. Often, at dinner, he would peer over his bowl of food at McCready and Carlita and giggle. Sometimes he would make kissing sounds, which his mother scolded him for, but she laughed. She adored McCready.

As the weeks went by, though, McCready felt a change in attitude from Carlita's father. He would catch him giving McCready a hostile stare every now and then.

Nothing physical ever happened between McCready and Carlita, as much as he would have liked it to. He thought the friendship and kinship that was growing between them almost transcended anything else. He knew that deep down he loved her totally, completely and unconditionally, and anything physical that might happen would happen whenever the time was right. Clearly though, Carlita's father was not so sure. The antics of Fernando at the dinner table didn't exactly help. One day he pulled McCready aside and told him he thought it was maybe time for him to move on. McCready was at first furious at the thought of having to leave, but when he had calmed down he could understand that, to Carlita's father, all he saw, was this foreigner come into town, sweep his innocent daughter off her feet, and then likely to disappear with her, never for her family to see her again.

McCready thought long and hard and came to a decision.

It was the hardest he had ever made.

When he told Carlita he had to go, she was distraught. She sobbed uncontrollably. She asked if her father had said anything to him. He replied that he hadn't. He wasn't sure if she believed him, but from then on she became sad and morose, but always still loving and caring when she was with him. Eventually, he realized he couldn't put it off any longer. One night he just left, walked out into the darkness and away from someone the like of which he knew he would never meet again.

He knew it was the right thing to do.

And he knew he would regret it for the rest of his life.

The day after he left, he was mad at the whole world. Life was so unfair. The worst part was that he could hardly think what she must have thought of him, just walking out like that. But later, when he had reached down into the bottom of his backpack to pull out some dry socks, he had found a cloth bundle he hadn't put there. He pulled it out carefully. It was neatly bound with string, and as he unwrapped it, a deep ache in the pit of his stomach developed.

Inside was a brown poncho with three bands across it. One was red—his favorite color. One was yellow—her favorite color. One was green, which she had always told him represented the planet. They were interwoven, and McCready now knew what Carlita had been doing when she had refused to see him some days. She had coyly said she was working on something private. The bands represented McCready and Carlita, bound together forever with the planet and all it had to offer. There had also been a little note, folded in among the fabric. When he opened it, he knew what it meant to suffer a broken heart.

There was a simple message.

> *My John, wherever you are, whatever you do, I will be there with you always. I love you forever.*
> *Carlita.*

He cried long into the night.

But he had learned a lesson. He was growing up. And when he returned to Scotland a few weeks later, he returned as a man.

Ever since then, he had kept the poncho close to him. It now hung on the wall of his living room, always there, always close to his heart.

Never forgotten.

When McCready had finished, Richards just stared at him. After a minute, he took a swig of whisky and plonked the empty glass back on the table.

"Okay, that beats an overweight Russian shot-putter." He glanced at the picture on his phone. "Sorry Kristi, my love." He put the phone down. "And you never tried to contact her?"

"When I got back to Scotland I wrote every week for six months. I never received a reply. After that, I gave up. I didn't want to bring any pain to her or cause any trouble with her family. We were from different worlds. It could never have worked."

He looked out across the bay, which was now dark and lit with stars.

Richards watched him for a moment, knowing full well that his friend didn't believe for a second that it could never have worked. He was about to say something when a text pinged on his phone. He picked up the handset.

"Great!"

"What?"

They've got problems on that film shoot back at HQ. You want to come in tomorrow and watch the circus in action?"

"Not particularly."

"Might do you some good. Take your mind off things. Brandy Carmine. World's hottest film star and all that."

McCready looked at Richards and grinned. "Okay, old man. Good idea!"

And with that, they both made their way inside. Richards managed to stumble up to the guest room on the first floor.

McCready closed the large glass panel that led out to the raised deck. He then walked over to the stairs. Before he turned off the light, he stood and stared at the poncho on the wall for a few moments.

Three intertwined bands.

Unconditional love.

He turned out the light.

Chapter Eleven

Clare was dressed in her smartest black business suit, with accompanying stylish black shoes. Her hair was tied neatly back and she wore a small pearl earring in each ear. She couldn't remember the last time she'd been so nervous going to work, but when you were going to meet the leader of the free world and the Russian president, it wasn't a usual day.

She stood just behind Walker, who was looking equally smart. In front of them was the curved drive-through at the entrance of the Omega Complex. A slick layer of smooth black tarmac swept round in a circle, and at its apex was a red carpet that led up five wide steps to the main entrance of the building.

As Clare watched, she saw the first of the limousines pull into sight. It was accompanied by a number of large SUVs with blacked-out windows. The first SUV swooshed past, a secret service agent climbing out after it had stopped. He walked into position to meet the limousine that followed.

As it pulled to a stop, the agent moved forward, checking left and right, and then smoothly opened the rear door.

Clare had never seen President Galt Stevens up close, but his reputation preceded him. He had swept to office after the dismal performance of his predecessor, and while his politics were similar, he was sharp, to the point, and seemed to have a plan that was backed up with logic and action. He was also a hard man, determined for America to have a leading role in the world order, but it would be from a position of cooperation and understanding, backed up with power rather than idiotic rhetoric with no reasoning behind it. He believed passionately in a strong military, and made it clear he would have no hesitation in using it if necessary. From what Clare had heard, he spoke his mind, but more worryingly, he was seemingly dismissive of women. This concerned her, but as Brad would be the main liaison during the stay, she would just be there in the background, to back him up if required, so it was unlikely to be an issue.

As the president stepped out of the car, Walker moved forward to greet him. The two men shook hands.

Stevens was of medium build, in his mid-fifties, and had clearly kept in shape. He had a lean face, but one that wore an expression that was somewhat distant—it was difficult to read the man. His dark brown hair was cut short and he was clean shaven.

Walker then introduced him to Clare. She stepped forward with a broad smile, giving the deference the office of the man before her warranted. What happened next did not bode well for the future.

Stevens barely looked at her, didn't take her hand, and what attention there was, was a cursory up and down glance, accompanied by an expression of such disdain that it sent chills up her spine. The man then turned back to Walker, who glanced helplessly at Clare, rolling his eyes slightly when Stevens wasn't looking. Inside, Clare was seething. She took a number of deep breaths and managed to maintain the smile until they had disappeared into the building. She was just about to follow when she heard someone approach from behind.

"Sorry about that. One of his less attractive qualities."

She turned to see the bodyguard who had opened the president's car door standing there. He was typical secret service. Tall, chiseled, with a black suit, shoes and glasses. A curly wire disappeared into his ear. She wondered if he was a fully paid-up member of the Men in Black.

"No worries, we're just here to make your stay as comfortable and as safe as possible," said Clare.

"Anyway," said the agent. "My name's Paul Murphy. Don't let him get to you." He smiled at her and followed his boss into the complex. Clare grinned, but she was still worried by Stevens' behavior. She took a deep breath and walked inside.

Once through the entrance she saw that Brad was halfway round the atrium pointing out the statue in the center to Stevens. The president was admiring the interior of the building. He seemed genuinely impressed. Next, she saw them cross over to one of the lift-track capsules and enter. Before they did, Brad glanced over at her and gave a reassuring smile. A few moments later she watched as the capsule rose up to the fourth floor, where the conference suite was located.

She crossed over to the lift-track at the side of the atrium and tapped her watch. She saw one of the capsules higher up move around the circumference until it locked onto a vertical track and then descended quickly toward her.

Once it reached the floor, the doors slid smoothly open. She walked in.

"Cocoon level."

"Destination cocoon. Please hold on," said the automated voice.

Clare gripped the handrail as the capsule moved around the atrium and then halted before descending into the ground. Five seconds later it came to a stop.

"Cocoon level. Doors opening."

She walked out into the pièce de résistance of the complex.

To enter, she had to pass through an airlock, which had a palm reader to gain access. It also had a numerical key code that could allow coded entry. As the inner door slid open she entered a large two-story cocoon that could be sealed against any form of attack. This included chemical, biological, even nuclear. It would be where VIPs and other dignitaries would be taken should there be any threat toward the complex. It was the last line of defense, and would keep occupants safe until overwhelming force could arrive from outside. And given that the main SEAL operations base was in San Diego, a mere forty minutes flying time, that wouldn't be long. It was also where the two presidents would be staying in secure quarters for the duration of the summit.

The capsule she had entered from was the entrance to the cocoon most visitors would pass through. There was a second lift-track station at the far end of the facility, but that was considered more of a tradesman's entrance.

She walked across the wide lobby. The whole interior had been designed to be a pleasant environment; to instill calm. The walls were neutral in color. Tasteful paintings and decorations adorned the walls, and a thick carpet deadened any noise, making the place feel safe and secure.

She left the lobby and walked through a set of double doors. They led out onto a raised gallery that looked down onto an open space below. This was the recreation room, or rec, where occupants would spend most of their time. There were comfy chairs and couches, a TV, and refreshment facilities. At one end was a small dining area for meals. To her left, at the end of the gallery, was a swing door. It led down a short passage and set of stairs to another airlock. This one, though, was far larger than the one she'd entered through. It opened out into a cave that had been hollowed out of the ground in order to build the cocoon. It was also where the entrance to the escape tunnel was located.

It was this that Clare wanted to check out.

She walked along the gallery, through the doors, and down the stairs to the airlock. The size of the lock was impressive. It was large enough to drive a small car through. She opened the inner door, through palm-print recognition, and then entered the space. It was essentially a reinforced corridor about ten feet wide by twenty feet long. On either side were see-through panels that looked out into the cavern beyond. At each end were controls that allowed air to be evacuated out or pumped in depending on the state of any contamination that may have entered from outside.

After walking to the end, Clare operated the second door controls and stepped out into the space beyond. She had a look around. There were a number of maintenance vehicles parked up. A couple of others were making last-minute deliveries. She found a small electric cart, like those you might find ferrying passengers around an airport. She climbed on board and pressed the accelerator. The electric motor whirred away as the small vehicle moved off, heading for the tunnel.

The tunnel was well lit and large enough to accommodate a semi-truck. She had been driving for a couple of minutes when she heard noises up ahead. Around a slight curve, there was a yellow pickup parked to one side. It was the same one she'd seen on the monitor in the security center.

She pulled over behind it and climbed out. As she did, two men turned to look at her. One was in a cherry picker on the back of the truck and was suspended up near the tunnel roof. He was holding an instrument against the wall. The other was on the ground, where a small channel ran the full length of the side of the tunnel. A stream of water was running down it. He was measuring the flow rate.

"Hi guys," said Clare with a friendly wave.

"Hi, Clare," said the man on the ground. He stood up and walked over. The man in the cherry picker merely grunted and waved.

"What can I do for you?" They shook hands.

"Just checking on your findings, Hank. Anything to worry about?" She was glancing at the small stream of water running down the channel.

"Nah, she's fine," said Hank. "You always get a small amount of seepage. There're bound to be a few leaks. It's designed for it though."

Clare nodded. She had a certain amount of experience with tunnels and water. "Great to know. Anything you guys need?"

The other man looked down from the cherry picker. "Yeah, filet steak—medium rare, with mustard, crinkly fries, and a cool beer."

Clare grinned. "Wow, Josh, never knew you had a sense of humor!"

He waved a dismissive hand, but he was smiling.

"Okay, guys," said Clare. "Keep up the good work. Let me know if anything changes."

She climbed back in the cart, and with a wave she drove back down the tunnel, feeling somewhat reassured.

After Walker had shown President Stevens around the conference facilities and ensured he had everything he needed, he pulled out a small walkie-talkie that worked exclusively in the complex, even down in the cocoon and tunnel. He pressed a button next to Clare's name. There was a beeping, a crackle, then he heard her voice. There was a degree of irritation in it.

"Great house guest you have there!"

"I'm sorry, Clare. It's not for long, and anyway, you shouldn't have much to do with him." He could hear the cart noise in the tunnel in the background. "Where are you?"

"On my way back down the tunnel. Just checking on the water seepage. It looks fine. What time is Petrovich due?"

"About half an hour."

"Okay, I'll see you out front then."

Half an hour later Clare and Walker were again standing at the front of the building watching a large black limousine pull up and stop in front of them.

President Viktor Petrovich had much in common with President Galt Stevens. They both considered themselves as hard men. Neither would back down if it meant losing face, a factor that would make the coming summit particularly difficult, given the issues involved. Somehow, sorting out the world's nuclear arms issues, as well as saving the planet, seemed an odd double bill for a summit, but both were pressing matters that needed to be resolved, and it was only so often the two leaders would get together in the same room to try and thrash out topics of this magnitude. There were certainly a volatile few days ahead for the participants. However, one area Petrovich did not ally with Stevens was in his demeanor and attitude toward women.

Once he had shaken hands with Walker, his gaze fell on Clare. This time, though, she didn't cringe, as although the president's eyes traveled over her body, it was with appreciation and respect, not disdain and contempt.

Petrovich was of similar age to Stevens, and although his frame was not as svelte, it was all muscle. He had gray eyes topped off with a set of thick eyebrows, and his mouth could often display a charming smile on a round weather-beaten face. It was, though, a smile that hid a darker side that would show no compromise if pushed into a corner. But now, when he looked at Clare, that side was nowhere to be seen.

As she held out her hand, Petrovich took it, bowed slightly, and then kissed it.

"My dear, if you are to be looking after us during our stay, I am sure we will be in the most professional of hands. I also fear we may all be thoroughly distracted." He smiled disarmingly. Clare found herself blushing slightly.

"Thank you, sir. My aim to be of any assistance I can in support of your stay here. Please let me know if there is anything you need."

Petrovich smiled again and glanced at Walker. "You have a good one there, Mr. Walker. Hang on to her."

"Oh, I intend to, sir," said Walker with a smile. "Now, if you will just follow me, I'll show you where you'll be staying for the duration."

As they walked off, he glanced at Clare. She beamed back, feeling far better than she had earlier. The smile, though, was quickly wiped off her face as Petrovich's bodyguard walked past. She knew his name was Ivan Igorov from the personnel list. He looked down at her with a superior expression.

"I, too, would very much like to be in your hands," he said with a thick Russian accent. "In fact, I will look forward to talking to you later."

He didn't give her another look and turned to follow his master.

Clare's skin crawled for the second time that afternoon. She was just glad that Brad would be handling all the face to face. She prayed nothing would come up that meant she had to be in close proximity to Stevens or Igorov.

If that happened, things could get tricky.

Chapter Twelve

McCready and Richards drove over to their HQ in Aberdeen the following morning.

Over the previous six months there had been many changes at the company. The most symbolic was the rebranding from Ocean Oil Exploration to Ocean Tech. This was on graphic display when they arrived, as the new name, spelled out in large blue letters, was currently being put in place on the front of the main entrance block. McCready could see a worker up a long ladder placing the T in 'Tech' as they drove in.

However, the sight beyond was not so good.

Huge plumes of orange smoke poured from one of the large buildings. They parked up and jumped out.

"Jesus! What the hell's that?" said Richards.

They both watched as smoke continued to billow into the sky.

They started running, but before they got halfway, they saw Graham Evans, one of the company's key technicians, heading their way from the building. He was patting the air with both hands, indicating for them not to worry.

Richards gave him a questioning look.

"It's that bloody film crew!" said Evans when he reached them.

"What have they done now?" asked Richards.

Evans shook his head in frustration. "Some idiot let off an orange smoke canister thinking it was a handheld flare. He'd been told several times but wouldn't listen. Don't worry, we've got the doors open. Should all blow through soon."

Richards and McCready relaxed and glanced at each other.

"Amateurs!" they both said together.

"Come on," said Richards to McCready. "Let's go enter the madhouse."

The newly named Ocean Tech was spread out over a number of acres on the outskirts of Aberdeen. It was located just to the east of the city on the coast. The original buildings were still in place, though there had been a significant amount of updating, along with a complete change of purpose for much of the infrastructure.

The focus of the facility was two large buildings running parallel to each other.

The first had originally been built for the construction and repair of equipment for the oil industry. It was a hundred and fifty feet long and fifty feet high. This had now been given over entirely to the development of technical equipment for underwater operations, both scientific and military. It was also where the Skyline delivery system was built. Gone were the welders and heavy-duty machinery from before; now there was an almost cleanroom vibe that was quiet and sedate.

Next to the construction building was the large test tank. It was housed in an equally tall building. The tank was a hundred feet long and fifty feet wide. It had a depth of twenty feet, with a 'deep' section that extended down to forty feet in the middle. The filtration system had been updated, but there were still no plans to heat the water; the volume was just too large. It meant thermally protective clothing had to be worn by anyone who entered the water. At one end, there was also wave simulation equipment that could create water conditions of anything from a mild chop to a raging storm with a swell to match.

As they walked through the full-height open doors, the smoke had started to dissipate. They could see that the doors at the far end were also open. A stiff breeze was clearing the particles that hung in the air like an orange mist.

The tank took up about two-thirds of the floor space and was located to the left, away from the entrance doors. There was a concrete surround around the sides, and at the near end, at the first-floor level, was an enclosed gallery that extended along the width of the building up to the huge doors. It consisted of a conference room, design studio, and Richards' office, with windows that looked out onto the tank below. An indoor metal stairway led up to it at one end.

The area to the side of the tank was currently taken up with the paraphernalia of a film crew. There were about twenty people in the throes of varying degrees of activity. It looked to be in a state of controlled chaos.

It had been decided that now Ocean Tech was no longer directly involved with the oil industry they would look at interesting and diverse projects the facility could be used for. So, while they were ramping up the tech design and development side of things, allowing film companies to rent the tank seemed like an appealing idea. McCready had worked on a film before when an old stuntman friend had asked for his help. He had found it hugely enjoyable to apply his diving skills to a different side of the industry.

The film shooting at Ocean Tech was called *Phoenix Rising*, a big Hollywood female action/spy movie, and sequel to *The Phoenix*, which had grossed over a billion dollars.

The experience had, however, been far from smooth. McCready had stayed well away, but the reports Richards had sent over, with the demands and problems the crew seemed to be having, had been endless. They had refused the help of any of Ocean Tech's staff and insisted on doing everything themselves.

Richards had been somewhat surprised by their lack of professionalism, particularly given that Brandy Carmine, currently the world's biggest movie star, was playing the lead. From what Richards could see, she wasn't particularly happy in the water. Her dive training had appeared to be minimal, which, again, was a surprise, given the somewhat challenging underwater sequences she had to shoot.

Things didn't look as though they'd improved, when Matt Castle, the first assistant director, or first AD, came hurrying over to them with a worried expression on his face. He was of medium build, mid-forties, and was normally pretty calm—the job demanded it—but right now, he looked considerably stressed.

McCready stood back and watched as Castle spoke to Richards. He was clearly harassed and looked like he was at the end of his tether.

"Craig, I am so, so sorry for all this." He waved an arm

at the smoke that was still floating around the building. "He was told a number of times, but you know these creative types…"

"No harm done," said Richards. "How's it going otherwise?"

"Arrrrrgh!" Castle acted pulling his hair out. "Not great. Brandy had another fit. She's in the water now, but the shots aren't looking good. She looks like a hamster every time she holds her breath. And when she does, she only lasts about ten seconds—not long enough to complete the take. Half the time she panics and comes spluttering to the surface. The director even suggested the stunt coordinator tie her to the bottom until they get the shot. We've only got a couple more days. No idea how we're going to get it done. You can only do so much with a double and face replacement, and there are some critical close-ups we need."

The walkie-talkie slung around his waist suddenly crackled to life.

"Matt! Matt! Where the hell are you? We're waiting to shoot."

"Got to go. Talk later." And with that he turned and scurried back to the edge of the tank.

Richards glanced at McCready. "Better them than us. Looks like a right balls-up."

McCready smiled. "What are they shooting?"

"Oh, you'll like this. The hero's trapped in a nuclear sub that's flooding and she has to get out."

McCready raised his eyebrows. "Bit close to home."

"Yeah, tell me about it," grinned Richards.

"Come on. Take a look. They're set up next to the observation window."

They walked down to a lower level that was used for tank maintenance and access to the filtration system. It also housed a twenty-foot-long window that looked out underwater.

The scene beyond the glass was certainly spectacular. McCready remembered the last time he'd been down here was when they'd been testing a submersible to lock onto a tunnel wall. Now, in front of them was a cross section of part of a nuclear submarine on a large gimbal that had been built by the special effects department. It extended above the waterline. At the director's whim, it could be maneuvered in any direction, making the sub tilt, roll, rise and fall, as required. It was an impressive piece of engineering. At the moment it was in a stable, upright position.

Around the set, about ten feet back from the gimbal, was an array of high-powered underwater lights. They were all focused on the middle section of the sub. McCready could see the cameraman lining up a shot. The large white camera, in a sturdy metal Hydroflex housing that would take two people to lift on land, floated perfectly in front of his face. Attached to the top of the housing, a video monitor showed what the camera was seeing. A cable snaked across the floor and up the side of the tank to where McCready knew there would be a surface monitor for the director to watch. There would also be an underwater speaker system over which the director and/or first AD could talk through the action to those in the water. The cameraman was wearing a full face mask with built-in comms, which would mean he could talk back to the director with questions or suggestions for the shots and provide feedback on how it was going.

But in the center of all this was the figure of a woman. It was the first time McCready had seen a real movie star. And right now, she did not look happy.

Brandy Carmine had made fifteen films in her relatively

short five-year career. She was twenty-eight years old and had burst onto the scene in an edgy, hard-hitting independent film made by Hollywood's latest *enfant terrible*, Henry Strong—the new Tarantino. Her performance had been electric. She'd soon become flavor of the month, adorning billboards, magazine covers, and appearing on all the late-night talk shows. This debut had resulted in a string of films that showed off her allure as well as her acting talent, which was considerable. This was no flash-in-a-pan, babe in a bikini, movie star. She was the real deal. She had a classic femme fatale appeal, but also a vulnerable side, which she could turn on seemingly at will. It had captivated audiences young and old and led to her having sixty million followers on Instagram and a bank balance that meant she never needed to work again.

As McCready stared out through the dirty glass window, across the twenty feet of water beyond, he mentally played back some of the scenes he had watched her in. None of them, though, would have prepared her for where she was now. She wore a sleek-fitting black and silver neoprene wetsuit that had clearly been shaped within an inch of its life to fit her body. Her face was covered by a dive mask, but this would shortly be removed for the shot.

She was currently receiving air from a safety diver, who was holding on to her to keep her steady. He had a six-foot-long regulator hose coming off a second cylinder on his back, from which Brandy was breathing.

Everything all looked smooth for now.

The difficultly would come when she removed the mask. She would then have to breathe through her mouth with nothing around her nose until the mouthpiece was removed and she could perform her scene. For inexperienced divers this was the most difficult time. The urge to breathe in through your nose was often too great, and if you weren't careful, could result in snorting water up your nose. This, in turn, could lead to panic and shooting to the surface holding your breath, something, that, depending on the depth, could damage your lungs, let alone ruin the take.

What was more worrying, though, was that McCready could see the thin tell-tale length of fishing line that attached her right foot to a large metal stage weight immediately below. There was a quick release buckle in place, but there would have to be someone to release it if she got into trouble. As of now there was only one safety diver and he was looking after her air supply.

He watched nervously. So much could go wrong.

A tinny voice echoed over the underwater speaker.

"Okay, darling, now remember, look left, right, and then above, as though you're desperately searching for an air pocket. And I want real drama. Real terror." McCready didn't think that was going to be a problem. "Okay, action in THREE… TWO… ONE… GO!"

The safety diver pulled the mouthpiece from Brandy's mouth. McCready cringed. He hadn't given her enough time to fill her lungs. He could see she was already desperate. Her cheeks were holding all they could. Her eyes were wide with fear.

"ACTION GIMBAL!" came over the speaker.

Immediately, the huge cross section of the sub started to rotate over, as though the vessel were sinking. The safety diver had moved away to get out of shot. In order to do so, he'd turned his back on Brandy. She was looking around in a state of panic, pointing desperately at her mouth—the signal that meant she needed air—when disaster struck. There was a massive groan from the gimbal supporting the sub. Suddenly, with an almighty CRACK, a strut holding the huge metal structure gave way. Even through the water and glass it sounded like a gunshot. The whole thing started to fall. The movement was dampened by the water, but it was only headed in one direction.

Straight on top of Brandy Carmine.

She was oblivious to the danger, tied to the bottom and out of air. She was desperately looking for her safety diver. He was way off to the side, only now just turning to look back at her.

McCready had seen enough. He ran up to the concrete surround, three steps at a time, pulling off his shoes as he went. From looking through the window, he'd mentally created a picture of the setup and relative position of everything in the tank. He didn't have time to grab a mask, but ran full tilt for the water and dived in. There were shocked looks from the crew.

"Who the fuck is that?" shouted the director.

When McCready hit the water, he oriented himself by the position of the lights. He knew Brandy was about ten feet in front of them, dead center. He could make out the silver of her suit in the glare. He could also see the sub was almost on top of her, still falling. He powered through the water, straight to her position. Once there, he reached down to unclip the line attaching her to the weight. He then unceremoniously grabbed her around her chest from behind.

The set was almost on top of them.

He swam aggressively away from the impact, smashing her shoulder into the sharp metal at the side of the falling sub. He could hear her cry out through the water. But that was the least of his worries.

He wasn't going to make it.

The sub was still falling.

He saw a dark shadow race across his view.

At the last second, he thrust Brandy away from him, beyond the fall of the sub, but then the massive metal structure was on top of him. It pushed him down to the bottom, pinning him to the floor, squeezing what little air he had left from his lungs.

Chapter Thirteen

As the massive structure hit McCready, he grunted with pain.

The air was knocked out of him. He scrabbled desperately, trying to free himself, but it was no good. He was trapped.

Moments later, he felt a darkness starting to envelop his mind. There was a strange gurgling sensation, as though water was running down his throat.

And then everything went black.

When Richards had seen McCready run out of the dugout, he knew what he was going to do. He followed him up and arrived just in time to see his friend's flying figure hit the water and disappear.

He watched for a few seconds, but as the sub continued to fall, he grabbed a spare mask and aqualung that had been lying where one of the divers had left it for a break.

There was no time for a suit. He jumped into the water just in time to see McCready thrust the girl out to one side and for the set to drop down, pinning him to the floor of the tank.

He glanced to his side. The safety diver had finally woken up to what had happened and swum over to Brandy and pulled her clear. But the cameraman was nowhere to be seen. He must have gone back to the surface.

Richards headed down to the bottom. There was only one mouthpiece on his set. When he reached McCready, he wasn't moving.

He took his mouthpiece out and pushed it into McCready's mouth, holding it firmly in place and pressing the purge button on the front. This would forcibly inject air into McCready. He stopped and watched a stream of bubbles come out. There was no way he could lift the huge collapsed set off his friend. He had to make a split-second decision. He took off the aqualung and pushed off for the surface. He broke through and looked round wildly.

"We need a jack. He's trapped!" He glanced round and saw Evans, who had crossed over to see what was happening. "Graham! Defib. O-two. Quick as you can!" And with that he ducked back down, not waiting for a reply.

When he reached McCready, he continued doing his best to keep air going into his lungs. After what seemed like an eternity, two special effects divers swam up to him. They levered a jack under the set and managed to raise it enough to free McCready's body. Richards dragged the inert form up to the surface. Before he'd even broken through, two strong arms reached down to pull McCready up onto the side. Evans and a second technician then got to work.

They checked his pulse. There was none. They started

to ventilate his lungs with a bag mask. Next, they ripped off his shirt and applied the defibrillator pads.

"Clear!"

McCready's chest jerked upward with the jolt.

Again the breaths through the mask.

"Clear!"

Again his body jerked up.

Evans looked at the readout on the screen. There was a sinus rhythm, but they still needed to ventilate his lungs.

Richards watched anxiously, oblivious to the fact he was standing in his clothes, dripping wet and shivering. All around there was a somber air as the crew watched on, now silent.

All, that was, except for Brandy Carmine. Once she'd climbed out of the water she shouted at the safety diver. At the same time, one of her assistants ran up with a thick toweling robe. Then, oblivious to the drama taking place a few yards away, she shouted to no one in particular, "What the fuck was that? Who was that bloody idiot who smashed my shoulder? Look! I'm going to have a massive bruise. I want him fired!" When nobody looked at her, she glared at the group clustered on the tank surround. "Immediately!" When there was still no response, she stalked off toward the rear of the building, her assistant in tow. "If anyone wants me, I'll be in my trailer."

At that moment, apparently no one did.

An hour later McCready was lying on a couch in Richards' office, gazing at the ceiling. Richards was on the phone. He ended the call and replaced the receiver.

After he had been stabilized, the paramedics had come to check McCready over and suggested he go to hospital where he could be monitored. McCready had declined, saying he felt fine. He just needed some rest.

Richards looked over at his friend. "Why, for once, won't you do as you're bloody well told? You should be in hospital."

McCready glanced at him. "I'm okay, Craig. Really. And thanks for pulling me out of there. Another one I owe you."

"The list is getting longer, though you did jump out of an airplane without a parachute to save me, so I guess we could almost be quits."

McCready smiled. "I just need to take it easy for a while."

Before he could say anything else there was a knock at the door.

"Come in," said Richards.

The door opened. A woman in her mid-fifties entered. She was about five foot two, had a severely short haircut and a hard, chiseled face. She stared at Richards for a second and then at McCready. He returned her gaze unwaveringly.

Pamela Franklin was the producer of *Phoenix Rising*. She was successful. She was intimidating, and she didn't take no for an answer, but right now she seemed to have a mellow expression on her face. She looked at McCready. "Thank you for what you did." And then Richards. "Both of you."

"Anything we can do to help," said Richards evenly. Then, after a pause. "You know, you guys have to get your shit together. There have been no end of problems on this shoot. It was an accident waiting to happen."

He watched her. He could see her bristling at the criticism, but there was nothing she could do. Richards and McCready didn't work for her, and the bottom line was, what he had said was true. It also looked as though she needed something from them. And to Richards, she didn't seem as though she was the type of person who would garner praise and thanks unless there was something in it for her.

"The thing is," she continued, "our dive supervisor has quit. Says he can't work with little Miss Sunshine anymore —she's too much trouble. Also, she really doesn't seem to have the aptitude for this, on top of which, she's refusing to go in the water again. We have to complete the shots in the next two days. After that we lose her to a premiere in London. Once she leaves, I bet she hightails it back to LA and lets her lawyers deal with the fallout."

"So, what are you saying?" asked Richards.

Franklin looked uncomfortable for a moment, as though she was chewing wasps—but she was the sort of person who would do anything to get things done, however distasteful it might be to her.

"I need your help."

Richards and McCready exchanged glances.

"And just how might we do that?" asked Richards.

Franklin took a deep breath. "I need someone to talk to Brandy. Someone who can get her back in the water for the final shots. Calm her down. Encourage her." As she spoke, her gaze slowly wandered over to McCready. "Someone who has her best interests at heart."

Richards looked incredulous. "Correct me if I'm wrong, but didn't I hear her say she wanted the person—no, 'idiot'—who injured her shoulder and caused her bruises fired, despite the fact he saved her life, which nearly cost him his own?"

Franklin looked straight at him. "She has her tantrums. She's a movie star, for God's sake! That's what they do. But she also wants to work again. She needs to finish this film. Now, will you help me?"

"Well," started Richards, "John obviously can't do it. He was effectively dead an hour ago. He needs to rest. He doesn't need the stress."

"Er, I am in the room," said McCready, sitting up on the couch.

Richards sighed. "Don't be stupid!"

McCready looked at Franklin. "I don't think it would work. From what I hear, she won't listen to advice. She thinks she knows best. I really don't have time for people like that. I'm sorry."

Richards chipped in. "Trust me. John McCready and Brandy Carmine, together in a confined space—you really don't want that to happen."

Franklin was getting frustrated.

"Look, we're burning through money here. I don't care what you say to her, how you do it. You have carte blanche to do what you like. We need these shots and we'll pay you to help us get them... I dunno, make the silly little cow fall in love with you or something. Anything to get her in the water." She looked McCready up and down, taking in the tall frame, the broad shoulders, the relaxed, almost laconic demeanor, even now, and the piercing blue eyes. "Yeah, try that. Shouldn't be too hard. You're just her type. Another one she can add to the list. Think about it, okay. But I need to know soon." And with that, she turned and strode out of the office.

"Jesus! What a bitch!" said Richards when she'd gone.

McCready just stared after her. He'd never experienced such a total lack of care or empathy for another human being. Anything to get the job done—even playing with someone's emotions and trust. He suddenly found himself feeling completely differently about Brandy Carmine. If this was the world she inhabited, how on earth could you not be screwed up? He also found himself desperately wanting to help her. For her to be able to prove them wrong.

And he was pretty sure he wouldn't have to make her fall in love with him for her to do that.

Chapter Fourteen

At the rear of the Ocean Tech buildings was a large backlot. It had previously been used for stockpiling metal plate, girders and construction equipment. It bordered a dry dock, which had a tall tower crane looming over it. There was also an area for parking, while the far end bordered the North Sea beyond.

Since the changes at the company, the backlot had been cleared to make way for a couple of new buildings. One enclosed a deep tank that extended down to a depth of sixty feet. A second housed a shallow pool where trials on more delicate equipment could be carried out, as well as testing and training with diving gear and instruments. It was the only tank at Ocean Tech that was heated, so there was no need to wear a suit when in the water. The rest of the backlot was taken up with a helipad and parking area.

Right now, much of this space was filled with vehicles and equipment from the film crew. When a production came to town it was very much like a circus. There were trucks for the lights and camera equipment, rigging, props, special effects, stunts, and so on. In the case of *Phoenix Rising*, a large flatbed semi was parked up that had delivered the massive gimbal and cross section of the nuclear sub. There was also a catering truck to make sure the crew were fed and watered, as well as a number of large trailers for the talent. In this case, three: director, producer, and Brandy Carmine.

It was to this final trailer that McCready now headed. It was late afternoon and the light was fading. Lights had come on in the buildings and twilight would soon be there.

The trailer itself was about fifty feet long. It had been delivered by a towing vehicle, which was now absent. A couple of sections extended out from the main body to give more internal space. On the roof was a satellite dish.

As McCready approached, the door flew open. A woman in her mid-twenties ran out. Booming music followed her as she slammed the door behind her. She had tears in her eyes. As she walked past McCready, she glanced up.

"You going in there?" she said, throwing her thumb at the trailer.

"That was the idea."

"Good luck with that!"

She walked on, back toward the main tank building. McCready raised an eyebrow and looked at the door in front of him. There were a couple of steps up to it. He walked forward and knocked assuredly. The music boomed on.

He knocked again.

Nothing.

He couldn't stand around all night. He pulled the door

open and walked inside. The place was larger than an apartment he'd rented in Edinburgh in his twenties. The music was even louder in here. Immediately to his right was a door that was currently closed. To his left, the space extended to the far end. It had a wide couch and a couple of chairs on one side, which looked across to a large TV on the opposite wall. Directly in front of him was a cooking area, complete with cooker, fridge freezer, wine cooler and the like. The music was annoying him. He spotted the hi-fi on a shelf. He crossed over and turned the volume down. He was looking around to see if there was anyone at the far end, when the door to his right flew open and Brandy Carmine walked through.

It was the first time McCready had seen her out of the water and close up. And even though her hair was wet from a shower and she was wearing no makeup, he could tell in an instant why she was who she was. Even without all the trappings to make her look her best, she looked her best.

She was wearing a thick toweling robe and was shorter than McCready had imagined, about five foot five. She had an oval face with large hazel eyes topped by immaculately trimmed eyebrows. Her dark brown hair was wet and hung down below her shoulders. She had a cute but strong nose and her cheekbones were high enough to imply disdain, while at the same time the eyes could convey a certain vulnerability.

When Brandy saw him, she stopped short with a cry.

"You turned the music down?" She looked him up and down. "And who the hell are you, anyway?"

"Yeah, sorry, it was a bit loud. My name's John McCready..."

Before he could continue, she interrupted.

"I don't care. I've never seen you before. Get out!"

Her eyes blazed. Her nostrils flared.

McCready stood his ground.

"I'm afraid I can't do that."

At that, Brandy just stared at him.

McCready continued. "You see, Ms. Franklin has hired me to help you out with the underwater shots. See if we can get you happy enough to complete them."

Suddenly, recognition came over her. "You're that guy in the tank. The one who smashed my shoulder. Have you seen the bruises you gave me? If you think I'm going anywhere near the water with you, you've another thing coming. Now, get out!"

It looked as though no one had told her what had happened.

"Yeah, that might be a problem. As I said, I've been hired to look after you. Make sure you're okay and are able to finish the film. So, I can't go—I might get fired—though I hear that was what you wanted. It won't take long, and you might be surprised what you can do."

He stared at her with those piercing blue eyes.

She looked at him, unsure.

She hesitated.

"This is unacceptable."

"I couldn't agree more. I'm really not sure I want to spend any longer in the company of a spoiled brat than I have to, but when you're hired to do something... well, you know... if I don't follow through..."

She stared at him. He returned her stare. She was about to speak... but stopped. He seemed to be totally unfazed by her.

"Well... well, how long would it take?"

"That depends on you. We have a small pool just over

there." He indicated the building at the side of the backlot through the window. "It's heated. We could go over and have a play around. See how you get on. You never know, might be fun. You might even like it." Again, there was that inscrutable look.

She looked like she was thinking it over.

"Maybe we could do that," she said slowly, looking up at him. "But it would have to be on my terms."

"Absolutely," said McCready, lying through his teeth.

But then she gave him a look he'd seen many times on screen—one of extreme vulnerability mixed with a certain pleading, wanting. For a second, McCready paused. There was something intoxicating about standing in front of the world's biggest film star. He knew it shouldn't make a difference. She was just a woman—but, of course, she wasn't. He mentally kicked himself and walked toward the door.

"Okay, then. Shall we say, half an hour at the pool?"

She looked at him as though deciding, then nodded slowly.

"Okay, half an hour at the pool."

McCready opened the door and made his way outside.

Once in the fresh air, he took a deep breath.

This might be harder than he had thought.

Forty minutes later McCready was standing over a scuba set at the side of the small heated pool. It had two regulators coming off the first stage, which was mounted to the cylinder. One of the hoses was the standard length, the other, far longer, like the one the safety diver had used in the tank with Brandy.

He was going through the equipment checks when she walked in through the door. It swung to behind her. He looked up. She was still wearing the thick white toweling robe, but as she walked toward him, she let it fall to the floor, revealing a black swimsuit that wrapped around her body, highlighting the many dips and curves of her smooth, tanned skin. When McCready managed to raise his eyes to her face he noticed there was a certain apprehension. The aggression and bluster of earlier had been replaced with uncertainty and, almost, fear; as though she was resigned to having to do this, but it was the last thing in the world she wanted to be doing.

She walked over and sat down next to him.

"Okay, where do we start?"

Over the next two hours he took things slowly. Once he was in his stride, focused on the job, all other distractions disappeared. What he was doing was important. The bottom line was that her safety was in his hands. Nothing could override that. At times she tried, like when she had failed at something for the fifth time and really didn't want to go on. She would give him a look that might have melted most men, or twisted them to her compliance, but it was water off a duck's back with McCready. Eventually she gave up and concentrated on what he was asking her to do. At one point she came spluttering to the surface, splashing the water with frustration. But rather than getting cross or impatient, McCready gently, but firmly, told her she could, and would, do better, and they had gone again. At no time did he shout or get angry. At no time did he lose his patience. He just kept reminding himself that at this time, for these two short hours, he was the most important person in the room.

As the session progressed, she found herself improving. She had given up trying to twist McCready to her whim and had buckled down. She found herself attempting things she never thought she could do, and finding she could do them. When she failed, he would pick her up. When she pouted, he looked at her with unwavering resolve and waited patiently for her to continue. And then, without realizing it, she almost burst into tears. No one had treated her like this before. She'd been surrounded by yes men for the last ten years. The totally implacable wall that was John McCready was like a breath of fresh air. She felt something shift inside her, and before long she found she wanted to succeed to please him. She felt giddy, like a schoolgirl trying to impress a teacher, and then, at a stroke, she realized... it was a teacher she fancied like hell. McCready wasn't just some pretty boy actor who was with her to raise his profile or get more Instagram followers. McCready probably didn't even know what Instagram was. The thought had made her giggle, and she'd come spluttering to the surface. He'd given her a stern look and she'd obediently gone back down and tried again.

By the time the two hours were up, she was feeling like a different person. There was someone in front of her who was real. The first in a long, long time. And she knew, then and there, she desperately wanted that feeling to continue.

She wanted John McCready in her life.

When they finished, she walked up to him, looked him straight in the eye, and reached up to give him a light kiss on the cheek. It wasn't forced. It was for the briefest of moments, but it was long enough for him to feel the warmth of her breath. She then turned, and without another look, walked from the pool and back to her trailer.

McCready watched her go.

He shook his head. *Pull yourself together, John. She's an actress. It's her job to manipulate people.* But he found himself fighting a feeling that just wouldn't go away; one that could only lead down a path he knew he really shouldn't go.

Chapter Fifteen

The sky was black and the stars were bright. It was cold.

Las Vegas was surrounded by desert, and while the strip and the main city were ablaze with light and noise, the edges of the metropolis were in the gray zone, between light and dark... in so many ways.

Lieutenant Gerry Grimes from the Las Vegas Police Department had just taken a bite from a Big Mac. He had been about to grab a handful of fries, when the call had come through to go and investigate suspicious behavior in a new warehouse district that had sprung up to the east of the city. He didn't mind the run out to the edge of town, but he'd been looking forward to having his calorie fix before a long night shift, and it pissed him off.

He was now on his way to the location, having berated the dispatch controller. It was probably nothing, just some kids, but he had to check it out. The sooner he called it in, the sooner he could return to his burger.

He turned slowly left onto North Hollywood Boulevard from Stewart Avenue. There were few street lights out here, but all the buildings were lit in a faint glow from the gigawatts of electricity that illuminated the city half a mile away.

The report had said people had been seen coming and going at weird hours from a warehouse down a side street further along. When he found the street, he turned into it. There were warehouses on all sides. All were dark. Nobody was around at this time of night.

He had driven about halfway down the street. At the far end he could see the desert beyond. He was about to do a U-turn to take him back to civilization, when he saw light coming from under a wide roller door at the front of one of the warehouses a hundred yards further on. He drove forward slowly, checking his police-issue thirty-eight was unbuckled in its holster around his waist. He drew up and stopped opposite the building and looked at it. The light was definitely there. When he turned off the engine, he could also hear noise coming from within. People talking. The clanking of equipment.

He climbed out of the car, checked his weapon again, and then walked toward the door. He was alert, checking all around. But the one thing he didn't see was a figure on the roof. It suddenly detached itself and disappeared into the darkness behind.

A minute later all sound ceased from the building. A second later, the light disappeared from under the door.

Grimes stopped. Listened. He moved forward more cautiously now. He was up against the wall. He drew his gun and approached the door slowly. The warehouses were in a row. They were separated from each other by gaps of about ten feet. As Grimes moved along the wall, toward the door, he failed to notice a shadow move out from one of the gaps and approach him from behind.

He had almost reached the door, cursing he'd got the call and that his food would be going cold, when he heard a twig break behind him. It was the last thing he ever heard as the bullet from the silenced pistol, at point-blank range, drilled straight through his head and out the other side, making a slight 'PHUT' sound as it impacted a wall further down the street.

Grimes slumped to the floor. The man holding the pistol moved forward and rapped three times on the door. It immediately rose upward. Two men ran out and dragged the body inside. One of them then ran to the police car and drove it away.

Once the roller door had clattered back down, the lights in the warehouse flicked back on.

Andriy Kozak walked back from the door into the middle of the large space. To one side was a semi-truck. Its long trailer had high canvas sides. Just behind the cab, a neat crane was folded in on itself, its cargo already aboard. To the side of the truck were two gray Toyota SUVs. Behind one of them was a trailer carrying a fast black RIB with twin outboards. In front of these, nine men were working at packing equipment into kit bags. Diving equipment was strewn across the floor. There were rebreathers, diver propulsion vehicles, an array of drysuits and a number of harpoon guns, all being meticulously prepared. There were also automatic weapons and boxes of ammunition.

Kozak stopped for a moment and surveyed the group. All the men had been hand-picked from his home country of Ukraine. Every one of them was dedicated to the cause. None of them had flinched when he had told them what he was planning to do. He had worked alongside many of them in the Ukrainian special forces. He trusted all of them with his life. But the one he loved and trusted the most was leaning over a box marked HEMOFILTERS—his brother, Ilya.

They had grown up together, along with a second brother, Mikhail, who was now dead. They also had a sister, but she had married and moved to Russia some years previously. They were not in contact much of the time, but Kozak knew she was equally dedicated to the cause. In fact, she had, in a big way, been responsible for the timing of the operation he was now undertaking.

As he watched Ilya check through the box of equipment, it was with a sense of pride. They had been a close family up until the point the Russian army had invaded Crimea. The war that had raged since had killed his parents. They had lived in the small town of Sorokyne in the east of Ukraine. Their family home had been taken over by Russian forces. It had been where they had grown up, where they had happy memories. But those memories had been destroyed forever. It was as though their childhood had been ripped from them.

Kozak had mourned for weeks, unable to come to terms with the loss. He had felt so impotent, so at a loss, but there was nothing he could have done. He had thought that as Russia had effectively invaded a sovereign country, then the West, and, more specifically, the United Nations and America, would have done something.

But nothing was done.

It appeared the great powers of the world were also impotent. Injustice was something Kozak hated. And it was injustice. It was about as unjust as you could get. He had vowed there and then, on the graves of his parents, that he would do something to avenge their deaths. Something that would strike a blow at Moscow and those who ruled over the corrupt and dangerous regime.

Then, when his brother Mikhail had been killed by American friendly fire while fighting with the rebels in Syria against the Assad regime, he knew others, too, needed to be made aware of their failings.

They had lost nearly everything. But despite that, it had taken some persuading to get Ilya on board. He had always been the quiet one, the one who took the path of least resistance. The one who wanted to talk things through rather than confront them. But Kozak had slowly persuaded him, little by little, bit by bit. He told him what the Russians had done to his parents. He had stopped short of telling him their mother had been raped and they had both been burned alive. He always needed something in reserve in case his brother wavered, but he wanted to spare him the details if possible. For now, those facts could remain untold, because, in his brother, he could already see he had ignited a desire for revenge as great as his own.

Kozak had found backing from an individual of great wealth and motivation, who would financially support his cause under the condition of absolute anonymity. That had been fine. He just needed the funds to pull it off. He was fully aware it was a probable suicide mission, but it was a mission that would change the world, and he was quite prepared to make the ultimate sacrifice if that was what it took. He had also convinced himself he could make the same decision for Ilya. His little brother had always looked up to him, followed him wherever he had gone. Death would just be the next great journey they made together.

He again looked at his men and the equipment they were preparing.

The time had nearly come.

He walked over to Ilya and ruffled his hair. The younger man looked up. When he saw Kozak, he smiled, if not a little nervously. To him it was all a big adventure with his big brother. It saddened Kozak that this might be the last they had together, but at least they could then be finally at peace and reunited with their parents and Mikhail.

"Are you scared, my brother?" asked Kozak.

Ilya looked up at him. "No, Andriy. I know you will protect me. It is a cause that is worth the sacrifice. I will always be with you."

"Well done, Ilya. You are a good boy." And with that he walked over to check on the rest of the men.

Judgment day was coming, and for some, it wasn't far away.

Chapter Sixteen

The next stage of filming on *Phoenix Rising* went better than anyone had any right to expect.

In fact, it went so well, there was a certain level of confusion on set. Brandy performed the underwater shots to perfection, and everyone had noticed a marked change in her whole demeanor. It was thought this was due to the fact McCready was acting as her safety diver. In fact, as they were climbing out of the water after the final shots, Franklin approached him with a knowing look on her face and gave him a wink as she passed. He stared at her, wanting to smack her one.

That was not what had happened.

Later that afternoon, McCready and Richards were standing in the main construction building. The nose cone of the crashed Skyline craft looked even more sorry for itself out of the water than it had strapped to flotation bags in Loch Lomond.

They walked around the battered vessel.

"So, any news on why the rocket failed?" asked McCready.

"We're looking into it now," said Richards. "Could be software, like you suggested, but more likely a defect in the triggering mechanism. Graham hopes to have some answers in the next few days."

"Hope so. If we ever get the Variant Two up and running, could be a whole bigger problem."

Richards looked at him. "You can say that again... By the way, looks like everything turned out okay with Miss Hollywood."

McCready was thoughtful for a moment. Richards looked at him curiously.

"Yeah, all things considered. She's not how she seems. She's complicated."

Richards was about to say something when he glanced up at someone over near the entrance. A delivery driver was walking toward them. He had a package in his hands. It was about three feet long and shaped like an elongated triangle. As he approached, he looked between the two men.

"One of you McCready?"

"I am."

"Delivery for you. Can you sign here?" He offered McCready a small PDA to sign digitally. McCready did so and took the package. He glanced at Richards. On closer inspection he could see that the top was covered in see-through plastic. Inside was a large bouquet of flowers.

Richards glanced at McCready, raising his eyebrows. McCready felt slightly embarrassed. No one had ever sent him flowers before. There was a note attached. He pulled it free, placing the flowers on a large metal trolley. He opened the note and read it. His face took on an inscrutable expression, and when he looked up he blushed slightly.

"Well, well," said Richards. "Are those from who I think they're from?"

"Like I said," said McCready, "she's complicated."

He turned to one side and reread the note.

> *John, I hope these will brighten your day. They are just a small token of my gratitude. Not only for helping me to find the courage and confidence in the water, but also, and more importantly, for saving my life. I never knew. I was only told today. Please accept my apology for the way I behaved. Sometimes I feel I am totally lost in this strange world I inhabit. You couldn't possibly understand. But if you would let me, I would love to buy you dinner tonight at my hotel so I may have a chance to explain more fully to you. I will, of course, understand if you choose to decline, but it would make my heart happy if you would be there.*
>
> *Love, Brandy. xx*

McCready folded the note and put it in his pocket. There was a faraway expression on his face.

Richards grinned. "Earth to John. Hello, anyone there?"

McCready turned to Richards, a smile starting to form.

"What?" said Richards.

"She wants to buy me dinner."

Richards shook his head. "Well, well. Guess you followed the producer's advice."

McCready looked shocked for a moment and shook his head. "It's just dinner."

"Yeah," said Richards, grinning, "of course it is."

The film unit had been staying at various hotels around Aberdeen. Most of the crew were in the Jurys Inn in Union Square, but the 'talent' was accommodated separately. The production had taken up the majority of rooms at the Marcliffe Hotel and Spa just outside the main part of the city. Situated in its own grounds, it provided a certain amount of exclusivity and privacy compared to others in the area.

The taxi carrying John McCready arrived at seven thirty. He climbed out and walked up to the entrance. He was shown into the bar where Brandy had told him she would meet him. He would have preferred to have gone home and changed, but that meant a four-hour drive each way, and he didn't have time. Instead, he'd showered and shaved at Ocean Tech and then borrowed one of Richards' clean shirts and a jacket. A tie would be going too far, but he did, at least, feel he had to make an effort. It was weird, McCready had never had a problem around women, but now he was going out for dinner with Brandy Carmine. Somehow, in this setting, out of the comfort zone of the water, where he was the important one, he was back in the real world where she was who she was, one of the most famous women on the planet.

He found he was getting butterflies in his stomach.

He'd been sitting in a large, comfy chair in the corner, reading a paper, when he heard a slight murmur from the others in the bar. He glanced up and his heart almost missed a beat.

Brandy walked toward him from across the room.

As McCready watched, he could see all eyes were on her

—men and women. In that split-second he had an inkling of what her life must be like. But he didn't have long to dwell on it. She was wearing a one-piece black dress. Not too long. Not too short. Just right. She had an elegant black leather choker around her neck, and when she lifted her hand he could see a fine gold bracelet made up of interlinked leaping dolphins—he wondered if this was for him. Her hair was brushed back, straight and dark, and fell down behind her as if a single mass of soft, luxurious fabric. She was, quite simply, stunning.

As she saw him, she smiled demurely. He stood up to greet her. She put a hand gently on his shoulder and kissed him lightly on the cheek.

"Shall we?" she said.

She linked her arm in his and they walked out of the bar toward the restaurant. All eyes followed them. As McCready risked a glance at the others in the room, he could see the men had slightly glazed, almost hostile, expressions on their faces, while the women wore open, inviting smiles. He furrowed his brow. Brandy glanced up at him. As they walked through the door she whispered in his ear, "People will look at you differently when you're with me." And then she added, "Particularly women."

McCready was about to say something along the lines of how outrageous and arrogant that statement was. But he couldn't. It was true. He had just witnessed it. He felt a tingle run up his spine.

When they sat down at a table in a corner of the restaurant that looked out over a large green lawn, the first thing McCready noticed about her was a total lack of tension. When she'd been on the set in the company of the crew, there had always been a nervousness to her. A wall of friction she clearly felt she needed to adopt to get through the day. He felt sorry for her. He could imagine there needing to be a protective wall when out in public—he had seen as much from the last few minutes—but when she was working with her fellow actors and technicians, it seemed a hell of a way to have to live. When he looked into her eyes now, though, that tension was gone. She was relaxed and smiling. The thought that his presence in any way made her feel like that sent a warm feeling through his body.

He hardly noticed the food. All he knew was that it had been delicious and they had managed to polish off a bottle of wine between them. McCready was about to order another when Brandy reminded him she still had some shots to complete the following day, and although they were all above water, she had to at least be coherent.

Throughout the meal he had listened to her as she had slowly unwound and told him her story. It may have been partly due to the wine, but there was something earnest about the way she spoke that made him feel she had wanted to tell someone for some time.

It was one of those fairytale Hollywood stories you think was almost written for the movies. But she had lived it.

She had been discovered while walking along Sunset Boulevard. That had led to commercials—one, in particular, that had involved a snake, a Ferrari and very little clothing, to promote a high-fashion perfume, had made people sit up. After this, Hollywood had taken notice. It was that alluring yet innocent image she projected, and could turn on at a whim, that had captivated them. It had also seemed to work on millions of others around the world, creating a combined box office for her films of over four billion dollars.

She told him of the time, as a young actress, when she'd been physically assaulted and had only survived the experience by zoning out and letting it happen. She'd reported it to the police, but the individual was high up in the industry, and back then, many things were overlooked. And no, his name wasn't Harvey. She explained about the time a video of her and a boyfriend had been leaked to the internet… by the boyfriend, who quickly became an ex. And then having her private life crawled over by the tabloids, who literally made up ninety percent of what people read.

As she spoke, McCready could see her eyes were welling up. He suddenly had an overwhelmingly protective feeling toward her—this young woman who had been used and abused in pursuit of the almighty dollar. He couldn't imagine what it must be like to have to live like that.

When she finally finished, she looked at him. Her eyes were still moist. She suddenly seemed to realize what she'd said. A fleeting look of panic flashed across her face, as though she'd revealed too much of herself and again had given away trust where it would be abused. But McCready looked at her with such calm assuredness and such kindness that the fear was replaced with a vulnerable look of helplessness, almost as though she were crying out for understanding.

But as she looked at him, almost pleading, McCready realized he was torn. How could he go down that path? As much as he wanted to sweep her up in his arms. As much as he would love to wake up next to her in the morning, his protective arm wrapped tightly around her, he knew her life wasn't for him. It would only lead to heartbreak for both of them.

She blinked and then looked deep into his eyes.

"Stay with me."

There was a slight smile on her face, but also a look so

wrapped up in pain and longing and love that McCready found it almost impossible to resist.

But he did.

He looked straight back at her.

"I can't."

A sad smile crossed her lips. She nodded slowly to herself, and then spoke softly, almost a whisper.

"I don't give up, you know."

She stood. McCready stood with her.

"You always get your way?"

As she turned, she spoke quietly. "Pretty much." Then she frowned slightly. "No, always." And with that she left the restaurant. All eyes followed her to the door. She briefly glanced back at McCready before he sat down. It was then he saw she had written her room number in lipstick on her napkin. He closed his eyes and took a deep breath.

Shit!

Ten minutes later he walked along the narrow hotel corridor on the first floor. There was a thick deep-pile carpet underfoot, which deadened the sound of his footsteps. He stopped opposite a door with the number fifteen on it. He paused, looking straight at it, as though imagining her on the other side. What she was doing. Had she gone straight to bed, or was she just sitting there watching TV? He walked up to the door. A loose floorboard squeaked under the carpet. He raised his hand, about to knock.

What the hell are you doing, John?

Inside the room, Brandy had slipped out of her clothes and pulled on a satin robe. It had a spiral design of a snake twisting around her body. She heard a noise outside the door as a loose floorboard squeaked.

When she'd come up to the room her heart had been racing. Normally, she had the men she wanted completely in her control. But that was the problem. Most of them were disposable. They used her. She used them. That was just the way it was. The people she met were largely from the industry and had the same vacuous philosophy. She rarely got to meet *real* people, at least not men she could feel she had a genuine attraction to beyond the superficial. But in the last two days all that had changed. She hadn't felt like this since grade school.

She was pretty sure he would come. She had that effect on people. They always came. When she turned it on, no one had resisted before, men or women. But before, she hadn't *needed* it to work. Now, somehow, she did.

At the squeak of the floorboard, she looked up. Her eyes shone. Her heart rate quickened. She ran lightly over to the door and peered through the spy hole. She could see McCready standing there, his hand raised. She prepared to pull the door open at his knock.

But it never came.

She watched in disbelief as he slowly lowered his hand, letting his arm fall by his side. He looked long and hard at the door, and then a second later he turned and walked off down the corridor.

Her immediate reaction was anger, her petulance coming through.

How could he?

But then an unfamiliar feeling of warmth spread through her. She returned to the bed, lay down, and smiled to herself. She curled up into a ball.

She now respected him more than ever.
She now wanted him more than ever.

Chapter Seventeen

The last day of shooting on *Phoenix Rising* was far less stressful than the previous few days. There was an end-of-term feel about it. Much of the crew would be moving on to new projects, and while many would work together again, they would never all be together as the same group. It truly was like a never-ending circus, just with different troupes. The top creatives would go into the post-production phase, holed up in an edit suite for several months, but right now was a transition time in the creation of the film. It also helped that the tension with Brandy had gone. The critical underwater shots had been achieved and there were just some last-minute in-water shots on the surface they could knock off well before lunchtime.

McCready watched from the periphery of the action that centered on the tank. The final shots were of Brandy appearing on the surface from underwater, swimming desperately for the upturned hull of the sub, which was now half in, half out of the water, and then climbing triumphantly up on top.

There was a palpable tension as things wound up for the final shot of the movie.

Brandy was in the water preparing herself by taking deep breaths in and out.

"Okay, waves!" shouted the first AD.

Immediately, the wave generators at the end of the tank started up, sending a rhythmic oscillation of water across the surface that created a realistic chop around the hull of the sub.

"Wind!" shouted the first AD.

The two wind machines cranked up close to the side of the tank. They consisted of two aero engines mounted on trailers. The operators swung them from side to side while using motorcycle accelerator grips to vary the speed. The effect was to send a hurricane-like gale across the water, adding to the chaos.

Everything was set.

"Turnover!" shouted the first AD.

Three cameras were covering the action. As they were shooting on film, not digitally, acknowledgment of readiness came with three shouts of "Speed" from the camera operators as the cameras ran up to speed.

Finally, the director shouted, "ACTION!"

On cue, Brandy took a final breath, submerged for a couple of seconds, so it would look as though she was appearing from out of the depths, then burst through the surface with a desperate, determined look on her face. She looked around, and then toward the sub. Then she struck out with a strong overarm stroke for the metal hull. When she reached it, she grabbed onto a protrusion on the side and hauled herself up. She climbed up on to the top of the hull, looking wildly around, her hair flying in the wind from the propellers spinning at a zillion revolutions a minute merely yards away. Finally, she pulled a walkie-talkie from her belt. She looked straight into the camera lens and spoke into the walkie-talkie.

"Mission accomplished! The Phoenix has risen!"

There were five seconds of her holding the pose.

"And cut!" shouted the director.

The waves flattened. The wind died down. Calm returned to the building.

"Check the gate!" came the order from the first AD.

The three cameramen checked there were no hairs in the mechanism that threaded the film through the cameras and could have ruined the take.

After a few seconds there were three confirmations.

"Gate clear."

"Gate clear."

"Gate clear."

The director stood up and looked around.

"Okay, everyone. That's a wrap!"

There was immediate cheering and clapping.

Brandy slid down off the sub into the water and swam across to the side of the tank. Her assistant was there with her robe. As she climbed out and slipped into it, Pamela Franklin walked over, arms out, a big smile on her face. But Brandy ignored her. She was looking for someone. She was smiling, but there seemed to be a sense of urgency on her face. Finally, she saw him, over to the side, away from the rest of the crew. She stopped for a second, then walked straight past Franklin and over to McCready. She was still wet and slightly bedraggled, but when she looked up at him, her eyes shone. She put her arms around his neck and gave him a long tender kiss. He didn't stop her. How could he? When she pulled away they stared at each other for a moment.

"I'm so proud of you," he said.

At that, her eyes moistened again.

"I have to go get changed. Things to do. Then let's talk." She smiled a warm, inviting smile that was full of affection, and then turned to head for her trailer. She was immediately lost in a scrum of bodies as the crew congratulated her. The director wrapped his arm around her and led her away.

McCready shook his head. How fickle could they be? It had only been a couple of days since they were slagging her off. But, hey, that's showbiz!

He turned and walked outside for some fresh air.

An hour later McCready was sitting in the conference room in the galleried section of the tank on the first floor. He was drinking coffee with Richards and chewing his way through a ham, cheese and pickle sandwich from a half-empty plate on the table. The door opened and Charlie Menzies walked in. Just behind her was Eugene Porter.

"Hi Charlie," said Richards. "Glad you could make it." He glanced at Porter. "Eugene, what are you doing here?"

"Well guv, you see, it's like this…" He was about to continue when Charlie cut in.

"Thought I'd bring the little dingo along. Seems to follow me around anyway." Porter looked a little embarrassed. McCready and Richards glanced at each other with *okaaay* expressions on their faces.

Charlie and Porter sat.

"If only Mac was here, we'd have the whole team," said Richards.

"Oh, yeah," said Porter, "where is our fine Scottish friend?"

Mac Logan had been a key part of the team that had been involved with the operation in London to retrieve the gold.

"He's taken some time off," explained Richards. "Joined an expedition exploring a network of flooded caves in Mexico."

"Hmmm. Kilts and sombreros," said Porter. "Never gonna work."

"Okay," said Richards, looking around the group, "I just wanted to go over the upcoming trials of the 737 with Charlie. You okay on these?"

Charlie leaned forward. "Just put me in the driver's seat, I can usually work things out from there," she said with a smile.

They looked at her dubiously.

"Come on guys. No worries! Yeah, I've five hundred hours on tankers. Bigger, if anything, but the 737's a good plane. Just give me a few flights to get used to the handling and we'll be good to go."

"One of Boeing's pilots will be with us for the crossover period, so you won't be completely blind," said Richards. "The only difference will be airflow and handling with the test module. When the Skyline system is finally deployed it'll be from a pylon beneath a wing, but so we can monitor things close up and test the Variant Two, the unit is housed inside the plane in a pressurized section. When she's ready to launch, we open twin doors in the bottom of the fuselage. She drops down. And off she goes."

"Just like an X-15," said Charlie.

"Pretty much," said Richards.

"Sounds fun. When do we start?"

"In a few days."

"Can't wait."

Richards was about to continue when there was a knock at the door. One of the runners from the film crew walked in. He glanced around. His eyes fell on McCready.

"Mr. McCready, Brandy would like to see you down by the tank if you have a minute."

They all glanced at McCready.

"Tell her I'll be right there," he said.

The runner nodded and closed the door behind him on the way out.

Everyone looked at McCready. He smiled at them innocently as he stood.

"What?"

"Have fun, John," said Richards.

When he'd left, Porter looked up. "Who the hell's Brandy?"

Richards looked at him, shaking his head. "Brandy Carmine, the actress? World's biggest film star?"

"What, she's here?"

"They've been filming the last couple of weeks," said Richards.

"Bloody hell!" said Porter. "She's hot!" Then he noticed Charlie staring at him "...ish. Hott*ish* is what I meant to say."

Charlie grinned. "Isn't he adorable?"

McCready walked out of the conference room, through the design studio, and down the set of metal stairs that led to the floor of the building.

He looked around and found her standing by the tank looking at the water. The special effects crew were in the process of removing the large gimbal and the set of the submarine using a mobile crane. As he approached, she turned toward him. She'd had a shower and was dressed casually in jeans and a white rollover top. Her hair was still damp and flowed down her back. When she saw him her face lit up.

She reached out her hand and he took it. With a mischievous grin she looked up at him earnestly.

"Come with me to London. I have a premiere to go to tonight. It might be fun. See some of the chaos and craziness that's my life."

She looked at him with such pleading, but also with a wicked gleam in her eye that he couldn't resist. He looked at her. Then he took out his phone.

"Stay here."

"Yes, sir," she said obediently. "Anything you say, sir."

He shook his head slightly, grinning. He walked a few feet away and pressed one of the speed dial buttons. She watched him every step of the way. A second later he spoke into the phone.

"Craig, you need me for the next couple of days?"

"Now why on earth would you ask me that?" said Richards with a smile in his tone.

"I, er, need to go away for a while."

"Of course you do, mate... We've just got the Skyline trials. Charlie and I can handle those. I'll see if Graham can get to the bottom of the glitch with the rocket system. We should be okay for a few days, but we need you back then. Go. Have fun. And John..."

"Yeah?"

"Don't do anything I wouldn't do!"

"You kidding, old man. I hope to do a lot of things you *couldn't* do!"

He clicked off the phone, took a deep breath, and

turned back to Brandy. She had an expectant but confident expression on her face.

"I'm all yours."

"I know you are," she said with that wicked gleam again. She walked over and hugged him.

"You won't regret this Mr. McCready. It's my turn to teach you a thing or two, and I'm a very good teacher."

From the windows of the conference room Porter and Richards watched McCready walk out of the main door, arm in arm with Brandy. She was looking up at him with adoring puppy-dog eyes and he was looking like the cat that had got the cream.

Richards was smiling. "All's well that ends well."

"What was that?" said Porter.

"After what happened in the Pacific and then with Clare. He needs to unwind. Relax. Have some fun."

"No danger that ain't gonna happen," said Porter with an inscrutable expression.

"Huh?"

"Well, it ain't gonna need me to make those two go bang!"

Richards looked at him and grinned.

Chapter Eighteen

President Galt Stevens looked around the conference room on the fourth floor of the Omega Complex. It was around thirty feet long and half as wide. The perimeter was curved to allow the lines of the building to sweep round. It was made up of floor-to-ceiling glass that looked out over a spectacular view.

There were eight people present. Four American. Four Russian. Each group sat on opposite sides of a large oval table and was made up of the respective presidents, their national security advisers and their chiefs of staff. There was also an adviser on each side who was there to add another voice to the mix and help document the proceedings. For the Americans, this was Randal Watson. While President Petrovich was almost fluent in English, his security adviser was not, and since none of the American delegation spoke Russian, translations were done in real time through small headsets using digital technology.

So far, little progress had been made, which was a shame, as the stakes couldn't have been higher.

Stevens' gaze came to rest on Petrovich.

"Viktor, it is in both our interests to reach an agreement on arms control. If we do not, our countries will become bankrupt. Neither of us can afford this in the current climate. Let us agree to stop all development and limit any new technology."

Petrovich fixed Stevens in his stare. Gone was the geniality he had shown to Clare earlier. In its place was the hard man of Russia who was so vividly displayed across TV screens. It was an image of a man in ruthless control of his country; one who had no limits in his desire to see Russia back to her glory days, but an image the rest of the world had moved on from and knew would never return.

"Mr. President… Galt. These agreements you speak of can only be reached through an understanding of mutual trust. You speak of limiting development in new technology, yet I am fully aware of the continued progress of your so-called 'Star Wars' system of orbiting laser weapons, and that you have been secretly deploying them over the last three years. It is to counteract threats like these that we have developed the hypersonic cruise missile system, as well as nuclear-armed autonomous underwater vehicles. We will soon have enough units in play that your weapons from space would only have limited time to acquire and destroy our missiles. And given we will be deploying these in the thousands, through land, sea, air and underwater launch systems, reacting in time, for you, would be impossible. Many would get through. The cycle of MAD continues. You say to me you will be giving up these weapons, then we can maybe talk. But somehow I do not think you will be saying this thing to me, do you?"

He let the question hang in the air.

Stevens fixed him in a hostile glare. He leaned over to

Harvey Danvers, his national security adviser. Danvers was a sixty-year-old veteran of conflicts over thirty years. He had been a senior general in the US Army before taking up the highest security position in the land. He did not frighten easily and he did not bargain away an advantage.

"What do you think, Harve?" said Stevens. "We can't go down that route. And how the hell does he know we've been deploying for the last three years?"

"Sir, he can't know the true capability. You can call his bluff. It just depends how far he's prepared to go in calling yours."

Stevens nodded slowly in agreement. He then looked back at Petrovich.

"Viktor, you cannot know our capability, as indeed we cannot truly know yours, which means it is more vital than ever that, while we may agree to disagree on certain things, we reduce our overall arsenal."

Petrovich returned the stare evenly. "Fine, Mr. President, you go first!"

Stevens leaned back in his chair in exasperation. It was going to be a long few days.

Clare was feeling tired as she walked across the rec room in the cocoon. The summit had only been going on for a couple for days, but already it had seemed like weeks. There were still things to check over to ensure all the systems were running effectively should the worse happen. She had a checklist she was working through, and, except for the leakage in the tunnel, which she was assured would be fine, everything seemed to be in order.

On the far side of the rec was an eating area, and beyond that a kitchen that could cater for ten guests, with enough provisions to last two weeks. Clare checked all the supplies and resources were in place and fully stocked and then took a walk up to the first-floor level. Here were located two sumptuous suites where VIPs could stay if they had to remain locked down for any period of time. There were also a number of smaller rooms. Given the nature of the current summit, the two presidents were staying in the cocoon for the period, just in case. On the lower level there was also a gym, which could be used for general fitness activities, and a small meeting room, in case there had to be private discussions between individuals.

Midway along the upper level was a control room. It had direct contact to the security center in the main building. Clare walked in and glanced around at the displays and systems. On the screens were views from CCTV cameras across the complex. One camera showed the security center above. She could see Patterson reclining in a chair drinking a coffee. She clicked the comms mike.

"Hey, Harry, stop slacking!"

She saw him glance around, looking for where the voice had come from. His gaze fell on a monitor just above his work station. He looked straight into the camera. Clare grinned as he smiled at her.

"Checking up on me, are you, little lady?"

"Someone has to keep the place safe."

"Well, seeing as you're on the clock, guess you don't need me," said Patterson.

"Guess not," said Clare. "See you later, Harry."

She saw him lift his mug in acknowledgment, and then turn to someone who had called him from across the room.

Clare smiled and walked out into the corridor and turned right. She headed down to the far end. This led to the second lift-track access point that connected them to the main building above. When she reached it, she checked the control panel was operational and also the airlock seal. When she tried a pressure test, all looked good. She took another glance around and then headed back to the rec.

Once there, she lifted the walkie-talkie.

"Brad, you there?"

A second later the speaker crackled. "Go ahead."

"All looks good down in the cocoon. I'll be up top in ten. Anything you need me to do?"

"All okay thanks. The delegations will be wrapping at four today, so they should be in their suites soon after. I've had a call from head office in NY. I may have to go over tonight. Sorry, I know about the time you had planned with Jade, but this can't wait. I'll have to confirm later. It'll mean, though, you'll have to be here overnight if I'm away."

"Jeez, that sucks!"

"I know, I'm sorry, hun. I'll make it up to you."

"Yes, you will! Okay, let me know when you know. Out."

She clipped the walkie-talkie back around her waist and then headed to the lift-track to go and check her room on the accommodation level. Both she and Brad had rooms within the complex to stay in when major events were on at the facility. And they didn't get any more major than this. At least one of them had to be on-site overnight for the duration. The summit was only meant to last five days, so it was no hardship, but it would mean she'd have to cut short her time with her best friend, Jade, if Brad had to go out of town. And she'd been looking forward to that for a couple of weeks.

As the lift-track arrived to take her topside, she took out her phone to call to her friend.

Chapter Nineteen

The limousine pulled up outside Claridge's Hotel in the heart of Mayfair in central London just after two o'clock in the afternoon. As the car pulled to a halt, a doorman, bedecked in a long, smart coat and top hat walked smoothly forward to open the door.

Brandy climbed out.

She was greeted by the head concierge.

"Good afternoon, Ms. Carmine. How lovely to see you again."

"Thank you, Martin. Looking smart as ever."

"We aim to please, madam."

McCready had walked around the car and joined Brandy.

"John, this is Martin. He's amazing. Anything you want in London, he can get it for you. You only have to ask."

"Welcome, sir. I hope you'll enjoy your stay with us," said Martin, flicking his fingers for a bellboy to collect their luggage from the trunk of the car, which had automatically sprung open.

"I'm sure I will," said McCready.

They walked into the hotel, their luggage following behind. *Their* luggage was probably not quite the right description as McCready had nothing with him. Brandy had said not to worry; she'd take him shopping. He had to look the part if he was going to a red carpet premiere with her. She'd seemed really happy at the prospect. McCready not so. He was sure the experience would, at some point, involve an encounter with a tie.

Check-in happened effortlessly—there was none—and they were led through the sumptuous interior that simply oozed class and sophistication.

They were escorted up to the second floor and the Prince Alexander Suite. Once the cases had been delivered and they'd been left alone, McCready looked around the elegant rooms. There was an entrance hall that led into a living room, two bedrooms with en suite bathrooms, and a small dressing room. The view outside was onto the redbrick buildings of Davies and Brook Streets.

Apparently, in 1945, it was the suite in which Alexander, Crown Prince of Yugoslavia had been born, hence the name. The family had been staying there after being exiled during World War Two. Winston Churchill had even ordered some Yugoslavian soil be placed under the bed and declared the room to be Yugoslavian territory for the day.

It was all exquisitely decorated and appointed. Discerning artwork hung on the walls and the furniture was appropriate and tasteful. There was even an original Gilbert & Sullivan grand piano in the main room.

McCready walked though into the smaller of the two bedrooms but realized the whole space had been transformed into a dressing room. Clearly the small one in the suite would not be big enough. The space where the bed should have been was filled with a wide table with a chair pushed neatly underneath. Resting on top was a large mirror surrounded by lights. Any other space was taken up with boxes of makeup and hair-styling equipment.

He walked back into the main sitting area where Brandy was happily smelling a large bouquet of flowers on a glass table next to the window.

"Looks like there's only one bed," said McCready.

Brandy spun round, a smile on her face, followed by a frown.

"Really, I'm sure I mentioned the suite needed to sleep two." She walked into the master bedroom and stared seriously at the Emperor bed. "Yep, I'm sure two can sleep there."

She then turned and walked straight toward McCready. When she reached him, she grabbed him round the waist and pulled him close. She then stretched up, to be next to his ear, and whispered, "But whether you get any sleep will be an entirely different matter."

Any willpower McCready had managed to hold onto went completely out the window. He locked lips with hers and they kissed for over a minute, tasting each other and reveling in it. When they broke apart, Brandy had a faraway look on her face, one that was a mix of pleasure and happiness he hadn't seen before. She grabbed his hand and led him back through into the main room.

"Now, we have to get you ready for tonight. We can't have you looking like a scruffy old diver if I'm going to show you off to the world."

"Hey, I'm not old!"

She stuck her tongue out at him.

The next two hours were a whirlwind. He was whisked through the high-class, high-fashion shops of London as

Brandy aimed to do the impossible: make McCready presentable for the red carpet. The premiere was in Leicester Square, the main entertainment hub of the capital. There would be celebrities by the limoful, as would be expected for a Brandy Carmine film. All the world's media would be there. It was the showbiz event of the month.

As this started to sink in, McCready felt a knot develop in his stomach. He was experiencing a rare thing for him— nerves. He was way out of his comfort zone.

When they arrived back at the suite, four people were waiting for them.

Brandy's manager, Raymond Shelby, was a small, thirty-something New Yorker, who either drank a whole lot of coffee or was permanently high on something else. Despite that, he seemed competent and on the ball. He was polite, or, rather, tolerant of McCready, but then almost zoned him out as he went through a million things with Brandy. There was a hair stylist and makeup artist who descended on her after Shelby had finished. They hauled her into the chair in front of the mirror in the second bedroom and set to work.

The fourth person was a stylish woman in her late forties with brown, shoulder-length hair, immaculately dressed in a fashionable skirt and blouse. She had laid out a collection of designer clothes for Brandy to choose from to make her look like the movie star the whole world expected to see.

Before hair and makeup had claimed Brandy, she'd whispered into the woman's ear and nodded at McCready. The woman had smiled and approached him. Before this, Brandy had given him a comforting and helpless hug— *welcome to my life*. And then she was gone as hair and makeup returned to their tasks.

The woman crossed over to McCready.

"John, my name's Stella. Let's get you looking like a million bucks."

McCready shook her hand and then followed her into the bedroom where Brandy had dumped the selection of clothes from their earlier shopping trip.

"Don't I recognize you from somewhere?" he asked.

"Maybe," she said. "Been doing this for a while. Also, my dad made a few records. Could be that."

McCready nodded, realization hitting him. "Yeah, think I've heard a couple of them."

An hour later and McCready felt like he'd been through the ringer. He'd showered and shaved and then put himself in Stella's capable hands.

When she'd finished with him, he walked back out from the bedroom, through the main suite and into the room where they were still working on Brandy. He walked up behind her. She was waiting for her hair to set from the construction job her stylist had completed. When she saw him, she let out a cry of delight.

"Well, well, the man scrubs up okay."

McCready looked at himself in the mirror. He'd only ever worn a dinner jacket and bow tie once before, and those had been borrowed. But he had to admit, he did feel like a million dollars. He turned to his side to look at himself. He then moved to reach up and pull his collar looser.

"Ah… Ah! No, you don't."

"But it's too tight."

"You'll get used to it." She stared at him for a minute, and that faraway expression came across her face again. "You look gorgeous."

They locked eyes for a moment and then the stylist intervened.

"Brandy, we need fifteen minutes."

McCready held up his hands. "Okay. I know when I'm not wanted."

He walked back into the main room and sat down on one of the couches, feeling slightly awkward, but also very good about himself.

Twenty minutes later she was finished. He could see her through the door as she walked into the bedroom to choose her outfit for the night, the one the world would see and would act as a billboard for one particular fashion label. It might also sell a few more of the designer's dad's albums.

When Brandy emerged half an hour later, McCready's jaw literally fell open. He stood up. There was nothing else he could do. She was dressed in a simple long-flowing black and white gown that seemed to cling in all the right places yet hang provocatively in others, revealing just enough flesh to stimulate the mind but err on the side of good taste. Her hair was piled up in a bundle of curls that flowed down over her shoulders, and she wore a necklace of glistening diamonds around her neck. She looked at him like a little girl seeking approval.

All he could do was stare for a moment and slowly shake his head with an admiring smile.

"Wow!"

She beamed back at him.

At that moment, Shelby burst through the door, eyes glued to his phone. Everyone looked up. He stopped, glanced around, checking people were ready.

"Great. Right. Car's downstairs. We need to move. Let's go!"

McCready barely had time to thank Stella for all her help before he followed Brandy and Shelby out of the door.

Downstairs, they walked through the hotel lobby to the waiting limousine outside. Everyone watched as they paraded through. There was the usual murmuring and a couple of gasps that accompanied Brandy wherever she went. Again, McCready could feel eyes on him.

A few seconds later and they were in the quiet of the car. He was starting to see what her life was like. As he looked at her going through last-minute details with Shelby, he actually felt sorry for her. While her position gave her great privilege and wealth, it stripped her of any privacy and a life that was hers and hers alone. She was property to be used and exploited—nothing else. An item in the financial strategy of a movie. If they pay this much for something—a special effect, a director, etc.—they get this in return. That was the only factor in the equation. If the film would bring in an extra hundred million because Brandy Carmine was in it, it was worth paying her ten million for a few weeks' work. Simple arithmetic. At the end of the day she was just a component in a product, an engine in a car, a screen on a television. He found it all rather sad.

Twenty minutes later the car pulled into a line of limousines heading down Cranbourn Street that led into Leicester Square. McCready could already see the crowds of people just beyond the police cordon. They were shouting and cheering, straining to see who was in the procession of vehicles that were arriving with blacked-out windows.

Brandy looked at McCready. She smiled and then frowned, shaking her head.

"What am I going to do with you?"

She reached up to his neck and redid the top button of his shirt that had somehow come undone.

"Ow!"

"You big baby!" She straightened the tie and leaned back to appraise her work. "There, that's better." She gave him a quick peck on the lips and then wiped off the lipstick that had stuck.

The limousine pulled to a halt. McCready saw a woman move forward to open the door. Behind her, the lens of a TV camera pointed at the car.

Shelby looked at Brandy. "Okay, kid. Knock 'em dead!"

Brandy glanced at McCready. She reached out and squeezed his hand, an excited gleam in her eyes.

"Come on, let me show you my world."

And with that, he noticed something change in her, as though a switch had been flicked. Now she was that confident, arrogant, almost brattish person he'd met in the trailer. It was transformative, and he watched in awe as Brandy Carmine, the world's biggest movie star, climbed out of the car to a roar of screams and cheers. As he followed, Shelby tapped him on the shoulder, looking at him ruefully. "I've never seen her like this with anyone before. Don't fuck it up!"

McCready climbed out of the car and was immediately hit by a barrage of flashguns.

Chapter Twenty

Clare checked her watch as she turned into Laurel Canyon in her Audi TT Roadster with a squeal of tires.

Dammit!

She was twenty minutes late. She'd told Jade she'd be back by midday but everything had run over at the complex. Coupled with the fact that Brad did now have to fly to New York, and she was going to have to return to the complex later and stay overnight. But she did at least have the afternoon free she could spend with her best friend. She'd told her to let herself in and make herself at home.

She screeched round the final corner, blipped the gate controls, and swept into the drive, just missing the high wooden barrier as it slid smoothly to one side.

She pulled up next to Jade's battered Ford and could hear barking before she'd even headed for the wide glass panel that made up the front door. She was barely inside when there was the dash of paws skidding on tiles and her one-year-old white retriever puppy, Max, came hurtling toward her. She had to put her bag down as he tended to launch himself from several feet away these days, and he was getting far too big for that sort of thing.

True to form, Max took off about three feet from Clare. He landed halfway up her body, barking excitedly, tail on full auto. She was ready for it, though, and braced herself.

"Come on now, you daft thing. I've not been away that long." The barking would suggest otherwise.

She picked up her bag and walked through the hallway into the large open-plan living room. Since moving in six months previously, everything now had its place. It was starting to feel like home. To the right was the kitchen. She could see Jade in there clanking around with pots and pans.

"Hey!" said Clare.

"Hey, yourself," said Jade.

"You didn't need to do all this."

"Well, figured you'd need to relax a bit when you got back."

Clare walked into the kitchen and gave Jade a hug.

"Thanks, that's really great."

"So, Brad's away for the night?"

"Yeah. He has to go see the high-ups at the head office in NY. Some foul-up re financing or something. Wish he'd given me more notice, though, what with all that's going on at the summit."

"So, everything all okay in paradise?" said Jade, looking pointedly at her friend.

"Yeah, course," said Clare, maybe a bit too quickly.

"Really?" said Jade.

Clare sighed. "I just wish he'd make up his mind when he's going to move in. He seems to like the fact he has his own place, which is okay, I guess, but if it's going to move forward... well, you know..." Jade looked at her with raised eyebrows. "I don't know, it almost seems like now we're together he's eased off the gas. Certain things aren't so important anymore." Jade's eyebrows were still raised. "It's probably just me. Paranoid from past relationships." Clare looked hopefully at Jade.

"If you say so... Spag bol, okay?"

"Perfect."

Clare crossed over to a wine rack and grabbed a bottle of Cabernet Sauvignon, opened it, and poured a glass for both of them.

She walked back into the living room, kicked off her shoes, and glanced at the large-screen TV above the fireplace. It was currently showing the latest edition of *Entertainment Tonight*. She looked briefly out through the space left by the glass panels that had been drawn back to reveal the external pool, which was built out on stilts with a view across Los Angeles beyond.

The TV then drew her attention. The eager, young blonde *ET* reporter was looking straight into camera. The Odeon in Leicester Square was behind her, a red carpet disappearing out of shot. A series of celebrities were trailing past. Every now and then the reporter glanced down the line to see who was coming next, and if they were worth talking to. She turned back to camera.

"We're still waiting for Brandy Carmine, the star of the new thriller, *Deception in Mind*, to make an appearance. I hear she's just left her car and is on her way, so we should be able to bring her to you any minute now."

Jade poked her head through the hatch from the kitchen.

"I wonder who Miss fancy-pants has on her arm

tonight. That girl goes through men like I don't know what."

"And women, from what I hear," added Clare.

Jade stopped to think. "Yeah, I'd do her." They both laughed.

The reporter was now all smiles. She turned back to the carpet. Brandy was just coming into view. The shot was framed on her face and so cut off the head of the taller man accompanying her.

Jade had walked through into the living room to watch.

The reporter grabbed Brandy and held the mike between them.

"So, Brandy, great to see you again. How you doin'?"

"Couldn't be better," Brandy beamed back. She waved at someone in the crowd who shouted at her.

"I watched the film last night," said the reporter. "What a ride! I never saw that ending coming."

"That's the idea," said Brandy. "Keeps you guessing all the way."

"So, what have you been working on recently?"

"Well, I've just finished shooting *Phoenix Rising* over here, which is the sequel to *The Phoenix*. In fact, we were doing the final shots this morning."

"Wow! That's cutting it fine. I hear you had to learn a whole load of new skills for this one, really amping up the action."

"Yeah, it was really cool. I had to ride a motorbike, and there were some underwater sequences, so I had to learn to scuba dive."

The reporter pulled a face. "How did that go?"

"Well," said Brandy, "it was really difficult until I met this guy." She turned to the man next to her, a huge smile on her face.

"I was going to ask you who this hunk is you're with tonight."

Clare and Jade leaned closer to the screen.

The camera tilted up to reveal McCready looking slightly awkward in his jacket and tie.

Clare let out a cry, nearly dropping her glass.

"What?" asked Jade, looking puzzled. But Clare didn't answer. She just kept staring at the screen, her hand to her mouth.

The reporter was smiling at McCready.

Brandy held tightly onto his arm, her face one of pure joy. Her eyes sparkling.

"This is John," she said. "He saved my life."

"Yeah, I bet he did!" said the reporter.

"No, really, he saved my life. I would have drowned without him. He's my hero."

And in that instant Clare found herself fighting for breath. She tried to speak but couldn't. All she could do was stare. She mouthed four words, but only a rasping whisper came out.

Jade looked at her with a quizzical expression. "Huh?"

Clare repeated it as though she was far away, and this time the words came out.

"But he's *my* hero."

"Who?"

She pointed at the screen. "McCready!"

Jade stared at her with shock.

"That's McCready?"

Clare nodded slowly.

"I thought you two were over. Past tense."

"Yeah... No... I don't know."

"Jeez, girl, you're in trouble."

They watched the screen. Brandy continued to look

adoringly up at McCready. He was smiling and charming the reporter, who was fluffing her hair and smiling back. Halfway through, he tried to loosen his tie, giving a slightly pained expression as he did so.

Clare found herself talking to herself. "And he hates ties."

Jade glanced at her again. "Girl, you really got problems. But I wouldn't worry. Her track record with men ain't too hot."

"But they weren't *him*."

"What's so special about *him*? Thought you'd found out he wasn't so shit hot?"

"Yeah, maybe. But look at the way she's looking at him."

"Whaaat?" said Jade. "She's an actress. It's her job to convince you of stuff. She'll probably dump him after the premiere... well, maybe in the morning." Clare looked at her sharply. "It's all a publicity stunt to show off *her hero*."

But Clare was feeling a pain inside she hadn't felt in a long time. "You can't fake that... Can't you see, she's in love with him?"

Jade looked at her. "Girl, you got it bad."

She looked helplessly at Jade. "Maybe I was in denial. I was so far away. I was still mad at him. But then he did write this sweet message, saying he wanted to explain."

"And did he?"

"I never gave him the chance. I wrote back saying I thought it better if we didn't continue. I'd met this old friend from college, who was now more than a friend, and I was going to be working with him over here. And that it was over between us."

"Don't look like it's over to me," said Jade, her eyebrows raised as high as they could go.

"What am I going to do?"

Jade just looked at her.

On screen, the reporter was wrapping it up. "Okay, Brandy, have a fab night, and I wouldn't let this one out of your sight."

"Thanks, Chloe, and trust me, there's no danger of that." Brandy pulled McCready close and kissed him deeply on the lips.

Clare jumped up and walked out onto the pool surround carrying her glass. She stood by the railing at the edge and looked across the LA skyline, taking a large gulp of wine.

A short while later Jade joined her. She was about to say something when Clare's phone rang. She answered it, listened for a minute, replied a couple of times, and then clicked it off. She shoved it back in her pocket.

"Shit! I have to go back in. There's some problem with the catering for the Russian delegation. I'm so sorry. I'll make it up to you. And we haven't even eaten." She looked at Jade imploringly.

Jade gave her a huge hug. "Hey, don't worry. It'll sort itself out. Try and forget him. Either he's a million miles away with her not thinking of you, or he's a million miles away not thinking of you. That boat has sailed, girl. Just think about work now… and Brad. I thought you guys had something good going on."

Clare looked totally lost. "Yeah, so did I." She smiled weakly. "Could you stay over tonight and look after Max till tomorrow?"

"What, you mean in this dump?"

Clare smiled and gave Jade another hug. She'd made her bed and now she'd have to lie in it. Anyway, right now she needed to focus on work. She forced herself to snap out of it.

She kissed Jade on the cheek and managed to negotiate a retriever at full sprint as she headed for the door.

But inside, her world had been turned upside down.

Chapter Twenty-One

It was approaching two o'clock in the morning when Gemma Morgan finished up her mug of coffee and turned to the man sitting in the chair opposite.

Gemma was twenty-seven. It was her third week on the job. The guy in the chair was her boss, Brett, and she'd been trying to get him to go on a date with her. Probably not the best course of action anyway, and he was ten years older, but she'd never let that stop her before.

Brett was witty, kind and listened to her when she moaned and groaned about her life—what more could you want? He was possibly carrying a few extra pounds, but hey, you couldn't have everything, right? So far, he'd been playing hard to get; at least, that was what she thought he'd been doing.

She stood up and walked over to him. He was wearing one of his numerous Pink Floyd T-shirts and was staring out of the main window of the dam control room that looked out over the Griffith Park reservoir.

"Hey, Brett, you wanna go to that Rams game at the weekend? Should be good."

Brett looked up at her with a smile on his face. "You don't give up, do you, Gem? I'm on shift this weekend."

She pouted at him. But then he sighed.

"Okay, how about the week after?" he said.

"Yes!" she said, pumping a fist in the air. "You won't regret it."

"That is yet to be seen. Hey, isn't it time for your patrol?"

She checked her watch and groaned. "Yep, looks that way. See you in about thirty."

"Don't fall in!"

"Ha, ha. I can swim, you know."

And with that she left the room. She walked down a narrow corridor and into a large locker room. She walked over to her locker and pulled out a belt with a holster and thirty-eight revolver already secured. She wrapped it round her waist and then stuffed a large flashlight into a holder on the belt. She then pulled on a lightweight jacket with SECURITY written large across the back in white letters. She zipped it up, closed the locker, and headed out of the building.

Once outside, she glanced around. It was fairly cloudy and there was a cool breeze. She liked these patrols. It got her out in the fresh air. She also liked to look down the high dam wall. It always amazed her that the concrete structure could hold back the mass of water contained in the reservoir. She allowed her gaze to follow it all the way to the bottom and then along the wide spillway that led into a tunnel that went under the I-5 and entered the Los Angeles River just beyond. Right now there was a steady trickle of water coming from the overflow, but there were gates that could be opened to increase the flow in emergencies, or after particularly bad weather if the dam was in danger of being breached.

She turned away from the drop and walked further along the wall. Her patrol was fairly straightforward. She would walk the full length of the dam checking for any cracks, leakage, anything unusual. In the past three weeks she'd found nothing.

Fifteen minutes later she reached the end. She had just started to head back, when she heard a noise from across the water.

The lake extended for about a mile and widened out to half a mile at its midpoint. The surrounding land, which was hilly and largely covered in trees, was open to the public during the day so families could make use of the area as a recreational facility. There was even a boat hire company operating at the far end of the lake that hired out sailboats and electric boats, as well as having a small cafe, shop and parking facilities. But the area was locked off at night, so there shouldn't be anyone around.

She had almost made it back to the dam buildings when she heard the noise again. It sounded like a number of vehicles driving slowly. One of them seemed large, like a truck. It could, of course, just be traffic noise blown in on the wind from roads in the surrounding hills, but there was also the distinctive crunching of tires on gravel that sounded like the gravel of the track further up the lake.

She walked over and jumped into the yellow utility pickup they used to get around the grounds. She started the engine, flicked on the lights and headed off along the narrow track at the edge of the water that would take her toward the public entrance.

She had been driving for about ten minutes and had

passed the first car park and was now about halfway along the length of the reservoir. She stopped and turned off the engine.

The noise was still there. The crunching sound was louder. She lowered her window and looked down at the track—definitely the same gravel. An owl hooted in the trees somewhere. She started the engine and headed on.

Five minutes later she rounded a bend and came to a screeching halt. She almost skidded into the fender of a gray SUV that was running with no lights. Behind it, in the glare of her headlights, she could make out a second SUV towing a trailer, and behind that, a large semi-truck. She picked up the radio and clicked TRANSMIT.

"Hey Brett, you there?"

The reply came a few seconds later.

"Don't tell me you've fallen in already?"

"Brett, there are a number of vehicles out by the picnic area. A couple of SUVs and a semi. All running without lights."

Brett's voice suddenly turned serious. "You know what they're doing?"

"No, I'm just going to find out."

"Okay, be careful. Check back when you know."

"Will do." And with that she clicked off the radio.

She climbed out of the cab and had taken two paces toward the first SUV when the bullet passed straight through her brain. She fell to the ground, a limp pile of flesh and bones of what, seconds before, had been a living, breathing human being.

Andriy Kozak lowered the silenced pistol and stepped out from behind the door of the lead SUV. He walked over to the body, glanced around at the pickup and then further along the track. He turned and walked back to the car. When he reached it he motioned to two men inside.

"Put the body in the pickup and drive it into the woods. She may have called it in. We need to be careful. Okay. Go!"

Two men climbed out. They picked up the woman's body and slung it in the back of the pickup. When it was off the track Kozak waved the other vehicles forward. The convoy moved on, heading toward the dam.

Ten minutes later they came to the car park at the picnic area. Immediately the lead SUV drove in and parked. The second SUV with the boat backed up to the water's edge. The men inside climbed out and quickly launched the RIB. Behind them, the semi drew up next to the water and parked parallel to it. Four men climbed out of the cab and set to work to pull the canvas sides and roof from the trailer. As they fell away, the lethal shape of the *Deep Intruder* special forces submersible was revealed. Fifteen minutes later it had been lowered into the water by the small crane at the front of the trailer. It now floated calmly in the water next to the fast black RIB.

Kozak watched his men with satisfaction. Things could not have gone more smoothly… well, maybe one less body more smoothly. As he looked across the water to the dam beyond, he was joined by his brother.

"It is a good night for it," said Ilya.

Kozak looked down at him with pride. "Tonight, we strike a blow for the evil that has been done to our country. Tonight, we right many wrongs."

Ilya looked up at his older brother. They held their hands in the air, clasped together, revealing two matching tattoos of a wolf's head with crossed swords on their wrists.

"For justice!" they both said together.

Kozak then turned to his men who were laying out their equipment in the car park. They were overseen by Alexei Masaev. The man was huge. His face was battered from previous aggressive encounters that had no doubt ended badly for the other parties. His arms were covered in tattoos, and he seemed to have a permanent sneer written across his face. He looked up as the brothers approached, his gaze falling on Kozak with respect and deference, but when he looked at Ilya, there was nothing but contempt. Kozak noticed the difference but said nothing.

"Are the men ready?"

"Yes," said Masaev. "They are ready for the sacrifices ahead."

They watched as the men checked the diving equipment and weapons. At the side was the box marked HEMOFILTERS. Kozak walked forward and pulled out the small packages with the wristbands. He handed them out to all the divers. They attached them to their arms and then dressed in their gear.

Kozak pulled out a tablet in a waterproof case and opened up a schematic. The map showed a layout of the reservoir in detail: dimensions, depth of water, where all the facilities were located. It also showed a specific shaded area in the reservoir, about fifty feet out from the dam wall. Kozak showed it to Masaev.

"This dark area is the tunnel. It is critical you place the charges directly above it for a distance of twenty yards. We need to ensure a large enough opening."

Masaev watched intently.

"Also," continued Kozak, "watch out for other patrols. I am sure the woman in the truck spoke to someone over the radio. If she doesn't report in they may be looking for her."

"I'll take care of it," said Masaev.

With that, Masaev called over two of the men who were now fully dressed in their gear. They climbed into the boat, along with a driver. Masaev also carried a silenced waterproof rifle with telescopic sight.

He gave a meaningful look at Kozak and then the boat disappeared into the night, heading toward the dam.

When Brett had put down the radio after Gemma's call, he'd been concerned but not unduly worried. She could handle herself, of that he was sure. It was probably a load of kids trying to go boating in the middle of the night as a dare. The report of a large semi-truck was concerning, but maybe she'd got it wrong. There were no construction or maintenance works scheduled at the dam this month, so what could a truck possibly be doing there at night? But just to be sure, he decided to check in with her.

He picked up the radio. "Hey, hotshot, anything to report from your mysterious nightwalkers?"

He released the button and listened.

There was nothing but static.

He tried again, but no response. He sighed and stood up. He made his way through the building and headed out onto the dam wall. He walked toward the center and looked out across the water. It was a dark night, but the clouds weren't too thick. The occasional shaft of moonlight gave him something to see by. He couldn't be sure but he thought he could hear some sort of noise coming from over by the picnic area. He moved closer to the side of the wall. Then, from below, he heard something else. It sounded like an outboard at low throttle, just ticking over. It came and went as the wind changed, but there was definitely some sort of noise coming from the water, and it wasn't far away.

After some minutes, the sound was closer. He peered over the edge, leaning right out to see if he could see anything.

A supersonic, high-velocity round, traveling faster than the speed of sound, hit him before he heard a thing. His body toppled over the edge to land with a dull splash. He was dead before he hit the water.

In the RIB, Masaev watched the body float silently, face down, for a few seconds. He then checked the tablet. He picked up a laser rangefinder and directed it at the dam wall. When he had a reading of fifty feet, he instructed the driver to move along until they were level with the center of the dam.

Once they were in position, he called a halt. The man at the front threw out a small anchor. It plummeted into the depths below, pulling a line behind it. Masaev knew it would come to rest at a depth of eighty feet.

When the anchor had touched down and the line was secured to the boat, he gave a signal to the two men who were fully kitted in their gear and they rolled over the sides. Once they were in the water Masaev handed them two large bags. They were about five feet in length and two feet wide. They appeared heavy. He also passed them a small buoy. It had a compact waterproof box of electronics and a coiled wire attached to it. They took them, and without a word, they slipped silently below the surface.

Half an hour later they returned without the bags and nodded at Masaev. They were hauled back into the boat along with the anchor. Masaev checked that the buoy with the wire, which now led below, was clearly visible. Once he was happy, they sped back to shore, where Kozak was waiting.

Kozak received Masaev's report. He then gathered the men around him. He looked them in the eye, one by one.

"My friends. We embark on an historic venture. Many of us will not return. But it is for our families, for our friends, and for our country, that we do this. I could not be more proud of you. When the day is done you will be able to rest well, knowing you did what was necessary to strike a blow at injustice and tyranny, and to send a message to those who think they are untouchable. They are not."

All the men crossed their chests with clenched fists and then headed quietly for the sub, entering through the hatch on the top.

Kozak and Ilya were the last to leave. Before they climbed in, Kozak pulled a small black box with a red button on top from his pocket. He extended a short aerial and handed it to his brother.

"Here, my little brother."

Ilya looked at it with eager eyes. So much power, yet so small. He glanced up at Kozak, who nodded. Ilya took the box and put his thumb over the red button. He looked out across the reservoir, toward the dam.

He pressed down hard.

Immediately there was a massive explosion of water that shot up a hundred feet into the air.

Ilya's eyes shone.

Kozak clapped him on the shoulder.

"Come, my brother. Now it begins."

Chapter Twenty-Two

The explosion ripped a massive hole in the floor of the reservoir directly above the escape tunnel from the Omega Complex.

Millions of gallons of water thundered through, the force widening the newly created gash in the roof of the tunnel. The water swept aside the cherry picker and equipment where the men had been inspecting and repairing the side of the tunnel, the leak now far greater than any they could ever have imagined.

It bulldozed all before it, sweeping into the underground area around the cocoon, shunting vehicles into a heap, like a pile of discarded toys. It filled the cave and then headed for the roof. The pressure built until it was too much for the floor of the atrium above. It exploded upward, killing anyone who had been walking there at the time. The massive statue was ripped from its stand as it was swept to one side.

Immediately the cocoon went into lockdown, the automatic systems doing their thing; pressurizing the interior so no water could get in.

In her room, five floors above, Clare was woken from her sleep. She felt a rumbling vibration in the building. It was accompanied by a strange, far-off roar. Her immediate thought was that it was an earthquake. The building had been designed way beyond the required standards, even for Los Angeles, but she had felt earthquakes before, and there was something different about this one.

She jumped out of bed, pulled on a set of sweat pants and a shirt, and then grabbed her phone and walkie-talkie and ran out of the room. There was a short corridor that led to the walkway around the atrium. All the time the vibration was becoming more profound. She ran to the walkway and then to the edge of the atrium. She looked over the side and reeled back in shock. There, two floors below, the whole building was filling with frothing, foaming water. It was creeping up the side at an alarming rate. There must have been some sort of catastrophic failure in the reservoir—they had told her a little seepage was okay—but this?

Her first thought was for Stevens and Petrovich. They were down in the cocoon, so they should be safe. Her second thought was how she could escape. The lift-track system should still be working. Her best bet was to get to the roof, where she could be evacuated by helicopter.

But then she paused.

Brad was away.

She was in charge.

It was her responsibility.

She could never live with herself if she didn't try and do something.

She tapped the app on her watch. She saw a capsule on

the floor above answer the call. It moved smoothly round to the nearest vertical track, dropped down to her level, and then moved toward her. All the time the water was rising.

It was now only one floor below.

A second later the capsule drew up. The doors opened. She stepped in. She was about to speak to the computer when she saw a confused Randal Watson stumble out onto the walkway.

"Randal! Randal!" He looked up. "Over here!" cried Clare.

Watson looked over at her, and then he saw the water. It was now lapping at the walkway. It seemed to galvanize him. He started running, his feet splashing on the carpet that was now soaking underfoot. He only just made it in time. He rushed into the capsule, slamming up against the far side. Clare shouted at the system.

"Cocoon. Entrance B!"

"Cocoon. Entrance B. Please hold on."

And with that the doors closed, just as water started to flow into the capsule. The small pod moved off around the atrium until it was over the track that led down to the rear entrance of the cocoon. Clare and Watson watched in horror as the water rose up the sides and then over the top to completely cover them. But then they were descending into the depths. As they looked out into the flooded atrium they could see debris from the force of the water. And then Clare gasped as several bodies floated past. They must have been from the night shift. She gave a cry as she recognized Sam, one of the security guards. None of them would see the light of another day.

They traveled down quickly. And then, suddenly, they entered the vertical shaft that led to the cocoon. A second later they came to a halt with a swoosh. Above them, water completely covered the cocoon, but the sides of the lift-track station were pressurized, so when the doors opened they were completely dry. Before leaving the capsule, Clare deactivated the controls so it couldn't be called elsewhere. Once she had a handle on just what had happened, this might be their only way out. When the capsule was secure, she turned to Watson.

"Randal, go and get the president and see if you can find Petrovich. Get them to the rec. I'll join you shortly. I have to talk to the security center, see what they know."

"Okay," said a visibly shaken Watson.

While he headed off to find his boss, Clare ran to the control room. There was no one there so she entered her code. The system came online, allowing her full access. The camera feeds showed the area around the cocoon, as well as the rooms and various spaces. Everything seemed to be intact for the moment. She flicked a switch to show the cameras in the main building. The water level was now up to the tenth floor and rising ever higher. A glance at the exterior cameras showed that it looked like the building was in full lockdown. The sensors had detected the 'intrusion.' All the doors had sealed. A large solid barricade had risen up against the exterior doors. Since all the windows were reinforced, pressure-proof and airtight, there was no danger of those giving way. Next, she grabbed the comms mike and hit the button.

"Security, this is Clare Kowalski in the cocoon. Anybody there?"

There was a crackle and then a reply.

"Hi, Clare, this is Rosa Hernandez. Are you okay? What happened?"

"I'm fine thanks, Rosa. It looks like there's some sort of failure at the reservoir. The water must have come down the escape tunnel. As you can probably see, it's rising up the center of the building. Are you guys okay in there?"

"All, good. The system's sealed, so at least it works okay. The problem will be if the water goes all the way to the roof. If it overflows, it'll hit Los Angeles. I've already informed disaster relief agencies. They should be here soon. Also, Harry's on his way in. How are the presidents?"

"I'm not sure yet. Checking in with you first. I'm going to see them now. I have my radio with me, so keep me updated, and let me know when Harry gets in. I have to go."

Before she left, she picked up a tannoy system mike. "Everyone in the cocoon, please make your way to the rec room. You may be aware there has been an incident. All is fine. The structure is built to withstand far worse. I'll talk to you all in a couple of minutes." She clicked off the mike, feeling somewhat more in control. She then paused for moment.

Why tonight, Brad… of all nights? I really wish you were here.

She then checked her walkie-talkie was turned on and hurried down the corridor to the rec. Anyone she passed, she ushered them forward ahead of her.

Before joining them she made a detour to check the other entrances to the cocoon to make sure they were intact. The main lift-track was secure, but there was no capsule there so it wouldn't make for an escape route. She then checked on the main airlock that led into the cave outside the cocoon. It too was secure. She looked through the glass panels on the door into the wide pressurized corridor that led to the outer door. So far there were no leaks. They had air. They could breathe, and the provisions had been recently stocked. They were in pretty good shape. She would just need to check on the house guests and find out who else was in the cocoon. And then coordinate with Harry in the security center as to how to get everyone out.

Hopefully, it should all be over by lunchtime.

When she walked onto the raised gallery overlooking the rec, she could see there were eight people there. Stevens and Petrovich were with their respective bodyguards. Watson was also with Stevens, while there was a blonde female adviser with Petrovich. There were also two night staff from the cocoon, both looking suitably anxious. There was the sound of general chatter and muttering. She realized, sadly, that the national security advisers and chiefs of staff of both countries had been up in the building above. She had to assume they were dead.

Clare took a deep breath. She moved forward until she was halfway along the gallery.

"Ladies and gentleman, if I may have your attention."

Slowly the muttering subsided. All faces turned to look at her. She saw a mix of worry and concern, but also a look of irritation on some of the faces. The two leaders were looking fairly stoic, if not completely relaxed.

"I'm sorry you've all been woken at this hour, but as you may have guessed, we have an unprecedented situation we're dealing with. It would appear there's been some sort of failure with the roof of the tunnel that provides an exit from the cavern outside the cocoon. It's allowed water from the Griffith Park reservoir to enter the tunnel and surround the cocoon. I have no idea what's caused this, but I've been in contact with the security center topside and all the appropriate authorities have been informed. You are perfectly safe here in the cocoon. We have supplies, enough for a couple of weeks, but hopefully you should all be out of here by lunchtime. We're just working on what will be the safest and quickest way to get you out. In the meantime, I suggest you stay in the rec area and grab a coffee, or even an early breakfast. I'll keep you up to date with any developments. Now, does anyone have any questions?"

She looked around the group, feeling somewhat more confident now she had their attention and had got her speech out of the way. However, her confidence was about to be well and truly shaken.

Stevens stepped forward, a thunderous expression on his face. He looked up at her with contempt.

"What has happened to my national security adviser and chief of staff?"

Clare took a deep breath.

"I'm afraid, sir, they were staying in the accommodation on the fifth floor, as were yours, President Petrovich. It's unlikely they survived. When I left there myself, the water was moving above the level. I didn't see anyone apart from Randal here. There wasn't time to get anyone else. I'm sorry."

"How on earth could you let something like this happen?" shouted Stevens. "And where is Brad Walker? Why isn't he dealing with this?"

Clare's cheeks flushed. "I'm afraid Mr. Walker is away in New York. He had to leave at short notice. Some corporate issue to deal with. But I can assure you, sir, I am more than capable of handling what we need to do."

"Yeah, right!" said Stevens.

Petrovich looked up at Clare.

"I'm sure Miss Kowalski will do all she can to keep us safe. I, for one, am more than happy to let her do her job." He smiled reassuringly at Clare.

"Thank you, sir. I'll do my best. Now please just relax. We'll all be out of here in no time."

She turned and headed back toward the control center,

all of a sudden not having nearly as much faith in the veracity of the words she had just spoken.

The wall of the dam that held back four billion gallons of water was designed in classic style. The top was far narrower than the bottom. It stood to reason, the base would take more of the pressure exerted by the water. Engineers had calculated the stresses caused by a certain volume and depth and the forces that would be exerted on the concrete wall. This, in turn, had led to a calculation as to how thick the wall should be at various depths.

What the calculation had not taken into account was the force exerted by a nearby detonation of carefully placed Semtex charges.

The effect had been somewhat negative.

The result was that thirty feet up from the bottom of the reservoir, several small fissures had been created, allowing the water to worm its way through the concrete.

Twenty minutes later it had progressed to within a hair's breadth of the outside of the dam wall.

A moment later, a small dribble, which quickly became a spurt, barely a quarter of an inch wide, erupted from the concrete. It left a thin wet stain on the otherwise dry wall as it gracefully tumbled to the slipway below, now free of the constraints of the lake behind.

Chapter Twenty-Three

Andriy Kozak peered out of the domed front of *Deep Intruder*. The visibility in the reservoir had reduced to a few feet following the explosion.

As he neared the entrance to the tunnel, he could feel the sub being pulled forward as millions of gallons of water flowed down, sucking them toward the large hole in the bottom of the lake.

He glanced back at his men in the rear. "Hold on!"

And with that, he steered the sub into the tunnel.

It was rough. The hull was thrown against the sides of the passage, and it was all Kozak could do to hold it steady. He had waited as long as he could to allow the water to fill the complex. He had previously calculated the depth of the reservoir in relation to the height of the main building. He had to make educated assumptions about the flow rate into the tunnel, not knowing exactly how large the hole created by the explosives would be, but he reckoned the water would almost completely fill the building, maybe even spill over the top, and that the flow would slow anytime soon.

His calculations proved to be correct. As they approached the end of the tunnel leading into the cave housing the cocoon, the flow rate started to slow. In fact, once he was out of the tunnel and had moved to one side, he could control the sub and bring her to a stop, settling on the floor of the cave. The schematics had shown the layout, but right now, debris and piled-up vehicles filled most of the space surrounding the cocoon.

He checked the weapon controls and lined up a small torpedo to blast the overturned cars and trucks out of the way. He squeezed the trigger and watched as the projectile sped through the water. It hit the center of the mass of vehicles. A second later a dull thud echoed through the water. The vehicles disappeared in a mass of bubbles and twisted metal. After a few minutes the visibility started to clear. Kozak could see the entrance to the main airlock. He pushed forward on the thruster controls, moving the sub closer to the entrance.

Once stationary on the bottom, he turned to his men.

"Okay, let's do this."

They donned their gear and carried their weapons in waterproof bags. Kozak led them out through the hatch in the bottom of *Deep Intruder* and over to the airlock. He pulled out a waterproof pad, checked the code for the entry door and entered it. A display confirmed the code had been accepted. A further message then said to stand by while equalization took place.

They watched the airlock fill with water, equalizing the pressure to the outside. Finally, a green light blinked and the doors slid open. The men swam into the airlock. Once inside, the outer door closed, and the procedure was repeated at the inner door. This time the water drained out of the airlock. When it was clear, the inner door opened.

Kozak looked in at the interior of the cocoon. A corridor led off ahead of him to some steps. He could hear the sound of people talking beyond double swing doors at the top of the stairs. He checked his men. They quietly removed their gear and dropped it to the floor. They then pulled automatic weapons from the bags. Once they were ready, Kozak indicated for one of them to stand guard at the airlock and for the others to follow him.

He held his weapon to his shoulder and aimed forward, moving with the precision and expertise of a soldier. He knew the layout by heart from studying the plans. He walked down the corridor and up the stairs that led to the gallery overlooking the rec. He pushed the door open and walked through.

As he looked down he saw a relaxed group of people. He had no real feelings toward them. But the two most important ones were to be protected at all costs. The others were expendable. He knew the construction of the cocoon could withstand the ammunition their weapons used, but he'd given strict instructions for his men to only fire when absolutely necessary. Should either of the presidents be killed or seriously injured it would have a major impact on whether they could achieve their objectives.

A second later he fired a short burst of automatic fire at the ceiling to get their attention.

It did.

All faces turned in shock to look up at the gallery. When they saw the armed men their reactions varied. The two cocoon staff tried to run for the door to the kitchen and were gunned down mercilessly by Kozak. It would send a useful message that there were consequences to resistance.

The presidents were unusually calm, merely looking up at Kozak and the men who had joined him on the gallery. It was immediately clear to Kozak who the bodyguards were. Only two of the group had looked around, gauging the options, the opposition and the odds. They had wisely chosen to do nothing for the moment, but Kozak knew who he had to be concerned with. They could be dangerous. They might have to be sacrificed as another example. There were only two other people in the room. He assumed they were assistants of some kind. At least the numbers were manageable. They might be here for some time. He wondered how many others were in the cocoon. He indicated for Masaev to take one of the men to find the control room and guard it, and then search the facility and bring anyone they found back here.

The group was still watching him. There was a palpable tension in the air. It was as though they wanted to speak but no one was willing to go first.

He stepped forward.

"My name is Andriy Kozak. I was a member of Ukrainian special forces." At this he could see a slight creasing of the forehead of Viktor Petrovich. "As you have seen"—he indicated the two dead staff members—"I will not hesitate to punish those who cause me problems or do not do as I instruct. However, my intention is not to harm you. But you need to understand that I am serious in what I ask, and I will not be persuaded to deviate from my path. Of that you should be very clear." He paused and looked at all the faces. "First, I would ask anyone who has a weapon to put it on the table below the gallery. I know which of you work in security, so please do not try my patience." He watched as no one moved. He then looked directly at the two bodyguards. A second later, Paul Murphy stood up and walked toward Kozak. He placed a small pistol on the table. Kozak then looked pointedly at Ivan Igorov. It took a ten-second stare-off before the Russian complied. When he did, he put down a far larger weapon on the table. As he walked back to his seat he sneered at Murphy, as though the size of the weapon somehow showed his superiority. Kozak smiled at the petty slight from the Russian.

"Now, you are probably wondering why we are here." He looked around the group. "We are here because of the actions of the Russian government, which nobody has seen fit to curb for many years. That is going to change."

Glances were shot at Petrovich, but for his part he remained expressionless. His eyes were fixed on Kozak with a deadly intensity.

Clare had been checking the integrity of the sensors in the control room when she heard what sounded like gunfire. At first she couldn't believe it could be, so she'd walked out into the corridor to see if she could hear any better. A few seconds later and there were two more bursts of fire. For a second, she hesitated. The only people who were armed were the bodyguards. Surely they couldn't have got into an altercation, though she knew there was no love lost between them. She made a decision and returned to the control room to check the monitors. As she flicked through the various cameras she eventually came to the rec. She operated the controls to move the camera round. When she saw the bloodied bodies of the staff on the floor she threw her hand to her mouth. Everyone else was accounted for. It was only when she rotated the camera further, to face the gallery, that she saw the armed men. She grabbed the mike and looked at the monitor that showed a view of the security center above.

"Rosa, this is Clare. We have a situation."

There was no reply for an agonizing few seconds. She then saw Hernandez sit down at the comms and look straight into the camera "Clare, go ahead. Anything new?"

"You could say that. We have armed men in the cocoon. There are at least six that I can see and they've shot…"

At that moment, a large hand grabbed her from behind and pulled her sharply backward. She cried out, falling to the floor. On the screen, Hernandez looked out with concern.

"Clare! Clare!"

Masaev looked into the camera and then shot it out. Immediately the image faded from the screen. A second man picked up Clare. She was struggling, trying to shout, but he clamped a hand over her mouth. Masaev looked over the control panel, found the camera controls and systematically clicked them all off. He then turned to Clare. She stared at him in fear. He smacked her across the face and then twisted her arm behind her back, driving it up toward her shoulder, causing her to cry out.

"Try to escape and I break your arm, okay?"

"Yes," was all Clare could manage through the pain.

He then grabbed the walkie-talkie from her belt and the phone from her pocket and smashed them both. He turned to the other man. "Stay here. Don't let anyone in. If anyone approaches you, shoot them."

The man nodded.

Masaev pulled Clare roughly from the room and headed down the corridor toward the rec.

Kozak looked around the group. His men covered every angle. No one moved.

"For years the government in Moscow has seen fit to

rape and pillage my country. They have annexed Crimea and are waging an unjust war against my people in the east. Thousands have been killed. No one is doing anything about it. You will be free to go when an agreement has been reached to end this war. For the Russian troops to withdraw. For Crimea to be returned to Ukrainian sovereignty and for reparations to be paid. Nothing less will be acceptable." He paused. "And this must be completed within the next forty-eight hours."

"Or what?"

The question came from Petrovich. It was said with an icy calm by the calculating hard man who had presided over the continuation of the war his predecessor had left behind. He was a man who didn't compromise. He had no intention of doing so now.

Kozak looked at Petrovich with such a relaxed assuredness and total commitment that it almost caused Petrovich to hesitate.

"Or, Mr. President, there will be an attack on New York so destructive, so definitive, it will make nine-eleven look like a minor car crash. The city will be wiped from the face of the Earth. There will be no mercy. There will only be death. Annihilation. Total destruction."

"Hang on a minute," blurted out Stevens. "I thought you said your problem was with Russia. Why is America being threatened?"

Kozak turned to Stevens, a scornful expression on his face.

"Because, Mr. President, any threats against Russia would be ignored by its president." He looked at Petrovich. "He would not care or act to protect people's lives if it meant he had to back down and face humiliation in front of the entire world. No, the only way he would back down is if you, Mr. President, exert pressure on him that is so overwhelming he has no choice. Something you and the UN should have done years ago but failed to do. Perhaps now you will have the incentive to do so."

Stevens stared at him in shock. Petrovich almost had an air of respect for Kozak on his face.

Stevens glanced around and then looked back at Kozak. "How do we even know your threat is credible? You could be bluffing."

Kozak looked at him evenly. "Yes, I could, but I am here, aren't I? You think this was easy? Taking out New York will be simple compared to this."

Stevens was thinking. "You say it will be worse than nine-eleven, which means you'll attack from the air. We can ground all aircraft. Have the air force patrol the skies. You wouldn't get through. We have a warning this time." He smiled, triumphant, but not completely sure. It was as though he realized the planning the terrorists had been through would not make things that simple.

"Indeed, Mr. President. You could do all of that, and I would tell you not to waste your time. It would make no difference."

Stevens was mulling this over when Masaev dragged Clare into the room. She looked around, wide-eyed, at the group. Kozak glanced at Masaev.

"She was the only one I could find. Dimitri is at the control center. He will keep an eye on things. She contacted the security center, but that was to be expected. They know we are here but they are blind."

"Good," said Kozak. "Put her with the others."

Masaev pushed Clare down the stairs to the lower part of the room. She walked shakily over to the group. Murphy smiled at her. She smiled weakly back.

Kozak turned to face them all.

"Now, you have much to discuss. My men are in control of the cocoon. If you do anything to try to leave, to get a message to the surface, you will be dealt with harshly. Other than that, you are free to move around. Do not test me and you will get through this. If I have cause to, I can make things much more unpleasant for you."

He then turned to the two presidents.

"You have forty-eight hours."

When the camera had been blown out in the cocoon control room there had been an abrupt flash on the screen in front of Hernandez. There was also a loud crackle through the speaker. She found it hard to take in what Clare had told her, but the presence of the armed men had meant she didn't have much choice. She was working out what to do when Harry Patterson strode into the room and marched straight over to her.

"What the hell's going on?"

After Hernandez had told an increasingly incredulous Patterson what had happened, he stood there for a moment processing what he'd heard. He was then suddenly all focus and concentration.

"Contact San Diego. Get me the duty commander. Tell him it's a Code Zulu and let me know when you have him."

"Yes, sir."

Patterson then walked quickly over to his own station and picked up the phone. He dialed a number. It rang eight times before being picked up. The voice at the other end was sleepy and not happy.

"Yep, Harry. Guess this must be urgent to call at this time," said Brad Walker.

"Yes, sir. It is."

Patterson relayed what Hernandez had told him. When he finished there was a pause.

"Have you been able to locate Clare?"

Patterson paused and took a deep breath.

"The bad news is there are no survivors from the main building, except here in the control center, which has been isolated and is secure. The good news is we believe she's alive. But I'm afraid she's in the cocoon with the terrorists."

There was silence from the other end.

"Sir?"

"Is she okay?"

"I can't be sure, sir. She was talking to Rosa when two men burst in and pulled her off camera. They then disabled the cameras and comms. We don't know her current status."

Again, there was a pause.

"Okay, keep me advised. I'll be back as soon as I can."

Chapter Twenty-Four

Ever since she'd been a little girl, Yana Kuznetsov had loved science. To her it was like magic made real. How chemicals could react together to produce something new; how animals had evolved through evolution; and most significantly, how the planets moved around the sun and the seemingly infinite number of stars and celestial bodies there were out there in the galaxies and ultimately the universe. It had blown her mind, so much so that she'd dedicated her life to the pursuit of the unknown, and taken the curiosity of a child and made it her life's work.

Now, in her early thirties, she had another purpose, one that had taken over deep inside and focused her attention beyond the dreams she'd had as a little girl. It involved her passion and her skillset, but fused with a calling she now knew she had, which was to right a wrong that had been done in the world. In fact, the calling had consumed her to the point that nothing else mattered. She was only glad her experience and position allowed her to help in such an important mission.

These and other thoughts were going through her mind as she arrived at the research station for what would be a stay of a few weeks, maybe less if her plans didn't turn out as she hoped.

The journey had been rougher than she'd expected, but she'd been warned about that. But now, in the confines of the habitat, sealed against the extremes of the cold outside, she could relax and get to know her fellow scientists and explorers.

The station was multinational, with contributions from many nations making the research and funding possible. She knew one of the other scientists on the team, Dr. Karl Gruber from Germany. The other one, Andrea Petersen from Sweden, she had heard of by reputation and was looking forward to meeting. As she made her way through the entrance, Gruber came forward, a big smile on his face, his arms held out.

"Yana, it's great to see you again. How was your trip?"

Yana hugged the huge man and smiled back. "Hi, Karl, good to see you too. Trip was interesting, but exhilarating."

"That's what they all say."

Gruber led her over to a small, intense-looking woman who was working on some equipment at the side of the space they were in.

"Yana, I'd like you to meet Andrea Petersen. She's on her final leg. Going home on the next rotation."

Andrea moved forward and smiled. "Hello, Yana, I've heard a lot about you. It's great that you're here. Too much testosterone around recently!" They all laughed.

"Now, I'll show you around," said Petersen.

While Yana knew the layout of the base, having trained on a mock-up of the facility, it was great to finally be in the real thing.

Gruber introduced her to the team commander, Jonas Jackson, a laid-back American from Kansas, who spoke slowly, but clearly had a whole lot going on upstairs. He even carried a 'lucky' cigar he brought with him on every trip to smoke when he returned home safely.

Once she'd settled in and found her sleeping quarters, she checked over the kit she'd brought with her. While she would be conducting experiments herself, she was also there as an electronics, software and communications expert. When you were miles from any form of rescue, you had to be as self-sufficient as possible. Her first task was to check the main computer control systems were all in good shape. While much of this could be done remotely, there had been a few glitches recently, which fell under her brief. It had been lucky they'd happened around now, given her time slot at the base had been planned months before.

The layout was fairly straightforward. It was of a modular design, creating a long structure with additional modules at various points along the side. Everything was grouped in relation to the contributing countries. Each had their own module where their scientists could work and sleep. There were additional modules for specific experiments and for exercising, as well as a command and control module where the main communications and computer systems were located.

Once she was happy things were as she had expected, she pulled out her laptop and went through a program she'd written specifically for the mission.

Ten minutes later she was sure everything was in order. She smiled to herself. It looked like all was set. She just had to wait for a message that would tell her it was time to start.

Chapter Twenty-Five

John McCready couldn't remember a time he'd felt more exhausted.

When they'd returned from the premiere, he'd been in a daze. However self-congratulatory, however gratuitous you thought the celebrity lifestyle was, until you'd experienced it from the other side, no one could really prepare you for what it was like. And while he knew full well he was just a fifth wheel in the process, he'd felt a thrill he'd never thought he would. The sheer number of people screaming for Brandy had been overwhelming. And by association, like she'd said, people looked at him in a way no one had ever looked at him before. And while he knew it was false and didn't really mean anything, he had guiltily found it exhilarating. It was the ultimate aphrodisiac.

When they'd returned to the hotel room and Brandy had hung the DO NOT DISTURB sign on the door, it was all he could do not to grab her, lift her off her feet, and carry her straight to the bedroom. And he would have done, if she hadn't grabbed him first.

What had followed had been a night like he'd never known. He'd always thought of himself as fairly broad-minded but this girl knew things he had never imagined.

Now, at six in the morning, half an hour since she had woken him, she rolled back onto her side of the bed, a look of mischievous excitement still on her face. She draped an arm over his chest. He could feel her heart beating fast, pressed close against him. He was breathing heavily and staring at the ceiling, a feeling of total contentment, if not exhaustion, spreading throughout his body.

She suddenly brought her face close to his and kissed him cruelly. While there was a vulnerable and innocent side to her, there was also a wicked and insatiable side that made being with her a new and delicious experience. A couple of minutes later she climbed back on top and looked down with that suggestive smile.

At that moment, McCready's phone rang. He tried to move, but she wouldn't let him, gripping him with her thighs. He tried again, but now it was a game.

"Don't get it, John!"

"I have to. It might be important."

"More important than me?"

He pulled a face.

"You get that phone, no candy for John."

He smacked her on the backside, which made her squeal with delight. He then easily rolled her off him, stood up naked and walked over to the table by the window to pick up his phone. He checked the caller ID. Craig.

"Morning. Little early for a call, isn't it?" He was still breathing heavily.

There was a hesitation at the other end. "You okay? You don't sound too good."

"It's nothing. Just a late night."

"Yeah, right, I saw it on TV. Almost didn't recognize you."

"Yeah, yeah."

"No, really, John, you should take it easy. Sounds like you need a brandy or something."

At this, McCready glanced over at the bed, where she was peering at him with those come-to-bed eyes peeking above the sheets.

McCready turned his attention back to the phone and grinned. "No thanks. Just had one."

"Okay, but look after yourself."

"So, why the call?"

"Sorry, mate, but you know I said we didn't need you up here? There's been a major problem with the Skyline system. We're going to have to make some big decisions that will involve you. Can you get back today?"

McCready thought for a moment. He glanced at Brandy, who was now pouting. He scrunched up his eyes and sighed.

"Yeah, okay, I'll do my best." And then added, "And I think I will take your advice."

"Huh?"

"Have another drink."

With that, he clicked off the phone and walked back to the bed. He slipped under the sheets and she wrapped her legs around him.

"So what was that all about?"

He took a deep breath.

"I have to go back to Scotland. Something's come up."

She looked at him with an innocent expression and then he felt her reaching down beneath the sheets.

"You are so right, Mr. McCready. What on earth are we going to do about it?"

Half an hour later, McCready climbed out of bed and walked into the en suite bathroom and straight into the shower. He let the water run hot and then cold to wake him up and return him to the real world.

When he emerged, with a towel tight around his waist, Brandy stared at him from the bed, a relaxed and satisfied expression on her face. The vulnerable, innocent woman was back.

"Do you have to go, John? I feel so great when I'm with you." Those innocent eyes stared up at him.

McCready crossed over and sat on the bed next to her.

"I've had one of the most amazing nights of my life." She smiled, and he thought he could detect the gleam of love in her eyes. "But you… and me… you really think it could work?"

She just stared at him. "Come back with me to LA. We could try."

"Stay here. We could try." His gaze was unwavering.

She sighed. "I can't. I've a million things to do. Meetings for my next movie. Sponsor commitments. Functions to attend. It's all part of the job."

McCready smiled. "I know, and I'd never want to take you away from that, but we're from different worlds. We're different people."

He thought he could see an instant of panic in her eyes, but then it was gone. Instead there was that pleading look that was almost impossible to resist.

"I'm not that person, John," she said sadly. "I hoped maybe you might realize that. 'Brandy Carmine' is just a product. It's not *me*." She looked imploringly at him.

"I know. I didn't think I would believe that, but I do. It's just that there is that other side. And I'm not cut out for that sort of life."

"What if I said I'd give it up?"

This he hadn't expected.

He hesitated.

He looked straight into her eyes, trying to see if it was the actress talking or the little girl. He decided he couldn't tell.

He chose his words carefully. "I would say that I could never ask, or expect, you to, and that if you did, I think you'd miss it. You'd eventually come to blame me, resent me, and we'd part badly. I would never want that."

She looked at him with such sadness that he wondered if she'd misunderstood what he'd said.

"I didn't…"

"No… no, John." She paused, then looked into his eyes. "You know, you're everything I ever dreamed of in a man when I was growing up, but you're right, my life took a different turn, and part of me would not be able to give that up. If I really think about it, deep down, I know you're right, but I'll never give up hope that I'm wrong, that maybe one day…"

"Brandy, if I'm honest, my heart tells me to go with you. But it's not enough. In the past I've always followed my heart, tried to do the right thing, which is probably why I'm still alone. I've hurt people I care about. I never want to do that again."

She looked at him sadly and smiled. "Which is why you're the perfect man I can never have."

She scrunched over to him on the bed. He lay down next to her quietly and stroked her hair as he held her gently.

Room service had brought up breakfast an hour later.

They'd eaten in bed, where little had been said between them. They'd both known they didn't have much time left together. Her flight was later that morning, and she would leave straight after she was dressed. She'd whispered in his ear that one day he'd realize how much he needed her and couldn't live without her. He'd smiled and held her tight. She'd told him the room was booked for the rest of the day, so to stay as long as he liked.

After breakfast they'd cuddled up again for a while.

Then, quietly, Brandy had climbed out of bed and showered and dressed. Before she'd even put on her makeup and done her hair, her phone had rung. And then, like before, it was as though a switch had been flicked. The film star was back, fielding calls from Shelby, her publicist, and her agent, who'd set up five meetings for her when she got back to LA.

Now, as she was preparing to leave, and the porter arrived to take her bags down to the car, McCready watched her with admiration tinged with a certain sadness. He would never forget his time with her. But he also knew he'd made the right decision. She was someone he would never—could never—forget, but he'd be able to observe her from afar, as he knew her career would go from strength to strength.

Though he would never be able to watch a Brandy Carmine movie again in quite the same way.

Chapter Twenty-Six

When the call had come in, Commander David Bryce had been asleep in his bed. He and his wife had had friends around the previous evening and a late night had been enjoyed by all. He was due a day off so he had indulged maybe a little more than he would normally have done, but you only live once, as they say.

However, when the duty commander at the base had told him what had happened at the Omega Complex, he'd been fully awake within seconds. When you had to fight through adversity, years of military training came to the fore, even if the adversity was caused by a bottle of Chardonnay and several whiskies.

As he drove through the security gate at the entrance to the base, his mind had already worked out three different scenarios as an initial response. It would, of course, depend on additional information he'd receive when he had a chance to talk to the security controller at the complex, but at least it was a start.

It was now fully light. He could see it was going to be another hot, clear day. There was hardly a cloud in the sky.

He pulled into his parking space next to his office just as Mitch Harley drew up in his Jeep Wrangler. Harley jumped down and walked toward him. He was looking fit and fresh. Bryce cursed his advancing years. He knew his men were young and fit, but it still reminded him of his mortality. He beckoned Harley over and strode into the building. He walked down to his office at the end with Harley in tow.

Once inside, he pushed the door to.

"Must be serious, sir. Haven't had a 'return to base' request for six months."

"It is, Mitch. Take a seat."

Harley sat down, a tingling sensation running up his spine. This was what he lived for.

Bryce looked at him for a second before he spoke.

"You know that new conference center over in LA?"

"The one where the president's meeting the Russians?"

"The very one. Well, it's been taken over by terrorists."

"Jesus!"

"That's not the half of it. The facility has an escape tunnel that runs under the Griffith Park reservoir. This appears to have been compromised by blowing a hole through the bottom of the lake. Right now, the Omega Complex is full of water. All two hundred feet of it. The pressure even blew off the roof."

Harley didn't say anything. He was trying to comprehend the enormity of what had happened. Then he looked up.

"And the presidents?"

"The facility has an underground cocoon that can seal against any form of attack. There's air and supplies to keep them going for a couple of weeks. It appears the terrorists have managed to circumvent the security systems and gained entry."

"So, we have our president and the president of Russia sealed inside a pressure-proof cocoon two hundred feet underwater with a bunch of terrorists?"

"That's about the size of it."

"Pheeeew."

"And you know what the real kicker is?"

Harley waited for the answer.

"It looks like they used *Deep Intruder* to gain access. The security center saw it on CCTV before the terrorists cut the feeds."

Harley just stared at his commander, but he found himself gripping the arms of his chair with increasing intensity.

"This is a big one, Mitch. Not only are the lives of two presidents at stake, but this is personal. You have to get these bastards. I don't want one of them left alive. You got that?"

"Loud and clear, sir."

"Okay, we need to be on-site as soon as possible so we can assess equipment and plan an approach. As a start, I want two chambers and a four-man team with full dive gear and weapons ready to go on the pad in one hour. There'll be two Sea Stallions ready and waiting. Can you do that?"

"Yes, sir."

"Good. Get to it, and bring Doctor Fletcher as medical supervisor. We may have to sedate the presidents to get them out. We'll need drugs and positive flow masks, like they used on that Thailand cave rescue in 2018. Have Fletcher source the drugs and go through any procedures with her. We have to be ready for anything."

"Sir."

Harley walked out of the office at a brisk pace. His mind

was whirling. The task ahead seemed impossible. But that was why he had joined the SEALs—to achieve the impossible.

He walked across the large car park just as two cars pulled in. One was a highly modded Trans Am, the other a new Ford pickup. He watched Miller and Garcia climb out and head over to him. They'd almost reached him when a third vehicle, a battered Land Rover Defender, raced in and skidded to a halt. Another SEAL climbed out.

"Hey, Anders," shouted Harley. "Over here."

Anders came over to join the group.

Ten minutes later Harley had briefed them on the situation. As he'd spoken, their expressions had turned from incredulity to a hard-set realization of what lay ahead, as well as a grim determination to avenge their friends and colleagues. There was no jovial banter, no horsing around. They left quickly to prepare their gear.

Harley then walked over to the medical block. It was still early but he knew Connie had been working on the next stage of the hemofilter research and was always in by six in the morning these days.

As he entered the lab, she looked up.

She smiled. "Wow, you're up bright and early." But then her face fell as she saw his expression. "Hey, what is it?" she asked with concern.

"It's bad, Con."

He explained everything quickly and again watched as her expression changed from shock and anger to a steadfast determination.

"Okay, give me five minutes to clear up here. I'll bring the hemofilters for your team and I'll source the drugs, medical supplies, and gas requirements for the chambers.

They're always prepped ready to go, but I need to double check."

"Bryce said one hour on the pad. I'll see you there."

Connie nodded, but Harley could detect a slight nervousness about her. She normally stayed on the base. For Bryce to ask her to go into the field was a big step. While they were on American soil, and she wasn't being sent into a war zone, they were clearly dealing with ruthless, dangerous people; who knew what might happen?

An hour later they were assembled at the side of the helipad. Bryce oversaw the operation. First, the dive gear and weapons were loaded into the Sea Stallions. Following this, the men and Connie climbed into one chopper. Bryce climbed into the other.

As the massive helicopters lifted off, the roar was deafening. When they had risen to a height of thirty feet, they moved slowly to the side of the pad in a stable hover. A thick cable hung below each helicopter. A ground crew waved them in line until they were exactly above two recompression chambers. One was larger than the other. The chambers were located in strong metal frames. Around each frame a series of long, fat metal cylinders were securely attached. They contained oxygen and helium for the rebreathers, as well as air for the chambers, and additional oxygen as a therapeutic gas for any treatment.

Once the cables were attached, a controller on the ground gave the all clear to the pilots. A moment later the engine noise increased to a crescendo as they lifted up, hauling the chambers into the sky. When they were at a height of a hundred feet and clear of the buildings, the two helicopters, with their important cargo slung beneath, banked smoothly round and headed north toward Los Angeles.

When he had been awoken at an ungodly hour, Gregory Mason, the manager of the Griffith Park dam, had not believed what he had been told. There had been some sort of incident at the reservoir that had led to water entering the Omega Complex tunnel and flooding the building. He had, at first, thought it was a practical joke, but the explosion of fury from the man called Harry Patterson, the security controller at the complex, had soon made him realize he was serious.

He had then high-tailed it over to the dam from his home in West LA. When he got there, he found the level of the dam had dropped somewhat. When he entered the main building, he found it deserted. There was no sign of Brett or Gemma.

He was walking along the top of the dam, looking out over the surface of the water, the light increasing all the time, when something attracted his attention. It was floating about thirty feet out from the wall. He moved closer. The object was about three feet long. It was black with something white on it. As a shaft of sunlight fell onto it he stopped in his tracks. He could now see he was looking at the back of a T-shirt that was still attached to its owner. The white he had seen looked like a series of building blocks piled on top of each other. In scrawly writing across it, he could make out the words *The Wall*.

He staggered back from the side and pulled out his phone. He dialed 911, though it looked like there'd be a whole load more departments up here if even half of what he'd been told was true.

He walked over to the other side of the dam, thinking things couldn't get any worse. But as he looked down the steep wall he noticed a dark patch about forty feet from the bottom. As he watched, what looked like a small squirt of water suddenly became a jet. It shot out ten feet, pulling some of the concrete with it. He looked at it for a second, but then his eyes moved up to the hundreds of homes and thousands of people that lay in the shadow of the dam.

"Oh my God!"

He lifted the phone again and noticed his hands were trembling.

Chapter Twenty-Seven

The meeting room in the cocoon was situated just beyond the rec. It could act like a mini conference center, and while it didn't have the space, facilities and view of the larger one up in the main building, it did give the leaders somewhere they could meet in relative quiet. Before he had left them, Kozak had told them he would be monitoring the CCTV in the control room, so they shouldn't think they could plan any form of takeover or escape while in there.

The two sides were now seated round the conference table. It was square and took up most of the middle of the room. At each end were two seating areas, consisting of a couch, a couple of comfortable chairs and a glass table. These could be used for more private conversations for the respective sides.

The bodyguards had been left outside. The only people in the room were Stevens, Petrovich, Randal Watson and Petrovich's assistant.

As Stevens had expected, they had reached an impasse.

"No, Mr. President, as I have told you, I will not... I

cannot withdraw forces from Ukraine, and I will certainly not cede Crimea back to them. I would lose all credibility at home and around the world."

Stevens was getting exasperated.

"But Viktor, if you do not, then we may well both die down here and there will be massive loss of life in New York. You have to see the bigger picture. Once we are free of this and the city is safe, we can talk about the future of the region in a way that is mutually beneficial for all concerned and gives you a way out without losing face. Right now, I am more concerned about saving lives."

Petrovich looked dubious. But he was thinking.

"We do not even know if this man has the capability of doing what he says," said Petrovich. "As you said yourself, you can ground planes. Anything that tries to get through, you will see coming a mile away and can shoot down. I say he is bluffing."

"But it's not Moscow he's talking about, it's New York," said Stevens in frustration. "How would you act if it was one of your cities being threatened?"

Petrovich's face hardened. "In exactly the same way."

And in that instant Stevens knew the man meant it. He also knew that Kozak had been right to threaten America. The Russian leader didn't care about his people. Image was more important.

"I need to discuss this privately," said Stevens. He walked over with Watson to the corner chairs and sat down. He leaned in and spoke in hushed tones. "Randal, what are we going to do?"

"It's tricky, sir. We don't know the exact form of any attack, or when it will come, but if this Kozak isn't bluffing, I don't see any way Petrovich is going to give in, so I'm sure the attack will come."

"We have to get word outside, so they at least have time to prepare. God, this is going to affect my numbers!"

Watson looked at him incredulously. "How can we do that? We're completely locked down."

Stevens looked around. Petrovich was deep in conversation with his adviser. "Go and get that Kowalski woman. If anyone knows how to, she will."

Watson stood up and left the room. Petrovich watched him go, before glancing over at Stevens with a superior look.

Five minutes later Watson retuned with Clare and led her over to Stevens. He looked up at her with a disdainful expression.

"Sit!"

Clare sat, her expression neutral.

It looked to her as though Stevens was having a hard time containing himself.

"Firstly, how the hell could you let something like this happen?"

"Sir, with the greatest respect, this is not something that could have been foreseen."

"Bullshit! It's your job to cover every scenario. Security is the most important factor. There will be a reckoning when this is over."

"I'm sure there will be," said Clare evenly, "but you're secure, you're alive, and everyone out there will be doing everything they can to try and resolve the situation."

"As may be. Right now, we have a bigger problem. The threat this maniac has laid out. We can't afford to ignore it. We have to be ready for whatever he has planned. Is there any way to get a message outside? Let them know what's happening."

Clare thought for a moment. She glanced around the room, as well as a quick look up at the security camera in the corner. It was at the far end so unlikely to be able to pick up their conversation from that distance. Even so, she hunkered toward them and spoke in a whisper. "There's an emergency hard line in the control room, but they have it manned and guarded, and there's only a narrow corridor to approach by. Unless we can create a distraction to draw them out, which is unlikely, that's a no-go."

Stevens looked frustrated.

"But there might be another way," she said, thinking. "There's a capsule that uses the lift-track system at the rear of the cocoon. They may know about it but I haven't seen any of their men in that part of the facility. If I could get to it I might be able to get a message out. Whether they receive it topside, that's another matter."

"Couldn't we try and escape that way?" asked Watson.

"It would be too dangerous. I've no idea what's happened above us in the main building, other than it's flooded. The track could be damaged. The capsule could leak on the way up. If you got stuck and it filled with water, you'd be dead. If there's just a message in there, nothing's lost. But people..." She let her words hang.

"Okay," said Stevens. "I'll write something out for you."

"Yes, sir. Include as much as you can about the terrorists —numbers, names you've heard. Anything to give them an edge."

Stevens glanced up, looking annoyed at being told what to do, but he nodded slowly and started to write on a pad.

Once Stevens had given Clare the note, she had to get to the rear lift-track capsule on the upper level without being seen. To do this she would have to somehow disable the cameras in the control room.

She made her way along the corridor from the meeting room into the rec.

Kozak and three of his men watched her as she walked in. The two bodyguards were also there. She had managed to talk to Paul Murphy earlier, and he had buoyed her spirits by trying to lighten the mood, which she appreciated. Igorov, on the other hand, had continued to leer at her. She looked at them all, a pleasant smile on her face.

"Like some coffee?"

Kozak glanced at the others and then back at Clare.

"Thank you."

"Thanks, Clare," said Murphy with a smile.

Igorov just glared, but nodded imperceptibly.

Clare turned and walked into the kitchen.

Five minutes later she emerged with a tray of nine mugs on it. Six she laid out for the men in the rec. She then carried the tray up onto the gallery and disappeared down the corridor that led to the control room. She didn't know how many men Kozak had in total, but there were the three in the rec, plus him. She had seen two earlier in the control room. There had also been another couple coming and going, so the total must be eight to ten, maybe more.

When she reached the control room she peered in the door. There were two men inside. They looked up as she entered. One of them she knew was called Masaev. She didn't like him. He'd looked at her with an expression of pure evil. She was sure he would be aggressive if given the chance. The second man she found hard to figure out. He was younger than the others, with a fresh, lively, and somehow softer face. He almost seemed out of place in the group. She had caught him looking at her a couple of times when she'd glanced in his direction. He'd quickly looked away. She'd seen him almost blush on one occasion. His look, though, had not been leery, more that of a teenager with a crush. This might be something she could use to her advantage.

"Would you like some coffee?" she asked, cheerily. Masaev glared at her with undisguised resentment, while the younger man smiled and took the tray from her. She smiled back, at which Masaev said something to the younger man in Ukrainian that was clearly a put-down. Clare couldn't understand what he'd said, but it hadn't been pleasant. The younger man shot back with far more confidence than she would have expected. Rather than argue, Masaev seemed uncharacteristically restrained. He glared at the younger man, and then, with a glance at Clare spat on the floor and walked out.

Clare looked at the young man. He seemed to be somewhat embarrassed at the man's actions.

"I am sorry about that," he said, looking up at her.

"What's your name?" asked Clare.

"Ilya," he said, avoiding her gaze.

"Ilya, that's a nice name," said Clare, smiling at him. He looked up, a bit sheepishly. She passed him one of the mugs, letting her fingers linger a second on his as he took it from her. He looked at her and she smiled openly. "My name's Clare."

There was an awkward silence for a second, and then Clare looked straight at him.

"Ilya, why are you doing this? You seem like a nice man. These men are not so nice."

Ilya glanced down into the mug, and when he looked back up his expression had changed. It was harder. There was a fiery gleam in his eye.

"It is for a great cause. My brother, Andriy, leads us to right a great wrong."

She could see there was real passion there. "So your brother is the leader?"

"Yes," he said proudly.

That was interesting.

Clare then looked up at him, a scared and vulnerable look on her face. "Do you think they'll hurt me?"

Ilya looked at her. "Not if everyone does as they are told. I am sure they will not hurt you. You are not one of them." He pointed upward, as though meaning the higher-ups or leaders. She noticed he was struggling to say something, as though he was wondering whether he should.

"I... I will try and stop them if they do," he said, again looking down as he said this.

Clare saw this as her chance. She reached out and held his hand, rubbing it soothingly. "Thank you, Ilya, that is so kind of you." As she said it, she looked for the controls on the desk that operated the cameras that led to the rear lift-track station. She took his other hand and squeezed it, at the same time turning his body away from the screens. "That means so much to me." She then noticed a tattoo of a wolf with crossed swords on the inside of his arm. "That's interesting. What is it?"

Ilya looked down. "My brother and sister have them also. To show our devotion to the cause and each other. It binds us together."

"Where is your sister?"

"Oh, she is far away. She is older. She married a Russian and moved to Moscow. I haven't seen her in years."

"That's sad," said Clare, rubbing his arm affectionately.

He smiled at her. She let go of one hand and then stealthily flicked off the cameras. Two of the screens on the wall behind Ilya's head went blank.

"I have to go now," she said. "But thank you, Ilya." And

with that, she leaned forward and gave him a light kiss on the cheek.

She then turned and left the room. Ilya was left sitting on the control desk. He touched his cheek and a smile spread across his lips.

When Clare was outside she knew she had to move fast. She didn't know how long she would have, and while Ilya may not notice the screens were blank, Masaev surely would if he returned.

She ran along the corridor and stopped at a storeroom. Inside, on one of the shelves, she found an empty glass jar about six inches long. It had a screw top and would be waterproof. She undid the top, folded the president's letter in half and rolled it up. She then slid it into the jar and snapped the top back on. After checking the corridor was clear, she ran on toward the lift-track station.

Ilya was sitting on the desk, drinking his coffee, when Masaev returned. He glared at Ilya, before looking round for Clare. He was about to say something when he stopped and looked at the line of screens on the wall. Two of them were blank.

"What is this?" he said, indicating the screens.

"I don't know," said Ilya.

"Where are those cameras?"

Ilya shrugged helplessly.

"You idiot!" shouted Masaev. "The woman tricked you. Where has she gone?"

Ilya now looked panicked. He glanced at the screens. They had a number written under each one as to which camera they represented. He looked down at a schematic on a laptop that showed the layout of the cocoon and the area each camera covered. They both looked at the area that was blanked out.

Masaev then ran from the room.

Ilya followed close behind.

He was scared Masaev would hurt Clare if he found her doing something she shouldn't. He'd never liked the man, and he was upset his brother put so much faith in him. He dreaded to think what he might do to Clare.

He couldn't let that happen.

Clare reached the lift-track station undisturbed. She could see water around the outside of the capsule.

She went over to the panel at the side of the station, placed her palm on it, and the doors slid smoothly open. She moved inside and put the jar, with the letter inside, on the central seat.

"Helipad station. Direct," she said.

The computer was speaking its confirmation when she heard running footsteps behind her. The words were lost in the deafening sound of gunfire. Clare ducked as glass splintered behind her. She turned to see what damage had been done in time to see the capsule disappearing upward at speed.

As she turned back, Masaev smacked her across the face. She cried out and fell to the floor. A second later Ilya arrived. He rushed over and helped her up. Again, Masaev shouted at him, furious. He then turned on Clare. He tore her from Ilya's grasp, smacking her across the face again. She stood her ground this time. Masaev shouted at her, but she couldn't understand him. Ilya ran between them, forcing Masaev to back down. Clare could see the growing anger in the larger man, but still he wouldn't hit Ilya.

Ilya then turned to her, a worried look on his face.

"You have to tell him what you have done. I do not know how long I can hold him off."

She was about to speak when there was a loud 'CRACKING' sound from behind. They turned to see a splinter extend out across the glass surround of the lift-track. It didn't break, but it wouldn't take much.

Clare looked at it with horror. "Oh shit!" She turned to Ilya. "This is bad. If that goes, the whole cocoon will flood."

"How long?" asked Ilya.

"I've no idea. Depends how strong it is, but if it breaks it will flood."

Ilya turned to Masaev, who still had hold of Clare's arm. He spoke in fast-talking Ukrainian. Masaev then pulled Clare from the room.

They arrived in the rec a minute later. Everyone looked up as Masaev threw Clare roughly to the floor. He then spoke to Kozak, explaining what had happened, nodding at Ilya as he did so. Murphy went to help Clare up. When Masaev had finished, Kozak turned to Clare.

"Is this true, what he has said? You sent something up in the capsule?"

"No," said Clare, defiantly. "I was checking the integrity of the structure. The airlocks are the weak point for the pressure. Everything was fine until your idiot shot up the place. If it leaks, you won't be able to stop it. The cocoon will compensate for the pressure increase, but it could give way at any moment. If it does, the cocoon will fill, and there are no pumps to remove the water. We'll drown."

Kozak looked at her, a deep anger crossing his face.

"Why do I not believe you?" He turned to Masaev. "I think she has outlived her usefulness. Kill her!"

"Noooo!" cried out Clare.

An evil smile crossed Masaev's face. He walked toward Clare, pulling his gun from his waistband.

There was immediate tension in the room.

Masaev was starting to raise the gun, when Ilya ran between them.

Masaev aimed. His blood was up.

"Stop!" shouted Kozak, shaking his head. He crossed over to Ilya and spoke in Ukrainian. "What is this?"

"She has done nothing wrong, brother. There's no need to kill her."

Kozak looked at Ilya and then Clare. She showed fear, but there was a strength there. He then looked back at his brother, whose face had lowered. A realization seemed to come over Kozak, as though he had put two and two together. He glanced at Masaev, who was gripping the pistol in anticipation.

"Leave her," said Kozak. "Maybe she will be useful."

Masaev was about to protest, but Kozak raised his hand to end the discussion.

He turned to Clare. "This is your only chance. Do not test me again."

He then strode from the room.

Clare nodded her thanks to Ilya, and took a deep breath.

It could have been her last.

Chapter Twenty-Eight

The situation was unlike any Officer Luis Rodriguez of the LAPD had ever encountered. It was probably unlike any situation anyone had encountered.

He'd been told to go to the new conference center and assist in any way he could. That had been it. When he'd turned up, there were already trucks and vehicles from other agencies there. There was the fire department, a number of police cars, and five ambulances. Even a truck that looked like it had something to do with the military. They were all parked up on the vast car park at the side of the building, part of which had been sectioned off to be used as a helicopter landing pad.

There was the continued whoop, whoop of sirens, which died as vehicles arrived and it was realized they weren't needed anymore. People were running everywhere. He saw a large semi with US Navy written across it drive in. It looked like some sort of command center and was bigger than the LAPD one that was already there.

When he'd climbed out of his squad car with slight

bemusement, he'd been beckoned over to a group of fellow officers who were standing next to the mobile command and control unit. He'd announced his name and been told to wait by his car; someone would come and allocate a duty to him.

Ten minutes later he'd been ushered over to one of the police helicopters on the pad. Next, he'd found himself airborne and watched in amazement as the chopper rose up to the top of the building. As he'd stared through the glass sides of the structure, it had looked as though there was something shimmering inside. He had a crazy thought but instantly dismissed it. That was, until the chopper climbed up over the top and set down on the helipad. The whole central section of roof was missing. Beneath where it should have been, he found himself looking at a core full of water. He couldn't believe his eyes. He'd been dropped off and told to watch and observe and report anything unusual—yeah, right—even the slightest thing. He should also mention if he noticed any change in the condition of the building or if the water level altered. If it rose, he wouldn't have to inform anyone, it would pour over the side and a lot of people were going to get very wet.

He'd been here for over an hour now and nothing had changed. He wished he'd brought a flask with him. How the hell was he going to get a coffee? He then wished he hadn't had that thought, as he immediately wanted to relieve himself and there was nowhere to go. He looked around, but there was nowhere. And then he slapped his forehead—duh! He turned to the water that filled the building. Talk about pissing in the pool! He had almost finished when he saw something in the water over on the far side of the core. It was a change in texture and tone. As he watched, the disturbance took on a more solid form. A few seconds later, he could see that whatever it was was attached to the side of the building. He quickly zipped up his fly and watched more intently. He had no idea what he was looking at, but it was rapidly coming closer. He crouched down, retreating behind one of the supports for the helipad. He pulled out his sidearm as he did so.

Suddenly, a large glass capsule erupted out of the water. Rodriguez could see it was attached to some sort of track at the side of the inner wall of the building.

He stayed in his position, not sure what to do. He knew he should call it in, but he'd always thought of himself as a bit of a hero, and right now might be the time to prove it. He edged out from his hiding place. There appeared to be no movement from the capsule. As the water ran off the curved glass side it became easier to see inside. He moved closer. It looked empty.

So why was it here?

He cautiously inched closer. He was now right next to it. He peered in through the glass and looked around.

It was empty.

And then his gaze fell onto a small jar on a seat. When he shielded his eyes against the reflection, he could see there was something inside the jar. He went around to the entrance doors. There was a panel with a keypad, but he had no code. He pressed a number of buttons. Nothing happened.

Fuck it!

He moved back and aimed his revolver at the center of the glass side. The sound of the shot reverberated around the rooftop, but the glass shattered. He climbed over the smashed frame and retrieved the jar. Inside was a rolled-up piece of paper. He crossed back onto the side of the roof, smiled to himself, and then he picked up his radio.

The glass jar was handed to Harry Patterson as he exited the security control center through the external entrance. The ranking police officer, Larry Hawkins, who had been on-site for half an hour and was personally handling the liaison between the different departments until the military arrived, had taken it from a second officer who had brought it back by helicopter from the roof. The chopper had rapidly been dispatched following Rodriguez's radio call.

Now the two men looked closely at the jar.

They walked into the mobile LAPD trailer and sat down. Patterson unscrewed the jar and carefully pulled out the piece of paper, He unrolled it and laid it out flat.

Five minutes later he'd read the text in full, which he'd noted was in President Stevens' handwriting.

"Jesus, this doesn't look good."

At that moment, there was a loud and distant 'WHUMP, WHUMP' that reverberated through the walls of the trailer. Both men walked outside in time to see two massive Sea Stallion helicopters approach from across the city. Immediately Hawkins ran over to his men, waving them to clear the helipad and the surrounding area.

Patterson watched as the massive machines circled round. As they did, two men from the military truck ran out to an area beyond the main helipad, directly below the swirling rotor wash. One stood in clear view of the pilot. The other ran to a space on the concrete parking area away to one side. The man in front of the chopper put his hands out, directing the helicopter into position. The pilot then maneuvered it so that it could lower the chamber slung beneath onto the ground. Once it was secure, a remote release jettisoned the cable from the chopper. It fell like a collapsing snake lying across the top of the chamber. As the second man ran to remove the cable, the second chopper was directed in and similarly lowered its chamber.

Once both chambers were safely on the ground, the Sea Stallions banked round to land in formation at the rear of the pad. As soon as their wheels touched the tarmac, the rear ramps were lowered and the occupants walked out.

Harry Patterson crossed over to greet Commander David Bryce as he strode toward him.

They shook hands.

"Commander Bryce?"

"That's right."

"Harry Patterson. Security controller for the complex."

"Looks like you've a lot on your plate, Mr. Patterson."

"Harry, please. Yep, you could say that."

"What's the latest?"

"Big development. We just received contact from the cocoon. Somehow, someone managed to get a note out from President Stevens. It looks like his handwriting, but I'm sure you guys can verify that."

"What does it say?"

"It basically gives an indication of the hostile force, but more importantly that there's a planned attack on New York that will make nine-eleven look like a picnic unless an agreement is reached in the cocoon between the two presidents, something President Stevens thinks is unlikely."

Bryce thought for a moment.

"How did you get hold of it?"

"It came up in one of the facility's capsules, part of the lift-track system. An LAPD officer posted on the roof found it."

"So there's a capsule at the top that came from the cocoon?"

"That's right."

"So that might be a way for us to get down there."

"Unfortunately, that won't be possible." Bryce looked at him sharply. "The officer shot through the capsule glass to retrieve the letter. It's going nowhere."

"Okay," said Bryce, knowing it would be only the first of, no doubt, a thousand setbacks he'd have to deal with today. He took the letter from Patterson and walked over to the military command post that was being set up close to the chambers.

To one side, Harley and the SEALs were unloading their equipment and laying it out ready for final checks. Meanwhile Connie prepared the gas cylinders on the chambers and looked through the medical supplies.

When Bryce entered the command trailer all the comms and electronic surveillance equipment was coming online. The technicians hurriedly connected up the final wires and power systems. With a flick of a switch it all went live. From here, Bryce had a direct, secure line to anyone, anywhere in the world.

His first call was to the governor of New York. He outlined the threat, though there were no specifics. Just that he should plan for every eventuality. Although the indication was an attack from the air, they should be ready for anything. Check all public places. Check all trucks. Check for bombs. Check ships coming close to shore. Ban all access to the Hudson. Use radiological and biological detectors… And no, he didn't know how long it would be for. His next call was to the chief of staff of the air force, a man he frequently played golf with and frequently beat. The call went as expected. The man was efficient and a true patriot. He would move heaven and earth to protect the city.

With that done, he strode back outside and over to Patterson.

"Okay, show me your control center and what you know."

As they walked over, Bryce shouted for Harley to join him. Together, the two men followed Patterson to the security center, entering through an external door. Patterson led them down onto the floor, stopping them in front of the panel of screens showing images from the cameras around the complex. There was also a plan layout of the building, the cocoon and the tunnel and dam.

Bryce cast an appraising eye over the information. "Okay, what do we have?"

Patterson explained the layout and showed them the cameras of the cocoon exterior and the cave surrounding it. As an image of *Deep Intruder* came on the screen, Bryce and Harley exchanged grim looks.

When Patterson had finished, Bryce thought for a moment.

"How the hell did they get in there?"

"They either had someone on the inside, and/or they had access to plans and protocols that should have been confidential."

"Cameras inside the cocoon?"

"Disabled."

"Is there anyone from the complex in there with them?"

Patterson turned to a laptop and pulled up a schedule list. "At the moment, the only people thought to be in there are a couple of staff, a cook and a cleaner, and Clare Kowalski, the assistant manager."

"What do we know about her?"

Patterson looked surprised for a moment. "Clare? She's as good as gold. No way this came from her."

"I think, at this stage, we can't rule anyone out," said Bryce seriously. "Where's the manager?"

"Brad Walker is… was… in New York for a business meeting with the parent company. He said he would be flying straight back. We expect him anytime."

Bryce looked closely at the schematics.

"What can you tell me about the tunnel?"

"It was built as an escape route from the cocoon in case the complex was attacked from above and they needed to get out. It runs under the reservoir—obviously—and exits just beyond the dam buildings." Then he added, "It's definitely the way they gained entrance. A number of vehicles have been found close to the reservoir, which it seems they used to get their gear on-site. Also, the bodies of two of the night shift workers have been found. They were both shot."

Again, Bryce thought for a second. "Okay, we need to get a SWAT team up there in case that's their escape route. In the meantime, is there any way we can lower the water level in the building?"

"We thought of that. The only way is by opening the sluice gates at the dam, which has been done. But that would only help marginally. If you look at this graphic we worked up earlier, you can see the problem."

Bryce and Harley looked at the graphic Patterson brought up on the screen. It was a stylized depiction of the relative positions of the Omega Complex and the reservoir shown in profile.

"Here, you can see the full depth of the reservoir in relation to the height of the complex and the cocoon. The bottom of the reservoir is higher than the base of the complex—where the cocoon is. So even if you managed to drain all the water from the reservoir, you still wouldn't completely drain the complex. And it would take weeks, if not months."

Bryce looked at the graphic. "Okay, so how about entering through the tunnel?"

Patterson looked at him. "You could, but there's no knowing what damage was done when they blasted through. Also, it's not that wide. It would be a bottleneck. They could have it boobytrapped and have divers lying in wait. Your men would be like fish in a barrel."

Bryce glanced at Harley, then back to Patterson. He was about to say something when Patterson's phone rang. He put a finger up to ask Bryce to wait, then answered it. He listened intently and spoke when necessary. "What? You're kidding... Okay, keep me updated." He clicked the phone off and the turned to Bryce who was watching, expectantly.

"You may not have a problem with emptying the reservoir after all."

"Why's that?"

"Apparently the explosion damaged the dam wall. It's leaking. Parts of the concrete are splintering. They've no idea how long it'll hold."

"Jesus!" said Bryce.

"FEMA have been informed," continued Patterson. "They have experts on-site as we speak, but they're looking at contingency plans to evacuate downtown LA just in case."

"Okay, Harry. Thanks for your help. We'll take it from here. Let me know if there are any developments. I'll be in touch if we need anything."

And with that, Bryce and Harley walked from the room straight over to the command trailer.

When they arrived, the other SEALs were waiting for them, their gear checked and ready to go. Connie was laying out the medical supplies on a wide portable table next to the chambers. Bryce called her over.

When they were all assembled, he looked along the line of serious, yet eager, faces.

"This is like nothing you've done before. Not only will you have the usual dangers to self and each other, you have the lives of the president of the United States and the president of Russia to think about. Your primary objective is to rescue those two men. If only one is possible you don't need to be told which one, but the repercussions of a Russian president dying on American soil do not bear thinking about. I'm open to any and all suggestions as to how you approach this. Mitch, what are your thoughts?"

Harley stepped forward and looked around the group.

"Thank you, sir. From what we know, it looks like the tunnel is a last resort. Too confined. Too much of a risk. If we go in from the roof there's more space to operate in and there are the floors of the building to use as cover if we're attacked. It's possible we could meet no resistance until we reach the cocoon, but they've been prepared and efficient so far, so that would be expecting too much. I suggest a four-man team, aerial entry to the water, and then proceed down to the cocoon, taking care of any resistance on the way. Once we reach the cocoon, we have the entry codes. There's a front and a rear entrance used by their lift-track system and there's the main airlock. I'm sure all will be guarded from inside, if not outside as well, but we need to be able to access all of them to give us options.

"Once inside, it'll depend on what opposition we meet and whether we gain entry undetected or there's a firefight. This is where things can go badly wrong. Clearly, they have very high-value hostages, so we need to be able to put the terrorists out of action as soon as possible. Assuming we make it to a position to extract the primaries, we need to be able to do so without worry for their life support." He looked at Connie. "You're up."

Connie stepped forward holding one of the constant flow full face masks. She raised it in front of her.

"This is how you'll bring them out. You've all used these masks before on missions, but these have been adapted to work on constant flow and so keep the user alive even if they're not conscious. To bring out the presidents you'll need to sedate them." She put the mask down and pulled out a small waterproof box. She snapped it open to reveal four syringes. "Each shot of this preloaded mix of drugs will knock them out. It's a combination of ketamine, Xanax and atropine. The dose should wear off in around half an hour to forty-five minutes, so you need to move and get them out as soon as possible after injection.

"Once we have them back here they'll need to go into a chamber due to the pressure changes their bodies will have experienced. I'll monitor and administer any further medication as required. You should all be fine from a deco point of view, given you'll be wearing hemofilters. As you may know, these were the people responsible for the deaths of Frank and Mateo. At the time of the incident they also stole a batch of hemofilters, so their divers will likely have the same protection as you with regard to depth/time considerations. Now, there's a pack of syringes for each of you. We don't know who will eventually be in a position to sedate the patients, and it's always good to have backup."

Connie stepped back. Harley spoke again.

"Thanks, doc... One final option is that *Deep Intruder* is down there. This is what they stole it for, so it may be possible to utilize it in any extraction plan. But that will be a mid-operational decision. Okay, any questions?"

They all looked grim. They knew what lay ahead.

There was only one question.

"Does it matter which order we kill them in?" asked Anders.

Bryce looked at him. "No, son, it does not. Just so long as you get them all."

"One thing to bear in mind," said Harley. "Given where they are, I don't know how they ever expected to get out alive, so we may be dealing with people more than happy to die for their cause."

"Fine by me," said Miller.

Bryce again looked over the faces. "Good plan, Mitch. It could work. We'll put a drone in the water to recce the building, but have your guys ready to go in an hour."

"Roger that, sir."

Chapter Twenty-Nine

Thirty minutes later, Harley and Bryce were standing in the command trailer watching a large screen on the wall. To one side of them an operator held onto two joysticks controlling a drone that had just taken off from outside the trailer. The camera currently showed the trailer disappearing out of shot below. The operator twisted the stick and the image spun rapidly round to face the Omega Complex.

"Okay, go in closer so we can get an idea of what we're looking at," said Bryce.

"Yes, sir," said the operator.

The two men watched as the image on the screen moved closer to the building. When it was around ten feet from the glass, at the fourth-floor level, the drone hovered so they could take in what they were seeing.

As the water from the reservoir was fresh and crystal clear, the visibility inside looked good. It was obvious, at this level, that the floor was completely flooded. They were looking at what appeared to be meeting rooms and small offices. They could see that desks and chairs had been rolled over as the force of the water had burst in. There were sheets of paper and blinds from the windows floating free as localized currents within the building moved them around.

"Okay, higher," said Bryce.

The drone moved up.

The next two levels were the same, though the usage of the rooms changed to the accommodation levels, with bedrooms and living spaces. At one point they grimaced as a body floated through the shot. As the drone proceeded higher, more bodies could be seen. Harley glanced at Bryce as he murmured to himself.

"Imagine that. Drowning in the sky."

On one level there had clearly been some sort of structural failure as the ceiling had collapsed. An airspace could be seen in a corner of the room.

"That could be useful," said Harley.

Bryce looked at him. "Make a note of any you see. Could be safe havens if you get into trouble."

They were nearly at the top.

"Okay, let's take a look inside," ordered Bryce.

The operator flew the drone over the top of the building. They could see an LAPD officer taking a drink from a flask, watching the drone fly over as it headed for the atrium.

The operator lowered the drone gently onto the water and shut down the propellers that had kept it in the air. Next, he flicked a switch. A small transponder detached from the side and floated on the surface. It would allow control to be maintained while underwater. He then powered up four small electric thrusters that allowed the drone to move smoothly thorough the water.

Over the next ten minutes they saw the full extent of the

damage to the inside. More floors had collapsed. Some had created air pockets. More bodies drifted into view, like some sort of macabre theater show as they hung lifeless in the water.

When they reached the ground level they could see where the force of water pressure had blown open the floor, allowing the building to flood in the first place. The range of the drone meant they couldn't go any further to see what was happening in the cocoon; that would have to be left to Harley and his team.

"Right, I've seen enough," said Bryce, standing up. He turned to Harley.

"Okay, Mitch. Over to you."

Harley left the trailer and ran over to his men, who were standing by the chambers. Their equipment had already been loaded into the chopper. As he walked over, he signaled the pilot with a whirling motion with his fingers. The pilot shot him a quick salute and initiated the start-up procedure. Before Harley had even reached his men, the massive rotors had started to turn.

The SEALs needed no bidding. At Harley's direction they ran over and climbed up the rear loading ramp into the Sea Stallion. Before he joined them, Harley walked over to Connie. She was at the chamber controls, going through a checklist. She looked up and smiled grimly as he approached.

"How does it look?"

"Not great, but we'll be fine."

"You'd better be, Lieutenant, you still owe me dinner at the weekend."

Harley looked confused. "What dinner?"

She smiled at him. "The one you're about to promise me you'll buy me."

"Ah, that one. Wouldn't miss it for the world."

They nodded at each other and then Harley walked over to the chopper.

As he left, Connie watched him go. She knew he was good at what he did, but she also knew what they were facing.

Good luck, Mitch, she said to herself. *Stay safe.*

Harley ran up the ramp and walked the length of the interior to the cockpit. He patted the pilot on the shoulder. Immediately the helicopter lifted smoothly off the ground, sending dust and dirt scurrying into the air.

Inside, the men were now all focus. They kitted up in their gear. Once they had the rebreathers on their backs and had run through the various gas checks, they made sure they had the drugs for the presidents. Each carried a set of the syringes in case they were the one who was in a position to extract the primary targets. They checked their weapons were locked and loaded and then looked to Harley. He glanced at them in turn and received affirmative nods to tell him they were ready. No more words were needed. The time for that had passed. They turned their gaze to the building. They knew that once they entered it, they may not all come out alive, but none of them felt any trepidation. This was what they trained for. This was what they lived for.

The helicopter powered up to the top of the complex. It swept out over the flooded core, the downwash blasting ripples across the water as it came in low over the surface.

A second later the four men jumped from the rear ramp. They held the DPVs in their hands. These would allow them to move through the water at speed. Each diver also had a large waterproof holdall strapped to their sides. It contained personal equipment, which included a weapon for use in the cocoon, as well as a small cylinder and full face mask to extract a single individual. It always paid to have backup, and no one knew who would be there at the final moment to make the escape.

Once they were in the water, the Sea Stallion lifted with a roar from the rotors and banked away to return to the helipad.

Underwater, the bubbles from the impact rose slowly, like a curtain, to reveal the SEAL team in its element. There were many branches of the US military, but the one that felt most at home under the water was the SEALs.

Miller, Garcia and Anders looked over at Harley. He could see their eyes through the full face masks and he could talk to them over comms. To allow him to talk to Bryce in the command trailer he had to fix a transponder to the glass wall of the building.

"Okay, guys, follow me down."

They descended to the floor below. All around them was the devastation and destruction caused by the water when it had flooded into the building. There were also, now, more bodies. Even given the restricted visibility of the depth, they could see about ten of them. The building operated 24/7, given the global nature of modern life. There would be many more behind the closed doors of the rooms they would pass as they descended.

Harley accelerated his DPV. The small torpedo-like device took him smoothly over to the side of the building. He pulled out the transponder from a large pocket on his drysuit and attached it to the window.

"Comms check. SEAL Alpha, do you copy?"

"Loud and clear, Mitch," said Bryce in his ear. "How's it looking?"

"Not good, sir. More bodies than we saw before. Do you have video?"

"One minute." There was silence for a second or two. "Yep, okay. I have four feeds. Miller's camera's a bit fuzzy, which could just be range. Yours is too angled."

"Roger that. We're heading down."

Harley adjusted his camera so it was pointing more forward, and then allowed the DPV to tow him back to the other three.

"Okay, guys, let's go."

They headed deeper.

Andriy Kozak walked into the meeting room and looked around at the occupants. He had been monitoring what had been going on remotely. There had seemed to be very little discussion between the leaders.

Stevens and Petrovich looked up as he entered. Their aides were also present, as was Clare.

"What progress have you made?" asked Kozak.

Stevens was the first to speak.

"What you are asking cannot be resolved in a couple of days. There are many factors that have to be considered and agreed. This is just not possible."

Kozak had no sympathy. "Then I am afraid, Mr. President, that many of your countrymen are going to die." He was about to say something else when one of his men came in and whispered in his ear. He listened, glanced around the room, and then followed the man out of the door.

He walked at pace to the control room. Masaev was

hunched over the screens alternating the camera views. He looked up as Kozak entered.

"You need to see this," he said, concern thick in his voice.

Kozak moved forward. "What is it?"

Masaev flicked a control. A view came up of the atrium. The camera was mounted high up on the inside, looking down. It showed four divers heading away from the surface into the depths. Another camera, lower down, followed their progress. From their equipment, it was clear they were armed. They looked highly professional.

Kozak thought for a moment.

"We knew this would happen. Go and prepare the men. I want those divers taken out. They need to know what they are dealing with. They will be wearing cameras. Make sure you put on a show to cast fear into any who follow."

"Yes, Andriy."

"Let me know your progress."

Masaev nodded before heading off to round up the men.

Kozak took a deep breath and walked back out into the corridor. He then pulled out his gun and checked the magazine. He put a bullet into the breach and replaced it in his waistband, then he walked purposefully back to the meeting room. Again, as he entered, all eyes looked his way. He stared evenly around at the three men and two women. Clare was seated in the corner away from the others, drinking a coffee.

As they looked at him they seemed to realize something was wrong. Something was about to happen. There was a stiffening of backs as they waited for what was to come.

Kozak walked forward and took a deep breath.

"It would appear the schedule has to be moved up. I

had hoped my initial threat would make you realize I was serious, but as you seem not to believe that I am able to carry it out, I can assure you I am every bit as capable of carrying it out as this."

Watson glanced around at the others. "As what?"

Kozak swiftly pulled the gun from his waist and shot Watson through the head. He then quickly shot the female Russian adviser. They fell to the ground without even a cry. In the small space the noise was overwhelming. Clare and the two presidents glanced at each other in total shock.

Kozak looked between the two leaders. "I suggest you speed up your discussions. The authorities have sent forces into the complex. They clearly think they can rescue you. This will not happen. My men will take care of them, but it has accelerated things. You need to confirm your commitment to my demands. If by some miracle they reach the cocoon, you will not leave here alive."

With that, he stormed from the room, leaving the smell of cordite hanging in the air.

The SEAL team was halfway down the complex when Harley stopped.

"Do you see something down there?" He pointed to the large gash in the floor of the atrium, about a hundred feet below.

"Yeah. Just to the right of the fallen girder," said Anders.

"That's it. Looks like five of them. There was a glint off a mask."

Harley checked they were all with him. "Okay, this is what we do. Spread out to the four quarters at the sides.

We'll keep level but head on down. If they attack, they'll have to split up, and we can take them individually."

He received three okays in his ear.

They moved slowly to the edge of the building at the four quarters. Harley was in no doubt the terrorists knew they were there. They would have been like sitting ducks silhouetted against the sky above.

Clare was still in total shock from witnessing the murders. But there was nothing they could do. She crossed over to the bodies.

"We have to move them. We can't just leave them here," she said.

Stevens and Petrovich looked at her, at first with anger, but then they relented and helped move the bodies to one side. Clare pulled a drape off the wall to cover the faces. Petrovich then turned to her. His expression softened.

"Isn't there anything you can do, my dear? Any other way of contacting the outside?"

"Not unless we can get to the control room. There's a hard line from there, but other than that, we used the only option to get President Stevens' message out."

Stevens turned to Petrovich.

"Viktor, you have to concede now. There is no other choice. As I have said before, we can revise the decision later, but for God's sake, now you have to agree. You want to live, don't you?"

Petrovich looked calmly at Stevens and then said in a low and determined voice, "Mr. President, I would not give in to those demands whatever the cost. It is just not possible."

With that, he stood and walked defiantly from the room.

Harley glanced across to the other SEALs spread around the perimeter of the atrium.

When he looked down again, he couldn't see anyone below. He was about to call in and see if any of the others knew where they were, when something appeared in his peripheral vision. He just had time to duck before a projectile smashed into the wall behind him, creating a small explosion. The shockwave sent him spinning out over the void, holding his ears and letting go of his DPV.

A moment later another projectile headed his way. It passed beneath him to explode harmlessly in a room behind. He turned back to the atrium. He could see where the threat was coming from. The terrorist divers had somehow managed to use the cover of the rooms around the edge of the building to get above them. He could see his men on the other side doing battle at close quarters. He quickly retrieved his DPV, engaged the propeller, and headed to help.

He was just reaching Anders when he saw a projectile hit him squarely in the chest and explode. Miller had also seen it. He returned fire with a harpoon, which skewered the terrorist through the chest. The man creased over and sank into the depths.

One for one.

Next, Harley could see Garcia fighting with a man using a long diving knife. They were struggling hard. Finally, he managed to cut one of the terrorist's rebreather hoses. The man didn't last long.

Two for one.

But before Garcia could turn to the next opponent, another projectile came out of the blue. He exploded in a mass of bubbles.

Two for two.

Harley could now see two of the enemy coming up behind Miller.

"Miller, look out!" he shouted into the comms.

Miller turned, but it was too late. One held onto him, while the other rammed a knife straight into his chest.

Two for three.

"You bastards!" shouted Harley into his mask and he aimed the DPV straight for them. But as he approached, the terrorists moved forward. One held onto Miller, blood oozing from his chest, while the other looked straight at Harley.

Harley could see Miller's eyes still flickering through the mask.

The terrorist then proceeded to take his knife and saw through Miller's neck. Harley saw his friend's eyes go wide for a second before closing forever.

When the man had finished, he pulled the now severed head from the body and dropped it into the depths. As he watched it fall away, the terrorist waved it goodbye before discarding the headless corpse. Thick, dark liquid spewed from the neck, creating a bloody trail behind the sinking body.

Harley hung there, unable to move for a second, and then he realized they knew he was wearing a camera. The brutal act had been for the benefit of those watching. He fought the desire to scream and tried to calm himself down. When he had his breathing under control, he spoke into the mike, his voice emotionless.

"Did you see that, sir?"

"Yes," came the subdued voice of Bryce over the comms. "You need to get out of there, Mitch. It's three against one, and these guys aren't taking prisoners. Come back to fight another day. We're getting the second team ready, but there's a problem with the chopper at Coronado. I'm not sure when they'll get here."

"I can't let this stand," said Harley.

"And it won't. But come back now. That's an order."

"I can't do that, sir."

"Harley!"

And with that, Harley clicked off the comms.

The three terrorist divers were now lined up facing him.

Harley checked his equipment. He tightened his straps and gripped the DPV with extra force. He knew there was no way to win out in the open in a straight fight. He spun the DPV and headed for the rooms and corridors at the side of the atrium. He had a plan of the complex in his mind and he had seen the collapsed floors and rooms from the drone footage. If they decided to follow him, he would have the advantage, even if he was outnumbered.

Then they'd see who won.

Chapter Thirty

Jade walked through into the living area of Clare's house.

She really hoped Max was asleep or had found something to play with out by the pool. Of late he'd become even more of a pain. While she had dog-sat for Clare many times, and she and Max had an understanding, it was a sort of love/hate relationship, which, right now, was definitely more hate than love. As he was growing up, so his independence also seemed to be growing. He seemed to take great delight in riling her whenever he could. Of course, around Clare he was all sweetness and light, and she couldn't understand what Jade was complaining about. But Jade was sure Max was working his way through the 'piss off Jade handbook' and it seemed like he was already on volume two.

Right now, there were more important things on her mind than an errant puppy. After a great night's sleep in the second of three bedrooms in 'the dump,' she'd had a leisurely breakfast and then relaxed by the pool enjoying the morning sunshine. She knew Max could be left for a period of time on his own, so long as he had food and water, but she needed to know when Clare might be back. She hadn't heard from her the previous evening. She also hadn't been able to get in touch with her this morning. None of her office numbers were picking up and her cell kept giving a 'this handset is not connected' message. She wasn't quite sure what to do.

She wandered back into the living room and Max came hurtling after her. He nipped at her ankles with a loud bark.

"Max! No!" She managed to make it inside and shoo him away. Max, feeling pleased with himself, woofed contentedly and trotted back into the garden, mission accomplished.

Jade went into the kitchen and poured herself a fresh orange juice. She then went to sit on one of the three couches arranged in a large U in front of the fireplace. She clicked on the TV to catch up with the latest news.

There was initially a report on the proxy war still raging between Saudi Arabia and Yemen in the Middle East, but then her attention was drawn by a large BREAKING NEWS banner across the bottom of the screen. The CNN anchor looked seriously, but excitedly, straight at the camera.

"Now, some breaking news to bring you. We're going straight to LA and our reporter Dan Metcalfe. Dan, what have you got for us?"

The screen changed to a shot of Metcalfe close to camera. There was a tall glass building behind and some hills beyond. All around there were trucks from various official departments, including the military. People were rushing around in the background. A couple of helicopters were parked to one side. There was a serious look in the reporter's eye.

"Thank you, Susan. I'm here at the Omega Complex in the Hollywood Hills where a crisis of international proportions is unfolding. You may have seen, in recent days, the arrival of President Stevens and the Russian president, Viktor Petrovich, to meet for an arms summit. Well, it appears that terrorists have taken over the complex and are holding the two world leaders hostage. The demands have not been made public, and the condition of the leaders is not known. The only thing I can tell you is that a recent assault by a SEAL team appears to have gone catastrophically wrong. No details have been forthcoming, but from the activity among the military, and the 'no comment' responses when asking for updates, things look like they're going from bad to worse."

A window appeared in the top right of the screen showing the news anchor in the studio.

"Dan, what do we know about how the terrorists gained entry? I thought the facility was chosen as it was one of the most secure buildings in the country, if not the world."

"That's supposed to be the case, and although conjecture at the moment, this is what we know so far." A graphic appeared on screen showing a cross section of the complex layout, including the reservoir and the tunnel. The reporter continued. "From what my sources tell me, it looks like the terrorists entered through a tunnel that runs beneath the Griffith Park reservoir. They blasted through the bottom and then proceeded to an area below ground level that is now flooded by water from the reservoir. This water has also filled the entire building—all two hundred feet of it. It's thought the presidents and their staff are in a secure cocoon below the complex. However, it appears they're effectively sealed inside with the terrorists. It's not looking good, and given the first rescue attempt has apparently failed, time seems to be running out for those trapped inside. There's no knowing how the terrorists will react to this action by the special forces. Now back to the studio."

The screen changed to the anchor full-screen. She looked into the camera with a serious face. "We'll bring you more on this breaking story as it happens. Now, for some environmental news…"

Jade found herself tuning out everything around her. She just stared at the screen that was now showing some climate change protesters dressed as icebergs in Washington. Then, as if in a trance, she stood up and walked out onto the pool surround. She crossed over to the edge and looked along the hills, knowing that her best friend was trapped, possibly dead, in the complex only a few miles away.

She was numb. She didn't know what to do. She thought back to the previous day when Clare had been there with her. They'd laughed together, drunk wine together… and watched the film premiere… And then something turned over in Jade's mind. An idea. A crazy idea. She seemed to be wrestling as to whether she should even entertain it.

But then she decided.

Clare was in trouble. Whatever she could do, however much of a Hail Mary it might be, she had to do something to try and help her friend, and hang the consequences.

With new vigor she made her way through the house into Clare's office. It was at the front, with a small window and not much view, other than over the parking area, but she didn't need a view for what she had in mind.

She sat down on the leather swivel chair at the desk and looked at the blank screen of Clare's twenty-seven-inch iMac. She reached round the back and turned it on. There was the familiar chime and the screen lit up with an underwater wallpaper and the login password request.

Okay, girl, now what would you pick? Let's start with the obvious.

She typed in…

u… n… d… e… r… w… a… t… e… r.

Hit return.

The entry line shook itself as if in disgust that she had got it wrong. She deleted the entry.

Okay, what else?

At that moment, Max peered around the corner of the door. He started with a low growl and then ran forward, but before he could reach Jade's ankle, she turned sharply to him. "No! Not now, Max! Bad puppy!"

He seemed to get the tone in her voice, and that now was not the time. He lay down with a slight whimper, his head on his paws, and looked up at her with soulful eyes.

Jade stared at him for a moment and shook her head. "Really not so tough, are you?"

But then a thought came to her. She turned back to the keyboard and typed in…

m… a… x.

Hit return.

Again, the computer shook the line of letters.

Jade looked out of the window for a moment, in frustration, as if searching for inspiration, and then she suddenly faced the screen. "It better not be this, girl, else you really is in trouble."

She typed in…

m… c… c… r… e… a… d… y.

She paused… hit return.

The screen opened up to Clare's desktop.

Jade shook her head. "Yep, you're really over him!"

She looked at the screen and clicked on the contacts

app. She scrolled down until she reached McCready's name. When his details came up, she sat back and stared at them for a moment. Should she be doing this? Then she thought of the news reports she'd seen earlier, and the stories Clare had told her about McCready. She didn't have a choice. She grabbed her phone and dialed.

It rang three times before being answered.

"Hello, John speaking."

For a second, Jade hesitated, then rolled her eyes.

"Is that McCready?"

"Er, yeah. Who's calling?"

"We have a mutual acquaintance."

There was a pause. "We do?"

"Clare Kowalski… My name's Jade, her best friend. Maybe she mentioned me."

There was another pause.

"Er, maybe… Black girl. Speaks her mind."

"That what she said?"

"The gist of it."

"Well, that would be me. Which makes you the arsehole white boy who sleeps around!"

The phone was silent for a moment. Jade thought he'd hung up. "Hey, you there?"

"Is that what she said?"

"The gist of it."

There was another pause.

"Okay, not what happened, but go on."

Jade was now the one who hesitated. She'd been expecting a tirade from McCready, but his simple response had somewhat blindsided her. She was all riled up ready for a fight. Eventually she pulled herself together.

"You there?" she heard over the speaker.

"Yeah."

"So, what can I do for you?"

Jade took a deep breath.

"Your girl's in trouble."

Again, there was a pause. "I'm not sure if you're up on current events, but she's not exactly 'my girl.'"

"Well, I can see how you could be confused over that."

"Confused? She told me as much six months ago… She's apparently now with some guy she knew from college."

"Like I said, can see why you might be confused. But she's all messed up, and that's all your fault. You need to turn on your TV and look what's happened in LA. She's stuck in the middle of that." At this, Jade had to take a second. Her voice was breaking. "I know you know what you think she thinks, but you're wrong." Her voice was really going now. "I mean, who the hell has the name of someone they want to forget as their computer password. That would be crazy, huh?"

There was silence for a moment.

"Yeah, that would be pretty crazy… Hey, you okay?"

"Not really. I don't know if you can help her. I probably shouldn't have called, but I had nowhere else to go."

Again, there was a pause.

"Listen, Jade, you were right to call. More than you know. And thank you. Let me take a look. I'll see what I can do. If it's in my power, I won't let anything happen to her. Okay?"

"Yeah, okay."

"Look after yourself, and don't worry."

With that, the line went dead.

Jade placed the phone back on the desk and looked at it. McCready's voice had been so calm, so collected, and his words were said with such resolve and determination that she felt herself almost float off the chair. He didn't even know what had happened yet. Realistically, what could he possibly do? But his confidence was infectious, and in that moment, she knew what Clare saw in him—even if he was a guy. Why she had fallen for him. And why she was definitely still in love with him.

She smiled to herself and started to relax. She let out a long sigh. Somehow, she felt calm, where before there had been no hope. Her gaze fell to the floor. Max was still looking at her, clearly aware something serious had happened.

She looked at him.

"You know, if all this goes wrong, you made the call, right? Nothing to do with me."

McCready had taken Jade's call as he walked to the car park at Aberdeen Airport after a late afternoon flight back to Scotland from London.

When he reached the Range Rover, he jumped in, closed the door and found a live feed of the BBC News Channel on his phone. He started to watch what would turn out to be wall-to-wall coverage. When he had flicked through various other channels and seen about four different versions of what had happened, and listened to numerous experts speculating on what was going on and what the outcome might be, he felt a deep dread spread through his body and something clutch at his chest. The defining takeaway from the reports was summed up by one of the American reporter's on-site, "…but the one thing we can all be sure about is that there now seems to be little hope for any of those held hostage inside."

He had tried to put Clare out of his mind. He had

thought that was what she had wanted. He had to move on with his life. It was as though he had compartmentalized her—that she was still out there doing her thing, but that maybe one day she would come back. His brain understood this wasn't going to happen, but he now realized his heart had never accepted that. Maybe that was part of what had held him back from Brandy, not the explanation he had given her—who knew?

And Jade was right, who the hell has an ex's name as their computer password if they want to forget them? No one, right? That would be nuts.

He brought up his speed dial numbers and clicked on one. It was answered on the fourth ring.

"Craig Richards."

"I'm at the airport. We need to have a chat about something. It's going to be a long night."

He didn't even wait for a reply.

He paused for a moment and then gunned the engine.

Chapter Thirty-One

Richards followed McCready into the conference room on the first floor at Ocean Tech. Once they were inside, McCready closed the door and walked over to a kettle, switched it on and grabbed a couple of mugs that had been drying on the side of a small sink in a worktop at one end of the room. Richards watched him dubiously.

"Am I going to need to put whisky in that?"

McCready hesitated. "We could just go straight to the Glenmorangie."

"That bad?"

McCready smiled, poured the coffee and placed the two mugs on the table. He then grabbed a remote and switched on the TV in the corner. He flicked through the news channels until he found one starting an update on the situation in California. He let it play through and then muted the sound.

Richards looked at him.

"Okay, I saw that earlier, what's it got to do with us?"

McCready took a deep breath. He knew the barrage of

objections he was going to receive, so he may as well get on with it.

"Oh no," said Richards, staring at him.

"What?"

"You have that determined, won't-take-no-for-an-answer look, where you come up with some sort of hair-brained, half-arsed scheme there's no way I should get involved with, and that, after very little consideration, I stupidly agree to and regret for the rest of my life."

"Good, now we've got that out the way."

Richards groaned and leaned back in his chair. "Okay, let's get this over with."

McCready took a deep breath. He nodded at the TV. "The cocoon the terrorists are holding the presidents hostage in… Clare's in there with them."

Richards looked at him in shock, his mind trying to catch up with where McCready might be going with this. Once all the worst-case scenarios had piled up in a corner of his brain, which he knew were probably nowhere near as bad as what he was about to hear, he managed to focus.

"Question still stands. What's it got to do with us?"

McCready looked at him as though he were stupid.

"I have to get her out."

Richards had been right, it was far worse than he'd imagined. He tried to process what he wanted to say but realized that would get them nowhere. He toned it down and came up with… "Are you absolutely freaking nuts?"

"You've used that one before."

"Oh, really?"

"Uh huh."

"For a start, how do you know she's in there?"

"I had a call from a friend of hers. She saw her yesterday before she went to work at the complex. She can't be a hundred percent sure Clare is in there, but she hasn't been able to contact her since, and as Clare is the assistant manager, she would likely have been with the presidents in the cocoon when they were attacked."

"That's a whole lot of ifs and buts."

"I know."

Richards paused. "So what happened to the fact she's moved on? She's with this other guy. Why is it any of your business?"

McCready looked at him, and Richards knew he didn't need an answer. It was clear he'd never really gotten over Clare and obviously still loved her. Any other considerations would be irrelevant. The fact she may well have moved on simply wouldn't compute in McCready's mind. He'd cross that bridge when he came to it.

"Okay," he said, slowly feeling his way carefully through the minefield he now found himself in. "Just for argument's sake, let's say she is in there. Just about every law enforcement agency in the US is on-site. The military's on-site. What the hell do you think you can do that they can't?"

"First off, the military seem to have screwed up. That was a SEAL team that was taken out, and those guys know what they're doing. If they're gone, the authorities will have limited options. Short of blowing up the building, there's not a whole lot they can do, and they'll never do that with Stevens and Petrovich in there, so we have to think outside the box."

"Outside the box? We don't even have a box! Listen to yourself. You've just described the perfect, iron-clad reason why there's nothing you can do. If a SEAL team is taken out, how the hell do you think you can do any better?"

The obvious didn't seem to faze McCready.

"They won't be expecting me. I have no rules I have to

stick to. No standard operating procedure. And, most importantly, I have a different objective. I'm not after the presidents. Even if they send another team in and attempt another rescue, they won't care about Clare. All they'll try and do is get Stevens and Petrovich out. Clare wouldn't have a chance. She'd be collateral damage. Expendable."

Richards had seen him this focused many times before, but maybe not to quite the same degree.

"Okay, there is a certain logic to that, but it doesn't change the situation. How the hell do you expect to get in? The place is surrounded with all the armed forces you can lay your hands on. From what I can see there are only two entry points. One, through the reservoir. You could maybe sneak in at night from the lake, but as the reports showed, there's a SWAT team on-site in case the terrorists try and escape that way. The only other option is through the top of the building, but how do you get close enough to somehow climb up and get in through what will no doubt be another heavily guarded area? It's just not possible." He sat back, happy he'd given McCready no room to maneuver and that he would see the futility of the task. He appreciated his friend had had to try, but the obvious impossibility would hopefully finally dawn on him.

He should have known better.

"What if they didn't see me coming?"

"And how the hell would that happen?"

"Come with me."

McCready led Richards out of the conference room, through the design studio, and then outside and down the metal exterior set of stairs. He then made a right that took him into the construction building that extended alongside the full length of the tank building.

The place would normally be a hive of activity, but now it was quiet as everyone had gone home for the night. At the end of the space was the battered hulk of the Skyline craft.

McCready walked straight past it and up to a door in a wall that divided the building in two. He typed into a security keypad, opened the door, and walked through. Richards followed. He closed it behind them and stood by the door looking out across the space. It was large, but not as big as the one they had just left.

This was where the more sensitive projects Ocean Tech worked on were located. While most of their work was involved with the development of equipment for use by the scientific community, for expeditions and underwater exploration, the other side of the business worked on government projects for the special forces and other clandestine services.

McCready walked over to the far right-hand corner. He had got about halfway when he heard Richards behind him.

"No, no, no, a million times, NO, John!"

McCready stopped next to a large vehicle that looked similar to the Skyline craft in the other part of the building. It was resting on a wheeled metal frame about six feet off the ground. The main difference was the size. This was larger than the one in the other room. Instead of a solid nose cone, the whole front dome of the craft was transparent. The main body was white, as with the smaller model. But this was a prototype. The final version would have a body covered in a matte-black radar-absorbing polymer-based material to provide stealth capabilities. Also, at the rear, where the engines were located, there was what appeared to be a large detachable section.

McCready turned to Richards.

"No, absolutely, no!" said Richards.

"Why not?"

"Which reason do you want? The first... or the five thousandth? She's never flown before. You saw the problems out on the loch. This was what I wanted you to come back to talk about. The engineers think we took the wrong direction with the thruster jets to slow her down. There seems to be an inherent design flaw in the concept. What they want to try is the second option they developed—the rocket propelled system that fires projectiles at the water. They explode, creating millions of tiny bubbles, aerating it, making it less dense. Cushions the impact, so it's survivable. But it's never been done before... let alone tried on an unmanned vehicle... let alone tried on a manned vehicle that's never even flown. The units are ready to go, but they've never been tested beyond being attached to a frame at a test site."

"But it could work, yeah?"

Richards just stared at him, shaking his head. "Yes, it could work, in the same way you could win the lottery on Friday night... but are you prepared to bet your life on those odds?"

McCready's expression gave him all the answer he needed. Richards clenched and unclenched his fists. "And if you give me the *this is the most important thing I've ever asked of you* speech, I swear I'll come over and smack you one!"

"This is the most important..."

"I will, John. This is beyond nuts. Do you really have a death wish?"

"I'm still here, aren't I?"

"Apparently miracles do happen. If you were a cat you'd have been dead years ago."

"Good job I've never had a problem with hair balls then," said McCready, deadpan.

Richards was almost shaking with frustration when he looked at McCready. But he knew it would pass. The sooner he transitioned through this stage of denial, the quicker they could get on with making sure whatever they ended up doing would work, and that there was a vague to slim chance McCready might make it back alive. He took a deep breath.

"Okay, what do you want to do?"

Over the next hour McCready told him the plan. And while Richards didn't feel any better—in fact, he felt a whole lot worse—he now had a goal, a task he could focus on, so that was what he did.

The Skyline X2, as it was known, was designed to carry a single person to any point on the planet at speed and with complete stealth.

It had been developed at the request of a man McCready had come to know only too well—Martin Steel. Steel worked for the British government on security projects but liaised with the special forces as well as all branches of the military. It was thought a vehicle of this capability could be invaluable in infiltrating special operatives behind enemy lines, or indeed anywhere there was a need to get a human being on the ground should a drone not be able to provide the necessary intel or carry out a mission. It had been developed alongside the unmanned version, as many of the technologies were similar. The obvious difference was that the manned version had to provide life support for its occupant, as well as have space for equipment.

There were also different options when it came to landing.

The land version would simply touch down using a parachute. The aquatic version, however, had to use a version of the rocket system to land safely in the water and ensure no harm came to any occupant.

Once in the water, the rockets would be jettisoned along with the main engines. It then had the added capability of acting as a one-man submersible. But as Richards had been at pains to point out, none of the aerial capabilities had been tested. The underwater trials had been thorough and had worked perfectly in the tank, but they had never been tried following a flight and landing. No one knew, beyond computer modeling, how it would actually work when the craft had flown at speed through the air and then impacted the water. If they went through with this, McCready was in danger of becoming the ultimate crash test dummy.

McCready's plan was for the X2 to be air launched (another thing that hadn't been tested) some way out in the Pacific off California. It would then fly in low over the ocean, minimizing detection by the US authorities as the prototype had no stealth capability. When it reached the complex, the craft would rise up high above the building, invert, and then drop vertically into the top of the flooded core. Assuming everything worked, and McCready was still alive, he could then use the underwater capability to descend to the cocoon and attempt to rescue Clare.

He clearly wouldn't be able to use the sub to get them both out, but he could take equipment with him that would allow them to survive underwater. Getting out, should, in theory, be easier than getting in. They could just come back to the surface, either in the building, or else make their way up the tunnel to the reservoir and simply surrender to the authorities.

There was, of course, always the chance of being shot at as potential terrorists, but as McCready had said, they would worry about that at the time. As well as that issue, it was entirely possible, if they made it out, that McCready would be thrown in jail for the rest of his natural life, but he had assured Richards a phone call to Martin Steel would sort that out. When Richards had looked at him skeptically, McCready had said he had an understanding with the man. Richards just wondered if Steel's understanding of the relationship was the same as McCready's.

So it was that Richards now found himself in the secure construction building, with his engineers, who had driven in for an all-nighter, preparing Skyline X2 for its first flight, one that would take McCready into the most heavily guarded and militarily sensitive piece of real estate on the planet.

He smiled grimly to himself—just another day—or night—at Ocean Tech!

The one other thing Richards had done was to ring Charlie and make sure she'd be at Aberdeen airport early the following day to prepare for the flight. The call had gone fairly well. He'd had to mention the fact that she might be away for a while, and no, this actually wasn't a training mission, it was the real thing and anything could happen. The reply from her had been "Ripper!" so Richards had taken that as her being on board with the whole fiasco.

Yet again, he found himself wondering if this was the last time he would see his friend. But then, as McCready had said, he was still here, though this time Richards couldn't help thinking he'd maybe bitten off more than he could chew.

Chapter Thirty-Two

Yana Kuznetsov had settled in well at the research station.

She had now found her way around and where everything was located. The first night had been a little weird, as the sleeping quarters were somewhat cramped and she couldn't really move around that easily in her sleeping bag, but after a while she had found the experience comforting and she was feeling good about things.

Karl had been a great shoulder to lean on, and while he had been showing her the ropes, they'd chatted about past exploits they'd shared together, from expeditions to the Atacama Desert in Chile, the driest place on Earth, and also to Antarctica. Those had all been in preparation for this mission. Petersen, though, had not been quite so forthcoming. Yana wasn't sure if the woman saw her as a rival or just didn't like the idea of another female on the base, despite her initial welcome.

Yana was working at the systems computer control panel when Petersen came over to her.

"So, what's your main research centered on?" she asked.

Yana looked up. "It's to do with the speed of photons in a vacuum. Trying to calculate if there are differences in different environments."

"Sounds interesting."

"It has its moments. And you?"

"I'm a biologist, so mainly looking at growth rates of different strains of seeds, to try to find the optimal conditions for growth."

"How's that going?"

"Great. We're on the fourth trial now. Should have all the data I need before I rotate out."

Petersen looked at what Yana was doing. "So, you're also an electrical specialist? I see you're working on the computer boards."

"Yep, that's right."

"What's exactly wrong with them? I wasn't aware of any issues before you arrived."

Yana concentrated on the boards. She needed to play this carefully. "Oh, just routine really. They need me to run diagnostic tests to understand what would happen if a certain percentage went down, that sort of thing. Probably out of your field as a biologist." She winced slightly, thinking she'd maybe gone too far.

"Yeah, maybe," said Petersen. "But I do know what you're working on has nothing to do with communications. That's the guidance and attitude control panel."

Yana froze for a moment. She didn't want to show her hand until absolutely necessary. Things could get tricky. "Yeah, the checks cover a number of systems. May as well be as thorough as I can while I'm here. Better safe than sorry, as they say."

She turned to smile at Petersen, her hand holding onto

the panel cover. As she turned, her sleeve rode up. Petersen noticed something on the underside of her wrist.

"Nice tattoo. Anything significant?"

Petersen glanced at the wolf's head with crossed swords before pushing her sleeve down to cover it up. "Just a family thing. Solidarity with my brothers."

"Cool," said Petersen, before moving away to concentrate on her own work.

Yana watched her go. She would have to keep an eye on her. The woman was clearly suspicious about something.

That and other thoughts were racing through her mind as she glanced out of the window at the Earth racing past at over seventeen thousand miles per hour, two hundred and fifty miles below.

Chapter Thirty-Three

It was nearly midday and the air was crisp and clear as McCready climbed aboard the modified Boeing 737 at Aberdeen airport. The plane was white with a sky-blue Ocean Tech logo and wording along the side. From the outside it looked like any regular passenger jet, but inside it was very different.

To the rear of the cockpit were the galley and toilet facilities. You then came to a seating area for eight people. These were all business-class type seats with appropriate legroom. This led into a space with couches and tables so discussions and meetings could take place. At the rear of the section was a console with computers and screens on the walls, beyond which was a pressurized bulkhead. There was a single door in the middle, which was currently open. The other side of the bulkhead was the cargo bay for the aircraft.

While there was a standard hold below the forward section, the rear half of the plane was completely free of fixtures and fittings. In the center was a cradle assembly that currently held the Skyline X2. It hung there, suspended from the roof, the transparent hinged nose cone swung open to allow access. The area could be pressurized and depressurized when the craft was launched through the two long double doors in the floor.

Right now, Graham Evans and a second technician were fussing around the X2, preparing it for the ultimate test flight. Some diving equipment was laid out on the floor.

McCready watched them for a while and felt a certain sense of pride. They had been up the whole night to get everything ready for the trip, but no one had complained, no one had grumbled, they had just got on with the work. At least there were now a couple of long flights they could get some rest on.

He walked back into the seating area and sat down on one of the couches. Richards was already seated, along with Porter, who had said he would come along for the ride. Both McCready and Richards thought it more likely to have something to do with his attachment to their Australian pilot than anything else, but he was good company, and it was always useful to have someone of Porter's skillset around.

McCready had just sat down when Charlie poked her head around the cockpit door, a smile on her face.

"Morning, guys. Good to go?"

"All set," said Richards. "You okay with the plane?"

"No worries. And your pilot guy seems to know what he's doing."

"Yeah, well he should," said Richards, smiling.

The pilot in question was Matt Carson, the test pilot Boeing had sent along to ensure everything ran smoothly after the reconfiguration of the aircraft. He would stay on to make sure Charlie was up to speed with the instrumentation and act as copilot for the trip.

"Just going through final pre-flight checks," she added. "Should be off in about fifteen minutes if we get clearance from air traffic."

"Thanks."

She disappeared back into the cockpit. Richards turned to McCready. There was no point trying to talk him out of it at this stage, but there was no harm going over the details again to make sure everyone was on the same page.

"So, you okay with the impact procedure?"

"Your guys told me the sensors are set for a hundred feet when the projectiles fire."

"Yep. Don't forget you'll be traveling fast. Once you pass a hundred feet above the surface, the rockets will fire from either side, same as the retros from before, only these will shoot small charges—think hand grenade size—into the water. They'll explode when they're about ten feet underwater. You'll hit hard, but the aeration should mean you'll be okay. Just make sure you're secured into the cradle harness as tight as you can. Don't want your head going through the dome. It would be awfully expensive to repair."

McCready gave him a look.

"Once you're underwater the rockets will drop away, giving you more maneuverability and less chance of entanglement. You'll have to manually jettison the engine pack. Be sure you're free before going anywhere. The main issues are going to be when you leave the craft. Obviously, you'll need to equalize the pressure, and, depending how deep you are, that may take a while. The cocoon appears to be over two hundred feet down, assuming the building is still full of water, so you need to make sure you're ready to get to the breathing gear in the cargo section before you flood the interior."

"Yes, Dad."

"John, I'm serious. There are a million things that can go wrong that we've thought of, and a million others we haven't."

"Yeah, I know."

As McCready leaned back into the seat, Charlie came over the speaker telling everyone to buckle up as they had clearance. Evans and the other technician made their way back into the main cabin, sat down and strapped themselves in.

Ten minutes later they were hurtling down the runway and smoothly lifting off the mile-long stretch of tarmac at the edge of the North Sea. The sky was clear, and as they banked round to line up for the long haul over the North Atlantic, McCready glanced down at the buildings of Ocean Tech and the city beyond. For a moment, he had the sobering thought he might never see them again. But he pushed it far back into his mind and settled in for the flight. They would refuel once they reached the States, but aside from that he would need to get all the rest he could. When they reached California, and he was released from the plane, there would be no rest until it was over.

McCready was awoken by a slight juddering. It was turbulence as they descended over the waters off the east coast of the United States. When he opened his eyes, he could see Richards staring out of one of the small windows in the side of the fuselage. It was dark outside, and as he watched, he could see the lights of New York glistening in the night.

A few moments later he felt the slight bump, bump of touchdown and then an increase in engine noise that meant the reverse thrust had engaged.

He relaxed back as they taxied down the runway and over to a refueling stand at John F. Kennedy Airport. They would be here for an hour and then there was the onward flight to California.

Five hours later Richards shook McCready gently. He opened his eyes and looked up blearily at his friend.

"Time to get ready," said Richards.

A moment later and McCready was awake. He made use of the facilities to have a wash and splash water on his face, and then he walked back through the plane to the console this side of the bulkhead.

Richards and Evans were at the computer. The technician was going over the calculated route for Skyline and inputting data. There was a map of southern California, along with GPS coordinates of various waypoints he was feeding into the system.

Richards glanced up.

"We're inputting your flight plan." He indicated a position on the map. "As you know, the whole flight is computer controlled. You don't need to do a thing. We'll drop you about ten miles offshore. The aircraft will be pointing away from land in case anyone is watching on radar. Once you're free of the plane you'll drop down to sea level and head out for a further mile. You'll then make a turn in a wide arc and head back for shore. Hopefully, by doing this you'll be below radar and will be on them before they know it. The terrain-following guidance system will then take you across LA just like a cruise missile. We're going to try and get you most of the way in the Los Angeles River."

"In a river?"

"It's a waterway that leads from Long Beach right up past the location of the complex. There's very little water in it this time of year. More like a large spillway—concrete sides and bottom," said Richards.

"The great thing is," said Evans, "that you enter at the coast and can stay low through the built-up areas, reducing the chance of detection and interception."

"Okay, so how far does it get me?" asked McCready.

"We can't get you all the way. It becomes too narrow further up and there are trees and obstructions, but we can get you eighty, ninety percent of the way."

"And then what?"

"We'll aim to pull you out probably around the Dodger Stadium. From there it's only seconds flying time to the end of the Hollywood Hills where the complex is," said Evans.

"So you don't want me to stop at any lights?"

Richards glanced at McCready, shaking his head.

"Once you're on final approach you'll gain altitude. This'll be the time you're most exposed. When you're a few hundred feet above the building, you'll rotate over one-eighty and fall straight down. At this point the main engines will cut out, so hopefully you'll be over the water."

"That would be nice."

"At a hundred feet the projectiles will fire. The explosions will cushion your fall. Once you're in the water, it's over to you. Any questions?" asked Evans.

McCready just looked at him.

"Hey, it was your idea," said Richards with little sympathy, though inside, now the plan was laid out, it seemed more like a suicide mission than anything else.

McCready looked at the final plot Evans was entering into the computer.

"How will we communicate when I'm inside?"

"Once we've landed, we'll try and get over there and get a transponder onto the side of the building somehow. No idea if we'll be able to, so assume we can't, but I'll contact you when I think we have a live connection."

"Okay, and where will you be?"

"The plane will land at Santa Monica Municipal, so we won't be far away. We don't want the scrutiny that would happen at LAX. We may need to make a hasty exit."

"Looks like we're all set then," said McCready.

Richards watched him carefully. He knew McCready better than anyone alive, and for the first time he actually saw a tenseness to him. He looked nervous. And McCready never looked nervous. He clapped him on the back. "Okay, let's get you ready."

They walked through into the rear section. The technician was making final checks to the craft. McCready's equipment was to one side. Due to size and weight restrictions, the breathing gear he would use, and that he would take for Clare, was a modified version of the Hydroid Aquabreather. It was basically a fully functioning rebreather built into a helmet about the size of a motorcycle crash helmet. It worked on the principal of having two canisters of sodium superoxide and potassium superoxide. These acted to absorb the exhaled carbon dioxide in the breathing cycle, and then convert it into breathable oxygen. The two canisters allowed for an hour's duration at depths of up to a hundred and fifty feet. The depth in the complex would be deeper, so they might run into issues of oxygen toxicity, but they would hopefully only exceed the operating depth for a short period of time, and anyway, it was all they had.

These were packed, along with McCready's fins, into the storage bay behind the main life-support compartment. When underwater, McCready would have to exit the craft to retrieve them while holding his breath.

Once the gear was secure, Richards helped him on with his drysuit.

He then went through the pressurization and depressurization procedures. This had to be carried out when McCready left the craft, but also if he had to get back in for any reason. There was a small control panel on the right-hand side of the main dome. It would take around five minutes to pressurize at the depths he was likely to go to. If he returned to the craft, it would take slightly longer to fully pump any water out.

Once McCready was happy, he stood up and looked at Richards.

"Thanks, Craig. As always, you know I couldn't do this without you."

"Tell me something I don't know."

They both smiled.

At that moment Evans poked his head around from the control desk. "Ten minutes to drop."

McCready and Richards glanced at each other. McCready then crouched down on the floor and reversed himself into the craft so he was lying prone, looking forward. Once inside, he made sure his shoulders were secure in the cradle and pulled the straps tight.

When he was set, he gave a thumbs up to the technician who was watching his progress. The man swung the dome shut, sealing him inside. Once this was done, he heard Evans' voice over the comms.

"Gas all okay?"

McCready checked the pressure readout on the digital

display just above his head. He could also hear the whooshing of gas as the machine pressurized.

"All looking good."

He could see Richards through the front dome. The second technician left the space and disappeared through the bulkhead door. A second later, Richards walked to the door and took a last look back. He raised his hand in farewell. There was nothing else to say. He walked through the door and closed it behind him.

McCready was alone.

He felt the plane make a slight bank and turn. They were heading out to sea. The next thing he heard was a crackle in his ear.

"Okay, John. One minute to drop," said Richards.

McCready looked down through the dome. A second later, the floor below him disappeared as the double doors in the bottom of the fuselage swung open. He could see the Pacific Ocean sweeping past two thousand feet below.

He found his breathing rate increasing.

His heart rate was going up.

Then Graham's calm voice came over the comms.

"Five…

"Four…

"Three…

"Two…

"One…

"Drop!"

The next instant he felt his stomach lurch as Skyline dropped out of the bottom of the 737.

Chapter Thirty-Four

He felt like he'd been falling forever, but it must have only been a few seconds before the rockets kicked in at the rear and he felt a punch in his back as he was accelerated forward.

Immediately, the view out of the dome changed from the static deep blue of the ocean to an ocean that was disappearing fast below him.

But then he had to focus.

Something wasn't right.

The trajectory was supposed to take him down close to sea level before turning back toward land, but that didn't seem to be happening.

"Hey, guys…"

"Read you, John," said Richards.

"Thought I should be losing altitude by now."

"Hang on."

McCready waited a few seconds. As he did, he felt, and saw, the craft turn in a wide arc and head back in the opposite direction. He could see the California coastline far ahead in the heat-haze of the day, but he was still too high.

And then he heard Richards' voice. He thought he detected a hint of concern.

"Yep, seems to be a slight glitch on the mapping. Working on it. You should be dropping down soon."

A second later, McCready felt his stomach heave again as Skyline dropped steeply down to just above sea level, before leveling out and heading for the shore at over four hundred miles per hour.

Lieutenant Callie Grainger looked at the radar plot in front of her.

The Rainbow Ridge Federal Aviation Administration radar site was located on the top of a mountain near Ferndale in Humboldt County, California, and it was used to track military and civilian aircraft within a two-hundred-mile radius. With the recent activity at the Omega Complex, they had been put on high alert to keep a lookout for any unusual or suspicious activity.

Grainger considered the activity on her screen to be highly suspicious. She clicked her mike control and spoke quickly and precisely.

"Vandenberg, we have a priority red. I repeat, priority red."

"Go ahead, Rainbow," came the fast and efficient response.

"Vandenberg, I recently had an anomaly approximately ten miles out from LA. The track showed two targets: one, a private 737 that had come in over land; two, a small and fast target that seemed to split off from the 737 track. It's now approaching the Los Angeles area at speed. It's also just descended below radar-tracking altitude."

"Roger, Rainbow. Thanks for the heads-up. We'll take it from here."

Grainger leaned back, still staring at the screen from which the small blip had disappeared several seconds before. She wondered what it was. But at least it wasn't her problem anymore.

The pilot of the lead F-16 received the message a few seconds after it had come through to Vandenberg.

Along with his wingman, he turned sharply to track in along the California coast toward LA. They had just completed a sweep and were at the northern end of their patrol area, a mile off San Francisco. They hit the afterburners and accelerated to Mach 2, the sonic boom ripping through the air, rattling windows along the way.

As they approached Los Angeles, the leader checked his radar. From his vantage point the equipment could look down on the ground, where altitude made no difference.

No one below could hide.

Within seconds, the system had tracked and locked onto a small, fast-moving object. It was approaching the Port of Long Beach at speed.

He spoke into his radio.

Instantly, the two jets peeled away and dropped altitude to race in and intercept the bogey.

McCready watched the world fly past a mere twenty feet below. The craft was still over the water. He had just narrowly missed a sailing boat, his slipstream almost blowing the boat onto its side. But he had no time to check. The shore was approaching fast.

But that was the least of his worries. Out of the corner of his eye, he noticed two fast-moving objects approaching from his left.

He glanced left.

"Oh shit!"

"What is it?" said Richards over the comms.

"Got two jets approaching from the north."

"You'll be fine."

"That's easy for you to say."

"We have you on the track. You're almost in the river. They can't afford to shoot you down in a populated area."

"Really? You want to tell them that?"

At that moment there was a roar as one of the aircraft flashed overhead. The fact there was only one was not reassuring. The most likely position for the other was right behind, ready to light up his tail with a Sidewinder missile.

But then the X2 raced over the docks and into the Los Angeles River.

As Evans had said, it was more like a concrete spillway than a river. A trickle of water flowed down the middle, but apart from that it was bare concrete, several hundred feet wide. He swore briefly as he shot under the first bridge, but his adrenaline was so high nothing could faze him now.

The sense of speed was exhilarating, but also disconcerting. He had no control. He was a passenger at the mercy of a computer program and sophisticated satellite tracking systems. But there was little time for fear or concern.

He glanced out of the dome, looking for the jets, but they appeared to have gone.

He looked forward.

Bridge after bridge shot overhead. There were slight curves to the right and left.

But then something distracted him to his right. He looked out of the dome and gulped. One of the F-16s had dropped down and was running parallel with him in the river. The pilot kept glancing over, his wingtip only feet from the hurtling Skyline. He suddenly jinked right to avoid the pillars of a bridge as it shot overhead. Out to the side, McCready could see the other F-16 keeping station just above the river.

A moment later and the jet disappeared behind. McCready dreaded to think what might be happening. Up ahead was a sharper turn to the left.

He was flying in blind.

The X2 suddenly banked sharp left.

As he turned, a missile flew past his right-hand side and hit an upcoming bridge. The explosion blew out the supports, throwing debris into the air. Shrapnel-sized pieces of concrete smashed and clattered against the dome as he flew through it, but then he was clear.

It was only the bend that had saved him.

Ahead, he could see more turns coming up. With a roar, he heard, and then saw, the F-16 shoot overhead. It was bugging out.

The next instant, he was pushed into the harness as the craft banked hard right, left, right. He felt the G-forces as he was flung from side to side. But the cradle held him secure. It was followed by a right and then a straighter section.

He flew under a freeway and was then pushed hard into the harness as the X2 shot out of the river and started to climb. He almost ducked as they raced past a large tethered blimp in the shape of a motorbike. Across the side was written BOB'S BIKES ARE THE BEST BIKES.

The buildings below started to recede. He could make out the range of hills ahead. He was climbing fast now, heading toward a point above the right-hand end of the hills.

He could also now see the F-16s. They were in a wide, fast turn over the city, banking round to reacquire their target.

The Hollywood Hills were coming up fast.

There was a flash of blue to his left as the Griffith Park reservoir shot past. But he barely had time to register it.

Below, he could now see the Omega Complex.

A second later the craft seemed to stall in midair. His stomach carried on without him. He felt somewhat nauseous, but he didn't have time to think about it. The X2 made an almost delicate bank over in the sky, and he suddenly found himself heading straight down for the center of the main flooded core of the building.

He prayed the rockets would fire. He barely had time to see the bemused figure of an LAPD officer standing at the side of the building, staring up at him, before he felt the two solid thuds of the rockets. He saw the trails streak ahead of him into the water below. After what seemed like forever there were two explosions.

Spray and water engulfed him.

And then he hit the water.

There wasn't the violent impact he'd expected. It was hard, but nowhere near as bad as he'd thought it would be. A few seconds later the bubbles started to clear. He found himself staring at an amazing space, but there was no time to take in the view. He pulled the ENGINE POD RELEASE lever and heard the clunk as the pod at the rear of the craft disengaged. He also saw the two landing rocket launch tubes drop away from either side. It improved his vision and made the craft sleeker and more maneuverable.

Next, he checked all the systems were working. He powered up the electric motor that drove the propellers and scanned the diagnostics on the digital display. Everything seemed in order. He checked off his depth. Currently he was at thirty feet. He then grabbed hold of the controls and tested the thrusters, making sure they handled as expected.

Happy he was back in control, he stared out at the void in front of him. And then his mind focused in on the single task ahead.

Why he was here.

To rescue Clare.

Nothing else mattered.

Despite everything, despite the challenges that lay ahead, he now felt he could relax.

He was back in his world.

He was back underwater.

Chapter Thirty-Five

Mitch Harley stared at the collapsed ceiling of the room.

He was sitting on a raised sloping panel that had clearly been dislodged when the water had swept up the building. And while the main glass walls had remained intact, the internal structure hadn't fared so well. Half of the room was acting as an air pocket. He could tell this wouldn't be for long as water was bubbling in from one of the corners, but it had at least provided some form of refuge after the attack when his men had been killed. Since then, he'd been lying low, trying to work out his best course of action.

He knew the correct thing to do would be return up the core to the roof and be evaced out to fight another day. The only problem with that was he was at risk of being spotted and killed as he did so. It would also give the terrorists time to regroup and defend any further attack.

With him holed up in the room for almost a day, he thought it would give them a false sense of security. They might assume he was already dead. He'd watched a couple of patrols move around the inside of the flooded atrium.

Once, they had even looked into the room, but he'd hidden beneath a collapsed girder. Their torches had swept overhead and then passed on. He had also not turned the comms unit back on. He would only get grief from Bryce, and right now he felt the element of surprise he could bring to the situation, and the fact he was working on his own, might be the single factor that could swing things his way.

It had also been a relief to be able to take the full face mask off in the air pocket. He was quite happy wearing the mask for extended periods, and had done so on many occasions, but even though he had a rebreather, it had a finite supply of oxygen, so the more he could conserve the better. The computer readings would be off somewhat given the change in mixture he was breathing, but he hoped the hemofilters, even though they were still experimental, would at least keep any potential damage to a minimum. He was just checking the rebreather display when he heard two dull explosions from above.

What the hell is that?

It was unlikely they'd mounted another assault. Bryce had said there was a problem getting another team on-site due to the transport issues. He thought he'd try the radio, just in case. He didn't want to go shooting any of their own men, creating a blue on blue situation. He plugged his earpiece back in.

"Control, this is SEAL Alpha, do you copy?"

There was a crackly silence for a few seconds.

"Go ahead, Mitch." It was Bryce. "You're clearly still alive." The tone wasn't particularly friendly. "What can I do for you?"

"I just heard two explosions, sir. Anything to do with us?"

"No. We're in the dark, same as you. Some kind of

aerial craft came in low over LA and then climbed above the building. According to an LAPD officer on the roof, it then dived for the water and fired two projectiles, which exploded just before it hit. It appears the craft is manned."

Harley hesitated for a moment.

"So, if it's not one of ours, then whose is it?"

"No idea. I've never seen anything like it before. I can't believe the terrorists would have access to that sort of kit, but then they should never have got their hands on *Deep Intruder*. If you come across anyone else down there, treat them as hostile."

"Will do, sir. Any sign of the second team?"

"They're on their way." He paused. "As you're back on comms, keep me updated with your status. When the team arrive, I'll brief them on everything that's happened, but I won't send anyone into the building until we agree a plan with you."

"Thank you, sir. Harley out."

He thought about what Bryce had said. Who the hell was out there? He pulled the mask back over his face, checked his gas, and then slid into the water.

It was time to go back to work.

McCready had taken only minutes to feel completely at home with Skyline in its underwater mode. They had done hours of trials in the flooded dry dock at Aberdeen and the craft had always performed flawlessly.

Now, as he headed deeper into the complex, he barely needed to think in order to maneuver through the water. He reached a depth of about sixty feet when he decided to take a look around the edge of the building. While his main objective was further down, over a hundred and fifty feet below, it was always good to know the challenges and dangers of the environment you were working in.

The controls were fairly simple. He had two joysticks that operated the main pitch, yaw and roll of the craft. He then had thruster controls located as pedals for his feet, which could increase speed.

He gently turned the left-hand joystick. The craft moved smoothly to the left, heading for the side of the atrium at the fifteenth level. He stared grimly out of the dome as he passed bodies suspended in the water. One brushed past the glass, the unseeing eyes staring blankly in at him.

He reached the side.

There was a walkway around the edge, and while most of the levels had rooms separated by walls, many of the areas were open-plan, and he could move freely through them. He reflected for a moment that this was where Clare had been working for the last six months.

He pushed on his left foot. The extra thrust propelled him forward through one of the open-plan areas to reach the side of the building. It was weird lying prone in the craft and effectively flying through the inside of an office block. It was even more weird to be able to look out of the glass side. Below, he could see a large number of vehicles parked up. Some were fire and rescue trucks, but many were military. He could also see helicopters and two recompression chambers. At least there was somewhere capable of rendering assistance if Clare had any issues when he brought her out. It never crossed his mind, for one second, he wouldn't be able to.

He moved back toward the center.

Before he reached the walkway, he noticed movement on the far side of the atrium. He stopped the craft and settled onto the floor.

On the far side, he could see a diver emerge from a collapsed section of floor. He looked to be wearing a rebreather and full face mask. He also had a DPV. He couldn't see any weapons, but the DPV had some kind of attachment on the top that looked like it could launch a spear or projectile.

As he watched, the diver moved to the edge of the atrium and peered over into the depths. Once he seemed to be happy all was clear, he looked up, as though searching for something. He then headed down, keeping close to the side of the core.

McCready watched for a couple of minutes. He didn't know if the diver was a good guy or a bad guy, but given he was on his own and being openly cautious, it was likely he was a good guy. The only issue was that he would almost certainly consider McCready to be hostile unless he had a reason to think otherwise. He decided it was best to stay out of his way for the time being.

He watched the diver head deeper.

The diver had been descending for about a minute when McCready noticed movement above him. There were two shapes on the floor above. They were tracking the diver's movements one floor below.

McCready was torn. He was here for Clare. He had no desire to get involved in anyone else's fight. If he did, it could create problems he really didn't want to deal with right now.

But the next second forced his hand.

One of the divers moved from the floor above and circled round behind the diver below. The other one stayed directly above the first diver, who was oblivious to their presence. The second diver, now behind the first, drew a weapon.

McCready could wait no longer.

He pulled back on the joysticks to bring Skyline up off the floor. He then pushed hard with both his feet on the thruster controls. The sub leapt forward, heading out over the void, straight for the second diver. The diver had now lifted the weapon and was aiming it at the unsuspecting person in front.

Skyline wasn't armed in any way, but a craft traveling at over thirty knots could certainly be used as a weapon. And it could certainly do damage to a diver in the water if there was a collision. McCready was determined to make sure there was one.

He was about twenty feet away when the diver on the level above spotted him. The two terrorists must have been in wireless communication because the second diver spun round to face him. He leveled the weapon at McCready, but before he could fire, Skyline crashed into him, pushing him back hard, pinning him against the wall. He was knocked out cold, but not before the projectile fired off harmlessly to crash and explode on the other side of the building.

At this, the first diver spun round. He took in the scene in front of him and stared straight at McCready. To McCready, he seemed completely calm, which meant he was highly professional and unlikely to do anything stupid. Through the transparent dome McCready urgently indicated upward. The diver glanced up to see the other diver drop off the level above and move down fast toward him.

The man finned up quickly, drawing a knife as he went. As they made contact, the two bodies struggled fiercely. McCready could see a knife in the second man's hand. It was touch and go, but after an agonizing minute the rebreather hose of the enemy diver was cut. He whirled around in panic, flailing in the water, desperate for something to breathe, but he was never going to get it. The first man looked into his eyes and held him there as he convulsed violently. After a couple of minutes he stopped moving. He let him go, watching briefly as his lifeless body sank slowly down into the deep.

The man turned to McCready and swam over.

The diver McCready had knocked out appeared to be coming round. The first diver swam up to him and swiftly cut his hose. He too convulsed briefly before slipping silently into the depths. The diver then approached the dome at the front of Skyline.

The two men stared at each other.

The man spoke, but McCready couldn't hear. He shook his head. The man held up a finger, telling him to wait a second. He adjusted a control on a small black box attached to the side of the rebreather. He then held up two fingers followed by seven fingers. McCready nodded. He glanced at the display above his head and turned the communications control switch. He retuned the frequency to 27 kHz.

"You hear me, now?" said a strong and confident American voice.

"Loud and clear," replied McCready.

"Nice toy," said the man.

"First test drive," said McCready. "Kind of a last-minute thing."

The man watched him with a slightly confused, but interested, expression.

"Thanks, by the way."

"No problem."

"Who the hell are you?"

"John… John McCready."

"Nice to meet you John. Mitch, Lieutenant Mitch Harley."

"Nice to meet you, Lieutenant. Good day for a swim."

Harley looked at him, not quite figuring him out. He smiled and then looked straight at McCready.

"What the hell are you doing here?"

"There's someone I need to get out of the cocoon. Don't worry, not one of your guys. I assume you're here for Stevens and Petrovich."

Harley nodded.

"Her name's Clare Kowalski. She's the assistant manager. To be honest I've no idea if she's even in there, but there wasn't much else on at the moment."

"You're doing all this for a girl?" Harley asked, incredulously.

"Yeah. Crazy, huh?"

Harley merely nodded, but also shook his head slightly. McCready could see a hint of a smile through a few droplets of water that had built up on the inside of Harley's mask.

"Yeah, I would say so." He looked like he was thinking for a moment. "We have reports that she is in there, and alive. Want to pool resources?"

"Maybe."

"What can that thing do?" He nodded at Skyline.

"She's just transport. I can get out, though, and I have gear to get the girl out. I really don't want to get in your way or have to worry about your guys. I'm only here for the girl."

"Okay, but let's play together until we have to part ways. Fair enough?"

McCready weighed things up. He didn't want to get involved in Harley's mission. It might leave him with difficult decisions down the line, but he could use the guy's help to get inside. And he was armed. It couldn't do any harm. He looked up.

"Okay, fair enough. But when the time comes we go our separate ways."

"Sure."

McCready knew he was lying, but what did he have to lose? He'd cross that speed bump when they came to it.

"I'll take her down to the bottom. Meet you there."

Harley waved acknowledgment.

McCready watched Harley swim away. He then adjusted the controls and moved out into the center of the atrium. Once done, he pushed forward on the joysticks. Skyline responded, heading deeper, and more importantly —closer to Clare.

Chapter Thirty-Six

Kozak looked at the screens in the control room.

He had seen the SEAL team encounter earlier, and the fact that he'd lost two of his men. He had sent two more out to sweep the area, sure one of the US forces was unaccounted for. Much later, he had then watched as a strange craft had entered the water and two more of his men had ended up dead.

With apparently two hostiles still alive and heading for the cocoon, he had reached a decision.

He placed a small box on the desk. He plugged a cable into a socket in the panel in front of him. He knew this would connect to the antenna at the top of building. He typed a code into the box and then pressed a small button on the side. A notification appeared saying the message had been sent. A minute later there was confirmation the message had been received. Kozak nodded briefly to himself.

He then walked with purpose from the control room

into the meeting room. As he entered, Clare and the leaders looked up.

Kozak looked at each of them in turn.

"It would appear the American forces are launching another rescue attempt. It is futile. My men will wipe them out. However, it has forced me to move things to the next stage. The attack on New York has been initiated. The only way this can now be stopped is for you to comply with my demands. And believe me when I say you do not have much time. I will leave you to decide what you wish to do, but be in no doubt, the consequences of doing nothing will be devastating. And they will be on your heads." He paused and then added, "The attack cannot be stopped unless I send a specific code through this box." He pulled out the small box. "So if anything should happen to me, that would not be good for you."

Stevens and Petrovich glanced at each other.

"What if we still don't believe you. The air force is on standby. The police and military are on the streets. You won't achieve your goal. You'll fail."

"I don't think so." There was a thin smile on Kozak's face, but there was no humor behind it.

"Prove it."

Kozak thought for a moment and then started to speak.

Yana heard a beeping from the pack she wore around her waist. She reached in and withdrew a small plastic device that had a screen on the front. She read the coded numbers that appeared on the screen and then pressed a button. An icon flashed indicating acknowledgment had been sent.

She then pushed herself away from her sleeping

compartment and floated effortlessly across to her work locker on the other side of the module.

It had taken her a while to get used to zero G, but now she had the hang of it she could move smoothly around the International Space Station without any problems. The trick was to use just the right amount of energy not to barrel into the other side, or wherever it was you were going. She found that a minimal amount of energy, just to start her moving, was usually the best approach. It wasn't like you needed to push harder to go further. Once you started moving you kept going until you grabbed onto something to slow you down.

She was currently in the Russian Zvezda service module, which was located at one end of the ISS. It had been the first main Russian contribution to the station. It was forty-three feet long by just over thirteen feet wide, and housed life support, data processing, and, critically, flight control systems. Attached to the outside was a ninety-seven-foot solar array that helped provide power to the station.

When she was at her locker she opened it up and pulled out a toolkit that contained a number of specific tools. She grabbed this, along with her laptop.

She then crossed over to the main computer control panel. She held onto the side to slow herself to a stop. When she'd steadied herself, she opened the toolkit and used a specific screwdriver to open up the main panel. She plugged in her laptop and made sure a diagnostic readout came up on the screen.

She then set to work.

She ran the program she had written earlier. Every now and then she would enter new code in the lines that scrolled up the screen.

Once she had finished modifying the flight control systems, she turned to the controls that would operate the adjacent Zarya module. This was now used primarily for storage, but it also had one other very special function she needed control over—the propulsion systems.

If the station needed to change orbit, there were a couple of ways it could do it. For occasional correction changes, it could use thrusters in the unmanned Russian Progress supply ships when they were docked. Using this saved fuel on the station itself. The second option, for more serious maneuvers, were thrusters built into the Zarya module. It was these that Yana needed to be able to control.

After ten minutes, she was still scrolling through the code, finding the lines she needed to alter, when she sensed something behind her.

She stopped and turned round.

In front of her the other astronauts were floating in a semicircle. None of them were smiling. It looked like a lynching party.

Jackson was the first to speak.

"Hey there, Yana. You need a hand with anything?"

Yana's gaze flicked from Jackson to Gruber to Petersen. There wasn't a friendly look from any of them.

"No, I'm fine thanks, Jonas. Just getting on with my work."

Gruber grabbed a handle on the ceiling and moved forward. He just about managed a smile, but he also looked slightly embarrassed. "Yana, Andrea has mentioned that you told her some things that are not entirely true. We're just a bit concerned."

"Really?" said Yana, a confused expression on her face. "What might those be?"

Petersen spoke. "I checked the log assignments and spoke with NASA. It appears you have not been assigned any diagnostic work. They say all systems are running fine and there are no planned checks until the next mission in a month."

Yana tried to look casual. "Well, they must be mistaken. I was definitely briefed on going through these checks. Anyway, what's the big deal?"

Jackson moved closer. "What exactly are you doing?"

"Just checking code. Thought I'd make sure it was all running smoothly."

"Let me see."

Jackson was about to move in to look at Yana's laptop. Before he could reach it, Yana spun to her right. She grabbed hold of a handrail above her head and kicked out at Jackson with all her strength. Taken by surprise, and unable to grab hold of anything, Jackson was pushed across the module, knocking Gruber out of the way as he went. Gruber spun to one side before grabbing hold of a locker and steadying himself. Jackson smashed into a food dispenser on the far side before being able to stop himself.

They all stared at Yana. She looked at them with a fierce determination.

"I didn't want you to find out this soon. It would have been much easier on you if you never knew, or didn't know until the last minute. But we are where we are." They continued to stare. "I have rewritten certain command codes for the orbital control of the station. Houston has been taken out of the loop. They can still monitor and receive automated feedback, but they can no longer control the thrusters or the orbital track; that is all now under my control."

They stared at her with shock and incomprehension.

"But why?" said Jackson.

For a second Yana appeared as if she were far away.

"You would not understand. You could not understand. And I am sorry you have had to become involved in this. But there are higher things at stake." She turned to Gruber and smiled. "Karl, you are my friend, so it is very hard for me to see you here. Jonas, you seem like a great commander and you have my respect." And then to Petersen. "Andrea, I hold no ill will toward you. I think we somehow got off on the wrong foot, and I do not blame you for being suspicious and concerned about me. Your instincts were correct. None of this is personal. But it is something I have to do. You cannot talk me out of it. You cannot stop me. That is just the way it is."

"But what are you doing?" Gruber asked the question everyone was thinking.

Yana thought for a moment. "I mentioned to Andrea earlier that I have a strong solidarity with my brothers." She pulled up her sleeve, revealing the tattoo. "Our family and our country have been ravaged and betrayed by Russian aggression. The world has stood by and let this happen."

"But I thought you were Russian?" said Petersen.

"I am Ukrainian. I married a Russian and moved there eight years ago. For various reasons, it helped protect my family." She paused. "Today, my brothers and I will avenge that aggression, either by forcing the Russians to pull back to their territory and return Crimea to its rightful sovereignty, or…"—and she hesitated now—"…or I will crash the ISS onto New York and make the Americans think of the consequences of their *inaction*—for once."

They stared at her as though she was insane.

"But Yana, you can't!" blurted out Gruber. "This is madness!"

"We will stop you," said Petersen defiantly.

Yana looked at her sadly.

"Andrea, you can't." She indicated the laptop. "The instructions have been entered. They can only be cancelled by a code I will receive if the demands are met. If that is the case I will gladly enter it in the laptop and stop the attack, and you may then do with me as you wish. But, and I must make this absolutely clear, without the code, nothing can stop the re-entry process."

As if in support of her words, there was a sudden jerk and a loud whooshing sound as the thrusters built into the Zarya module started to alter the course of the station. They felt the movement and had to hang on as they were jolted from their positions.

The normal track of the ISS took them in an orbit over the United States from west to east, but its exact position varied. Now, slowly, the orbital correction initiated by the thrusters was sending them toward a track that would take them directly over New York. Once this was set, the next stage would be to lower the altitude by reducing speed until they began to skim off the Earth's atmosphere. At this point the station would start to burn up, but enough of it would make it through to strike the city, wiping it from the face of the Earth.

Jackson looked straight at Yana. "You know we can't let you do this."

"Jonas, there is nothing you can do," she said simply. "I am sorry." She paused and then looked up at them again. "You are all free to leave in one of the Soyuz capsules. I will not stop you, but I must repeat, there is nothing you can do to save the station, except pray I receive the code before it is too late. And that is in the hands of President Petrovich."

They glanced at each other, the magnitude of the situation starting to sink in.

"You have got to be shitting me!" blurted out Stevens when Kozak had finished speaking.

"I am not," said Kozak. "Now I will leave you to discuss this, and I only pray you will come to the right decision."

Kozak walked from the room. When he left, there was a stunned silence, then Stevens turned to Petrovich. "Viktor, you have to accede now. There is no way to stop this."

Petrovich looked at him calmly. "As I have said before, Mr. President, I cannot. The loss of face would be a permanent scar on our country and my presidency, from which it would be hard to recover. I suggest you try to get a message out and see if they can stop the action on the ISS. If not, it will be very bad for you."

Stevens just stared at him.

Petrovich stood up.

"I am sorry, Mr. President, but I cannot agree to the demands. I never will."

He smiled thinly and headed for the door.

Stevens took a deep breath and stood up himself. Petrovich had almost reached the door.

"Then, Viktor, there is one thing you need to know."

Petrovich turned, an uncompromising look on his face. "And what is that, Mr. President?"

Steven's eyes were unwavering as they locked onto Petrovich with a laser-like intensity. "If you do not agree to the demands, and if this madman successfully carries out his threat to attack New York, it will be considered an act of war by the United Sates. As such, there will be an immediate response against Moscow. We will retaliate with all force at our disposal." He paused. "Including nuclear weapons... Do I make myself clear?"

All the niceties were gone.

Petrovich thought for a moment, and then looked at Stevens. He appeared almost sad. "Then, Mr. President, I am afraid we both know where that will end. I will not accede to the demands."

He turned and strode from the room.

Chapter Thirty-Seven

McCready eased back on the controls and brought the X2 to rest just next to the large hole in the floor of the Omega Complex atrium.

He now had to go through the procedure to leave the safety of the sub. He started by powering down the main systems. Next, he reached over to the controls on the side, which would start the equalization process. He pressed the sequence of buttons. Shortly after, he heard, and then saw, water start to enter the interior. He felt the slow squeeze of pressure as the drysuit was compressed around his body. He had to make sure he had enough air to exit the sub and retrieve his helmet rebreather from the equipment compartment.

He breathed in and out to saturate his bloodstream with oxygen.

The water level rose up across the dome until it filled the interior. When the pressure had equalized, there was a beep from the console. A green light blinked to his right.

He reached over and undid the clamp assembly that

held the dome closed. He slowly pushed it open. It swung back on the hinges and McCready pulled himself out. His vision was blurred by the water. It was also far dimmer because of the depth.

He swam round to the rear and opened the equipment compartment. He pulled out his helmet, along with two of the canisters he would need to allow him to breathe. Once you activated them there was no way of stopping the reaction, so he couldn't have put them in before. He undid the twin flaps at the rear of the helmet and inserted the canisters, shut the flaps and pulled the helmet over his head, widening the neck seal to squeeze into it.

Once it was on, he flushed out the water with air from a small cylinder built into the top of the helmet and turned on the computer display that was above the faceplate. He made sure all the functions were operating correctly. It showed him a readout of his depth, along with the dive time, and how long the canisters would last based on his current breathing rate. He had brought spares with him, which he shoved into a pocket on his drysuit, but it was always good to know how things were going. Once he was happy everything was functioning correctly, he lifted the second helmet out of the compartment, along with his fins.

He pulled the fins on and then moved back to the front of the sub, closed the dome, and made sure the craft was secure. It was unlikely he would need it again. It couldn't fit two, and, in his mind, there was no way he was leaving if Clare wasn't with him.

Once he was ready, he looked up. He could see Harley descending toward him.

When the SEAL reached the bottom he slowed to a stop.

"Nice hat," he said over the comms.

"Does the job, but limited on time and we're pushing the depth."

Harley took another approving look at the helmet and then spoke.

"There's a main airlock that accesses the cocoon. It's where the terrorists gained entry. That's our best bet. It may be guarded, but we have to try. If that's not possible there's a second option at the rear of the cocoon."

Harley led McCready over to the large gash in the floor. The force of the water had curved the floor upward, leaving little integrity in the structure. McCready was careful not to rip his suit on the jagged metal as they made their way through. He was feeling slightly dizzy from narcosis caused by the depth. He would have liked to have had a rebreather that could use helium and oxygen, like Harley, but he was stuck with what he had. Hopefully it wouldn't be long before they were inside the cocoon.

When they reached the floor of the cavern below the atrium, they could see the devastation. Apart from the hole they'd just negotiated, the cave was strewn with detritus swept down from the reservoir, as well as cars and vehicles lying in a heap at the side.

They swam past an overturned delivery truck and, as they saw what was beyond, Harley stopped dead. In front of them was a high-tech submersible. McCready had never seen anything like it. Its ownership was given away, though, as US NAVY was written in black letters down the side.

"One of yours?"

"Yeah, they killed some friends of mine to steal it."

"I'm sorry."

"They'll wish they hadn't."

"I'm sure they will."

The sub looked intact and Harley made his way around

it. On the far side they saw the cocoon straight in front of them. It was impressive. McCready thought it looked like a massive two-story recompression chamber. It was made of metal and the sides were white. But it was huge. He'd never seen anything like it. He could only marvel at the work and expertise that had gone into the construction of the complex. It was just a shame, from a security point of view, that it had all come to naught.

"This way," said Harley.

McCready cautiously followed the SEAL round to the large airlock that extended out like a corridor from the side of the cocoon. There were windows along the side. He moved closer and looked through. At the far end, he could make out two men on the other side of glass panels in the inner airlock door. Both were armed. McCready moved back to Harley at the outer door. A control panel was lit up with lights and there was a keypad. Harley was about to enter the code.

"I wouldn't." Harley looked up. "They've got armed men just inside the inner door."

Harley stopped. "You sure?"

McCready nodded. Harley thought for a moment. "Okay, plan B."

McCready smiled. He loved a plan B.

"Follow me," said Harley.

They swam back up through the gash in the atrium floor and over to what would be the far side of the cocoon below, eventually reaching a track that extended up the side of the building. It also disappeared into the ground below.

"This is part of the lift-track that acts as a transport system within the complex. Sort of an elevator," said Harley. "This one's like a back entrance. It may not be guarded." McCready followed him over to the track.

"So what's the plan?" asked McCready.

"Your lady friend was able to get a message up from here, using a capsule, so that means there's no capsule down below. It should give us access to the airlock and then into the cocoon." Harley glanced at McCready. "Okay, let's go."

Harley went first. The shaft through the rock was wide and easily accommodated both men as they made their way down. Soon, they saw a glow of light shining up from below.

They touched down on the bottom and Harley crossed over to a control panel at the side of the airlock door. He checked an iPad in a waterproof housing for the appropriate code. Before he entered it, he warned McCready.

"Hold onto something. When this opens, the water will fill the airlock."

McCready moved back to the side and made sure he had a grip on Clare's helmet. He nodded at Harley, who entered the code. The door slid smoothly open. As it did, water rushed in to fill the space, flowing up against the inner door. When it had calmed, the two men swam in. At the touch of a button on the inner control panel, the outer door slid closed. Harley then went through the procedure to flush the airlock of water and open the inner door.

Five minutes later they were inside with the inner door closed. McCready took off his helmet and placed it on the floor along with Clare's. There was no point in taking off the suits as they would inevitably have to leave quickly later.

Harley dekitted his dive gear and unclipped the equipment bag he had at his side. He checked through the contents and then pulled up a plan of the cocoon on the iPad.

"We've no idea where anyone is. The intel said there

were around ten terrorists in total. At least four are gone, which leaves at least six in here."

He pulled a Glock from the bag.

McCready looked at him. "Okay, this is where we part company."

Harley stopped. "Not yet. I have to find Stevens, then you can go find your girl."

"That's not the agreement."

"Hey, I got you in, didn't I? Where would you be if I hadn't had the code?"

McCready had to concede this. "Okay, fair enough. But as soon as you have him, I go."

Harley looked at him and made one final check on the pad.

"We'll try Stevens' quarters first."

McCready followed Harley down the corridor. He could see the man was good. He was minimal in his movement and he was alert and held his weapon with confidence. Given the circumstances, McCready actually felt fairly safe.

Harley suddenly put up a fist to one side. McCready had seen enough movies to know he should stop. From down the corridor they could hear footsteps. Harley indicated for McCready to stay where he was and stay quiet. He then inched closer to the junction with another corridor from where the sound was coming. A second later a man appeared around the corner.

He saw the two men and his eyes went wide.

Before he even had time to reach for the weapon that was slung casually around his shoulder, Harley moved forward, quicker than McCready could register. He thrust a knife deep into the man's throat. There wasn't even a gurgle as he covered his mouth and laid him down on the floor. He then pulled the body out of the way without a sound.

"One less to worry about."

He led McCready down the corridor the man had come from until he reached a door on the right. Harley again held up his fist. He drew the Glock, placed his hand on the door handle and pushed it open fast, at the same time moving in and covering the angles. From his position outside, McCready could see Harley's body language suddenly relax. He walked in and found himself face to face with the president of the United States.

The man looked in complete shock. Harley quickly checked the rest of the room and then returned to the president.

"Mr. President. My name is Lieutenant Mitch Harley. I'm here to get you out."

The president just stared at him for a moment, and then McCready saw a wave of relief wash over him. Harley glanced at McCready. "This is John McCready. He's with me."

The president nodded at McCready and then turned to Harley.

"Thank God, Lieutenant. You're certainly a sight for sore eyes."

"Do you know how many of them there are, sir?"

"I'm not sure. They're spread around the cocoon. Could be as many as ten or eleven."

"That's okay. They're down on numbers. Where would the leader be?"

"Probably in the rec. That's where he's been based, but they also have people in the security control room. That's never left unmanned."

"I'm afraid most of my team have been killed, so I have to get you out as quickly as possible, sir."

Stevens watched as Harley pulled out a small plastic box and opened it to reveal a number of syringes.

"What's that for, Lieutenant?"

"I'm going to have to sedate you, so I can evacuate you with a dive mask."

"So how are you going to get President Petrovich out?"

Harley stopped for a second. "I can't. The other gear was taken when my men were killed. My orders are just to get you, sir."

Stevens suddenly stiffened.

"We have to get Petrovich. There's more at stake than you can possibly imagine."

Harley looked at him. "That's not going to be possible, sir. I'm sorry, but I have my orders." He continued preparing the syringe.

Stevens looked between the two men, deciding something.

"If Petrovich doesn't agree to this terrorist's demands, the man is going to crash the International Space Station onto New York. He has a code he has to send to someone on the station. If the code isn't sent, nothing can stop the attack. Petrovich needs to be made to do this. Without him New York will be destroyed. I've told him if that happens we will retaliate against Moscow with everything at our disposal. You do know what that means, Lieutenant?"

Harley stopped, his face serious. "Sir, we don't know what *may* happen. I can't get Petrovich out. I have my orders."

Stevens looked at Harley coldly. "Then, as your commander in chief, I override those orders and instruct you to rescue Petrovich along with me. If that man dies on American soil we will never live this down, let alone what the consequences will be."

Harley stopped preparing the syringe.

McCready stepped forward. "Excuse me, sir, do you know if Clare Kowalski is in the cocoon?"

Stevens just looked at him.

"She's the assistant manager. I understand she's down here."

Stevens then focused. "Yeah, and a fat lot of use she's been. It's all her fault. This place was supposed to be secure. There'll be hell to pay when this is over, I can assure you."

McCready found himself taking a deep breath to calm himself. His fists were starting to clench. Harley watched him, not sure where this was going.

"But she's safe, yes?" said McCready evenly.

Stevens looked at him. "Why the hell do you care? She's around here somewhere. Probably down in the rec on the lower level. But if I had my way I'd smack the stupid woman, and then some." He turned away as if the subject was of no more interest.

Harley was watching the two men. McCready caught his eye. A barely perceptible shake of the head told him not to do anything stupid.

McCready was becoming impatient. "Okay, so what are we waiting for?"

"I have to do what the president has instructed. I have to try and get Petrovich out," said Harley. He then looked at McCready. "And you have to help me."

"That doesn't work for me," said McCready. He looked pointedly at the syringe. "Just do it!"

"While the president's not incapacitated, I have no choice. My comms won't work down here. I can't get instructions from my chain of command."

Stalemate.

This was too much for McCready. He stepped toward

Stevens. "Well it's a good job I'm not an American citizen then." They both turned to him.

"Why is that?" asked Stevens.

"Because you're not *my* commander in chief." He stepped forward and punched Stevens in the face with all the force he could muster. The blow knocked him off his feet. He landed in a heap on a small couch, unconscious.

Harley just stared at him.

"There, he's incapacitated," said McCready. "Now get him out. I'm going after Clare."

"Creative," said Harley. But then he stopped and slowly looked at McCready. "You can't. Not now."

McCready looked at him.

Harley continued. "You have the second helmet. You have to get Petrovich."

McCready shook his head. "Not why I'm here."

"This is bigger than that," said Harley. "You have to do this."

A million things were running through McCready's mind. He found himself shaking his head again. He watched as Harley laid the president on the floor and injected the drugs.

"I'm sorry, I can't."

Harley glanced up at him. He passed McCready the iPad with the plan of the complex and the security codes for the airlocks. "Here, you might need this." He then thought for a second. "You used a handgun before?"

"Couple of times, on a range, but you probably wouldn't want to be anywhere near me when I did."

Harley pulled out the Glock and showed McCready the basics. "Just in case."

"Thanks."

Harley then hoisted the president over his shoulder and

walked to the door. He glanced back. "It's your decision. You just have to know if you could live with yourself if all this goes wrong. If you could have done any more… Do the right thing, John. Good luck."

And with that, he turned and left to head back to the lift-track.

McCready watched him go. He had to make a decision.

But it was an impossible decision.

Chapter Thirty-Eight

Andriy Kozak paced up and down the rec.

It had been over an hour since he had spoken to the presidents. Time was running out for their answer. He was starting to think about the options for an exit strategy when one of his men came running down the stairs from the gallery.

"Andriy. Andriy. Come quick!"

Kozak ran for the stairs. His heart rate started beating faster. A minute later he arrived at the security control room. Ilya was at the monitors. He glanced up when Kozak arrived.

"Look, Andriy, someone has escaped."

Kozak leaned forward to look at the screen. He could see a diver towing what looked like a body. The man was unmoving but was wearing a full face mask and had a small cylinder attached to his back. Bubbles were flowing from the mask. From the look of his clothes, it was obviously Stevens. Kozak smashed his hand down on the desk.

He looked around the screens. "Where is this?"

Ilya checked the information in the corner of the feed. "I think it's close to the second lift-track. They don't look far off the bottom, but they're heading for the center of the atrium."

Kozak thought quickly. He turned to the man who had alerted him. "Sergey, go! Take Anton and bring them back. The whole operation depends on this."

"Yes, Andriy." Sergey ran off, and Kozak turned to watch the screen.

It hadn't taken Harley long to get the equipment onto Stevens. Although awkward, at least he hadn't had the man complaining or asking questions. He'd treated him like a slab of meat, getting the gear on as fast as he could. Once they were out in the water they would have a far better chance of survival than if they were found in the cocoon. He could also call on help, because, once out of the cocoon, his comms to Bryce should work. While he could take Stevens up to the surface on his own, it would be far safer to put him under pressure and keep him there and not risk the inevitable decompression issues that would arise. He just prayed they wouldn't be spotted until he could summon help.

Now, out in the water, he finned to the middle of the atrium, towing the president behind him. Once he was in position, he set Stevens down on the floor. He then clicked the talk button on the comms.

"Control, this is SEAL Alpha, do you copy, over?"

There was static for a few moments, then Bryce's voice came over the small speaker in the mask.

"Mitch, good to hear from you. The backup team

arrived in a Black Hawk half an hour ago. What's your status?"

"I can't talk now. I have POTUS. I repeat, I have POTUS. No time for the team. But I need immediate evac with a chamber from the atrium." He glanced up and saw two divers approaching from the large gash in the atrium floor.

"And I need it NOW! I have to go!"

He turned to face the approaching divers and stood between them and Stevens.

He then made a decision.

There were two of them. He was unlikely to be able to keep one of them from getting to Stevens if he left him where he was to engage with them. Before they could reach him, he pulled a small inflatable lift bag from one of his drysuit pockets. He secured it to the webbing on the cylinder strapped to Stevens. He then injected some air into it and it floated up above the president. As soon as the bag became taut against the short line, it started to lift the president slowly up. Harley adjusted a valve on the top of the bag that set the blow-off pressure. It wasn't that precise, but what he didn't want was the president shooting up to the surface out of control, resulting in him suffering the bends. With the valve set, he could minimize this.

As Stevens started to float up, Harley turned his attention to the divers, who were now only ten feet away. His aim was to prevent them from separating. If they did, one of them could attack him while the other grabbed Stevens.

One of them moved forward. The other swam off to the side. Harley lunged at the nearest, managing to pull his gas supply from his mouth. The terrorist had to retreat to replace his life support. While he did, Harley moved round to shield the president, who was now twenty feet above them.

This time he made contact with the second man.

They grappled in the water, twisting and turning. The man pulled a knife. He tried to cut Harley's breathing hoses, but the SEAL managed to keep out of range. Out of the corner of his eye Harley could see the other diver bringing a harpoon gun to bear on Stevens. He had to protect the president. But before he could extricate himself from the terrorist, he watched in horror as the harpoon was unleashed. The spear sped upward, straight for the president. But Stevens hadn't been the target. The spear pierced the small lift bag.

It imploded, instantly losing all buoyancy. The president began dropping back down.

As Harley watched, everything suddenly became darker. He looked up the hundred and fifty feet to the surface. The light continued to darken. And then there was a mighty crash as something entered the water above.

All of them looked up.

A few seconds later he could see a large chamber sinking quickly toward him. It was attached by a cable to what Harley knew would be one of the Sea Stallions.

Bryce had come through.

With renewed vigor he kicked the nearest terrorist in the stomach, causing him to double over. He then ripped the breathing hoses from his mask and watched as he convulsed several times before going still and dropping into the depths.

He then swam as fast as he could to catch the president's sinking body. He caught it on the move, with one hand, and finned quickly for the rapidly approaching chamber. Bryce must have been watching through the video feed, as the chamber stopped at just the right depth for him to swim to the door at the end. He reached it before the remaining terrorist could catch him.

There were only seconds to spare, but he managed to pull the outer airlock door open and push Stevens inside. He then hauled himself in after and slammed the door before the terrorist could reach them. He quickly turned the locking handles, sealing the door shut, and hit the DRAIN button. Immediately there was a whooshing sound as gas entered the small airlock, expelling the water.

There was no way the terrorist would be able to get through the thick steel of the chamber.

They were safe.

Once the water had drained, Harley opened the inner door. He pulled Stevens through into the main section of the chamber, immediately dragging an oxygen mask over his face. He then slumped back against the hard metal side, exhausted from the fight. He hit the comms.

"Okay, get us up!"

A couple of seconds later he felt movement as the helicopter hauled the chamber out of the water.

He had just removed his gear when he felt, and heard, something else. There was a series of bangs and clanks on the side of the chamber. He heard a loud hissing sound.

Shit!

If the gas feeds from the cylinders attached to the chamber were damaged, they could lose all pressure inside. He made a quick check on Stevens, then moved back through into the airlock. There wasn't time to put his gear back on.

He sealed the inner door and then flooded the airlock. He took a couple of deep breaths, swung the door open, and moved quickly outside to confront the enemy.

The man was on the side of the chamber. He was

hacking at a brass pipe attached to the bank of cylinders. Harley moved forward. At the last second, the man looked up, pulled a knife and lunged at Harley... just as the chamber burst through the surface and started rising above the complex.

A few seconds later, the chamber was fifty feet in the air and rising.

Harley advanced on the terrorist. The man backed away, climbing on top of the chamber, throwing off his mask and rebreather. The Sea Stallion was now moving over the side of the building, the soft landing of the water rapidly fading if either of them fell.

Harley climbed on top and the two men faced each other. The terrorist grinned. He was enjoying this. The man undid his weight belt and came at Harley, flailing the belt like a weapon. Harley ducked, but slipped on the wet metal. The belt hit the metal with a loud clang. Harley tripped the terrorist. He fell over, losing his grip on the belt, which slipped over the side for the long fall down to the concrete below.

The two men now wrestled on top of the chamber. It shuddered and jolted with their movement, causing the outer door to fly open. Metal clanged on metal as it swung to and fro on its hinges.

The terrorist now launched himself at Harley, almost throwing them both over the side, but at the last second Harley grabbed hold of the swinging door and held on. The terrorist's momentum carried him out over the void but he managed to grab hold of Harley's body. They were both now being pulled over the edge.

Harley gripped the top of the swinging door. His life depended on it.

The terrorist was hanging onto Harley's waist. Harley

repositioned a hand so he could hit him in the face. The man slipped lower and Harley grabbed back hold of the door with both hands. The terrorist was slipping down Harley's legs. Harley shook himself from side to side. The man was now round his knees. Harley kicked out at him, and then, with a final massive effort, he kicked him in the teeth.

The man fell away with a scream.

Harley watched him fall… all the way—two hundred and fifty feet to the ground below. As he hit, Harley could hear the distant 'SPLAT'. The body exploded, deforming into something that looked more like a human stain on the concrete than a man.

With the threat gone, he slowly hauled himself back on top of the chamber. He lay there for a minute, exhausted. He just managed to give the pilot a brief wave through one of the glass panels in the nose of the Sea Stallion before collapsing onto his back.

He watched the clouds pass peacefully overhead as the chamber was carefully lowered back down to the ground.

Chapter Thirty-Nine

After Harley had left, McCready took stock of the situation.

He had the somewhat surreal thought that in the same week, he'd slept with the world's biggest movie star and knocked out the leader of the free world. He knew which encounter he'd enjoyed the most. But thinking about it, maybe it was a close-run thing. He was pretty sure both would have their consequences at some point, but he couldn't deal with that now.

He looked at the screen on the iPad Harley had left him. It showed the layout of the cocoon. He needed to find where Clare was and work out how he was going to get her out. Stevens had said she would probably be in the recreation room on the lower level. He was currently on the upper level.

The layout showed he had to make his way along two corridors and past the security control room, so he'd have to be careful. He pushed the pad into a large pocket on the thigh of his drysuit. Then he picked up the pistol Harley had given him and checked the safety was off. He had never really liked guns, but he realized there were times when having one could save your life. This was one of those times.

He made his way out into the corridor.

There was no one there.

He walked carefully to the first junction and poked his head around the corner. It was clear. He turned right and padded down the passage until he reached a corridor that led off to the side. He looked down it. It was short, but at the end was the control room. He could see a series of bright screens through the open door. He could also see the back of a man in a swivel chair. He moved quietly until he came to another corridor off to the right. He glanced into it. There were signs on the wall for men's and women's rest rooms. He carried on, walking quickly.

About ten yards further, he could see the right-hand wall open out. Just around the corner a set of stairs led down to a lower level. Ahead was a wide gallery that looked out over what he assumed to be the rec room. There were three pillars spaced evenly along its length. He could hear talking.

He moved across to the gallery and over to one of the pillars and stood behind it. He needed to get an idea of who was there. He risked a peek low down.

His heart almost missed a beat.

Clare was sitting on a couch on the far side. She didn't look good. Her hair was a mess and she seemed physically drained and exhausted. There was a man sitting on the couch next to her. He looked American and was tall and fit. Could be one of Stevens' bodyguards. On another couch was an equally in-shape guy, but this one looked menacing... and Russian. He didn't seem to be pleased to be there, therefore not one of the terrorists—possibly Petrovich's bodyguard. But then where was Petrovich?

There were three other men in the room. One carried himself in the manner of someone who was in charge—could be the leader. Another was younger and looked like he didn't belong there. The final one stood at the end of the room, making a coffee at a machine against the wall.

McCready looked along the full length of the gallery. At the far end, on the right, it looked like there was a similar set of stairs, leading down, but there was also a door that led off to another part of the cocoon. He turned his attention back to the rec. Somehow, he had to get Clare's attention. The problem would be that she wasn't expecting to see him and the shock might make her cry out. He was still thinking about this when he heard her speak.

"I need to go to the rest room."

McCready peeked up over the gallery surround. The leader glanced at her, as though deciding. He turned to the man with the coffee.

"Stefan, go with her. And watch her. Enough's gone wrong already. Don't let her out of your sight."

The man put the coffee down and unslung the automatic he had over his shoulder. He indicated with the muzzle of the gun for Clare to get up.

Clare glared at him, and, with a contemptuous glance at the leader, she walked toward the stairs not ten feet from where McCready was crouched. There was no time to move. He just had to hope they didn't look his way.

The man called Stefan led Clare up the stairs, ensuring he kept her in front of him. They reached the top and turned left, away from McCready. As he'd seen the rest rooms on the way there, he was pretty sure where they were headed. He assumed the man wouldn't go into the room with Clare, so there might be the chance of confronting him without risking her safety.

He let them disappear down the corridor and then ran quietly after them. He reached the side corridor where the rest rooms were down to the left. He heard a door open and then bang closed on a spring. He waited thirty seconds and then peered quickly round the corner. The man was leaning against the wall. He was ten feet away, his gun hanging at his side.

He clearly wasn't expecting any trouble.

McCready didn't want to use his weapon unless he had to. He took a couple of deep breaths and ran around the corner.

He was banking on surprise.

The man noticed him a couple of seconds too late, his eyes opening wide. McCready could see he was calculating what to do. He didn't seem to know whether to shout for help or try and bring his gun to bear. Before he'd done either, McCready had reached him and smashed him in the head with the butt of the gun.

He collapsed to the floor.

McCready caught him. He quickly dragged his body into the men's room. As he did this, he heard a toilet flush, the sound of running water, and a few moments later, a door open and close. He gave Clare a couple of seconds to realize the man wasn't there and then walked back out into the corridor, silently closing the door behind him. Clare was standing in the middle of the passage facing away from him. It looked like she was thinking what to do as Stefan wasn't there. She was about to walk off when he whispered to her.

"Clare."

She froze. And then very slowly turned round to face him.

"Shhhh!" He had his finger to his lips.

Her eyes went wide. Her expression was one of total and complete shock. She was about to say something. McCready smiled at her. Again he put his finger to his lips, his eyes pleading for her not to make a noise. But a second later she ran forward and threw her arms round him. He hugged her tightly and then indicated for her to go back into the women's room. Once they were inside, with the door closed, she turned to him, her eyes still wide, but now with hope in them.

"What the hell are you doing here?"

He smiled back at her. He'd forgotten how she made him feel. He couldn't stop smiling. "It's a long story. One we don't have time for now. Suffice to say, Jade called me."

At this, Clare's eyes went even wider.

"Jade?"

"Yeah, she's quite a character."

Clare smiled. "That she is."

"We have to get you out of here."

Clare nodded enthusiastically.

"But…"

She looked at him with concern, worry on her face. "But what?"

McCready almost couldn't look her in the eye. "I have to get Petrovich. Apparently, if he doesn't make a deal with Stevens we could have World War Three on our hands."

Clare stared at him.

"Where is he?"

She thought for a moment. "I haven't seen him for a while. He's probably in his quarters on the other side of the cocoon."

McCready pulled out the iPad. "Show me."

Clare checked the layout and then put her finger on a room that was down a corridor that ran parallel to the gallery above the rec. McCready looked at it, committing it to memory. He was trying to work out a plan.

"Okay, this is what I want you to do. I have some gear at the rear lift-track airlock. It's how I got in with a Navy SEAL who took President Stevens."

"I heard something about that. They're really pissed."

"Yeah, I'm sure they are... Look, make your way to the airlock and stay there. I'll go and get Petrovich."

Clare looked at him. She still couldn't believe he was there. When he glanced at her he saw there were tears in her eyes.

"You came for me," was all she could say, a tear rolling down her face.

McCready looked at her curiously. "Of course I came for you."

"But after everything I said?"

"You had your reasons."

She just stood there, another tear running down her cheek. Then she hugged him hard. He gave her a few seconds and then gently pushed her away.

"We can talk later, okay?"

"Okay," she said with a sniffle.

McCready put the pad back in his pocket, checked the Glock, and then stepped out into the corridor. He gave her a quick glance.

"See you at the airlock."

Before he could leave, she grabbed his face and kissed him on the lips. When she broke away he could see her mouthing, "Thank you."

He smiled and was gone.

To get to Petrovich's room he had to pass close to the rec, so McCready hoped he wouldn't encounter any hostiles. The only problem was that Clare and Stefan had been gone for some time, so a search party might be sent out.

A couple of minutes later he reached Petrovich's door. He took a deep breath and knocked softly. He heard footsteps on the other side and then the door was pulled open, revealing the second world leader he'd met that day.

Petrovich stared at him, not fully comprehending. McCready walked into the room and closed the door behind him.

"President Petrovich, my name is John McCready. I'm working with the American forces to try and get you out of here. You need to come with me, sir, as quickly as possible."

Petrovich looked him up and down. He appeared completely unfazed by the situation, which was probably why he had lasted so long in control of his country. McCready could see he was a hard man, but there appeared to be more to him than that. He would need everything he had if they were to get through the next hour. He still didn't know what he was going to do.

He had two helmets… and three people.

"How are we going to do this, Mr. McCready?"

"John, please, sir. There's an airlock on the far side of the cocoon. Clare Kowalski is waiting there with some gear. I may have to be creative as to how we get you both out, but I have been described as pretty resourceful in the past, so don't worry… By the way, sir, you can swim, yes?"

At this, Petrovich raised an eyebrow. "I was on the Olympic team in my youth. Good enough?"

"It'll do," said McCready with a grin.

Petrovich watched him for a second. "I think I like you, John. Lead the way."

With that, McCready walked out into the corridor with Petrovich behind, and they made their way through the cocoon. They were doing really well, right up until they reached the corridor with the rest rooms. Just as they walked past the end of the passage, the door to the men's room flew open. Stefan stumbled out, clearly feeling the worse for wear. He saw McCready and Petrovich, obviously couldn't quite put it together, but then it seemed to dawn on him. He reached for his weapon.

"Stop!"

"Run!" shouted McCready.

The two men ran down the corridor. Behind them they could hear Stefan crashing into the walls as he found his feet.

They got as far as the corridor that led to the airlock when gunshots echoed round the confined space. They were aimed high and hit the ceiling, but they were still deafening.

Ahead, McCready could see Clare at the lift-track station. She was watching them, fear on her face.

"Okay, stop there!" ordered Stefan. The gun was leveled straight at them. McCready and Petrovich turned to face him. Clare was behind them at the air lock.

"You don't want to fire," said McCready evenly, but there was a certain amount of stress in his voice. "You kill this guy," he said, indicating Petrovich, "I don't think your boss would be too happy."

"Maybe," said Stefan with a smile. "But I don't think he would miss you. He sent a round into the wall right next to McCready's head, splintering the plaster into tiny pieces. One entered McCready's eye. He winced, blinking hard to remove it.

"Now move, all of you."

Petrovich stayed where he was.

"I said move!"

"Hang on a minute," said McCready. He bent down to try to sort out his eye. "Give me a sec."

Stefan watched, waiting for him to rise.

The piece had been out of McCready's eye before he'd even crouched down. He now slowly moved his hand to a side pocket in his drysuit where the Glock was located.

Behind him, Clare could see what he was doing.

"Hey, Stefan," she called out, trying to distract him.

Stefan looked up. "What do you want?"

"How long do you think we'll be down here?"

"That depends on him." He indicated Petrovich.

"Okay," said Clare. "And then what happens to us?"

At this, Stefan smiled. "I guess you'll find out." He was about to continue when McCready pulled the Glock from his pocket and fired. He hadn't fired a gun for many years, and the description of his skill level to Harley earlier was proven correct. Rather than hitting Stefan in the main part of his body or head, it merely grazed his shoulder. Enough to cause pain and for him to cry out, but also enough to make him grab the automatic and fire down the corridor.

They threw themselves to the floor.

"Okay. Anyone move, they die!" yelled Stefan.

Slowly, they raised themselves to their feet, but when they finally managed to stand up, only two of them were standing.

McCready looked down at the body on the floor, and a wave of helplessness came over him.

Petrovich lay on his front, a widening pool of blood streaming from his head.

Stefan seemed to hesitate for a moment, not sure what to do. Eventually he pointed the weapon at them.

"Come with me!"

McCready glanced at Clare. It was a look filled with

more confidence than he felt right now. A confidence that was reduced even further when he looked behind her. The helmet he had brought to get her out was full of bullet holes.

And the confidence dropped to zero as a sudden loud splintering sound came from the airlock.

A massive jet of water shot into the corridor, quickly covering the floor.

One of the bullets had breached the cocoon.

Chapter Forty

The Sea Stallion downwash sent dust and leaves scurrying as it descended slowly to the car park close to the Omega Complex.

Four naval ratings shielded their eyes as it came lower. The recompression chamber slung beneath swung slightly in the breeze. In order to get the president out safely he would first be transferred to the larger chamber on the ground that had more therapeutic treatment options. This involved mating the smaller mobile chamber to the larger one. The pressure could then be equalized between the two and the president could be moved from one to the other to complete a phased reduction of pressure until he was safely back at surface pressure.

Ten minutes later both chambers had been locked together, the lift cable had been detached, and the Sea Stallion had moved off to land further down the car park.

Once the chambers were secure, Harley jumped down. As he hit the ground, Connie came running over. Bryce wasn't far behind.

"You okay?" she asked.

He glanced at her wearily.

"Yeah, I think so."

"No, aches, joint pains?"

"No, I'm fine. Looks like your toys work."

Connie helped him off with his drysuit and then grabbed his wrist, turning over the hemofilter. She carefully removed it, pulling the small needles from his flesh.

"Ow!"

She gave him a look and smiled. "Kept you alive, didn't it?"

He nodded slowly.

Bryce had now reached them.

"You need him for anything, doc?"

Connie looked Harley up and down. "I think he should be okay, sir. At least as far as his brain goes, there's not much to damage, but I'll need him back later for tests."

Harley gave her a look.

"Okay, let me know how the president is," said Bryce. "It would be good to talk to him when he's had some rest."

"I think you'll want to talk to him sooner than that," said Harley.

Bryce looked at him sharply. "Okay, come with me."

Harley followed Bryce to the command trailer. As they walked over, he waved at the second SEAL team that was hanging around the Black Hawk that had brought them. He knew all of them and received waves and thumbs ups in return. He wondered if they would get to see any action.

Once inside the trailer, Harley and Bryce sat down on a narrow couch.

"Okay, Mitch, tell me all."

Over the next ten minutes Harley gave Bryce a blow-by-blow account of what had happened inside the complex.

When asked about the third party, he gave a concise description and appraisal of McCready. The report was favorable. Bryce wasn't so sure. He never liked elements he couldn't control, but he had to concede that McCready had saved Harley's life and seemed to be on the right side of the situation.

"And while his priority was the girl," said Harley, "I got the sense, when push comes to shove, he'll do the right thing. I wouldn't give up hope for Petrovich, but I would plan for the worst. The most critical thing, sir, is the threat the terrorist made, which would suggest they have control over the ISS, and, however far-fetched that might seem, they plan to crash it onto New York. This man Kozak has planned everything down to the last detail. I don't think you can ignore this and assume he's bluffing."

Bryce watched him for a minute, thinking.

"We have to talk to the president. See where he is with this." He paused. "On another note, what do we know about this Kowalski woman?"

"Er, nothing, other than I understand she's the assistant manager and a friend of McCready's."

"Okay, but McCready turning up like that—I mean, where the hell did he get that sub from?—just to rescue a 'friend.' Seems a bit improbable." Harley said nothing. "I'm sure he's connected to this in some way. I just can't figure out how."

"He seemed genuine to me, sir."

"They always do." Bryce again seemed to be mulling something over. He looked up. "Okay, Mitch, good job. Go and see the doc and let her run the tests she needs. I'm sure she'll enjoy them more than you."

Harley stood up. "Thank you, sir. And, yes, I'm sure she will."

Eugene Porter pulled up at the entrance to the Omega Complex and looked out of the front of the SUV. Charlie Menzies sat in the passenger seat.

"What do you think?" she asked, as they stared at the security and police presence at the gate in front of them.

After they had quite literally dropped McCready off over the Pacific, Charlie had taken the 737 in to land at Santa Monica Municipal airport. They had parked up on the stand and Richards had gone through the necessary paperwork with the airport officials. The flight had been planned and registered, so there shouldn't have been any problems. However, a report from a controller at the Rainbow Ridge tracking station had meant a few awkward moments. It had taken a while to resolve, thus delaying everything else. This frustrated efforts to try and set up a comms link to McCready.

Eventually, when everything had been cleared, Richards had hired an SUV and sent Porter and Charlie off to see what they could do. They had a link they could use if they could get close enough to the building and attach it to the glass. If not, there was a laser mike that could pick up any signals that could be detected in the water inside the core of the complex, but again, they had to get close enough to use this.

Neither system was ideal.

Couple that with how long it had all taken, and who knew what had happened to McCready in the meantime. Porter had also brought a number of items of 'personal equipment,' just in case. He now found himself with Charlie working out the best course of action.

She looked at the line of vehicles queuing to get through the security cordon. Some private cars were being turned away. A police car drove through. A large limousine waited while credentials were checked and was then allowed in.

Also in the queue was a local TV news truck. It was about five back from the cops at the gate.

"Wait here," said Charlie.

"Where you going?" asked Porter.

She just gave him a wave as she hopped out of the vehicle and walked over to the truck.

Charlie approached from behind. She checked the two side mirrors by the cab doors. There were two people in the cab that she could see. One was a guy. One was a girl. She made a quick judgment. The guy looked like he was in his forties and pretty stressed. Probably the cameraman or some technician. The girl, on the other hand, looked like a PA of some sort and seemed to be pretty chilled by the delay. There would no doubt be a presenter, but he/she was maybe in a different vehicle. Anyway, they wouldn't be any good for what Charlie had in mind. She made a decision and walked round to the passenger side where the girl was seated in the front. At that moment the driver got out and walked toward the security gate.

Charlie reached the cab and put on a frustrated expression.

"Jeez, takin' a long time."

The girl glanced up. She was in her twenties and looked bright but impressionable.

"Sure is," she replied. "You with a crew?"

"Yeah, we're stuck way back down the line." Charlie noticed a necklace round the girl's neck. "Hey, that's pretty. Just the look I love."

The girl smiled enthusiastically. "I know, isn't it so cool?"

"Do you mind?" The girl nodded. Charlie reached in to hold the gold cross hanging from a delicate chain. She brushed the girl's neck as she did so. Charlie smiled at her. The girl smiled back.

"Beautiful," said Charlie, looking into her eyes. The girl continued to smile.

Out of the corner of her eye, Charlie saw the driver returning from the security gate. The vehicles in front were moving. She also noticed the girl's ID pass clipped to her breast pocket.

"Well, looks like you might be on the move."

"Looks that way."

Charlie withdrew her hand from the necklace, gently brushing the girl's breast as she did so. The girl blushed, not taking her eyes off Charlie.

"Maybe see you on the inside," said Charlie.

"Maybe," said the girl.

At that moment the driver climbed back in the cab.

"Bloody hold-ups! Don't they realize we're press and have a right to access?" He started the engine and drove forward.

Charlie watched the truck move off and then turned to Porter, indicating for him to drive over quickly. He moved forward and pulled into the space created by the news truck. A horn blared from behind. Charlie waved and gave a thumbs up to the frustrated driver. She climbed back into the SUV.

"What was all that about?" said Porter.

Charlie held up the TV crew pass, a grin on her face.

Porter looked at her with even more respect, if that were possible.

"Ain't you just bloomin' marvelous!"

The SUV moved forward behind the news truck. When the truck was waved through they quickly followed. Charlie covered up the photo but flashed the pass to the hassled security guard.

"We're with them," she said, pointing at the truck in front.

He waved them on.

"Now comes the tricky bit," said Porter.

They followed the truck up the main drive to the complex. As they approached, they could see all the activity in the area. There were police and military personnel everywhere.

And then they saw the complex.

Both of them were awed as the massive building came into view. A little further on they followed the news truck as it was directed to a parking area at the side of the building. There were a number of other trucks and vans already parked there. Some had satellite dishes set up on top and had clearly been there for some time, providing the broadcasts the world had been watching for what was the biggest story of the day, if not the month or indeed the year. After they had passed the last officials Charlie told Porter to drive a distance away from the truck. When he glanced at her, she simply replied, "Don't want to risk being asked on a date."

It went over his head, but he complied and parked further down the car park. The building was now to the right of them. As they climbed out, Charlie admired the collection of helicopters that were parked in a row. They were located not far from two chambers that were mated together. There were two Sea Stallions and a Black Hawk. She'd flown Black Hawks when she'd been in the Australian forces. People normally concentrated on fixed-wing or rotor aircraft, but Charlie had been fascinated by both.

"Er, we're not 'ere to sightsee, luv," said Porter.

She turned to him with a smile. "Best get to it then, matey. What do you suggest?"

Porter looked across at the main building towering above them. It sparkled in the sunlight. He also checked around at all the military hardware, which included what looked like a command trailer bristling with dishes and antenna on its roof.

"Probably a bit risky to use the laser. Either it'll interfere with some critical systems, or they'll be monitoring anything unusual. Might get us caught. I reckon we go for the limpet mike on the glass."

"Okay, where's best?"

Porter looked at the building. "Ideally as high as possible. We don't know where John might be, but higher is always a good bet."

He looked over at the base of the building. There were a number of trees that ringed the area close in. They looked like they were hiding some of the building's utility systems.

"Those trees look like a good bet. If I can reach over from them, could get it maybe twenty feet in the air."

Charlie looked at him with surprise. "You, Eugene?"

He looked up, confused. "Yeah, who else?"

"Er, what about me?"

"You? But you're…"

She shook her head, smiling. "Look, while I'm sure you know what you're doing, you're not, how shall I put this, the most physically sprightly among us, now, are you?"

"Well…"

"Which completely disqualifies you for the part. So, give me the mike, I'll be back before two shakes of a rattler's ass!"

Porter just looked at the open hand. He obediently

reached into the bag slung around his neck and passed her the mike.

"Ripper!" said Charlie, and headed for the building. Porter watched her go.

"Bloody marvelous!" was all he could manage.

He was still watching her, slightly in a trance, and not really concentrating, when he saw two cops approach her.

What followed was some sort of argument that Porter watched with increasing concern.

She was then handcuffed, with her hands behind her back, and marched quickly away.

"Holy shit!" was all Porter could manage. "We can't be having that. We can't be having that at all!"

Chapter Forty-One

McCready and Clare were led at gunpoint by Stefan back to the rec. They had been joined by Masaev, who had heard the shots and come running from the control room.

When they appeared over the gallery, Kozak looked up. He frowned slightly at the sight of McCready. As they were marched down the stairs he stood and crossed over to them. But before they were even halfway, a surge of water followed them down. It started as a trickle, but by the time they reached the last step, it was a torrent. Everyone in the rec looked nervously at the new development.

"What is this?" asked Kozak.

Stefan looked at him in fear.

"They were trying to escape, Andriy. I had to shoot. One of the bullets must have hit the airlock at the rear capsule station." He hesitated, now looking really nervous. "And there's something else."

Kozak looked up. "Yes," he said, calmly.

"The Russian president is dead. He was hit in the exchange of fire."

Kozak fixed Stefan in his gaze, and then, without emotion, calmly pulled out his gun and shot him. He was dead before he hit the floor.

He glanced at the water flowing into the room and turned to Clare.

"Can you stop this?"

She looked at him incredulously. "You serious? No way. There's too much pressure. We don't have the equipment or the time to seal a leak like this. And it's only going to get worse. The hole will enlarge, creating a faster flow. It could even completely give way."

Kozak looked pensive, working out his options. "How long do we have?"

"Who knows? An hour. Five. It's impossible to tell. But less than a day."

Kozak clenched his fists and looked at Clare. "Go and sit on the couch." He turned to Ilya. "Stay with her. Watch her!"

Ilya nodded. But he looked scared.

Kozak turned to McCready, who was standing in the middle of the room, water sloshing around his ankles. Masaev had picked up Stefan's gun and trained it on McCready.

"And who might you be?"

McCready stared back evenly. "I'm just here for her." He nodded at Clare.

Kozak looked at him curiously. "You have come down here, through everything, risking all... for her?"

"Yes."

Kozak was clearly slightly bemused.

"Look, whatever you were trying to achieve, it's failed," said McCready. "Let everyone go. We probably won't get out of here alive anyway. There's no need to do this."

Kozak stared back at McCready. "You know nothing about our cause. Why we are here."

"So, enlighten me."

Clare watched Kozak question McCready. She had to try and do something. She glanced at Ilya sitting next to her. He looked scared and slightly lost.

"Ilya," she whispered. He glanced at her nervously. "There's nothing you can do now. You have to get your brother to stop this madness." She could tell he was torn, but he remained silent.

Clare continued. "If he goes through with his plan, it could start a war. Many thousands, maybe millions, of innocent people will die. Do you want that to happen?"

It looked as though he didn't. He seemed desperate to say something. She put a hand gently on his knee. At first, she felt him twitch slightly, but then he relaxed. When she looked at his face he had clearly decided something.

He glanced at her but then looked down at his feet as he started to talk in a whisper.

"But I cannot stop anything. Only Andriy has the ability to send the code to stop the attack. And he will never do that unless his demands are met."

"Do you know what the code is?"

At this he looked uncomfortable. He wrung his hands slowly together.

"Yes."

"Then tell me. It may do no good. I mean, how can we get out of here? But if we do, I can try and stop this."

Ilya was sweating. It looked like he was in great pain, wrestling with an impossible dilemma.

He finally took a deep breath.

"The code is made up of eight characters—numbers and letters. They are as follows." Again, a deep breath. "Z... 7... 4..."

Clare was concentrating, making sure she remembered it, but out of the corner of her eye, she noticed Kozak's attention had been drawn away from McCready to look over at them. He seemed to focus on Ilya.

"U... 3..."

And Clare saw recognition cross Kozak's face. His expression turned to thunder.

"Ilya!" he shouted.

Ilya turned to look at his brother. There was fear across his face. He looked up nervously.

"Yes, Andriy."

Kozak indicated for Masaev to watch McCready. He crossed over to the couch, looking down menacingly.

"What are you doing?"

"Nothing, Andriy. I was trying to tell her not to worry. It will all work out." He looked up pleadingly.

Kozak stood there fuming, but then a quiet calm came over him. He smiled.

"It's alright, my brother. We are all stressed, but I do not think you were telling her not to worry." As he continued, his face hardened. "I think you were telling her the code to stop the attack."

"No... Nooo," stuttered Ilya.

Kozak looked at him with a deep sadness.

"After everything that happened to our family. After the rape of our mother and the burning of our parents." He saw the shock on Ilya's face. "Yes, Ilya... and after the death of Mikhail. After our sister had to leave to live in Russia to protect us, her remaining family." He paused. "They have to pay. The Russians. The Americans. They have to pay."

There was silence in the room, save for the steady flow of water that now covered the whole floor to a depth of six inches.

All eyes were on Kozak and Ilya.

"Do not tell her any more!" said Kozak.

And then, as if he was fighting for his place in the world, Ilya defied his brother for the first time in his life. He stared straight at Kozak, determination in his eyes.

"P…"

"Don't do it, Ilya!" screamed Kozak. He pulled out his gun and pointed it at his brother. The barrel wavered slightly, but it was aimed straight at his brother's head. Ilya glanced at it and then looked into his brother's eyes.

"8…"

The sound of the gunshot deafened everyone.

Ilya's head jerked back. A splatter of blood and brains sprayed across the wall behind. Clare cried out. Masaev watched, a thin smile on his lips.

Kozak stared at the body of his brother. At first there was disbelief in his eyes at what he had done, but then they hardened. He slowly lowered the gun and stared around at everyone in the room.

His eyes then focused. He turned to Clare and brought the gun to bear. There was nothing McCready could do. But he noticed Masaev's attention was on Kozak.

Murphy jumped forward, but before he could reach Clare, Kozak fired. The bodyguard went down. And then, as if he thought Igorov would also be a threat, Kozak fired at him before he could even move.

He then brought the gun back to bear on Clare.

And pulled the trigger.

The gun clicked.

It was empty.

In that instant, McCready threw himself to his right, knocking the gun from Masaev's hand. It disappeared into the ever-rising water some way away and the terrorist went down. McCready didn't have time to find the gun, so grabbed a glass bowl from a nearby table. He brought it crashing down on Masaev's head, knocking him unconscious. He hit him again and again, gashing his forehead open. Blood poured down his face.

He left him there, not knowing if he was alive or dead, and then watched as Kozak dropped the empty gun and ran for the gallery, heading for the main airlock.

Clare stared at McCready. She was still in shock.

"Did you get the code?" he asked.

But she couldn't concentrate, couldn't focus. She was trembling. McCready grabbed her and shook her. She looked up at him.

"Clare!"

She seemed to regain some sort of control. "Almost," she said shakily. "Seven out of eight. There was one to go."

McCready thought for a second as more water thundered down the stairs. It was now two feet deep.

"I have to stop him."

With that, McCready ran after Kozak. Clare followed.

They ran up onto the gallery, through the doors and then down the stairs that led to the airlock. There was the chance Kozak had found another weapon. They had to be careful.

Clare now led the way. They turned the final corner and the airlock was in front of them, but Kozak was nowhere to be seen.

Clare crossed over to the control panel, now more composed.

"Shit!"

"What?"

"He must be already through. The lock's full of water."

They crossed over to one of the windows and peered in. There was water beyond the glass—all the way to the ceiling. They could also see a figure at the far end in diving gear. It had to be Kozak. As they watched the doors open, he moved out into the underground cavern beyond. More importantly, they saw him head straight for the unmistakable shape of *Deep Intruder*, twenty feet away.

McCready turned to Clare. His face showed pain and despair. She looked at him, knowing what he was going to say.

He could barely look her in the eye.

"I have to go after him," he said eventually.

"I know," she said calmly.

"But I came for you," he said, slamming his hand into the wall in frustration.

"I know you did, and that means everything, John."

When he looked at her he could see all the feelings he had ever had for her wrapped up in her eyes and reflected back at him.

He stared at her for a second and then headed for the gallery. She followed him, wading through the water that was now a foot higher.

Once on the upper level they ran back to the lift-track station. When they reached it, McCready grabbed his helmet. She watched him as he efficiently swopped out the canisters and checked the computer display was up and running. When he was finally ready, he stopped and looked at her.

There was a hesitation. He was torn.

"I can't. I have to get you out." He looked into her eyes.

"No, John, you have to do this. You know you do."

His stare was unwavering. "I'll come back for you."

She smiled, but they both knew he wouldn't make it before the cocoon flooded.

"I... I'm sorry for everything," she said.

"Don't!"

"We came so close..."

He looked down for a second, and then back up at her with a confident, determined expression. "I know. But it's not over yet."

"Go... Go and save the world."

There was nothing else to say.

He turned and made his way into the airlock, picking up his fins. The river of water rushed past him as he operated the controls. The door closed, sealing him in. He pulled the helmet over his head and pulled on the fins as the small chamber flooded. A second later the outer door opened.

He glanced back.

Their eyes locked for one last time, and then he turned and disappeared up the shaft.

When he'd gone, Clare looked around her. The water was powering in faster now.

It wouldn't be long.

She looked down the corridor. The water must have made it to the upper level as it was now nearly a foot deep and rising.

She had to do something.

Anything.

But what? She headed off down the corridor.

She had never been so scared in all her life.

Chapter Forty-Two

For about ten seconds after McCready left the airlock, he was thinking about Clare.

He knew, as well as she did, the likelihood of him making it back before the cocoon flooded completely was next to zero. But he also knew there was always hope. Even if something wasn't mathematically possible to achieve, or win, such as in backgammon, he would continue on to the bitter end. Some called it foolish and stubborn, and he couldn't argue with that—it was just the way he was. It was a way of reminding himself that you never give up, whatever the odds.

Moments later he had consigned the impossible thoughts to the back of his mind, realizing he now had to focus on what lay ahead. Everything depended on him reaching Kozak and making him give up the final piece of the code.

That was all that mattered.

He was heartened by knowing there was only really one place Kozak was likely to go—up the tunnel to the reservoir, where there was a whole series of armed forces, including the SWAT team, waiting for him. The only trouble was they were as likely to shoot him as take him in for questioning. He also hoped Harley had let people know there was a good guy on-site, and to ask first, shoot second.

He swam out of the shaft that led to the cocoon and made his way across the atrium to the small white craft that was sitting where he'd left it.

When he reached it, he had to get himself back inside. He pulled open the dome at the front. He was unlikely to need the helmet again, so he backed himself into the sub, and then, after taking a series of deep breaths, pulled the helmet off. He dropped it outside and pulled the dome shut.

He reached over to the control panel and started up the sub's systems. While his vision wasn't great due to the lack of a mask, the panel and controls were clear to see. The lights came on. The sub came to life. He was still okay holding his breath but now was the moment of truth. He hit the DRAIN button and waited for the water to be expelled from the interior.

Nothing happened.

His heart rate started to increase. He glanced over at the fuzzy figures on the panel. Again he hit the control.

Nothing.

He was starting to run out of air.

What have I done wrong?

He thought for a second and then glanced back at the panel. He hit the control again, and this time there was a CONFIRM button below. There was a sudden inrush and howling of gas as the sub pressurized and the water started to flow out. Before it had dropped by even a few inches, he had pushed his face up into the rapidly expanding airspace and gulped in the much-needed air.

Once the interior was free of water, he took a minute or two to calm down and then checked all the systems were up and running. He then pulled back on the controls and rose up off the floor.

There was no time to lose.

After Kozak had made it to *Deep Intruder* he was full of emotion.

Why hadn't Ilya stopped?

Why had he forced him to kill him? He was torn with his feelings. But he had no time to dwell on them. While he was quite prepared to die for the cause, and would never give up the code unless his demands were met, he didn't want to die unless it was absolutely necessary.

As he powered up the sub, he thought about his options.

There were two ways out. One, by ascending to the top of the building. But when he reached it, he would be trapped with no way to escape. Two, back up the tunnel. But this would lead to the reservoir and no doubt a hostile reception. There was really only one choice. He would have to take his chances with the reservoir. He could keep a low profile, maybe sneak over to one side and exit the sub while it was still underwater. Maybe no one would see him. He was still wearing his hemofilter so there was every chance he would escape any decompression issues, but he wanted to get as far away as possible before he had to deal with any of that.

When the sub was ready, he lifted smoothly off the bottom. He twisted the joystick to the right. *Deep Intruder* spun on a dime and turned to face the tunnel entrance. He pushed the stick forward and moved into the tunnel.

He assumed everyone in the cocoon would be killed

when it flooded. At least he didn't have anything to worry about from behind.

It was just what was ahead that would shape his future.

Clare ran down the corridor, heading for the control room. She had to get a message out, let them know what was going on.

She reached the small room and walked in.

There was a concealed hard line to the security center that was deliberately kept hidden. She just hoped the terrorists hadn't found it and disabled it in any way.

As she looked around, everything was pretty much as she expected. Some damage had been done to one of the screens, but they were all still working otherwise. She reached behind the back of one of the monitors and pressed a catch. Immediately a small panel opened to her left. In it was a wired handset. She pulled it out and pressed the only button on the top.

She heard a ring tone.

She waited.

In the security center, most of the operational control had been handed over to the military. After Patterson's initial talk with Bryce, they hadn't had much contact, other than to see if any of the cameras were working that could give an idea of what was going on in the cocoon, but they were all down.

While there was still a presence in the room, there were only a couple of people. So when a small red light started flashing on one of the consoles, nobody paid it much attention. It took more than a minute before Patterson noticed it. He quickly crossed over to the handset and picked it up.

"Hello."

"Oh, Harry, thank God!"

"Clare?"

"Yes, it's me. Look, you have to listen."

Patterson knew when to listen and when to shut up.

"Shoot."

"The terrorists are gone. Petrovich is dead, but they've set in motion an attack on New York. There's only one way to stop it. Kozak, the lead terrorist, has a code. He's currently taken a sub and is probably making his way up the tunnel to the reservoir. If he's killed, there's nothing that can stop the attack. I managed to get most of the code. It's a mix of eight numbers and letters. I only have seven. You got a pen?"

"Go ahead."

"Z... 7... 4... U... 3... P... 8..."

"What about the last one?"

"That's it. I don't have it. There's a man called John McCready, who managed to get into the cocoon—don't ask—He's gone after Kozak." And now there was real pleading in her voice. "Please make sure no harm comes to him. He's trying to get the final character. Don't let anyone shoot him."

"Okay, I'll see what I can do." He paused. "How are you? Can you get out of there?"

There was a pause. "I'm not sure. There's no one left. The cocoon's filling with water. I'm going to try and find some gear and see what I can do." Her voice was faltering. "But I'm not sure there's going to be enough time."

"Hang on in there, little girl."

"I'll do my..."

And then there was a piercing scream over the handset.
"Clare! Clare!" but the line was dead.

Clare screamed for a second time as the hand smashed across her face, knocking her to the floor. When she rolled over and looked up, it was apparent that Masaev had not died in the rec. He was bleeding heavily from a gash in his head, and his face wore an expression of pure evil. His eyes were blazing and they were fixed on her.

She backed against the side of the room but there was nowhere to go. As she looked at her options, none were good. She struggled to stand.

"Hang on a minute," she tried to say calmly. "You don't need to do this." But she was breathing fast.

"Oh, I think I do."

"We might find a way out of here together, but if you kill me you may be stuck down here."

Masaev sneered. "I don't think so. It's just you and me, and if I'm going to die, I'm going to have some fun first."

Clare's expression suddenly showed one of shock.

"I thought you said it was just you and me." She was looking beyond Masaev, out into the corridor. He turned to look. She took the only chance she knew she was going to get.

She kicked him in the groin, using all the force she had.

Her life depended on it.

Masaev screamed with pain and crumbled to the floor.

Clare ran over to him, adding a kick to the face, which broke his nose, as she went. She didn't even look back as she fled down the corridor. But the roars of pain and anger that followed made her realize that if he ever got to his feet she would receive no mercy.

Deep Hostage

She had to get out of there.

Chapter Forty-Three

Since Gregory Mason had called 911 earlier, a whole lot had happened.

He had found himself in a completely different world. The dam and the surrounding area had been swarming with police. One team had fished the body of Brett Stanley out of the water. He had also been told the body of Gemma Morgan had been found in one of their pickup trucks parked among the trees near the picnic area. Both had been shot. A SWAT team was now encamped on the walkway on top of the dam, as well as around the sides of the reservoir.

He had been interviewed several times. There was no more he could help the authorities with. His prime concern now was the state of the dam. The reservoir held over four billion gallons of water. If there was a catastrophic failure, all that would head straight down into Glendale, and then on into the downtown area. The police were well advanced with the necessary evacuations, but there would be no way they'd be able to clear the area in time if the worst happened.

However, he did have hope.

For the moment, the spillway was doing its job: taking the flow down under the I-5 freeway to join up with the Los Angeles River, which flowed through the city and on to the ocean beyond.

Mason watched as a man dangling on the end of a rope halfway down the dam wall assessed the flow of water. He hung next to the leak and was looking at the hole to work out how likely it was to grow larger and at what rate. Mason could see him lift a walkie-talkie. He heard the one around his neck crackle.

After a five-minute conversation, Mason was somewhat reassured. The man was convinced a valve could be fixed onto the wall and the flow rate capped, similar to controlling a blowout on an oil rig. It was a temporary measure, but it could work.

In the meantime, all the sluice gates had been opened. The water was being drained as quickly as possible. Mason was pleased to see the level in the dam had dropped considerably.

Even so, he wiped a handkerchief across his brow.

A lot more sweat would be lost before this was over.

Over a hundred and fifty feet below where Gregory Mason was standing, and around a quarter of a mile away, Andriy Kozak moved steadily up the escape tunnel from the Omega Complex. The sub was working well. He still had the problem of what to do when he reached the reservoir, but he was feeling confident. If none of the options he had gone through earlier worked, he did have one final idea. It was a nuclear, or Armageddon, option, but one he was prepared to take if all else failed.

After all, he was not afraid to die.

When McCready had set off in pursuit of Kozak, he was under no illusion as to the stakes.

If he couldn't find the man, extract the code, and stop the attack on New York, there was every possibility the world would suffer a nuclear war it might never recover from.

It was that black and white.

But McCready had always liked black and white. It made things simple.

While, of course, there were instances where the color gray had to come into play, where different scenarios and outcomes had to be considered to work out the best way out of a problem, McCready had always functioned better when the stakes were abundantly clear. It allowed him to focus, to use all his energy and skills to accomplish one individual task. That made it simple, however complicated it might actually be.

He brought Skyline up and over the mass of twisted metal surrounding the hole that led into the cavern below the atrium. He stopped for a moment and looked at what lay ahead.

The hole was quite large, but there were various obstructions around the edge. He would have to be careful. As a diver, it would have been easy to twist and turn to maneuver through the gap. But in the sub, it was a little more tricky.

He pushed the controls forward and moved toward the hole. He raised the profile into a more upright position, which wasn't natural for the craft, and then slowly advanced into the hole.

As he entered, he heard a clang and felt a nudge at the rear. He feathered the throttles, careful to make no sudden movements.

When he was sure he was clear, he cautiously pushed the throttle forward and drove the sub down into the cavern below.

He was free, but he had lost valuable time.

He could see the pile of vehicles he had swum past with Harley earlier. He could also see the long snout of the airlock protruding out from the cocoon. He had a pang of guilt as he realized Clare was still inside, somewhere beyond those walls. It made him all the more determined to find Kozak, as only then would he be able to return for her.

Now clear of the debris and obstructions, he accelerated. He had no time to lose. The small vessel raced up the tunnel, happy to be free of its constraints, and to be heading toward whatever fate awaited it.

Chapter Forty-Four

Yana stared down at the Earth through one of the small observation ports in the side of the Zvezda module.

It looked so beautiful down there.

A single blue orb in the blackness of space. And, as so many had said before, a view that from up here showed no borders, no countries, no problems—it was one world and should function as such.

Unfortunately, that perfect world didn't exist. She wondered many things as she stared down. And while she was a strong believer in science, and had never been persuaded by the religious argument, it was strange that so many people devoutly followed stories from the past in the hope that someone was looking over them, guiding them, making sure everything would be alright, and then, when they died, that they would transfer to a higher plane that would be quite literally heaven.

She had to shake her head.

When you were up here, closer to the heavens, you could maybe think like that. It was impossible not to think of the billions of stars and planets out there, and not try to work out where it had all come from—or who had created it. But it was an impossible question, with an answer, she was convinced, no human being would ever find.

The flip side of the argument was when you returned to the planet below that from up here looked so idyllic and peaceful. As she circumvented it every hour and a half, she could look down on all the beautiful geography—of oceans and land masses, mountains, deserts and ice caps, all without any of the trials and tribulations endured by the human occupants. But below her was the misery of millions of lives, intertwined with corrupt regimes, greed and avarice. No, it was not a beautiful planet. And she felt sure that any 'god' looking down would not be impressed. In fact, any 'god' that had created the humans that inhabited the planet should be ashamed of himself. He had totally and utterly screwed up.

"Yana."

She came out of her reverie and turned to see Gruber floating on the other side of the module. He wasn't too close. It looked like he didn't want to alarm her.

She smiled at him.

"Yes, Karl, what can I do for you?"

"Yana, this is not the way. Can't we talk about it? Isn't there some sort of arrangement we can come to?"

She smiled again, but this time there was a sadness to her.

"As I said, it is beyond my control now. I cannot stop it even if I wanted to."

"But surely you have someone you can contact?"

"The person who can stop this can only contact me. I can send a coded message to confirm or deny something, but I cannot talk to him. I do not want this to happen, Karl, but sometimes we have to take a stand for what we believe in. Sometimes people must be made to pay, even if that means others have to get hurt. I am sorry."

He looked at her and shook his head.

"So am I."

He turned, pushed away from the side and floated over to the entrance of the module, where Jackson and Petersen were watching him.

When he reached them, he grabbed hold of a handle to steady himself.

"No, she still says the same thing. There's nothing she can do unless she gets a code from this man. She is hopeful, but we can't rely on hope… Oh, and she's sorry."

"Do you believe her?" asked Petersen.

"I'm not sure. I think so," said Gruber. "I've known Yana a long time. This is so out of character. I would never have thought she could be capable of something like this. What I do know is that she believes in what she's doing, and if her past behavior is anything to go by, I don't think we'll be able to get her to change her mind. If it's true what she says about having to receive a code to deactivate the station trajectory, then there's nothing we can do anyway."

At that moment the whole station juddered. They held onto something solid and glanced around.

"We're starting to skip off the atmosphere," said Jackson. "There has to be something we can do." He then received a beeping in his earpiece.

"This is a NASA priority red."

He glanced at the others.

"Hang on a minute."

The others watched as he drifted slightly away and into the narrow passage that linked the Zvezda module to the rest of the station.

Yana also watched him, but then lost interest, returning to stare out of the port.

Jackson was now all focus.

The 'priority red' indicated a classified message from NASA. As commander, there were times when messages and information from mission control were for his ears only. It was an emergency backup in case of complicated or delicate situations, and while this definitely qualified as that, he was sure the controllers had never envisaged something like this.

He pressed a TALK button and spoke quietly.

"This is Jonas Jackson."

He listened for ten minutes, nodding occasionally. At one point he wrote something down in a small notebook and placed it in the breast pocket of his flight suit.

When the conversation was over, he backed out of the narrow linking tunnel and glanced at Yana. She was still otherwise occupied. He then made his way over to the other two astronauts. They watched him approach with questioning expressions. When he reached them, he turned his back so Yana couldn't see his lips move—he'd seen *2001*.

"Okay, that was Houston," he started. "There have been a number of developments. President Stevens has been rescued." At this, the others smiled and glanced at each other. "They don't know his condition yet as he still has to come out of a forced sedation, but it looks good." He paused. "However, the bad news is that Petrovich is dead, and the lead terrorist has left the cocoon. This leaves him with no incentive to carry out the attack, but he hasn't chosen to call it off, which is not a good sign. It would suggest this goes further than trying to prize demands out of the presidents. It looks like he wants revenge for some reason, which doesn't put us in a good position."

They looked at each other grimly.

"That said, some information has come to light that may, or may not, help." They were all ears. "Someone has apparently been able to get hold of part of the code." At this, Petersen looked hopeful and was about to say something. "BUT... and there's a very big 'but.' It's a partial code. The full code is made up of eight characters. We only have seven."

"Couldn't we try and enter it. Maybe guess the final one. How many combinations could there be?" said Gruber.

"The code I have is a mix of numbers and letters. The last one could even be a symbol of some kind, so we could be talking in the hundreds," said Jackson.

"So, what do we do?" asked Gruber.

Jackson thought for minute. "We have a couple of options. The other thing NASA said was that someone was in pursuit of the terrorist. If they can get hold of him, they may be able to extract the final character, then all we would have to do is overpower Yana and enter it ourselves. The problem is that may never happen, and even if it does, it may be too late."

"The other option?" asked Petersen.

Jackson looked between them. "The other option is we overpower her, enter the partial code, and try and guess the final character. It's a hell of a long shot, but it might be the only one we get."

Gruber and Petersen glanced at each other.

"I say we vote on it. Go with the majority," said Jackson.

Again, they looked at each other and then nodded in agreement.

"Okay," said Jackson. "Andrea. What do you want to do?"

She looked pensive, glancing round the group. "I say we go for it. Take her computer and try our best."

Jackson looked at Gruber. "Karl?"

Gruber look worried, torn over his decision. "If we do that, we may lose the possibility of waiting for it to be resolved with the right code. And what happens if the computer gets damaged or there's some sort of safeguard on the program? We may lose any chance at all. It's too risky. I say we wait."

They both looked at Jackson. He had the deciding vote.

He glanced over at Yana, then took a deep breath.

"I say we try. We can't just sit here. Taking action is the only way to go."

He glanced at the others. "You okay with that, Karl?"

Gruber nodded slowly. "It's a democracy, even up here. Let's go for it."

They all turned their gaze to Yana just as there was another violent vibration from the station around them. She had stopped looking out of the port and was now staring straight at them.

Chapter Forty-Five

After leaving Masaev in agony on the floor of the control room, Clare had fled into the passageways of the cocoon.

The facility wasn't large, and it wouldn't take him long to find her, but she knew it inside out and that had to give her an edge. But even more importantly, she had to work out how to get out. Although she knew McCready would come back for her if he could, she had to be realistic. It was unlikely. It would either take so long to catch up with Kozak and make him give up the code, by which time it would be too late, or else, and she shuddered at the thought, he might be killed somehow in the process. He might even be dead already.

No, she had to think of something on her own.

She found herself running though ever-rising water along the gallery above the rec. She stopped halfway. Each of the terrorists must have had a set of dive gear. Since a number of them had been killed in the cocoon, there had to be some sets lying around.

If only she could find them.

She ran further along the gallery and through the door at the far end that led to the airlock. It was more than likely any gear would have been left down there. The only problem was the whole lower level was now flooded.

She pushed open the door and looked into the stairwell. She walked up to her chest in the water on the stairs and took a series of deep breaths. It was freezing. She gritted her teeth, took a final breath, and ducked below the surface to swim down to the lower level. The lighting was still working, so despite the blurriness caused by the water, she could see where she was going.

She reached the bottom of the stairs and felt fine. She could normally hold her breath for one to two minutes, but it was cold and she didn't think she could last that long.

At the bottom was a short corridor and then the airlock. She swam along it. Her air was rapidly depleting. She wouldn't have much longer. She was about to turn round when she saw a reflection of light off something in the corner. She moved closer. Her heart leaped as she saw a rebreather with a full face mask lying on the floor. She desperately swam over to it, grabbed the mask and pulled it over her head. She breathed in.

Nothing.

She sucked harder.

Nothing.

She scrabbled around until she found the computer display. It was flashing large red letters…

O2 SUPPLY 0%.

She pulled the mask off in despair. Now she needed air.

She turned around and swam quickly back up the stairs to the gallery.

When she reached it, she climbed out, shivering, gasping for breath. She waited a minute to calm herself down and then pushed through the door onto the gallery.

And froze.

Masaev was standing at the far end, a couple of steps down to the rec. He was staring around, as though looking for something. He then turned and climbed back up onto the gallery.

In the time it had taken him to do that, Clare had quickly moved behind the pillar at the end and down a step of the stairs. She was in the water and still shivering. She was sure he would be able to hear her teeth chattering from the other end. She stood there, her back to the pillar, trying to listen for any movement.

She must have been there for a full minute, and she hadn't heard anything, so either he was standing still, unmoving, or maybe she'd missed him exiting the gallery and hadn't heard the door close as it was dampened by the water. She risked a quick peek around the pillar.

Her heart nearly stopped.

Masaev was creeping slowly along the top of the rec. He was ten feet away. He noticed the movement, and for a brief moment stared straight at her. An evil smile spread across his face. He didn't rush forward. He had time. He was stronger than she was, and she had nowhere to go.

She glanced desperately around—assessing her options. She couldn't get past him. She thought about heading back through the door, but that only led down the stairs, which were underwater. She glanced quickly across the rec.

And then she remembered something.

Back when they had all been in there. When McCready had been questioned. When he had attacked Masaev. Something had happened. She looked down into the water in the rec. Looking for something. Her gaze focused on an object halfway across the room.

And she knew what she had to do.

Masaev was closer now. He was in no hurry. She looked up at him as confidently as she could and then suddenly turned and dived below the surface. She had as much air as she could take in, but she knew it wouldn't last long.

She swam down to the bottom. The object she had seen was to the right of the couch on the far side. She reached the floor and made her way across. She could see the furniture laid out as she remembered it from above.

She was now at the far side.

She could feel the couch.

And then the lights went out.

She almost panicked, but she had to stay calm. It wasn't far. She was doing everything by touch now, her hands grappling across the floor. Then she had contact with the couch. She worked her way to the right. It was just beyond the couch, as she remembered.

She reached the end.

There was open floor.

One hand moved out from the end of the couch, the other held on in case she lost her bearings.

It had to be here.

But she couldn't find it.

She tried to search like a diver doing a series of concentric circles out from a datum point—the corner of the couch. Her air was running out. Her lungs were burning. She was about to give up and race to the surface when her finger moved over the cold steel. A wave of relief washed over her as her hand took hold of the grip of Masaev's gun, which had landed where McCready had knocked it from his grasp.

But now her problems were only just beginning.

Now she needed air.

The advantage of there being no light was that Masaev wouldn't be able to see her either, but he could turn the lights on at any moment.

But she had to get air.

She came slowly to the surface and poked her head up. She tried not to gasp, but she was desperate. She breathed as fast, but as lightly, as she could. Even so, she felt she was making too much noise. She had taken about six breaths when she started to swim toward the stairs at the kitchen end of the room. She stopped about halfway. Her breathing rate was still fast, but it was starting to come under control. She listened. She couldn't hear anything except the occasional metallic groan from the structure around her as components and girders moved fractionally with the stresses and strains upon them.

She moved off again. The stairs were right in front of her. It was still pitch-black. She felt her foot bump up against a step. She reached out to gain purchase. She had a second foot on the step when something massive hit her body. She was pushed under—no way of stopping it. He must have been lying in wait for her. There were only two ways out of the water and he'd guessed right. She hadn't even had a chance to get a breath before she'd been pushed below the surface. The impact had also forced her to drop the gun.

Now, large hands grabbed hold of her. She struggled fiercely, lashing out with arms and legs, but she was held in a vice-like grip. She could tell Masaev was standing half in, half out of the water, holding her under. She felt his hands reach up around her neck and start to squeeze. She couldn't hold on much longer. Her vision was blurring. She felt a blackness approaching—Not visually, there was no light, more primordial—like her soul was clouding over, shutting down. She gave up trying to fight him. She would never be able to.

There was only one chance.

She fumbled around with her hands on the steps.

The blackness was almost complete.

She felt it was too late, and then, like a beacon of light on a dark night, her fingers reached around the butt of the pistol for the second time. She channeled all her concentration into holding onto the gun. It was as though she was in a trance. Things seemed to be happening in slow motion. Like she was watching herself from afar. She saw her other self move the gun round to point at Masaev. She wasn't sure if it would work underwater, so she saw herself lift her hand above the surface and aim at where his head must have been.

It was still pitch-black.

Suddenly, there was a loud roar and a flash of light from the muzzle. As if by magic, the grip around her neck relaxed and was gone. She wasn't sure if she could control her body, but something must have happened subconsciously, because the next thing she knew, she was upright, shaking, gulping in massive breaths of air.

She stayed like that for five minutes. Just breathing. Just experiencing still being alive. She had been dead. She knew she had. But somehow she had come back from the other side.

After she was calmer, in control, she dropped the gun in the water and managed to walk hesitantly forward. She pushed Masaev's body out of the way and slowly walked up and onto the gallery. She sat down on the floor, but the water was now almost up to her chest. She didn't feel the cold. All she felt was the warmth of life coursing through her body.

It was still dark everywhere, but her enemy was dead. She was alive. The only question now was for how long?

And in that moment, she thought of McCready.

How he had appeared out of nowhere. How he had come for her when she'd had no right to expect him to. How he had brought hope and possibility back into her life, only for them to be cruelly torn apart so dramatically.

And she knew, beyond any doubt, if she ever got out of this, she was never going to let him go again.

Chapter Forty-Six

Andriy Kozak pulled the throttles back on *Deep Intruder* and stopped all forward motion.

He had reached the end of the tunnel. To advance further would take him out into the main body of the reservoir. This was where it would get interesting.

He went over the options again.

His best bet was to take the sub into the reservoir and then move to one side, maybe against the wall of the dam, and surface to check the lay of the land. Hopefully, he could then move to a shallow area, exit the craft underwater, and swim to shore and slip away. He could even wait until dark. There was plenty of life support in the sub. If he was seen, he would have to deal with that at the time.

And there was always the nuclear option.

He pushed the throttles forward and moved smoothly out into the large body of water. Once he was clear of the hole, the visibility improved. He could see around thirty feet. Looking up, he could see light coming through from the surface above. He moved slowly over to the dam. It was solid concrete and had algae growing in patches across its side. He slowed to a stop and then gently started to rise up the wall.

As he got closer to the surface, it became lighter. He was at about a depth of ten feet when he stopped. He could now see through the surface and up to the top of the dam. He realized that if anyone was looking directly down they would see him. He would just have to risk it. He rose up so the top of the dome was clear and glanced around.

There appeared to be no one on the top of the dam looking down. He was several hundred yards from each side, pretty much dead center. On the far side, to his left, there was a lot of activity. Construction trucks, a crane, and what looked like engineering vehicles were parked close to the water. He could also make out a number of armed men. No one was paying him any attention. He checked the other side of the lake. This was just barren grass and sloping ground that led up into trees. There was no road and so access was more difficult. He decided to descend and move over to the slope and wait until dark.

He settled himself into his seat and moved the craft away from the wall, then slowly dropped to the bottom. The tunnel exit was right in front of him. He was about to turn *Deep Intruder* away, when a small white submersible emerged from the hole. It came up at speed into the lake. Clearly the driver saw him, as it banked round like a plane, coming to a stop right in front of him.

He couldn't believe it.

He was staring straight into the eyes of the man called McCready. How the hell had he got out of the cocoon? As he stared at him, he saw the grim determination and unwavering commitment of a man who would stop at nothing until he had Kozak where he wanted him.

This changed everything.

The white sub moved forward aggressively. It thumped into *Deep Intruder*, pushing him back.

Kozak grabbed the controls and retaliated, pushing forward, trying to slow the action of the sub.

It seemed to be working, as the power of *Deep Intruder* was greater than that of the smaller craft. But then, suddenly, he realized that wasn't the issue. McCready was trying to corner him against the dam and push him upward, so he would be visible from the surface. In a panic, Kozak pushed forward on the controls. The white sub moved underneath. Kozak suddenly felt an upward motion. It must have been pushing straight up from below. In his haste he accelerated. It made the sub leap forward, but combined with the upward motion of the other sub, it merely caused *Deep Intruder* to shoot to the surface. It rose six feet above the water before crashing down in a wave of spray that couldn't fail to attract the attention of anyone in the vicinity.

Out of the dome, Kozak could see the armed men on the side of the lake. Some others had also appeared on the top of the dam. They all turned to face him. Many of them drew weapons.

He grabbed the controls that would send him back down, but before he could submerge, a hail of bullets struck the sub. Some missed. He could see their trajectories as linear streaks of bubbles through the water in front of him, but many hit their mark. There was a sharp pinging as they bounced off the hull. They wouldn't breach it, but a couple smacked into the dome inches in front of his face, causing it to crack and splinter.

Now he didn't have a choice.

He dropped deeper into the water and turned to face the dam wall, steadying the sub. He wasn't sure where the other craft was, but it didn't matter. In a couple of minutes he may well be dead anyway.

He pressed a button on the control panel.

On the outside, the weapon pods folded down and snapped into place.

Kozak took a deep breath. He selected his weapon of choice, said a quick prayer, and squeezed the two red fire control triggers.

Immediately, two torpedoes sped away from the sub and slammed into the wall of the dam. There were two sudden and dramatic explosions. Bubbles exploded out from the wall and instantly there was no visibility.

Moments later, Kozak could hear a rumbling. It was growing louder by the second. It then became a roar. And suddenly he found himself being pulled forward.

There was nothing he could do.

The torrent of water was all powerful, as millions of gallons poured out of the now breached dam wall and down into the valley below, carrying with it two men in two small, vulnerable machines.

Chapter Forty-Seven

Once McCready had found *Deep Intruder* in the reservoir, his plan had been to force him to the surface, where he could be dealt with by the forces he was sure would be there. What he hadn't counted on was the action the terrorist had now taken.

He braced himself as he became a passenger in the small sub as it was swept down into the valley below. The last time he'd had no control, he'd known he was in the hands of Craig and Graham as they had programmed the flight data into the computer. This time he was literally in the hands of the gods. He could see no way he came out of this alive.

All he could do was hang on and hope for the best. At least he was well secured in the craft.

He looked out of the dome only inches from his face but could see nothing. What he felt, though, was the power of massive kinetic energy at work.

He was pushed through the water with frightening

speed and force. First it was this way, then that. At one point he crashed into a large piece of the concrete wall that had been blown apart by the explosion. Next, the wall disappeared out of view and then seemed to come hurtling back to slam into the sub. He couldn't tell who had slammed into who, but it hardly mattered. The impact was the same. He was whirled from side to side, as though in a washing machine.

After about five minutes, which seemed more like an hour, he could see light above him. It came and went as the sub was tossed and spun around by the water. But gradually the light stabilized to remain constantly above him, the dynamics of the sub taking over in the flow.

A few seconds later he found himself on the surface. It looked like the Colorado River in full flood. There was debris and massive concrete blocks flowing down beside him. He found himself in a wide river. Remembering the layout of the area Craig had showed him when they were on the plane, he figured he must be in the Los Angeles River that ran past the end of the spillway from the reservoir—the upper end of the one he had flown up some hours previously.

For as far as he could see, there was water. Roads and houses either side were almost completely submerged.

He grabbed hold of the controls and tried to steer himself away from obstacles. It was like one of those video games where you have no control of the speed of the vehicle you're in and there's no way of stopping. You just have to steer to avoid being wiped out by some obstruction that comes hurtling toward you. In his case, the obstructions consisted of trees, large containers, even the walls of houses.

And then suddenly there were two cars alongside. They

seemed to be racing him. One veered away as though turning off but was barrel-rolled through the water. The other managed to overtake him somehow.

He must have traveled for several miles.

Eventually the speed started to ease off and the water level drop, but there was still debris and detritus everywhere. McCready thought this was what it must be like to be caught up in a tsunami.

He glanced ahead. There was some sort of blockage in the flow. As he got closer, he could see a number of telegraph poles and trees had become wedged against a bridge. They were matted together, creating an obstruction, like a dam built by beavers. But what was of more interest was what was caught between two of the poles.

Deep Intruder.

He was approaching at speed.

As he drew level, he saw the top hatch open and a man pull himself up slowly on top of it. It had to be Kozak. The man looked around. When he spotted McCready, he stared at him for a moment. He then reached back inside the sub and pulled out a gun, walked shakily over to the side of the river and climbed up onto the roof of a building.

McCready had to follow him.

He now had more control. The propulsion system was capable of over fifty knots. The shape was aerodynamic and would move through the water with ease, but it had been designed to move *through* the water, not on top of it.

He took a bearing on the side of the river and dropped the craft a few feet below the surface. He would be able to use the speed of the flow to help him. He aimed for the side and applied full throttle. The craft accelerated through the water, but he couldn't see where he was going. All he could do was aim where he thought he wanted to go and hope for the best.

A second later the sub impacted the concrete slope at the side.

It hit hard. But it didn't stop. It shot up the bank, powering up through the surface. It flew fifty feet through the air, over some low buildings, and then crashed down a slope, skidding into the middle of a freeway. Cars and trucks blared their horns as the sub shot across into the outside lane.

It came to a grinding halt in the middle of oncoming traffic. A large semi blasted its horn, jamming on its airbrakes. As it tried to stop, the rear trailer skidded to one side, coming to a screeching halt inches from the glass dome of the sub. When McCready opened his eyes, he was staring at a large chrome fender.

He breathed a sigh of relief and checked for broken bones. He thought he was okay, but he was going to be black and blue after this.

But there was no time to relax.

He had to find Kozak.

He undid the clamp and pushed the front dome of the sub open. He then climbed out and watched as bewildered drivers got out of their cars and stared at him.

He jumped on top of the sub and looked back up the road toward the blockage in the river. He could see Kozak run into the road. There was the sound of a gunshot. The door of a gold-colored Mustang was pulled open and the driver's body thrown out. Kozak jumped in and skidded off. It looked like he was heading south.

McCready looked around. He couldn't exactly hijack a car.

Over to one side of the freeway there was a large warehouse-style building. Floating above it, a hundred feet in the air, was a blimp in the shape of a motorbike. Scrawled across it was a banner stating BOB'S BIKES ARE THE BEST BIKES—*yeah, been there, done that!*

McCready ran across the road and over to the warehouse, then ran inside. There were a couple of customers, but most were looking at the water outside. One of the staff came up to him with a large grin on his face. Never say a little catastrophic flooding should get in the way of a sale. He didn't even comment on the drysuit McCready was still wearing.

"Hi, I'm Bob," he said, beaming at McCready. "Anything in particular you're looking for today, sir?"

McCready glanced at him. "Yeah, there's a Yamaha 500cc trial bike outside. Any chance of a test ride?"

"Of course, sir. Just let me get the keys." As he did so, his phone rang. He answered it as he went to look for the keys to the bike. McCready ran back outside. He could just make out the gold Mustang turning off at a junction a few hundred yards away.

He turned back to the shop to see Bob still on the phone but beaming at him as he brought the keys. McCready climbed onto the bike, waiting for Bob to get there. As Bob proffered the keys, McCready inserted them, kick-started the engine and looked at Bob.

"Anything else I can do for you, sir?" said Bob, still with that smile.

"Yeah, can I borrow this?"

Before waiting for an answer, McCready grabbed the phone out of Bob's hand, dropped the clutch, and raced away. He shut off the call and stuffed the phone into his pocket. He skidded the bike out onto the freeway and headed after the Mustang.

Bob watched him go, still not quite comprehending what had just happened.

McCready twisted the throttle as far as it would go and the bike leapt forward.

He reached the turn and followed the direction the Mustang had taken.

It was nowhere in sight.

He cursed. He had to choose. He revved hard and then sped off down the road, checking side streets on either side. Eventually he pulled over and grabbed the phone from his pocket. Bob's attention to security seemed to extend to his phone. It had no lock screen. He dialed. A couple of rings later it was answered.

"Hello, Craig Richards."

"Craig, I don't have much time."

"John! Jesus! Where the hell are you? You okay?"

"I'm on a bike on…"—he glanced around him—"somewhere just to the south, south-east of the Dodger Stadium, I think. The lead terrorist, Kozak, has escaped. He's in a gold-colored Mustang. I was following, but I've lost him for the moment. Petrovich is dead and Clare's still inside the cocoon. I have to find Kozak. He has a code that could save millions of lives. Too complicated to explain. But you need to let the authorities know about Clare. Someone has to try and get her out. I'll be in touch when I can."

He ended the call and rode on past some more streets. At the third one, he pulled up sharp. There, at the bottom of a long slope, he could see the Mustang. Just beyond it was the perimeter of what looked like a small airfield.

He was about to set off after the car when he felt a sharp pain in his shoulder.

Shit!

This was not what he needed.

He knew what it was.

He realized what it meant. But he had to put it out of his mind for now. He knew, though, that it would only get worse.

He revved the engine and sped off down the hill.

Chapter Forty-Eight

Porter had managed to follow the police officers as they had led Charlie away from the side of the complex. She had been taken to an LAPD mobile command trailer set up a few hundred yards from the military facilities.

He had driven closer to the trailer to get an idea of what was going on and to see if he could help her.

He went to the rear of the SUV and grabbed a bag from the trunk. Inside were a few 'useful' pieces of equipment he had brought from Scotland, but there was also the laser listening device. He pulled it from the bag and connected up a set of headphones. It had a long barrel, like a rifle, but with a highly compact butt. The part you held was a handle packed with sophisticated electronics.

He placed the headphones over his ears and then leaned back in the seat. He lowered the car window and pointed the device at the window of the trailer where they had taken Charlie. After adjusting the controls and sound levels, he concentrated on what he was hearing.

As he listened, he could hear the background noise of

cops chatting and receiving information over radios and phones. That wasn't what he wanted. He moved the angle. Eventually, he could hear Charlie's voice.

She was being interrogated.

The questions didn't sound promising. He could understand why. Given the current situation, they had to consider anyone a threat who wasn't who they said they were and had no good reason to be there. So far, the questions had ascertained she was nothing to do with the press, and the pass she had shown to the security guard at the gate wasn't hers. He was listening to the follow-up and what her options might be, when his phone rang. He picked it up.

"Yeah."

"Eugene," said Richards. "Forget the mikes. John's managed to get out, but he might need some help."

"Ah, well, you see. It's like this…"

Porter explained everything to Richards, who then gave him an update on McCready and what was going on. Porter listened intently. When he hung up, he realized the game had changed. He listened through the laser mike for another couple of minutes, but when he heard the cop say, "…and so we're going to remand you in custody until…" he'd heard enough.

He packed the equipment away and reached down into the depths of his bag.

It was time to have some fun.

Charlie had been in the LAPD trailer for half an hour when things started to turn serious.

The initial questions had been fairly routine, but when they realized she wasn't who she had claimed to be, their whole demeanor changed. A more senior officer had come to talk to her. They kept asking what she was doing there, a fact she couldn't enlighten them with. She tried charm. She tried humor. But it seemed they'd had bypasses for both.

She was just pondering if there was any way she could chat up one of the younger officers who had looked approachable and given her the occasional glance earlier, when she heard a loud explosion. It didn't seem that close, but it was enough for everyone in the trailer to glance at each other and for a couple of them to head outside to see what was going on.

A few seconds later one of them came back in, saying a news truck's engine had suddenly combusted and was on fire. They returned to their tasks. Ten seconds later, three explosions in quick succession ripped through the air.

And they were a lot closer.

This time, everyone ran outside.

Charlie was left on her own.

"Psssst!"

She glanced around.

"Psssst! Over here!"

Charlie looked toward the rear door of the trailer. She grinned as a serious-looking Porter beckoned urgently to her. She glanced round quickly, but everyone was gone. She ran over to him and out the back of the trailer.

"What happened?"

"Ah," said Porter. "If they leave their cars in the blazing sun, inevitably something's going to happen to the fuel tanks."

She followed him outside, but as they ran for the cover of some trees at the side of the car park, Charlie stopped and stared in awe at three upside-down police cars burning furiously. When they reached the trees, she grabbed Porter's face and kissed him hard on the lips.

"You beauty!"

Porter wasn't quite sure what to do. All he could manage was, "Thanks luv." He then turned serious and told her about the call from Richards, explaining what had happened to McCready.

She thought for a moment, all the while gazing across the open parking area at hardware, equipment and personnel. Finally, she stared at him with a determined expression.

"Eugene, I need you to do something for me."

When she had explained, Porter looked as if all his Christmases had come at once.

Ten minutes later, Charlie found herself at the edge of the military compound that had been roped off to keep people out.

One side butted up against a small wood. She walked over to the rope and stepped under it. In front of her was the full might of the US forces operation. At the far end were the recompression chambers. Next to those was the military command center, into which people entered and exited on an almost continuous basis. But what she was really interested in was the hastily prepared helicopter operations pad that was closest to her.

There were three helicopters sitting there. Two Sea Stallions and one Black Hawk. She had been in Sea Stallions but had never piloted one. She was pretty sure she wouldn't have a problem, but she'd rather go with something she had tried and tested, so to speak. The Black Hawk was like the sports car of troop-carrying helicopters. It was sixty-four feet long, could carry eleven troops fully laden with equipment, and had a top speed of over 220 mph. It also had a range of three hundred and sixty miles, though she noticed the one on the pad was fitted with a long probe that extended forward from the right-hand side of the cockpit to allow midair refueling, thereby giving infinite range, so long as it could rendezvous with a tanker.

To one side was a large semi-truck with a tanker trailer. It clearly carried aviation fuel for the choppers.

She watched the activity around the helicopters. All was calm and collected. Nobody was expecting any trouble. In fact, given what Porter had just told her, it was almost as though things were winding down, as the main activity switched from active engagement at the complex to the search and apprehension of the terrorist who had left the building, so to speak. She was sure the choppers would soon be in use, so the quicker she made her move, the better.

She finally worked out her approach.

There was a man sitting in the open rear door of the Black Hawk leaning against the side. He looked relaxed, was wearing shades, and was currently absorbed with something on his phone. There was no one else close by.

She set off, striding purposefully toward him. She was about ten yards away when he looked up. She smiled. He smiled back, but then glanced around. He put his phone away and jumped down from the doorway.

"Sorry, ma'am, but you shouldn't be over here. It's a restricted area."

Why are Americans always so damn polite? Charlie smiled a broad smile at him.

"Hi, name's Charlie. Just admiring your ride."

At this, he seemed to relax a little. He probably didn't often get to talk to people about the helicopters he flew, far less an attractive redhead. He smiled at her.

"They're really great. Nothing they can't do."

Charlie looked over the khaki-colored military machine with awe and respect.

"So, what do you do?"

He seemed to stand a little taller. "I'm the pilot."

"Wow, you actually get to fly this thing?"

"Sure do, ma'am."

"I've always loved choppers. It's just so amazing what you can do with them."

"She's the backbone of the US Army and Navy, ma'am. Nothing like it," he said proudly.

"I don't suppose I could have a ride sometime," she said with a suggestive smile.

The pilot looked at her. "I'd love to, but we're on duty right now. Anyway, we're down on fuel. Waiting to fill her up later on."

"That's a shame," said Charlie, but a movement had caught her eye over near the fuel tanker. She watched for a moment. The pilot was about to ask her something when she threw her hand to her mouth and pointed over to the fuel truck.

"What's that? Oh my God, she's going to blow!"

The pilot immediately turned to look where she was pointing. As he did, his eyes opened wide. A strip of grass was alight. The fire seemed to be shooting along in a line, heading straight for the tanker. If it ignited, the whole parking area would be devastated. The pilot's attention was fixed on the tanker. He ran away from the Black Hawk without a second glance at Charlie. As soon as he'd gone, Charlie climbed up into the cockpit and scanned the controls, taking in its status. They were identical to the aircraft she'd flown in the past. There were a couple of dials that seemed to have been repositioned in this model, but otherwise she slipped into the pilot's seat like a well-worn coat.

She reached forward and flipped the master switch. She then clicked the ignition and pressed a small button on the end of the collective to start the engines. She heard the slow whine as they started up. She didn't have time to go through all the usual pre-flight checks. She assumed the navy were pretty much on top of that.

When the twin General Electric T700 turboshaft engines were up to speed, she engaged the rotors. They started to turn slowly above her head, the narrow shadows of each blade passing over her face becoming faster and faster until it was like a canopy of shadow above her.

She watched the revs and power. When she was ready, she buckled up her straps and looked out across the parking area. She could see the pilot was halfway to the fuel tanker, but he stopped when he heard the Black Hawk start up. He was torn which way to go. Eventually he ran back toward the helicopter, waving his hands desperately. He was twenty feet away when Charlie pulled back on the collective and took the chopper up into the air. She grinned at him as she rose higher.

"Shouldn't leave the keys in the ignition!" she shouted above the roar. He'd never hear, and anyway, he was cowering beneath the rotor wash. She then banked round, away from the trees, and looked below.

She saw the strip of fire that had been heading for the tanker.

In fact, it was about thirty feet in front of the tanker and would never have been a risk to anyone. It was just the perspective from the position of the Black Hawk that made it look like it would be. She also saw Porter standing to one side, watching her. She gave him a big smile and a big thumbs up. He gave her a wave. Next, she called Richards to let him know she was airborne, and to let McCready know, if possible.

She then settled back into the seat and the task ahead. She would try and help locate the terrorist any way she could.

Her only worry was fuel.

The tank wasn't exactly full.

The roar of the Black Hawk taking off made everyone in the military command trailer stop talking until it had passed. Once it had gone, Bryce looked at President Stevens, who was sitting in a high back chair at the end of the table.

The trailer was divided into two halves. One half was where operations were conducted from, which housed technicians and operatives who monitored communications and security intel. The other was a meeting room—soundproofed and shielded against electronic eavesdropping. It was secure and private and was where sensitive operations were discussed and planned. It was where the president was while still under medical supervision from Dr. Fletcher.

After he had arrived in the chamber, still unconscious, Connie had gone inside, waited for the pressure to equalize, and then checked his vitals. She had conducted a bubble flow test to see if he had any enlarged bubbles within his bloodstream that could lead to decompression issues. The test had gone well, and she had since supervised and monitored his condition until he had come round from the sedation, aided by a reversal drug that had woken him up.

Since then he had improved in leaps and bounds. There had been a period where he'd had to decompress slowly, but that was routine. He was just glad to be out in the real world again after his ordeal.

Now, as he sat at the end of the table and learned of Petrovich's death, he wore a solemn expression. He had gone over everything in his mind. He still had the dilemma that the ISS was likely going to crash onto New York if he didn't do something. That meant two things. First, he had to get agreement from Moscow, and Vice President Slavov's approval, to meet Kozak's demands. And second, even if he managed that, they still had to find Kozak to let him know so he could stop the attack.

He held a receiver in his hand. It was connected to the Kremlin and ringing.

A second later, a gruff, heavily inflected voice came over the earpiece.

"Hello, Mr. President, I am so happy to hear you are okay," said Kostas Slavov, the vice president of Russia.

"Thank you, Kostas. It was very difficult." Stevens paused. "But I am afraid I have some very bad news."

The line was silent for a moment.

"Go on."

"I am afraid I have to report that Viktor Petrovich was killed during operations to free him."

Again, there was silence on the line.

"That is most unfortunate, Mr. President. How did this happen?"

"I don't have all the details, but it would appear he was shot during an exchange with the terrorists as he was trying to escape. I can only offer my deepest condolences and those of the American people at this difficult time."

"Thank you, Mr. President." Stevens noticed a hardening in the tone. "I trust those responsible are now in custody or are dead."

It was Stevens turn to pause.

"Not at the moment. We are conducting an operation to catch the lead terrorist. There is also an ongoing investigation looking at how they were funded. Initial reports indicate one of your countrymen may have been involved." He paused. "But there is a more pressing matter we need to discuss."

"And what might that be?"

"Certain demands were made by the terrorists that President Petrovich felt he was unable to agree to. If these demands are not met, one of my cities will be destroyed. It is essential we reach an agreement with regard to this to prevent the attack."

Again, there was silence.

"Mr. President, you contact me to tell me that our leader has been killed and then in the same breath demand we agree to something he would not agree to. That is impossible."

Stevens clutched the handset harder.

"Listen to me, Mr. Vice President, or should I say Mr. President, if you cannot agree to this, even in the short term, and if we are attacked because of this, we will be left with no option but to retaliate against your country in a strong and meaningful way. You should be in no doubt what that means. Do I make myself clear?"

Again, a pause.

"Yes, Mr. President, perfectly. And if you do, you know what will follow. There is nothing more for us to discuss."

The line went dead.

Stevens just sat there. He slowly replaced the receiver. All in the room watched him.

When he looked up, his face was tense.

"Where are we on finding Kozak?"

Bryce responded. "We have no direct leads, sir. The last we knew, he was in a submersible in the reservoir before the dam collapsed. The sub has been found wedged at the side of the Los Angeles River a few miles downstream. But Kozak was nowhere to be seen. It's possible a man called McCready"—at this, the president looked up sharply—"may be following him. This came from a colleague of his, Craig Richards, who contacted us. Other than that, we're in the dark, but we're making every effort to track him down."

The president looked at Bryce.

"So, what you're telling me is that the only lead we have to try and stop World War Three is a guy who no one seems to know where he came from, who he really is, or where he is?" He absentmindedly rubbed his jaw.

"That's about it, sir," said Bryce.

"That's just fucking great!" said the president.

Chapter Forty-Nine

The vibration was now more violent.

The ISS shook and juddered in a way that had never been envisaged by its designers. Space was a hostile environment at the best of times, but couple that with the forces applied when starting to reenter the Earth's atmosphere, and you were dealing with what was effectively the most sophisticated machine humans had ever built being slowly and inexorably torn apart.

Jackson could see the damage being done from a viewing port in the US Destiny module. There were already tears in some of the massive solar arrays designed to provide power to the station. Some of the ends had been pitted, even torn away in places. When he had last checked the temperature readings from sensors across the station, they had all risen dramatically.

He now stood by the main control computer with Andersen and Gruber next to him. They had come here to make final preparations for action. Currently, they were looking at the trajectory information on the screen. The usual orbit of the station was changing. It was moving to a track that took them across the Pacific, over the southern United States, lining up to fly directly over New York.

And there was nothing they could do about it.

Jackson smacked the side of the station in frustration. He then had to grab onto something to stop the momentum from sending him across to the other side.

The others shared his sentiments.

"Okay, are we ready?" asked Jackson. He looked at the other two.

They nodded slowly, clearly nervous at what they were about to do.

"Okay, let's go!"

They set off through the ISS back to the Zvezda module at the far end.

When they reached it, Yana watched them enter, single file, and array themselves in front of her.

She turned to face them.

Jackson was the first to speak. "Yana, we have to try and stop you. I'm sorry it's come to this. It's your last chance to be reasonable."

She said nothing, her expression firm.

Jackson sighed and moved forward. She waited until he was close, then she lashed out with a knife she had concealed behind her back. It took him completely by surprise as the blade ripped into his flight suit. He felt a burning welt across his chest as the steel penetrated his skin. He reeled back in shock, but then his face hardened. He moved forward, this time more aggressively, as small red droplets drifted out from the tear in his suit and floated in the air.

The ISS was not a great place to have a fight. Every action had an equal and opposite reaction, so anytime you tried to exert force on something, you had to think of the consequences. If it hadn't been so serious, it would have been comical.

The three of them now came at Yana—from all angles. But they were moving through space and Yana was secure against the side of the station. She could easily push or kick them away, so long as she held onto something solid.

After regrouping, they came from the sides. Now they could grip onto the structure as they approached.

She must have realized her time was up. She suddenly pushed off from her position, shooting between them.

They watched, curiously, for a moment. She crossed over to her sleeping pod and disappeared inside. At least she couldn't do any damage in there. But then she emerged carrying a hammer.

She pushed off from the pod, heading up through the station.

Jackson suddenly had a thought—she was heading for the main communications hub in the US Destiny module.

He realized what she was going to do. With a roar, he pushed off after her. Petersen stayed with Yana's computer, while Gruber followed Jackson.

You could only accelerate in space if you used the force of pushing against something—you couldn't just 'run' or 'swim' faster and you would move faster.

Jackson followed Yana as she flew through the Zarya cargo block.

She was then into the Unity module, one away from Destiny.

He desperately grabbed the bulkhead above his head, pulling himself faster through the air. It sent him flying down the station like Superman, but he was going to be too late. He could see she had reached the console. She knew exactly where the most damage could be done. She was the communications officer after all. She ripped off the panel, revealing the electronics behind.

Jackson was ten feet away, still speeding through the air, when she gripped hold of the side of the rack and brought the hammer down. She managed ten blows before Jackson reached her. He didn't even bother to try and stop himself. He crashed into her, pulling her away from the panel. They grappled in midair until they smashed into the end of the station where the Shuttle used to dock.

Yana struggled desperately, but it was no use. She managed to hit Jackson in the face, cutting his cheek, but the stronger man finally grabbed the hammer. Once it was free, he smacked her head against the bulkhead. He was so incensed he hit her again and again. He had to be stopped by Gruber, who had now caught up with them. Gruber gently pulled Jackson's hand away from Yana's head. When he stopped to look at her, she was unmoving, her face a bloody pulp. Jackson was breathing heavily. He looked at Gruber.

"Now we have no comms."

They both looked up as Petersen floated toward them. When she reached them she stared at Yana.

"You killed her!" she said in shock.

Jackson looked at her, his face emotionless.

"It looks like she's about to kill millions. She took out the comms. There's no way we can get the code even if they have it."

Petersen looked at them both with horror. She then glanced at Yana; all empathy or goodwill she may have had for her was gone.

"We have to try the code," said Petersen finally. "There's no other choice."

They headed back to Yana's computer. When they reached it, Jackson looked at the screen.

It was divided into two. The main lower area showed the current orbit of the ISS. There was also the predicted orbit the program Yana had input into the system was trying to reach, along with an altitude readout and a display that estimated the number of orbits it would take to get to the predicted track and perfect altitude to hit the target.

There weren't many left.

The second window, at the top of the screen, was smaller. It was simply an elongated rectangle with eight small square boxes. There was a blinking cursor in the first box. It was clearly where the code was supposed to be entered, which would stop the descent and bring the station back into a stable orbit.

Jackson glanced at the others.

"Okay, we enter the code as we have it, then we have to decide what to do."

"Agreed," said Petersen.

"Agreed," said Gruber.

Jackson pulled the small notebook out of his flight suit on which he'd written the code. He took a deep breath and typed…

Z

When he hit return there was a beep.

"Confirmed," said the computer.

He glanced at the others. He typed…

7

Again, a beep and "Confirmed."

He repeated this for the next four characters.

He came to the seventh one. He typed…

8

A beep and "Confirmed," came from the computer.

They were all silent, looking at the screen. Finally, Petersen spoke.

"One character to save the world. So near, yet so far."

Before anyone could say anything, there was a massive jolt. It sounded like an impact.

Jackson pulled himself over to the closest port and looked out. He could see that a whole solar array had been ripped away.

"Shit!"

"What is it?" asked Gruber.

"We're skipping closer to the atmosphere. I've no idea how long we have."

Jackson turned back to the computer. "Okay, final character. Who wants to take a guess?"

"So it can be anything?" asked Petersen.

"All the others have been letters or numbers, so I would assume it's one of those," said Gruber.

Jackson nodded. "Good point. Narrows it down. Also, none have repeated." He paused. "Okay, let's do this." He looked at Petersen.

Petersen glanced around for inspiration and then looked at the screen. She was trying to discern some sort of pattern, but she couldn't find any.

"X."

Jackson turned to the screen and entered X.

All the numbers flashed red.

"Unrecognized," said the computer.

They were about to go again when a message appeared in a box in the middle of the screen.

AFTER TWO MORE ATTEMPTS THE SYSTEM WILL AUTOLOCK
NO FURTHER INPUT WILL BE ALLOWED

"Dammit!" said Jackson.

There was now sweat on Gruber's brow.

"Okay, Karl, go ahead," said Jackson.

Gruber looked hard at the screen.

"One," he said simply.

Jackson entered 1.

"Unrecognized," said the computer.

AFTER ONE MORE ATTEMPT THE SYSTEM WILL AUTOLOCK
NO FURTHER INPUT WILL BE ALLOWED

Jackson moved back from the keypad.

"Okay, that's it. You guys have to leave."

They both looked at each other and shook their heads. Petersen spoke.

"No, Jonas. If you stay, we stay."

Jackson shook his head.

"I can't allow that. You both have families. I have none. Think of them. This isn't some big hero thing. If there's any way I can save millions of lives, I'm going to stay here until the last second. You don't have to do that. There's nothing you can do anyway. Like I said, think of your families. They need you. There's no point in us all dying… I'm not going to argue. As commander of this mission, I am ordering you to leave."

Petersen and Gruber moved away to one side and spoke briefly. A minute later they turned back to Jackson.

"Okay, Jonas. Thank you," said Gruber. "We'll make sure your actions are known, recognized. You will not be forgotten."

Jackson waved him away. "I don't care about any of that. We'll all be gone one day… Now get going!"

They hugged briefly, and then Petersen and Gruber moved quickly. The station was vibrating even more.

There were two options. Both involved Soyuz craft that had either brought them there or been used as food and cargo carriers. They moved over and down the narrow passage to the first capsule that was docked to the Rassvet module, just beyond Unity.

There was no time to carry out full flight checks. They just had to do the basics and go.

Jackson could leave in the second capsule, between the Zarya and Zvezda modules, if the station hadn't dropped too far and the capsule hadn't been damaged in any way.

Ten minutes later Jackson pulled the hatch closed on his fellow astronauts. He saw their concerned faces as the metal clanged to. He then moved away from the airlock to watch through one of the observation ports.

Five minutes later, the small spacecraft drifted away from the station. The maneuvering jets changed its attitude. Within minutes it was out of sight.

Jackson couldn't waste any more time. He prepared to leave. He checked the second capsule, going through the pre-flight checks so he was ready to go in case he had to make a last-minute dash. He then made his way back to Yana's computer.

He was trying to think of what he would enter as a final choice when the time came.

It was a tough decision.

One click to save millions.

Chapter Fifty

Andriy Kozak had thought his time was up when the dam had given way and he had been hurled into oblivion along with millions of gallons of water and the debris from the wall.

The sub was hydrodynamic, more than capable of withstanding the pressure, but it just wasn't possible to maintain any form of control. He had had to go with the flow. This had meant being rolled and tumbled over and over as *Deep Intruder* had been swept down into the valley.

After the initial shock, the flow had taken him into the Los Angeles River, where he had continued to be swept downstream. The sub had righted itself, but he still had no control over his destiny.

His journey had finally come to an end when the current had swept him into a tangle of trees and poles next to one of the many bridges that spanned the river.

Once he was sure he was stuck fast, Kozak had reached up and undone the hatch. He had half climbed out, when he had remembered something. He'd reached back into the sub and grabbed his gun. He had then emerged from the battered hull and looked around. He had to get away from there, disappear into the streets and downtown LA before the security services arrived.

He ran across the top of a building and down a bank on the other side to a freeway. There was water on the concrete surface but there were still cars and traffic on the road. He ran over to a Mustang, shot the driver, pulled him from the car, and jumped in. He then turned a full one-eighty and sped off in the opposite direction, causing cars to swerve left and right, blaring their horns in protest.

A minute later he turned off at a junction. He was now headed through a maze of suburban streets.

He had a destination in mind.

When the operation had been planned, he had worked out a number of exit strategies depending on how things played out. The original plan, if his demands had not been met, had been to evacuate through the tunnel and then escape from the surrounds of the reservoir, either by car or on foot, but that hadn't been possible. The plan he was now following involved reaching a small airfield that was used for military traffic in the area. It was a staging location for helicopters and military transports bringing supplies and spares for aircraft and other military assets. It had been built on an area that had previously been used for train freight and was located just north of the intersection of the I-5 and the I-10.

With a background in special forces, he had been trained to fly many types of aircraft. He felt sure he would be able to find one to make his escape in. Also, it would likely be easier to move around on a base, as once he was in, he would be assumed to have passed security and would therefore not be stopped or questioned, so long as he didn't act suspiciously. At a civilian airport there were the continuous security checks. And by now he was sure his photograph would be on the phone of every cop and with every law enforcement agency across the state.

He turned off New Mission Road and into Richmond Street. There was a gentle slope with small warehouses on the right. Both sides of the street were lined with parked cars, but he could see his destination. At the bottom of the slope was the chain-link perimeter fence of the LA Central Air Force Base.

He drove down the slope and stopped. To his left, in the distance, were the skyscrapers of downtown LA. Directly in front of him was the fence that bordered the south side of the base. He made a sharp turn to the right and drove parallel to the fence, oblivious to the Yamaha trial bike that was following a few hundred yards behind.

There were some commercial properties on his right, but the area was run-down. There was what looked like a heap of scrapped cars piled high behind a gate. A couple of dogs roamed free, barking and chasing each other through the dust. Several hundred yards further on, the road ended in a dead end.

But Kozak's interest lay with the airfield to the left.

He had to somehow get through the fence. He wasn't too worried. There were usually places where there had been damage, wear and tear, or where an animal had dug underneath. He ideally needed somewhere close to a building, where, once inside, he could slip into the infrastructure and not be noticed while he worked out his next move.

He drove a further hundred yards to where a large hangar butted up to the perimeter. He pulled over and watched the facility for a few minutes.

Fifty yards back, the Yamaha pulled up and stopped.

There wasn't much activity at the airfield. He couldn't see any helicopters, which would have been his preference, but then he turned his attention to the hangar. He could see partially inside. There was what looked like a C-130 Hercules transport aircraft with its nose sticking out the front. It was unlikely to be undergoing maintenance as it would have been fully under cover to be protected from the elements. It must be loading up some sort of cargo. It looked like an option.

He checked to his right. Most of the sheds and small business holdings seemed to be shut up. There was little road traffic, being a dead end. And right now, no one was walking around.

Kozak looked back along the road. He could see a trial bike parked about fifty yards behind him, but there was no one on it.

He made sure he had his gun concealed under his jacket and then climbed out of the Mustang. He walked toward the hangar, and as he went, he checked the fence. There were a couple of places where there had been some sort of damage to the links, but nothing large enough for him to squeeze through. They were also too exposed.

He was coming up to where the hangar adjoined the fence when he saw his chance. Where the fence came into contact with the rear wall, it stopped. The back of the hangar then contributed to the perimeter. Presumably the fence continued on the far side. But where the two joined, the fence didn't have a pole holding it up. It had been bolted onto the hanger wall itself. At the bottom, a couple of the bolts had come loose.

Kozak checked to confirm the coast was clear and then removed the two lower bolts. He could now prize the fencing away from the wall and just squeeze through.

Once inside, he pulled it back into position. From afar, no one would know it had been disturbed. He then made his way carefully down the side of the hangar and risked a glimpse inside.

It was large. There was only one plane: the C-130. Up close, it looked huge. He had jumped out of these on many occasions. He had also been in the cockpit and knew his way around. And while he had never flown one, if push came to shove, he might be able to manage. But if what he hoped would happen, he would only need the pilot to get him through the various air traffic protocols and into the air. He could then dispose of him. So long as they were flying on the right heading on autopilot, he wouldn't even need anyone to land it for him.

As he looked across at the aircraft, he could hear voices coming from the far side. Beneath the tailplane he could see the wheels of a large truck. It looked like equipment, or supplies of some kind, were being loaded on board. He could see the loading ramp was down.

He looked around the rest of the hangar. To his immediate right was a row of offices and what looked like locker rooms. He started down that side, walking out in the open as though he had every right to be there. There was no one in the first office. He came to a locker room, pushed the door open and walked inside. A man was shutting a locker. He was dressed in flight gear.

"Hi," said Kozak.

The man glanced up, nodded, and then turned and left the room.

Kozak looked around.

He pulled open locker doors until he found a flight suit that might fit and then changed quickly. If you had the right clothes you were even less likely to be questioned. He made sure to transfer everything from his pockets. He then walked back out into the hangar.

He crossed over to the plane and round to the back. He could now see the truck. There was a forklift working to load equipment into the C-130. He wasn't sure what they were loading, but there were a series of long, thick hoses. Some had wide conical ends, others, just adapters for extending their length.

As he watched, the final load was put on board. The forklift drove over to a corner of the hangar and parked up. The driver climbed out and jumped into the truck, which drove away. Kozak then watched the man he'd just seen emerge from the locker room walk out of one of the offices and over to the plane, where he made his way up the ramp and disappeared inside.

Kozak followed.

Inside the plane it was dim. There were no lights, only what spilled in from the hangar. Kozak walked past the cargo that was stacked neatly in the middle. Most of the space was empty, except for a few crates and the hoses that were coiled up on the floor and stood several feet high. There were all the fixing points and layout Kozak remembered from the aircraft he'd been in before.

It looked like the man had gone into the cockpit at the far end. Kozak moved further down the hold until he came to a locker on the left. If he was right he would find what he was looking for inside. He pulled it open. It squeaked. He stopped, glancing forward, but no one had heard him. He looked inside and smiled.

There were two parachutes.

Good.

He then made his way quietly over to the flight deck.

The door was half open. He moved closer, pulling the gun from his pocket.

At the last second, he slowly opened the door. Again, there was a squeak. The man in the pilot's seat looked round in surprise.

Kozak leveled the gun in his face.

"Do exactly as I say and you won't get hurt."

McCready had followed Kozak down to the airfield.

He'd climbed off the bike and hidden behind some trees to see what he would do next. He'd watched him leave the car and head toward a hangar further along the street.

McCready followed his tracks and squeezed through the fence at the side of the hangar. He was now inside the perimeter of the base.

He was walking slowly down the outside of the hangar when he heard the engines of a large aircraft start up. There was the whine of the starter motors as each of four sets of propellers began to turn. Then the noise settled down to a constant roar.

There was no longer any need for stealth.

He moved quickly to the end of the hangar and risked a look inside. He saw a huge C-130 sitting there, its propellers spinning at full speed. He glanced at the rear. The tail ramp was starting to lift. He had to make a decision and quickly... and then the clincher. In the light of the cockpit he caught a glimpse of Kozak. He had a gun in his hand.

He had to move fast, so he ran across the hangar floor, heading for the ramp. It was moving up slowly, the angle against the rear of the plane growing more acute by the second. McCready was at full speed. At the last second, he leaped into the air and grabbed hold of the side of the ramp eight feet up. But the gap was closing all the time. He inched his hands along toward the end. He was now ten feet off the ground. He hauled himself up with all his might.

The gap was closing… closing…

…and then he rolled inside, just as the end of the ramp shut fast against the body of the plane. He landed with a bump on the floor.

He'd made it.

But just then he was hit with a piercing pain in both shoulders. The pain was also in his knees. It was like needles were being driven into them. He rolled on the floor in agony, trying not to make a noise. After a few seconds the pain subsided, but he knew it would be back. He closed his eyes, resting for a moment. When he was able to, he sat up and pulled out the phone he'd taken from Biker Bob.

He dialed.

"Craig Richards."

"Craig, you have to move fast."

"Where are you?" There was no small talk, just get to the facts.

"I'm at an airfield just off Richmond Street. Looks like some sort of small air force base. I'm on board a C-130. Kozak has the pilot at gunpoint. We're about to take off. I've no idea where we're going, but he doesn't know I'm here. You need to track the plane."

"Okay, I'll see what I can do. Charlie's managed to get hold of a Black Hawk. I'll let her know. See if she can find you."

McCready was speechless for a second.

"How the hell did she get hold of a Black Hawk?"

"Dunno. Didn't explain. Must be that Aussie charm! Stay in touch."

And with that, Richards was gone.

McCready leaned back and then looked around the hold. He moved across into the shadow of the pile of hoses to hide. He didn't know what was going to happen next, but he had to think of a plan.

And he had to think of one fast.

Chapter Fifty-One

Clare was cold.

The water temperature was around fifty degrees and she was shivering uncontrollably. She had to do something to try and stay warm. The water was still rising.

Soon there would be nowhere to go.

She turned the lights back on, so at least, she could see, and looked around the rec. Aside from Masaev, there was also Stefan's body. She saw it floating in the water close to the side of the room. He had his drysuit on. The air inside was keeping him afloat. He'd been shot in the head, so the suit would still be waterproof. She reckoned he was about her size. She waded back into the water and dragged the body over, then hauled him up onto the gallery.

Ten minutes later she'd managed to strip him of the suit and put it on. As she had taken it off, she'd noticed a device strapped around his wrist under the suit. She looked at it closely. There was a screen with details of bubble absorption and gas percentages in the blood. She'd heard of research into devices like this that could minimize your gas loading under pressure and reduce the possibility of the bends. She had hoped they'd be available for sports divers one day, but she didn't know they actually existed. She would need all the help she could get if she was going to get out of this alive.

She pulled the device from Stefan's arm and noticed there were two small trails of blood coming from where needles had been in his veins. She screwed her face up and paused. Did she really want to do this? But she had no choice. She looked at a diagram on the base of the device that indicated where the needles should go. She then placed it on her wrist and pushed down hard in the manner suggested. She winced as they pierced her skin.

"Urgh! Hope I don't get rabies!"

And then it was on.

She secured the strap around her wrist and looked at the display. There was a reset/calibrate button, which she pressed. She then watched as it rebooted. There was a spinning ball while an initial calibration was carried out. A reading then came up showing it was functioning correctly. It showed a bubble rate that was within acceptable limits, but it also showed the pressures. As the cocoon had pressurized when the leak had occurred, she would need anything this gizmo could do to minimize bubble formation once she left the cocoon.

If she ever left the cocoon.

As she pulled the drysuit fully on, she saw there was a transparent window in the material that allowed her to read the display.

She made her way to the control room, but there would be no help there. As the water level had risen, it had shorted everything out. All the screens were down, along with the comms.

She had to think.

The main airlock was a no-go. Even if she managed to get out somehow, she would still have to get back up to the atrium, and she had no idea of the route or how badly damaged the floor of the atrium would be. Also, as she hadn't managed to find any working dive gear, she wouldn't be able to hold her breath long enough.

But then she had a thought.

The second lift-track, at the back of the cocoon, where the leak was. If she could get herself in there, it was straight up, no difficult route to navigate. She would have to do what was called a free ascent, which was doable but on the edge of what was possible. But with the water level rising by the second, she didn't really have a choice.

She quickly made her way back to the lift-track and the airlock.

When she reached it, the leak was even bigger. She had to force herself against the flow to move through it.

She looked around.

If she walked to the side of where the water was powering in, she would be directly in front of the airlock. As the airlock had reset itself, expelling the water after McCready had left, there was air in the lock and rising water where she was, and it would mean that when the door was opened, the flow would sweep her inside. Then all she had to do was close the inner door, open the door that led to the shaft and swim up to the surface.

Simple.

Yeah, right!

She readied herself.

First, she brought one of the cuff seals of the drysuit up to her mouth. She pulled the seal aside and breathed heavily into it several times. This inflated the suit. It would mean she would have additional buoyancy once she was out of the cocoon, which would propel her faster toward the surface. As she ascended, the air in the suit would continue to expand due to the reduction in pressure, thereby accelerating her even more. Getting up wasn't the problem. Still being conscious when you got there was a whole other thing.

The same principal would apply to the air in her lungs. As she rose, it would expand. To stop her lungs from bursting, she would have to breathe out all the way. The trick would be to do it at just the right speed to avoid overexpansion, but at the same time keeping hold of enough oxygen to support the functioning of her body.

Either way, she was soon going to find out if she could get the balance right.

She walked up to the airlock and punched in the code. The door opened immediately. She was swept in with the cascade of water and she let it fill up till it matched the height in the cocoon, which was about four feet from the roof. She then closed the inner door.

Next came the tricky part.

She steadied herself and started to breathe in and out deeply and slowly. This would saturate her bloodstream with as much oxygen as possible before the ascent. When she was sure she was ready, she quickly punched in the code for the outer door. There was a hesitation, but then the door slid open. Immediately, water poured in from outside, pushing her back against the inner door. The buoyancy of her suit then pushed her up against the airlock roof. She had a desperate thought she might get stuck there, like some sort of aquatic Garfield on a car window, but then she managed to pull herself to the edge of the shaft.

A second later she was in the shaft and heading up,

accelerating fast. All she could do was stare through fuzzy eyes as she shot upward. She tried to gauge, by the pressure on her chest, how her lungs were expanding, but it was impossible. Eventually, she decided to just keep a steady dribble of bubbles coming from her mouth.

She could feel herself moving faster and faster.

It was getting lighter.

And then she could see the surface fifty feet above.

She was going to make it.

But the oxygen in her body had dropped to dangerous levels.

Her vision started to blur and darken.

And with the brightening surface rushing toward her she blacked out.

Luis Rodriguez of the LAPD was bored.

It had all started out as an exciting adventure. He even thought at one point he would be the one to apprehend a dangerous terrorist. But as time had worn on, nothing had happened. After the strange craft had entered the water, which he had to admit had been quite exciting, since then—nothing.

He'd also started to get sunburnt. He was wearing short sleeves and there was no shade on the top of the building. He could feel himself starting to burn. He had called for a helicopter to take him back down, but his captain had told him to stay put—just in case.

Well, 'just in case' just happened.

Rodriguez had been looking through some binoculars at a number of girls by the TV news trucks below, when he heard a sloshing sound from behind. The noise made him glance over at the atrium, but he couldn't see anything.

He moved closer to the water. And now he could see something.

There was a body in the water.

He immediately dived in and swam strongly over to it. It was a woman.

He quickly dragged her to the side, hauled her out, and laid her on the ground. He pushed down on her chest to expel any water and was about to start CPR when she coughed and spluttered.

He had reached her just in time.

He rolled her onto her side while she coughed up more water. A few moments later her breathing rate calmed and she opened her eyes.

She looked up at Officer Rodriguez.

"Who the hell are you?" she asked with a puzzled expression.

Chapter Fifty-Two

Twenty minutes later Clare found herself lying on a small examination bed in a mobile medical unit on the car park outside the Omega Complex.

She had been brought down from the roof by a helicopter after thanking Officer Rodriguez profusely.

As soon as she had landed she'd been put on a gurney and wheeled into the unit. The first person she had seen was a young, blonde doctor who introduced herself as Connie. She had given Clare a quick check over. She'd been particularly interested in the fact she was wearing a hemofilter on her wrist. She carefully inspected it and complimented her on how she'd attached it. She had looked at the display, muttered a few things, and then plugged it into a computer on the other side of the room.

Five minutes later she had crossed back over to Clare.

"It all looks good. There's no major bubble formation, so you should be fine." She gave Clare a reassuring smile and then turned to her conspiratorially. "I'm afraid the bigwigs want to talk to you. A guy called Bryce. Don't let his brusque attitude scare you. He's a pussycat really." She smiled again and then left.

Shortly after she had gone, a tall man in a naval uniform walked in. He crossed over to Clare, sat in a chair next to the bed and smiled.

"Ms. Kowalski, I'm Commander David Bryce, but please call me David. I work over at the Coronado naval base in San Diego. I've been running the operation here today. I understand you managed to escape from the cocoon. I must say, that's some balls you have there." He then realized what he'd said and looked slightly embarrassed.

Clare smiled.

"Thank you, and it's Clare." He nodded. "Well, I've dived for years and know the theory, but I never thought I'd have to do an ascent from two hundred feet. Theory seems to work okay, though."

Bryce then turned serious.

"I'd just like to go over a few things with you."

"Sure."

"I understand you're the assistant manager of the complex."

"Yes, that's right."

"I also understand, from one of my men, that a man called John McCready risked his life to enter the complex with the aim of trying to rescue you." He looked straight at her.

Clare found herself blushing slightly.

"Er, yes, that's also correct."

Bryce glanced at her. "He took quite a risk."

"Yes, he did." Then she looked up. "Do you have any information on where he is?"

"I'm afraid not. As I understand it, he's gone in pursuit

of the lead terrorist, Andriy Kozak. Is there anything you can tell me about that?"

"Only that this man, Kozak, made threats against the US, and that unless the Russians agreed to his demands New York would be attacked."

Bryce nodded, as though it was confirming what he already knew.

"Do you think your friend has any chance of finding Kozak?"

He looked directly at her.

She looked back, equally directly. She was starting to feel herself again. She nodded slowly. "Well, if anyone can, he can."

Bryce could see the fire in her eyes. He smiled. "Thank you, Clare. Now, there are a couple of people from the FBI who would like to have a chat." He stood.

"The FBI… What do they want?"

Bryce walked to the door without another word. After he'd left, two men in dark suits entered the small unit. They took off their shades simultaneously and placed them in their top pockets, then walked over and sat down opposite Clare.

The one on the left spoke. "Ms. Kowalski, my name is Agent Sims, this is Agent Brock. We'd like to ask you a few questions."

"Go ahead."

"How long have you known Brad Walker?" asked Sims. He seemed to be the one in charge.

This wasn't what she'd expected.

"Er, I knew him when I was at college, then I hadn't seen him for years until earlier this year when he offered me a job at the complex. Why do you want to know?"

"But you are in a relationship with Mr. Walker?" said Brock.

They looked at her, expectantly.

"What has that got to do with anything?" They remained silent, watching her. "Yes, I am."

"So, between college and being offered the job, you had no contact at all?" Brock continued.

"No, none."

They glanced at each other.

"Didn't you think it a bit strange, suddenly being offered a job by someone you hadn't seen in years?" said Sims.

"Well, er, yes. But, you see, we'd been close at college and he'd said he kept an eye on me, and when he'd seen I'd been going through a rough time he thought he might be able to help."

Agent Sims seemed to ponder this and then looked up.

"Do you know if Mr. Walker speaks Russian?"

"Russian?" She looked between them. "Well, no... I mean, I don't know. I have no reason to believe he can, but he could, I guess."

"Have you heard him speak about a man called Alexi Lobanov?" asked Brock.

Clare looked blank. "No... Guys, what's this all about?"

Agent Brock glanced at Agent Sims. Sims turned to her.

"Alexi Lobanov is a Russian oligarch who fled from Russia eight years ago. His life was under threat from the administration in Moscow. In fact, he's survived two assassination attempts. He has since been living in exile in the UK. Given his position, he was of interest to American intelligence agencies. They have an ongoing investigation into his whereabouts, movements and known associates. We became involved when we were told about one of those associates: Brad Walker."

At this, Clare's eyes went wide.

Sims continued. "We were even more interested when further investigation revealed large deposits to an offshore bank account of a shell company that can be traced back to Mr. Walker. The origin of the deposits could also be traced. They came from Alexi Lobanov. Now, why would a known anti Moscow agitator pay large sums of money to a lowly manager of a conference building? Seems odd, until you realize that very same conference building is hosting the meeting of the American and Russian presidents."

Clare couldn't believe what she was hearing.

Sims continued. "Investigations have also uncovered a link between Andriy Kozak's activities and the funding by Alexi Lobanov. I would think almost anyone would be able to come up with a not very satisfactory connection between the events of today and the actions of Mr. Brad Walker. What do you think, Ms. Kowalski?"

They both stared at her.

Clare looked between them, complete shock written across her face. She didn't know what to say.

"I can't believe it. I just can't believe Brad would be involved in anything like this. It's not possible. I know him."

"Do you?" asked Brock.

"So, where do you think he is?" asked Sims.

"Er… he's over in New York at the head office. He had to go at the last minute. Something to do with funding." She looked at them helplessly.

Sims checked a notebook. "Unfortunately, that doesn't appear to be the case. There has been no record of Mr. Walker at the parent company head office for four weeks."

Clare was looking more shocked by the minute.

Brock again. "So, you can seriously tell us you know nothing about this, yet you are living with the man?"

She looked up sharply. "We're not actually living together. He hadn't decided to move in yet."

Both agents raised their eyebrows.

"It's an old story, Ms. Kowalski," said Sims. "A man gets a woman he thinks he can easily manipulate and then sets her up to take the fall. He clearly thought you would cave under the pressure of the events and would offer no resistance to the operation. If he had been here, he would have been expected to be in the building when the terrorists attacked, yes? Very convenient that he wasn't."

This whole new angle hit Clare like a thunderbolt. The mere fact that Brad could have been involved in any way—for money—was bad enough, but the thought he had used her, manipulated her, made her want to be sick. She glanced across to a side table by the bed and grabbed a glass of water. She found her hands were trembling as she lifted it to her lips. After a sip, she placed it slowly back down and looked at the men from the FBI.

There were tears in her eyes.

Sims' face seemed to soften a little. "Ms. Kowalski, from what I've heard of your actions today, I don't think you are in any way involved in this. In fact, I would like to commend your courage and the way you have handled yourself. I'm sorry to have broken the news to you in this way."

Clare nodded, still in a daze. She looked up at them.

"Do you know where he is? What will happen to him?"

The two agents glanced at each other, as though deciding whether they should tell her something. Sims nodded to Brock.

"We picked him up three hours ago," said Brock, "at Miami airport. He had a one-way ticket to Cuba. I think you can be assured he will be out of circulation for quite some time. Thank you for your cooperation."

When the two men left, Clare sat up on the bed. She could hardly believe what they'd told her. She wanted to cry, to scream. She wanted to understand how she could have been so stupid. So used. She felt so… dirty.

And then, more than anything in the world, she wanted to know where McCready was and if he was okay.

Chapter Fifty-Three

John McCready was sitting behind the pile of cargo in the hold of the C-130.

The pain had come and gone in his body from the bends. Each wave seemed to be more pronounced. He had been feeling nauseous and he knew it would only get worse. He had to act now or he wouldn't be able to. He pulled himself to his feet and walked unsteadily down the length of the plane.

Transport aircraft were not designed for comfort. The soundproofing was somewhat lacking to say the least. The noise would mean, though, that it was unlikely he would be heard moving around. Every now and then there was a judder and vibration from the airframe as they flew through unseen air pockets.

He had almost reached the cockpit when the door swung open and Kozak walked out. When he saw McCready, there was a moment of shock and hesitation. But then he calmly reached behind his back.

It was now or never.

McCready threw himself forward.

He hit Kozak in the midriff, smashing him back against the door, flinging it open.

The two men crashed into the cockpit.

The pilot looked up in shock as McCready tried to wrestle the gun from Kozak. McCready grabbed his arm so he couldn't bring the weapon to bear.

And suddenly there was a BANG, deafening in the confined space.

The pilot cried out as he collapsed onto the controls. The plane lurched, the nose starting to point down as it went into a steep dive.

Kozak lunged at McCready, smashing his head against the side of the cockpit, drawing blood. McCready could feel it running down his face. Again, he tried to keep Kozak's gun arm away, but he had to do something or they were going to crash.

He pushed Kozak hard against the bulkhead.

There was another shot.

The bullet ricocheted, zinging off the metal walls, finally embedding itself somewhere in the dashboard.

McCready pushed Kozak back against the door, but then a piercing pain ripped through his joints. He collapsed to the floor. Kozak backed away, an evil smile spreading across his lips. He lined up the gun. McCready was running out of options. Using all his remaining strength, he leaped up, crashing into Kozak and knocking the gun from his hand. It skittered down into the footwell below the pilot.

Unreachable.

McCready collapsed again. Kozak was about to hit him but then glanced out of the window. The dive was getting steeper. They were going to crash. He pulled open the cockpit door and ran into the cargo bay.

McCready made it to his feet, only to see the ground filling the view through the cockpit window. He climbed into the copilot's seat and pulled back on the controls but couldn't move them. The pilot was slumped over the yoke on his side. McCready reached across to pull the body free. When he had, he was able to pull the controls back on his side. The pain coursed through his body from the expanding bubbles, but he had to pull the stick back or nothing else would matter.

He finally managed it. The aircraft started to level off.

Once they were stable, he climbed to a height of two thousand feet and looked out of the cockpit to try to get his bearings. They had been traveling along the coast, the ocean on the right, so they were heading south. He wasn't sure how the next few minutes were going to pan out, so he turned the aircraft on a heading that would take them out over the water, just in case the worst happened. He didn't want to crash on a populated area. He then looked around the instrument panel. After a minute he found what he was looking for. He flicked on the autopilot.

Now he had to get to Kozak.

Again, there was a piercing pain in his shoulder that brought him to his knees. He managed to stand and stagger into the cargo bay. He could see Kozak over by a locker on the wall. The rear loading ramp was opening. The wind was howling and screaming around the hold.

Kozak had pulled a parachute from the locker and was putting it on. McCready stumbled toward him. He could see a second chute in the locker. Kozak looked up. He now had the parachute strapped to him. He smiled at McCready, grabbing the second chute. He then walked out into the middle of the hold and threw it out of the rear.

"So long, Mr. McCready, or whoever the hell you are." And with that he turned and ran for the ramp.

McCready lunged at him in a rugby tackle style dive. He missed his legs but just managed to tag his ankle, sending Kozak tumbling to the floor.

He threw himself at Kozak and they wrestled on the floor. The pain was still coming at McCready in waves, but he had to focus and stop Kozak from jumping. He held onto his leg as the terrorist tried to crawl to the ramp. He was barely managing to hold him back when his hand scuffed across a discarded nail on the floor. It was steel and about six inches long. He picked it up and brought it down with all his strength into Kozak's thigh, making him scream in pain. He turned to McCready, kicking him with all he had.

McCready had one final chance. As they rolled across the hold, he brought the nail down onto the pack on Kozak's back. It ripped through the nylon material and through the fabric of the parachute. It would be brave man who would jump with that on his back.

Brave or desperate.

Kozak roared again, but this time in fury, not pain.

He rolled over and kicked McCready in the face. Kozak was now all about survival, and if not that, then revenge. He grabbed a metal loading weight to his right and lifted it up, about to smash it down on McCready. He rose up, the weight high above him, and then he leaped forward, almost in a dive, using his full force and mass to drive the metal block at McCready's head.

At the last second, McCready moved his head to the right and shut his eyes. At the same time, he reversed the six-inch nail in his hand to point upward. He held it securely with one hand, resting the blunt end in the palm of the other. He pulled it to the middle of his chest, the sharp end pointing up.

Kozak fell, with all the force he could muster, down onto the nail.

It went straight through his heart.

The terrorist slumped on top of McCready, the large weight slamming into the floor an inch from McCready's head.

McCready lay there for a minute, exhausted. Then he rolled Kozak off him but remained on his back, panting, trying to get his breath back.

He was alive.

But he had failed.

He hadn't been able to get the final piece of the code from the man. Now, the attack could not be stopped.

He lay there, a tide of despair washing over him.

Slowly, he managed to pull himself up. The waves of pain from the bubbles in his body were becoming more frequent. They were increasing in intensity.

He looked down at the man on the floor. There was nothing he could do.

He bent down and started to go through Kozak's pockets.

There was a small black box with a screen. But when he tried to turn it on, nothing happened. He noticed a large crack on the back. It must be broken, whatever it was. There was a wallet. He flicked through it. There wasn't much. A few dollars. An old and slightly faded picture of a family. He figured it was Kozak's parents and brothers and sister. And in that moment, it brought something home to McCready. Despite everything. Despite the death and destruction. This had all started because a wrong had been done to an innocent person, or persons. It in no way condoned the actions, but at the end of the day, Kozak was just a man who had ended up in extraordinary circumstances because he had made extraordinary decisions.

He was about to put the photo back in the wallet when he noticed something written on the back. He looked closer. It was scruffy and well worn. The writing was in Russian, which he couldn't understand, but just below it was something else.

He froze.

He stared at the paper.

$$Z-7-4-U-3-P-8-6$$

"Jesus Christ!"

The code.

6 was the last character.

He reread it. He had to move.

He hauled himself to his feet and staggered back to the cockpit. He had to get the message out.

He slumped into the copilot's seat and reached for the radio controls.

And stopped dead.

The stray bullet from Kozak's gun had smashed them to smithereens.

"Arrrrgggh!"

Could anything else go wrong?

He thought for a moment and then shook his head at his stupidity. He reached into his pocket and pulled out Biker Bob's phone. He looked at the screen.

NO SERVICE

He looked out of the window. They were still heading

out to sea on autopilot. At this point he nearly passed out with the pain that came from his shoulder.

Once it had subsided, and he could think straight again, he was about to reach forward to disengage the autopilot so he could return to the coast and get within cell range, when he heard a low throbbing roar from outside.

When Charlie had taken the call from Richards, letting her know about McCready, she had immediately headed out over the city in the Black Hawk to try and locate the terrorist in the car.

She had done several sweeps of the area, but to no avail. There was just too much traffic, even with the fact the Mustang was a distinctive gold color. There had been a couple of potential targets, which she had gone to investigate, but she had quickly realized they weren't who she was looking for.

The first had been a woman with a couple of kids, whom she had nearly frightened off the road by effectively flying alongside on the freeway with the Black Hawk's wheels skimming along the tarmac at over sixty miles per hour. The kids had seemed to find it fun, but the mom had been none too pleased. The second had been a man who looked like he was in his seventies. Not him.

She had been thinking of her next move when a second call had come in from Richards telling her about the C-130. She had swung the Black Hawk in a wide turn and headed quickly toward the location of the airfield.

She had also heard there was the equivalent of an aviation APB out on the helicopter. She would have to look out for 'hostiles.'

She had flown over the airfield just in time to see a C-

130 in mid ascent. It had then headed south along the coast. She had tracked in behind and followed it, wondering what to do next. She had then watched with concern as the plane had gone into a steep dive. Shortly after, it had returned to a steady altitude but had turned to head out to sea. Moments later the rear tail ramp had started to descend.

She followed a little longer but nothing seemed to be happening. She then drew forward and level with the cockpit. She was about forty feet away when she saw McCready's pained and bloodied face appear at the window.

He stared at her with shock. She gave him a wave and smiled. It seemed to take him a minute before he recognized her, but then she saw what looked like a wave of relief wash over him. He then looked very focused. A moment later he held up six fingers.

What the hell is that about?

When she shrugged at him he seemed exasperated.

He then held up a hand as though for her to wait. A moment later she saw him crease up with pain.

What is going on over there?

At that moment, one of the four propellers of the C-130 spluttered. Smoke came from the exhaust vent in the side. The propeller died. The blades came to an idle rest, no longer providing forward propulsion.

McCready waited for the pain to pass. He was reinvigorated now that Charlie was there, but how could he make her understand about the code? There had to be a way.

He then saw the outside propeller on the port side splutter and die.

He glanced down at the fuel gauge.

It was reading close to ZERO.

Shit! Shit! Shit!

A moment later, a second propeller died, this time the outer one on the starboard side. He was now flying on two engines. He was sure it would soon be less.

He had to think. He glanced back into the hold. His eyes came to rest on the cargo and his brain suddenly clicked into gear. He moved over to the side of the cockpit and glanced at the Black Hawk. He was focused on one particular piece of equipment specific to that model.

Yes, it could work.

He was now awake and alert. He had a plan. He was sure he could fight though the pain that kept hitting his body. He looked over at Charlie and indicated for her to pull in behind the plane. She nodded and the helicopter dropped back out of sight.

He hobbled through the cockpit door and back into the hold. He moved as quickly as he could to the mass of hoses lying on the floor. He looked around for an attachment point. The hold was full of them. He picked one in the center of the floor and then ran across to the nearest hose. He found one end. There were large metal screw clamps to secure it with. He hauled it over to the plate on the floor and screwed two of the clamps to it. He hoped it would hold.

It had to.

His life, and the lives of millions, depended on it.

He then hauled the hose toward the rear of the plane. It was around six inches in diameter and heavy. He could barely lift the full weight of its length.

Once he reached the loading ramp, he lined the coil up in the center. He could see the Black Hawk about two hundred feet behind, keeping station. He kicked the end of the hose out of the rear. It started to uncoil, until it finally pulled up tight with the connector on the floor of the C-130. There was a slight judder to the airframe.

McCready could now see the hundred-foot refueling hose trailing out the back of the plane.

He looked across at Charlie in the cockpit of the helicopter and indicated for her to come in toward the hose. He was looking pointedly at the long probe on the front of the chopper.

He had to get the code to her, even if he had to take it to her himself.

Charlie stared at McCready in shock.

She realized now what he was going to do. She couldn't quite believe it. She pushed herself deep into her seat. Total concentration.

She became even more focused as she saw the third engine die on the C-130. The port wing dipped slightly as the autopilot fought to stabilize the plane, which was now operating on only one engine.

Okay, she knew what she had to do.

Focus.

"Let's do it!"

Just then, two F-16s screamed past, their afterburners on full heat.

Chapter Fifty-Four

Charlie looked forward out of the cockpit of the Black Hawk.

She could see the lone figure of McCready standing at the top of the tail ramp not two hundred feet away. He couldn't do anything until she had made contact with the fuel hose.

She glanced at the long refueling probe to the lower right-hand side of the helicopter cockpit. She clicked the switch that extended its length, but it was a delicate operation to bring it in line with the conical basket on the end of the trailing hose a hundred feet ahead.

She was about to move the helicopter forward to complete the maneuver when there was a crackle in her headset.

"Black Hawk. Black Hawk, this is Overwatch flight. You need to follow us back to shore and land at a location designated by us."

Ah, come on, guys!

She clicked TRANSMIT.

"Overwatch, this is Black Hawk. I'm kind of busy right now. But happy to oblige once I've picked up a passenger from the Herc. Have to go. Talk later."

There was silence for a moment.

"Black Hawk. This is Overwatch. You must comply with our request or we will be forced to fire upon you."

Jesus!

Charlie again glanced left and right. She then fixed her gaze on the pilot to her left who was watching her. She made a point of pulling off the comms headset and pointing at her ear and shaking her head. She then turned her focus forward.

They would do what they had to do.

At that moment, the fourth propeller shut down on the C-130. It started to go into a shallow dive.

"Oh shit!" said Charlie.

The F-16s must have seen it too, as they pulled back a respectful distance. Somehow she didn't think they were going to shoot her down, and anyway, she had more important things to worry about right now. She focused intently on the small wavering cone that was being buffeted in the slipstream from the C-130, and brought the probe in line.

Now all she had to do was thread the needle and connect the two, while heading for the ocean at over two hundred miles per hour.

McCready stood at the top of the tail ramp holding onto the side of the fuselage.

He had seen the two F-16s fly in close formation to the Black Hawk. He could only wonder what they were thinking, but he didn't have time to worry about them. His total attention was on the progress Charlie was making with bringing the probe in to mate with the cone at the end of the hose. When they were connected he could try and make his way across to the helicopter.

He was just looking round for something he could use to attach himself to the hose so he didn't fall, when he heard the fourth engine die. While it wasn't exactly quiet now, the vibration and juddering of before was gone. What he also felt was a slow dip in the attitude of the aircraft. It was starting a slow dive to the waiting ocean below.

"Come on, Charlie," he found himself saying.

He watched as the probe came closer and closer. The wind wasn't helping. It buffeted the end of the hose, making it jerk around like a kite on the end of a string.

Three times she nearly had it.

The C-130 was steepening its rate of descent. It was now a massive glider heading in only one direction. He glanced at the air force jets. They'd pulled back even further. They could see what was going to happen.

When he glanced back at the end of the hose, she was so close he could almost feel her concentration. And then, with a final push, the Black Hawk moved forward and the probe slotted in.

He heard a loud 'THUNK' as they connected.

He waited a few seconds and then glanced at Charlie in the cockpit. She looked like she was checking something on the instrument panel. She looked up, grinned and gave him a thumbs up.

This was it.

He grabbed a piece of rope he'd found in the hold and made a loop at each end. He then threaded his left hand through one loop and walked to the back of the ramp. He sat with his legs over the side and lopped the rope over the hose. He then put his right hand into the second loop. He was now attached to the hose. He looked ahead. The Black Hawk was level with the C-130, the hose slightly dipping as it stretched between them.

He eased himself over the edge and swung his feet up to grab onto the hose. He then started to shimmy down the hose toward the Black Hawk. His added weight made the hose sag. He moved as fast as he could. He then found himself starting to slide as the angle increased. He hoped Charlie was paying attention. It would be down to her to control his rate of descent by altering the height of the Black Hawk in relation to the C-130.

He slipped all the way down to a halfway point. Then he stopped. The helicopter was slightly above him now, but it was pointing in a downward position, as it had to fly in formation with the rapidly descending C-130. He had to now pull himself up the hose.

He risked a quick glance down. His heart rate increased, if that was possible. The ocean was coming up fast. He glanced desperately at Charlie. He could see her face was a mask of concentration.

McCready started to move faster. Hand over hand. Hauling himself to the connection point. There were only seconds to go.

Another few feet and he reached the cone.

He scrambled to grab it. He had one hand on the cone and one on the metal probe. He glanced briefly up at Charlie. She was screaming something at him and pointing. He risked a glance in the direction she indicated. The ocean was merely feet away. In a desperate lunge he slung the rope across the probe of the helicopter.

The second Charlie saw the rope was over the probe she pulled back hard on the collective, at the same time applying full power to the rotors. The effect was to rip the probe from the cone and pull the Black Hawk into a near vertical position, nose up.

A second later the C-130 smashed into the Pacific in an explosion of spray, completely covering the Black Hawk. The helicopter was still moving forward in a near vertical position. Charlie could feel resistance from the tail. The engine roared.

The rear tail rotor was in the water. It sent spray up like a massive Catherine wheel above the surface. Gradually, as the airframe came under control, the nose tilted down and the tail lifted out of the water, still shooting spray in all directions.

Charlie breathed a sigh of relief as she felt the helicopter respond beneath her. She glanced forward and could see McCready hanging from the rope slung over the refueling probe. She now just had to get him inside.

She brought the chopper into a hover and flicked on the autopilot. The Black Hawk hung in the air, all control handled by the computers, keeping the large machine perfectly stable.

She then moved over to the copilot's seat, opened the door and leaned out. McCready was three feet below. He looked exhausted. He was hanging from the probe that extended just below the door, back to the forward undercarriage.

"Hi, John," she said with a grin. "Quit hanging around out there!"

He gave her a look.

She leaned down to help him. Once McCready had undone one of the loops, he reached up to grab her hand.

She pulled him inside. When he was in, he collapsed into the copilot's seat. She could tell he was near the end of his tether. He suddenly creased up in pain.

"What is it? You okay?"

"Not really," was all he could manage. "I have to get to a chamber."

She suddenly realized the seriousness of the situation. Although they were already pretty low, she dropped altitude until they were flying barely twenty feet above the water. The higher the altitude the lower the pressure, the greater the danger from the bends.

"Okay, just hang in there."

"No, there's something else."

She looked at him.

"You have to get a message to the authorities. They'll understand. Tell them the final character in the code to stop the attack on New York is six."

She wasn't sure, but she put her headset back on. She was about to hit the transmit button, when a voice came over the comms.

"This is Overwatch flight. I've no idea what you're doing, but I must ask you again to follow us back to shore." There was a pause. "By the way, that's some of the best flying I've ever seen."

Charlie clicked the TRANSMIT button.

"Thanks. But we've got an emergency."

She repeated McCready's message to the pilot of the F-16. She was initially met with incredulity, but he carried out her request. When he'd received a reply, the news had not been good. However, he had repeated the demand she follow him back to shore. Charlie had said she needed to get her passenger to a recompression chamber. The pilot had made a couple of calls and then given her clearance to proceed to the Coronado naval base in San Diego. There would be a team on standby. He'd signed off with, "Good Luck." He'd also asked for her number. She'd grinned, but declined, saying she didn't think he'd be able to keep up with her.

After the F-16s had left, Charlie turned to McCready. He was slumped in the seat in ever-increasing pain.

"Okay, John, we have the good news and we have the bad news."

He looked at her as though he was going to throttle her.

"Okaaay. The good news is there's a chamber waiting for you in San Diego. Flying time about twenty-five minutes."

He looked at her again. She knew he wanted the bad news.

She paused.

"The bad news is it's impossible to get the code to the ISS. There's no way to contact them. All the comms are out."

He stared at her incredulously.

After everything they'd been through.

He had the last character of the code. All they had to do was get it to the station. How difficult could it be?

He slumped back in the seat, resigned to the reality of the situation. He felt about as low as he'd ever been in his life, and at times, he'd been pretty low.

Charlie applied full power, heading for Coronado as fast as she could go.

Ten minutes later they were still over the ocean.

McCready's gaze was focused on the water flashing past

rapidly below. Apart from the stabs of pain that wracked his body every few minutes, he felt numb.

They flew close by a large ship plowing through the waves, its crisp white wake extending out far behind, those on board oblivious to the danger the world now found itself in.

They flew on.

But then suddenly McCready's eyes became alert, his mind focused, as though something had come to him. And even through the pain, he found a smile spreading across his lips.

There was still hope.

Chapter Fifty-Five

McCready sat up straighter in the seat, wincing at the pain in his joints.

Charlie glanced at him.

"We'll have you back in no time, John. Don't worry."

"No."

"No?"

"We need to turn round."

"We do?"

"That ship we passed a while back." Charlie looked at him. "We need to get to it."

She glanced at him strangely. "But we're ten minutes from the chamber."

He just gave her a look.

She remembered what her Uncle Craig had told her about McCready; there would be times like this. She decided not to question him further.

"Okay, give me a sec."

She glanced down at the instruments, checking the status of the helicopter.

"We should be able to get there, but you'd better pray they have somewhere to land, cos there's no way we're getting back to shore on this fuel load."

"We need to go."

"Okay, skip. Let's go."

And with that, she banked the helicopter round, away from shore, away from safety, and headed back out to sea.

When they arrived at the ship, they could see it was a cruise liner. The massive number of block-like decks made it literally look like a floating hotel. Charlie gave it a wide sweep, looking for places to land.

There was a helipad amidships, but right now it was covered with some sort of entertainment equipment that was being constructed. Not an option. All other areas were too small or covered with aerials and antenna. At the rear was a swimming pool, but there was nowhere surrounding it large enough for the Black Hawk to set down.

Charlie made a second sweep. They could see the ship was called the *Ocean Star*, registered in Panama.

McCready looked at her anxiously. She glanced at him.

"Craig tells me you're up for thinking outside the box," she said.

"It has been known."

"Ripper!"

"What did you have in mind?"

She changed the frequency on the radio and paused. She glanced at McCready.

"You can swim, yeah?"

There was no response.

"Just checking."

She clicked the mike. *Ocean Star... Ocean Star*, this is the

Black Hawk helicopter currently circling your vessel. Do you copy, over?"

There was static for a couple of seconds. Charlie had now brought them level with the bridge and was tracking it as the ship plowed through the waves. Through the large windows, they could see a man in uniform pick up a mike on the main console. He turned to look directly at them.

"Black Hawk, this is *Ocean Star*. Captain Carlisle speaking. How can I help you?"

Charlie was about to speak when an alarm flashed on the instrument panel. It was accompanied by a rapid beeping. A large FUEL LOW light flashed at them.

Charlie looked across at the captain, her concentration total.

She spoke to him for five minutes, after which McCready looked at her with a new respect.

"You really are as nuts as Craig said you are," he said, smiling.

Charlie shot him a glance. "And then some!"

"Let's hope so," said McCready.

Charlie pulled back on the controls, moving the helicopter away from the ship, ignoring the continual beeping from the alarm.

She brought the Black Hawk round to the front of the vessel. She gauged the height of the tallest antenna and then hovered sideways on to the ship, which was now steaming straight for them. She then made a couple of adjustments and clicked on the autopilot. She could now take her hands off the controls. The Black Hawk stayed perfectly stable in a precise hover.

"Come on," she said to McCready.

She unbuckled her straps and helped McCready out of his seat. They climbed into the rear, Charlie moving to the side door and sliding it open. Immediately the wind tore in, along with the scream of the engines and rotors mere feet above their heads. The ship was now passing directly beneath them. Charlie realized she had maybe not got the height quite right as one of the ship's antenna scraped along the bottom of the Black Hawk before springing back on the other side.

A second later, there was a splutter from the engine. The fuel was nearly dry.

Another splutter.

The airframe wobbled, the autopilot fighting against the resources from the fuel tank. McCready could feel the aircraft starting to slip out of the sky.

As it started to fall he saw the ship's swimming pool come into view below.

Charlie held onto his shoulder for a second.

"Wait."

The helicopter was slipping further.

"Wait."

A second more.

"NOW!" yelled Charlie.

They both pushed off the side of the chopper that was now in free fall.

They could just see the Black Hawk crash down behind the ship, the whirling rotors smashing off the ensign at the stern.

And then they landed in the pool with a splash.

The water was refreshing.

McCready bobbed to the surface, shortly followed by Charlie. As they looked up, twenty camera phones looked back.

They hauled themselves to the side and were helped out by a couple of the passengers who were gathered around the pool. When they stood up, they could see the imposing figure of Captain Carlisle striding toward them. The passengers parted like the Red Sea. Carlisle looked them over and then signaled for them to follow him.

"You'd better have a bloody good reason for this!" he said. And then added, "And you owe me a flag and a pole."

As they followed him away from the pool, Charlie whispered to McCready.

"And the US government, one Black Hawk."

McCready and Charlie were still dripping wet when they walked onto the bridge and stood in front of the captain.

"Okay, let's have it," said Carlisle.

McCready spent the next ten minutes explaining what he wanted him to do. When he'd finished, Captain Carlisle looked at him incredulously.

"This is a joke, right?"

Chapter Fifty-Six

The vibration had increased on the ISS to nearly unimaginable levels.

Since the Soyuz had left, Jonas Jackson had thought of all the options he had. None of them had been good. The only thing he had come up with was what character he would use as the final choice for the code.

Now, as he held onto the side of the station to stop himself from being constantly thrown around, he decided to go and check on the orbital time he had until the station fell out of the sky.

He pushed himself away from the side of the module and floated over to the laptop. It was showing two orbits before they entered the atmosphere on a collision course with New York.

The time had come. He had to act.

He looked at the laptop and the section of the screen where he had to input the code. The cursor was blinking in the final small square that held the fate of the world within it.

He stared at it for a moment. It wouldn't give him long to get to the second Soyuz if it all went wrong, but he thought he could make it.

Before he pushed his finger down on his chosen character, he took one final look out of the window onto the world below.

The station was continuing its orbit over the Eastern Pacific, coming up on the continental United States. The air was clear below. No clouds for miles. He was watching the ocean, when he thought he could detect something at odds with the uniform blue of the surface. He took his hand off the keypad and moved closer to the window.

He hadn't been mistaken. There, down in the water off California, there was something in the ocean. It wasn't large, but against the continual blue backdrop, it was clear.

It looked like a number.

He stared, trying to make sure he wasn't seeing things; that it wasn't some strange cloud formation or atmospheric anomaly. He pushed himself off the side of the station and crossed quickly to a small locker on the opposite wall. He had to verify this before the station moved over land and out of view of the ocean.

He reached the locker, grabbed a pair of binoculars and pushed back to the other side.

He put the glasses to his eyes and stared down at the water below. And he was now in no doubt whatsoever as to what he was seeing. The edge of California was coming into view. The large number in the water was moving away.

But he was sure.

It was definitely a number, and it had been written by the wake of a cruise liner. Through the binoculars he could see the ship just finishing a loop after crossing the tail of the number with its own wake.

It had to be a message, and it had to be for him.

A new wave of hope spread through his body.

Just then, there was a massive vibration. He looked through the port to see a communications dish fly past the window.

He had to act fast.

He moved over to the laptop and made sure he had his finger above the key for the number NINE... and pressed down. He saw the number appear in the box. He then moved his finger over the RETURN key and was about to press it when some force stopped him from doing so.

His gaze had wandered to a locker above the laptop with a number written on it.

1069

He stared at the last two digits.

He stared in horror at what he had been about to do.

What if he'd seen it upside down?

What if it had been a 6 and not a 9?

Trembling, he pulled his finger away from the keyboard and backed away from the computer. He was shaking. He had to think.

Had it been a six or a nine?

The odds were down to fifty-fifty. But it was still fifty-fifty.

He couldn't even toss a coin.

It took a full orbit—the last orbit, for Jackson to make a decision. He crossed over to the laptop as they were coming over the Pacific for the final time. He looked down at the ocean. But the number was gone, absorbed by the ever-shifting pattern of waves.

How could he decide?

He stared at the ocean for a few more seconds before the ISS swept over land and the view was gone forever.

He didn't have much time. He looked at the window on the computer.

He had to decide. Was there one small thing—anything—that could tip it one way or the other?

He had to think.

Hard.

Anything.

But nothing came to him. He sighed. He would go with what he had first thought.

He would go with NINE.

His finger was again descending on the RETURN key, when he stopped.

His finger hovered above the key for several seconds, and then a faint smile spread across his lips. He closed his eyes briefly…

…and then he pressed the BACKSPACE key, removing the 9.

He hit the SIX key, and without further hesitation, with the fate of the world in his index finger, he pressed RETURN.

He held his breath.

The computer beeped…

"Confirmed."

He let out a sigh and watched the screen with relief as a new window appeared.

ORBITAL CHANGE UNDERWAY

He could feel the maneuvering jets on the Zarya module applying thrust to increase their speed and gain altitude.

He took a deep breath.

He thought for a moment about how close they had come.

It could have gone either way, but when you write the number six, you start at the top and draw down to the loop and cross the upright. When you write the number nine, you start with the loop and end with the tail. When he had looked down at the Pacific, the liner had been crossing the upright, having finished the loop.

He pushed himself through the station until he came to the Tranquility module, just off Unity. Here, there was what was effectively a large bay window, known as the Cupola, which extended below the station. It consisted of multiple windows that allowed you to look out over a wide angle onto the Earth below.

On his way over he had grabbed an item from his personal possessions. It wasn't something he had ever thought he would use on board the station, but it had symbolic meaning for him. He'd carried it on his first ever solo flight as a pilot, thirty years earlier.

He stared out through the viewing port and watched the Earth—the beautiful Earth—rotate below him. He almost cried as he saw New York sweep past.

He was suddenly overcome with emotion. How easily it could have gone the other way.

His eyes moistened, but then a deep contentment spread throughout his body.

There was also another reason for his relief. He had not been entirely honest with Gruber and Andersen. He did have a family. He had an eight-year-old son from a previous marriage. The relationship had ended badly and he had been awarded custody. His son was looked after by his parents when he was on missions.

They lived in a brownstone on the Upper West Side of Manhattan.

He smiled.

He pulled the 'lucky' cigar from its case in the top pocket of his flight suit. He carefully unwrapped it and then lifted the small lighter he had grabbed from his possessions. He paused. This wasn't strictly allowed. No, it was emphatically NOT allowed.

What the hell!

He lit the cigar and then stared out across the vastness of the planet below.

In the background, a series of alarms started up. At first there was one, then there were two. A third added to the mix.

Jackson took it as a celebratory fanfare.

If he had been in the main body of the station, he would have seen SMOKE ALARM flashing on many of the screens.

After Captain Carlisle had completed writing the number six in the ocean with the ship's wake, he had turned to McCready. He still wasn't sure if he believed the man, and that this wasn't all some sort of practical joke that was going to go viral on YouTube. But he had been assured by a certain Commander David Bryce, from the US Navy, that he should do whatever McCready told him to do, so he had duly gone about the task with relish.

All they could do now was wait to be told of the outcome.

But they didn't have time.

McCready collapsed in agony on the bridge. He drifted in and out of consciousness. A few minutes later the ship's doctor arrived with pure oxygen. A mask was swiftly pulled over McCready's face and a hundred per cent oxygen administered. It was all they could do.

The Coast Guard was called. They needed a chopper fast. McCready's life depended on it.

He had to get to a chamber.

Before McCready finally blacked out, he said one thing. "Find out about Clare."

Chapter Fifty-Seven

Brandy Carmine walked through her palatial home.

It was situated not far from Rodeo Drive in Beverly Hills. Handy for all the shops and not far to go when she had meetings at the studios.

She made her way in from the mezzanine, through the tall ornate hallway, and into the living area. The room looked out onto a courtyard where a fountain bubbled away in the middle of a large pool filled with koi carp. On the far side, a series of high stone arches led through to a tennis court and swimming pool, beyond which was a five-car garage.

The tall windows were open. A warm breeze flowed through the house. The forecast had said rain later, but it was fine and sunny for now.

Since she'd returned from London it had been a whirlwind. The premiere of *Deception in Mind* had gone down a storm. The initial box office receipts from Europe were breaking all records. The film was yet to open in the States, but the tracking and test audiences indicated it was going to be another hit.

As she walked through into the main living area, Raymond Shelby hurried over from the courtyard.

"There you are. The studio is going nuts over the figures. They want to fast track a sequel and line up a project for you and Joaquin to work on. It's going to be your year, Brandy… again."

"That's great," she replied, still making her way across the living room. A maid walked through from outside.

"Oh, Carmen, could you get me a jug of iced water and…"—she looked at Shelby, who nodded—"two glasses?"

"Yes, ma'am." She hurried out toward the kitchen.

Brandy slumped down in one of the large couches that were spread around the room. A TV was playing on the wall. The sound was down.

Shelby sat across from her.

"Now, we need to go through the offer from Marvel for the miniseries. You've always wanted to play a superhero."

Brandy glanced at him. He was about to continue when she saw a 'LATEST NEWS: LA TERRORIST INCIDENT' banner on the screen. She held up her hand.

"Hang on a minute."

Shelby looked frustrated as Brandy turned up the sound.

The anchor was looking seriously out from the screen.

"Now, an update on the rescue off the coast of California. A Coast Guard operation was underway earlier today to save the life of a man believed to have been involved with the terrorist incident in Los Angeles. Not much is known about him, other than he's British, but sources say he was responsible for helping to avert a disaster in New York."

The screen changed to show a Coast Guard helicopter close to a large cruise ship. Someone was being winched up from the deck. "These pictures are of John McCready being taken off the *Ocean Star* cruise liner. He has now been transferred to the recompression facility at one of the naval bases at Coronado in San Diego. Sources say his life is in danger and it will be touch and go whether he survives. We'll have more on this breaking story later in the hour…"

Brandy stared at the TV. Even Shelby was looking at it in shock.

She hadn't had much time to think about McCready since she'd returned to LA, but late at night, when she'd been lying in bed, her mind had drifted back to the brief time they'd had together, and what might have been. She had wondered if she would ever see him again. Now, as she watched the report, she knew what she had to do.

She looked sharply at her manager.

"I have to get to San Diego. Now!"

Shelby knew when not to argue.

After Clare had been debriefed by the FBI, Connie had come to check on her. She had taken a blood sample and checked her heart rate and other vitals. She'd smiled and said that all was well, and that if she took it easy, she was free to go.

Before she had gone, though, Connie had introduced her to Harley. They had got on well. Harley had told her about his encounter with McCready and how much respect he had for him.

Later that day, Harley had contacted her to let her know McCready had managed to get the code to the ISS, effectively saving New York. There were many people who were going to sleep a whole lot better that night because of his actions, including the president, despite his sore jaw.

He'd told her that McCready was in the recompression facility at Coronado. He'd said he would be able to get her in to see him if she came down to the base.

She was now at the gate, having driven all the way from Los Angeles. The last time she'd made the trip was when she'd met Brad, after all those years, and he'd offered her the job at the complex. She shuddered at the thought. That journey had been filled with hope. This one was filled with dread.

It was now night-time.

The rain that had been forecast had arrived with a vengeance. It was all the wipers of the Audi could do to keep the windshield clear. The headlights showed what was almost a wall of water falling from the sky.

A rating at the security gate came back from a phone conversation confirming her access. He nodded briefly at Clare.

"Right, ma'am, if you drive straight for about four hundred yards you'll come to a large tank. Take a left, and the recompression facility will be right ahead. Lieutenant Harley will meet you there."

She thanked him and then drove off through the rain.

As she drove, she wondered what she would say to him when she saw him again. How she could explain about the last six months and how she now felt. Also, how she would explain about Brad.

She stared, unseeing, at the buildings as they passed by the window. Many were low and squat, like equipment stores. She came to the large tank the rating had told her about, made a left, and then saw the building at the end. It was a medium-sized, two-story affair with a roller door at the front. It looked a bit like a unit on an industrial park.

She pulled up next to a sign on the wall that said RECOMPRESSION FACILITY.

As she came to a stop, she saw Harley run out from a side entrance and over to the Audi. She lowered the window.

"Hi, Clare," he said. "If you'll just come with me."

She climbed out of the car and quickly made her way to the door at the side of the building. As she hurried though the rain, she saw a long black limousine parked next to a navy Humvee. Through the window, she could see a chauffeur reading a newspaper, the interior light illuminating his face and uniform. It seemed a strange place to find a limo.

Once they were inside, Harley led her up some stairs to a room that had windows overlooking the chambers. There were four, all interlinked, so patients and doctors could transfer from one to another and depressurize at different rates, as required.

As Clare looked down, she could see a group of three men at the side of the cavernous space. There was also someone standing at a glass port in one of the chambers. She couldn't see the figure clearly as it was partly obscured by a pillar.

"Coffee?" asked Harley.

"Yes, thanks, that would be great," said Clare.

"How you holding up?"

She wrapped her arms around herself.

"Oh, you know, coping. I'm just really worried about John," she said, anxiously.

Harley looked at her, his face serious. "I won't lie to you, he's suffered serious decompression problems. Things weren't helped by the time he spent in the plane and helicopter." He paused. "Dr. Fletcher, who you met, is doing all she can for him. She's the best, but even if he pulls through he's not out of the woods. He'll have to stay here for monitoring and observation for several days."

"Can I see him?" asked Clare.

Harley was hesitant for a moment.

"Er, yeah, sure. But there's someone with him right now. We can go down when she's finished."

"She?" said Clare. "I didn't know he knew anyone out here?"

Harley looked at her.

"It's all a bit hush-hush. Some actress, I think. Someone at the studios knew the commander and pulled a few strings."

At this, Clare looked shocked. Tears sprang into her eyes. She stood and ran for the door.

Harley jumped up. "Clare, you can't…"

But she'd already gone.

Clare entered the lower level of the large facility from a door in the corner at the bottom of the stairs. She looked across the plain concrete floor to the massive chambers. From down here they looked imposing, menacing.

The cluster of three men were still huddled to one side. They all wore smart, expensive suits and looked like they were talking business.

She walked forward, as though in a trance. The chambers were large and white, cylindrical in shape. Massive couplings connected them together. There was a series of pipes and tubes leading into each of them. These would carry the different gases used to pressurize, and ultimately treat, any occupants.

As Clare walked forward, she could feel her legs trembling. Standing at one of the glass ports of the lower chamber was a woman. She had her back to Clare. She wore a stylish, full-length black coat with a high collar and seemed to be looking in through the port with an intensity Clare found hard to watch.

Before she had crossed half the distance, Clare noticed Connie walking toward her, a concerned look on her face. As she reached her, she smiled, but her expression was serious.

"How is he?" asked Clare.

"He's very tired. He'll be here for a few days, but we're hopeful."

Clare's gaze was fixed on the woman at the port.

"How long has she been here?"

"About thirty minutes."

Clare was silent. She just stood there, staring.

"Can I see him?"

"Yes, when she's gone... He nearly died, Clare. He's very weak. If it wasn't for the Coast Guard bringing him in when they did, he wouldn't have a chance."

"Will there be any long-term effects?" Clare hesitated. She almost couldn't bring herself to say it. "Will... will he be paralyzed?"

"It's too early to tell. We'll do all we can. I promise." She put her hand on her shoulder.

Clare was still looking at the chamber when the world's biggest movie star turned away from the port and looked around the room. When she saw the two women, she stopped. She seemed to be appraising Clare closely.

Clare could see she had tears in her eyes. She obviously cared deeply for McCready. Clare wanted to cry herself. How could she compete with that?

She managed a few more seconds and then turned to leave, any fight drained out of her.

She walked slowly back toward the stairs, her head down, the tears forming more readily now.

"Clare?"

A pause.

"It is Clare, isn't it?"

Clare turned slowly. Brandy Carmine was standing in the middle of the room, halfway between the chamber and the doorway. She was staring at her.

Clare just stood there. Brandy started to walk over. Clare didn't move, but she could feel herself shaking.

Brandy reached her. Her eyes were moist.

"Clare, yes?" said Brandy.

All Clare could do was nod slowly.

"Hi, my name's, Brandy." She managed a smile, offering her hand.

Clare wasn't sure what she should do, but she shook her hand. They stared at each other for a few moments.

"He saved my life, you know," said Brandy, simply.

Clare almost smiled. "Yeah, he has a habit of doing that. One of his more annoying ones."

Brandy smiled, but she was trying to blink away the tears that were forming in her eyes. She looked straight at Clare.

"You know, you're a very lucky woman. I'm glad I met you."

And then, with a nod to Connie, she turned and walked for the door. Immediately, the huddle of men ran over to join her. One of them threw a look at Clare and then they were gone.

Clare just stood there, not quite comprehending what had happened.

Connie smiled, but gave her a moment to collect her thoughts. She then put a hand gently on her shoulder.

"Would you like to see him now?"

Clare looked at her. The trance had been broken. She wiped away a tear, nodding eagerly.

Connie led her over to the small round window in the side of the chamber, and then, with a pat on the back, left her there.

As she walked away, she noticed Harley leaning against the door, watching. She smiled at him. He winked back at her.

Clare walked slowly up to the viewing port and looked in.

She could see McCready lying on a narrow bunk on one side of the chamber. He was plumbed into drips and monitoring equipment. A transparent oxygen mask covered his nose and mouth. He looked terrible.

She watched him for several minutes.

But then, as if he sensed her presence, his eyes flickered open. He turned his head to look at her. As soon as he saw her, he smiled that lopsided grin, or at least a weakened version of it. She couldn't help but smile back.

There was a microphone in the chamber next to the port.

"Hey," she said.

"Hey," he said.

"So, saving the world more important than me, huh?"

"Man's gotta do what a man's gotta do." He winced as he spoke.

Clare smiled.

"Also seems you've been to the movies recently."

He looked at her, that inscrutable expression on his face,

and when he spoke his voice was barely a whisper. "Yeah, but I'm still waiting for the main feature to start."

Clare's eyes welled up.

She could see he was fading. Could see his eyes closing.

"I am so going to look after you."

But he was already asleep.

Chapter Fifty-Eight

One week later

John McCready had slept long and he had slept deeply.

And he had dreamed.

He had been in a jungle, which was lush and filled with the sounds of the wild, but he was being chased by two big cats. One was fluffy and friendly, the other cruel and stealthy yet somehow hypnotic. They had both been pursuing him. He hadn't known what to do to shake them off. For some reason he had to choose between them. There were aspects of both he loved, but in the final analysis he didn't know what to do. It had got to the point where he'd realized it was a dream, but he couldn't wake up from it. The crunch had come when one of the animals had lashed out at the other and come close enough for him to feel her breath, her teeth inches from his face. The cat had been about to pounce when he'd felt himself jolt out of the dream and into the real world. He hadn't been able to open his eyes, but he could sense he was back in reality. The feeling of warmth and security that swept over him was like a tidal wave of relief.

He relaxed for a moment and then opened what he thought were his eyes. But as he did, he froze. Only inches from his face were two rows of sharp teeth belonging to a ferocious beast. It was panting heavily.

What the hell?

At that moment he heard footsteps, and then…

"Get him, Max!"

The mouth rushed forward, jaws open, and then a wet pink tongue was licking his face.

McCready groaned and sat up. Immediately, Max leaped up onto the couch and snuggled in against his stomach.

"Looks like you've got a friend for life," said Clare with a beaming smile. She came over and kissed him.

"Looks that way."

McCready stroked Max's ears. A contented sigh came from his lap.

"So, how are you doing, sleepyhead? I've just got back from a whole shopping trip downtown." She dumped a pile of bags on the floor. McCready could see the labels of various high-end stores scrawled across them.

"Still pretty knackered."

"It's going to take a while. You nearly died."

"Tell me about it." He yawned. "Think I'll take a shower. Wake me up."

"Okay. And then I'll have a nice clean John all to myself." The emphasis was on the *myself*. She gave him a knowing look.

McCready sighed. It had been awkward at the naval base. It had been wonderful to see Brandy again, but, if anything, it had driven home more than ever that however much he loved being with her, her life wasn't for him. And while he didn't think Clare would ever watch a Brandy Carmine film again, he might sneak one in occasionally when she was out, but that would definitely be the limit of his foray into the film world from now on.

He heaved Max off his lap and plonked him on the floor. The pup gave an indignant woof and wandered off to find his bowl.

McCready arched his back. He still ached from the ordeal and the hours in the chamber, but the navy doctor had said he should be fine. He had her contact details if there were any complications. She had also given Clare strict instructions as to how McCready should be looked after. The two had seemed to get on far too well. He was sure there was some sort of conspiracy to clip his wings—at least until a certain film star was off on her next shoot. If only Clare had known she didn't have anything to worry about, a fact she would shortly know beyond any doubt. He wondered how she'd react.

He watched her as she unpacked the bags from her shopping trip, and then he stood up and walked into the large bedroom with the wide balcony and an unrestricted view across LA. He stretched his back again, still feeling the aches and pains, and then walked into the shower. He let the jets pummel and massage his tired body.

Once he'd soaped himself down and stood under the hot water for another five minutes, he walked back out and grabbed a towel to dry himself off. He was mostly dry when he crossed over to the top drawer in a chest she'd allocated him to be going on with.

He couldn't wait any longer.

He pulled the drawer open and pushed a pile of socks out of the way to reveal a small black drawstring bag. Even in his condition, he had realized there was something he needed to do. The previous day he had managed to go on a shopping trip all of his own while Clare had been going through the aftermath at work. He stretched the top of the bag open and withdrew a small, square, velvet-covered hinged box. As he opened it and glanced inside, he smiled, and then all of a sudden found himself feeling extremely nervous.

In the background he heard a phone ring.

He took a deep breath and headed for the door.

Clare had almost finished going through her purchases and was putting the last bag back down on the floor. She had smiled to herself and felt a stab of joy when she'd come back into the house and seen McCready asleep on the couch. It was also great that Max had taken to him. In fact, he'd taken to him so well she'd wondered if he even noticed her anymore, but she didn't care. She finally felt at peace with her life. All the elements were in place—the right place, and in the right order. She felt nothing could upset this wonderfully contented idyll she now found herself in.

She had heard the shower in the background. It was all she could do to stop herself from creeping in to watch him through the glass, but she knew if she did she wouldn't be able to stop herself from joining him, and who knew where that might lead. And the doctor had told her what he was, and what he was not, capable of doing right now, and *that* was not on the list.

She was about to pick up the bags and take them into her bedroom when she heard McCready's phone ring. She glanced up. Although the shower had now stopped, he would still be getting changed. She crossed over to the phone and saw there was no caller ID displayed. It was still ringing. She picked it up.

"Hello, John's phone."

At first there was no reply, then there was a crackle and what sounded like some sort of blast and then a series of fast, loud bangs. She held it away from her ear in shock. When she put it back, she could hear a woman's voice. "Hello! Hello, John. Can you hear me?" She sounded scared, desperate almost, and was breathing fast.

Clare frowned. "Hello, who is this? I'm a friend of John's. I can hardly hear you."

There was more crackling. The line cut in and out, and then the woman tried to tell her, her name. And then the line went dead.

McCready walked through from the bedroom, the towel wrapped around his waist, his hands clasped behind his back, one of which held the small velvet box.

As he entered the living room, he found her staring at his phone, a concerned look on her face. He started to bring the hand holding the box round in front of him.

"What is it?" he asked.

She looked up. "You just had the weirdest call. At least I think it was for you."

"From who?"

"That's it. I have no idea. It was a really bad line." She hesitated. "It couldn't have been, but it almost sounded like… gunfire in the background."

"Gunfire?"

"Yeah, and there was this woman's voice. She was terrified. It was really unclear. She said her name was…" Clare tried to think, to focus. "Marl… Marl something… No, wait, Carl… Yeah, that was it, Carlita."

Clare looked up, but her face turned to shock as she saw McCready's expression.

"John, what is it? Do you know her?"

McCready was frozen to the spot. All he could do was look straight at her; all that was, except tighten his grip on the small velvet box and return his hand behind his back.

He found he was shaking.

Next in the John McCready Series

vinci-books.com/deep-control

Trust is an illusion.

When John McCready answers a cry for help from the past, he uncovers a chilling conspiracy: a billionaire's radical plan that could kill thousands to save the Earth.

As the countdown begins, McCready races from the heights of the Swiss Alps to the depths of the Indian Ocean to stop an uncertain future from which there would be no going back.

Turn the page for a free preview…

Deep Control: Chapter One

One month ago

The nine-inch rat scuttled along the narrow tunnel sniffing the air as it went. It was trying to search out something to eat. Dark gray in color, it had long white whiskers that stuck out from either side of its nose, allowing it to feel its environment, even when it was pitch-black.

Several hours earlier it had found a quiet place to hide up and rest. But its ever-vigilant senses had alerted it to possible danger, springing it awake, ready for any threat to its well-being and safety.

The rat was well used to the concept of fight or flight, and while its usual response was flight, it had no problem, when cornered, in fighting to the death if necessary, though for obvious reasons it hadn't found the need to do so yet.

However, when it had been woken, there had seemed to be no immediate threat. It was merely noise that was the disturbance. There had been a clanging and banging coming from about ten feet from where it had been hiding.

Deep Hostage

It had carefully moved forward from the dark corner and watched through the slatted metal ceiling a few inches above its head as a number of men maneuvered a large object on a cradle-like trolley into the area beyond its hiding place. The object was about thirty feet long and cylindrical in shape, and partially hidden by the thick metal bars of the cradle. It was being pushed by a small vehicle and it looked like it was heavy. Not that the rat would have noticed, but on the side was a symbol. It was black and yellow and similar to how you might imagine a whirling propeller to look. Immediately above it was the Chinese word for CAUTION, and immediately below, the one for DANGER.

After the men had positioned it in the middle of the space, the vehicle had disappeared. The men had then grabbed a series of wide webbing straps and secured the object to the floor.

They had then left.

About five minutes after they'd gone one of them had returned and headed straight toward where the rat was hiding. He had been carrying a small metal box with wires protruding from both sides. He'd approached the dark corner and reached down to a section of the floor. He'd then pulled it up, revealing a large compartment beneath.

The rat had wanted to run, but the smell of something the man had been eating overpowered any fear it had. As the man had worked in the compartment he'd placed a half-eaten burger in a wrapper on the floor. The rat had wanted to grab the food, but it was too close to the man. Too risky. The man had his arms in the compartment and was using some sort of tool. He worked away for several minutes. As he did so, he kept glancing around nervously.

Clearly, he wasn't meant to be there either.

Finally, he was finished. He had peered down into the compartment to make a last check.

At this, the rat had scuttled away, not wanting to be caught. It had stopped a few feet down the dark tunnel and looked back.

A second later and the top of the compartment had been closed with a bang, causing the rat to scurry further along the space beneath the floor.

After about twenty minutes there had been another loud noise. At first there had been a mechanical boom, as though something was closing, then later, a high-pitched whine that grew louder and louder. The rat had scurried deeper into the crevices and hidden in fear of this new danger. It had stayed there for quite some time, even managing to sleep.

But when it had awoken, it was still hungry.

So now, with renewed confidence, it was heading back along the underfloor space to where the man had been working, and from where there was the lingering smell of food.

Once the rat reached the compartment, it looked around. From all sides there was a steady drone and vibration, but it was more concerned about finding something to eat. The burger was gone, but some sauce and bits of meat had fallen into the compartment in the space beneath the floor.

The rat squeezed through a hole in the back and found the food. What was left of the meat was wedged behind some wires leading from the box the man had put in place. The wires led off either side and disappeared into other parts of the surrounding structure. On the front of the box was a screen. The rat had no interest in this, but if it had, it would have seen four numbers displayed on a digital display.

The first was a zero. This was followed by an eight. There were then two dots aligned vertically. The last two numbers were three and six. Every minute, the right-hand number reduced by one. Above the screen were two lights.

One had the word TRANSMIT next to it. The light was on and glowing red.

One had the word ARMED next to it. The light was on and glowing red.

The rat ignored the display and grabbed the wires with its front feet. The meat from the burger was behind the wires. It would be difficult to get to.

Fifty feet from the rat the captain of the Boeing 767 banked the massive machine round to follow the air corridor to the west of Thailand and on over the Bay of Bengal.

The two-man crew were members of the Chinese military and their mission was of the utmost secrecy. Even the aircraft being used was decked out to look innocuous and unremarkable. There were windows down the sides, but all the seats had been removed to allow the interior to be filled with cargo. The outside was white, with no markings, and a loading ramp had been added at the rear. But this flight was carrying only one thing; a very special item that was the property of the Chinese government.

The captain checked the systems and then settled in for the rest of the flight to South Africa, their final destination.

They had originated from an air base in the Guangxi region in southern China. The flight had no digital identifiers or beacons of any kind and would be blind to all tracking software used by people across the globe to follow aircraft as they sped through the skies.

The plane, for all intents and purposes, did not exist.

The rat was becoming ever more desperate. It could smell the food and it was driving it mad. But the wires were in the way. It reckoned if it could just get through them it could reach the meat lying on the other side.

It moved forward and opened its mouth, revealing two long razor-sharp incisors.

Rats had been known to gnaw through concrete to get to where they wanted to go, so the flimsy plastic coating of the wires was no trouble at all. Even the wire itself was made fast work of.

It bit through the final red wire in a cluster at the bottom and then cautiously moved forward for its prize—the morsels of meat behind.

It was completely oblivious to the screen on the box.

If it had looked, it would have seen that when it bit through the final wire, the numbers started changing rapidly. What had previously been a slow, predictable reduction of digits every minute now became a rapid torrent of falling numbers, heading in only one direction—00:00.

The numbers on the left were now at ZERO.

The two numbers on the right were counting down fast.

A second later and the right-hand number reached ZERO. There was a beep, a moment of silence, and then a large BANG.

The explosion took out the box and the cables and wires surrounding it.

The cables that led off into the plane were completely severed. Also, at the top of the box, the now cracked light with the word TRANSMIT next to it was no longer glowing.

The rat was hurled back by the blast, knocked unconscious with the impact on the far side of the compartment.

After a few minutes it came to. When it worked out where it was, it stared briefly at the remains of the box and then scuttled away as fast as it could.

There had to be easier ways of finding food.

In the cockpit, Captain Zhao and the co-pilot heard the explosion. It was not loud, muffled by the noise from the aircraft and the depths of the hold from where it originated, but there was a sudden judder to the airframe and the captain's instinct told him something wasn't right. He exchanged a glance with the co-pilot. He was about to stand to go and investigate when there was a violent dip in the plane's attitude. He looked back at the controls and instruments and his face filled with shock and horror.

All the screens were blank.

And the aircraft had gone into a dive.

The reason for this was soon apparent. The quiet in the cabin indicated the two engines had shut down. The plane was now gliding steeply and was on a one-way ticket to the waiting water below.

Zhao leaned back in his seat and tightened the double harness over his shoulders. He gripped the controls and pulled back on the U-shaped yoke. The plane started to respond, but you could only do so much with an airliner-sized aircraft with no engines.

The co-pilot grabbed the radio, but when he tried to send a distress call he didn't even get static.

It was also dead.

And because of the secrecy of the flight, no one knew where they were and that they were in trouble.

They were on their own.

Zhao glanced out of the windows. The night was clear and the weather fine. There were stars across the sky. The bright gleam of the moon cast a pale glow over everything. At least they would be able to see where they were going. The forecast had been good, so the sea would be flat when they eventually reached it, which by current reckoning would not be long. They were losing altitude at around a thousand feet per minute. He knew from his training that at their current cruising altitude of 29,000 feet they could glide for around a hundred miles. What he didn't know was their exact position. And while under normal circumstances he would have turned and headed for shore, there was no way he was going to try to bring the aircraft down in this condition on land, and definitely not with the cargo it was carrying. Any attempt to do so, even if they survived, would be met with brutal punishment, possibly even death, from his superiors. No, he'd just have to try and put her down in the water and see what options they had if they were still alive.

Zhao was trying to work out their location when the moonlight revealed the glassy water below. It was the perfect night to attempt a landing, but there were no guarantees as to the outcome.

He nodded at the co-pilot. Both of them steeled themselves for what they knew would be the most terrifying few minutes of their lives.

The huge aircraft dropped ever lower.

Out of the corner of his eye the captain noticed a large cargo ship about a thousand feet below them, but then it was gone and his focus was back on the rapidly approaching water ahead.

It came closer and closer and then he braced himself.

At the last moment, he pulled back on the yoke, aiming to pull the plane up at an acute angle and stall the airframe in the hope it would flop back onto the water.

It almost worked.

The plane rose up in the air but then rolled to one side. The port wing hit first, flinging the 767 round, almost ripping the engine from the wing. The nose smashed into the water. The pilots were thrown forward hard, the G-forces knocking them unconscious, but the seatbelts saving them from being hurled through the windows.

The plane spun horizontally, throwing a massive plume of spray high into the air and an impact wave off toward the horizon.

It then settled in the water.

A minute later all was quiet.

But beneath the waterline damage had been done to the belly of the beast. A section midway down the plane had been torn open. Water thundered in, slowly rising up through the compartments and spilling over through holes and cracks in the superstructure caused by the crash.

When Captain Zhao came to, water was seeping under the cockpit door. He glanced around in a daze, trying to remember what had happened. It came back to him all too quickly as the water sloshed around his ankles. He undid his straps and looked over at the co-pilot. He was still in his seat, but it was clear he was dead—it looked like the whiplash from the impact had broken his neck. He stood up and crossed over to make sure. He raised the co-pilot's head and checked for a pulse, but it was no good. He laid his head gently back down and then looked around the cockpit for the emergency equipment. He knew there was a raft in the cargo bay, but basic supplies like food and water, a knife, flashlight and flares were kept in a locker at the rear of the cockpit. He crossed over to it and pulled the door open. He grabbed the pack and hoisted it onto his shoulders. He then took a last glance around in case there was anything else that could be of use.

There was nothing.

The water was now halfway to his knees. He could feel the angle of the aircraft starting to shift. He didn't have long.

He moved to the door and grabbed the handle.

He turned it and pulled.

And nothing happened.

He yanked it as hard as he could, but it was no good. It was stuck fast. The impact must have twisted the frame.

He started sweating. His heart rate was thumping. He dropped the backpack and tried again, putting all his strength into opening the door. It was quite literally the door to the rest of his life.

The water was up past his knees now, the plane tipping even more. It was at forty-five degrees. He didn't have long.

He reached for the handle, put one foot against the bulkhead at the side, and pulled for all he was worth.

But it was no good.

The water was now above his chest. He was about to make one last effort when the fuselage jerked alarmingly. Out of the window, the captain could see the black of the night sky and the myriad of stars, and he knew he was not long for this Earth. He said a quick prayer, and a brief, final message to his wife and daughter they would never hear, and then the waters closed around him, sealing his fate forever.

The plane slipped almost silently below the calm waters of the Bay of Bengal.

There was barely a ripple as the nose was fittingly the last to disappear. There were a few spouts of gas that had been trapped in the fuselage, which were expelled like the breaths of impatient whales, but then she was gone.

For around a minute there was nothing to see across the surface, but then one by one a number of objects started to appear. Somehow they had become dislodged from the sinking plane and their buoyancy had brought them up.

One of the objects was a large wooden box of food supplies that had been in the galley. It broke through the surface and bobbed innocently in the vast expanse of water.

A couple of minutes later there appeared to be movement from within. The box wobbled. A broken splinter of wood was pushed to one side, and the inquisitive nose of a rat appeared. It sniffed the salty air and then ran out of the box and onto the top. It looked around. There was nothing to see in any direction. It paused for a moment, adjusting to the new world it now found itself in, but then it ran back inside. It wasn't particularly worried, the pile of biscuits and crackers it had found would be more than enough to keep it going for quite some time.

Deep below the rat, the plane headed into the depths. It sank fast, coming to rest on a sandy seabed at a depth of seven hundred and fifty feet. It had miraculously remained largely intact. One of the wings landed first, pulled down by the weight of the dislodged engine, but then the airframe folded itself down onto the bottom, sending up a wave of silt into the surrounding water.

A couple of other objects managed to break free from

their watery grave and make their way up to the surface. But one object that very definitely didn't move was the cargo in the rear of the plane. It remained secured to the floor, sitting there, dormant, its massive power unable to be unleashed so long as it was held captive.

For the safety of the world, it would be better if it was never found.

Deep Control: Chapter Two

Today

John McCready cast an imposing figure as he leaned against the glass surround of the pool area of a spectacular house built high in the Hollywood Hills overlooking the city of Los Angeles. He was barefoot and dressed in a casual light blue cotton shirt and tan knee-length shorts as he soaked up the rays from the early afternoon sun.

Normally, his relaxed, easy-going demeanor would have shown a man at ease with the world. But right now his piercing blue eyes stared out over the city with a concerned, worried intensity that implied a state of mind that was far from calm and relaxed.

The house belonged to someone he loved dearly and, in fact, had come within seconds of asking to marry, when he'd been stopped in his tracks by the greatest shock he'd ever received in his life.

As he gazed out over the city, he tried to take stock of

what had happened over the previous few weeks, which, for some, would have been enough for any lifetime.

Put simply, he'd nearly died on multiple occasions after traveling halfway round the world to save the woman he loved and whose house he was now standing in.

Her name was Clare Kowalski.

In doing so, he'd ended up helping to thwart a terrorist operation that could have resulted in a nuclear war between East and West that would have killed millions.

He thought that would have been enough for one week, but now, seven days on, and just as he was starting to heal and recuperate, there had been the phone call.

Phone calls can change your life—for both good and for bad. They could be the bearer of tragic news, such as the death of a loved one, or the joyous tidings of a new baby, or of securing a job—but this one, this one was different.

When he'd been eighteen, off discovering the world for the first time, he'd met a girl in Peru. Her name was Carlita. She had captured his heart in a way no one else ever had. And while Clare was now the woman he wanted to spend the rest of his life with, at eighteen, your first love was something that could never be repeated, never replicated. At that age you were full of hopes and dreams and the fairytale of living happily ever after. As you grew older, you realized things were not always quite that simple, but for McCready, back then, it was real. On top of which, she'd saved his life. He owed her in a way it would be hard to describe. But events had not turned out how he had imagined. Her father had not been happy with the way Carlita and McCready were becoming so close. He'd asked McCready to leave. It had pained him to go, but out of respect, he'd honored her father's wishes. When he'd left the small mountain village he'd been distraught. The feeling had only grown when he'd found something Carlita had made for him and hidden in his backpack before he'd left—a poncho with colored stripes representing the two of them intertwined together... forever. When he'd returned home, he'd written to her every week for six months. He'd never received a reply. But he never forgot her. How could he? The poncho had hung on the wall of every house he'd owned since, including the one he'd built over a number of years on the west coast of Scotland. Barely a day had gone by when he hadn't thought of her in some way.

And now, after twenty-five years, she'd called out of the blue.

But it wasn't just any call.

Clare had answered the phone, and what she'd told him had filled him with dread. There had been shouting and screaming, what had sounded like gunfire and loud blasts... and in the middle of it all, the desperate, terrified voice of a woman asking for John and saying her name was Carlita.

And then the line had cut out.

He had tried to call back but it was dead.

His mind had been in turmoil ever since.

What he had done, though, was place the small velvet box he'd been about to present to Clare back in a drawer in the bedroom until he could work out what to do. But there was one thing he knew for certain: it wouldn't stay there forever.

He was still gazing out over the city when he felt a hand softly touch his shoulder.

He turned and smiled down at the beautiful green eyes that gazed up at him.

"Hi," he said.

"Hi," said Clare.

As he looked into her face he realized there was

nowhere else he would rather be. But there were things that had to be done, a debt that had to be repaid. He just wasn't sure how he was going to explain everything to her, or if she would even understand.

"Do you want to talk about it?" she asked gently.

McCready paused and then nodded slowly.

"Yeah, there're some things I need to explain."

She reached up and kissed him on the lips. She then led him back into the house through the large sliding glass panes. As they opened, Max, Clare's one-year-old retriever, shot out, barking at the indignation of being cut off from his human playthings. She opened her arms, fully expecting him to leap up, like he usually did, but instead, he raced straight past her and jumped into McCready's arms. Clare looked at him and shook her head.

"Traitor!"

But she was smiling.

They crossed over to one of the wide, comfy sofas in the modern open-plan living space. She fetched a couple of glasses of orange juice from the fridge and then sat down next to McCready. She looked straight into his eyes.

"So, who is she, John? Who is Carlita?"

McCready looked at her and took a deep breath…

…and told her the story.

Grab your copy…
vinci-books.com/deep-control

About the Author

Throughout my life I have always tried to seek out adventure, whether real or imaginary. Much of this has taken place in, on, or under the water.

My love of diving has allowed me to explore the oceans of the world and also work extensively in the film and TV industry.

This spirit has filtered through to my creative writing, which includes the John McCready thrillers – a smart, fast paced action/adventure series with twists and turns right up to the end.

In the real world, LIGHTS! CAMERA! SUB ACTION! takes you behind the scenes of underwater projects in the film and TV industry.

But the one thing all the books have in common, is a sense of excitement and the unknown; whether journeying with a hero battling the odds on thrilling and dangerous adventures, or diving sunken shipwrecks and coral reefs in the company of sharks, manta rays and other creatures of the deep.

Lights! Camera! Sub Action!

A behind-the-scenes look at working on underwater projects in the film and TV industry.

Available in all good bookstores online